VAMPIRE

KHAN

The Immortal Knight Chronicles
Book 3

Richard of Ashbury
and the Mongol Invasion of Persia
AD 1253 to AD 1266

DAN DAVIS

Vampire Khan

Copyright © 2018 by Dan Davis

For information contact :
dandaviswrites@outlook.com

ISBN: 9781980640165
First Edition: April 2018

PART ONE
CONSTANTINOPLE
1253

THE BANNERS OF THE KNIGHTS whipped and snapped in the wind, framed by the vivid expanse of blue above. To my right, timber stands held the cheering spectators beneath the banners and blocked my view of the mighty walls of Constantinople on the horizon.

Through the eye slits of my helmet, I could see little enough. Straight ahead across the field, the line of knights struggled to contain their horses. Beside me, on my left and right, the men of my own side held their lances ready. Our horses stomped and shook their heads as the riders fought their beasts into submission and growled threats at them.

My destrier trembled. He was a monster. Too big and too slow for most knights and long in the tooth. Do not ride him into battle, a Burgundian man-at-arms had joked with me when I had purchased the animal, hitch him to a plough instead. But the beast rode as straight as an arrow in the charge and feared nothing. And he had a terrible anger when roused and would tear chunks from another horse's neck in a fight.

My enemies that day were twenty knights from France, Navarre, Aragon, Acre and elsewhere. My side was twenty knights from all over Christendom. The tourney was a French invention but it had spread immediately to the English, who knew a good thing when we saw it. And it had, over the years, become popular in many kingdoms of Christendom. That day outside Constantinople we even had two knights from the Kingdom of Poland, three from Bohemia, and two from the Kingdom of Sicily.

And me. A knight of England, who had no lord and nothing to offer but his lance and his sword. My coat and shield were black, emblazoned with a single red chevron.

The others were a riot of red, blue, green, white and gold, with blazons of crosses, stripes, lions, eagles, and chalices. Lances raised, pennants flapping in the wind like a flock of exotic birds.

It was best to enter a tourney with a companion or two, at least, who will fight alongside you and watch your flanks while you watched theirs. Some tourneys had companies of ten or more men fighting as brothers. While I, close to friendless in a strange land, had to make do with two young Breton knights who pretended they were granting me a favour by allowing me to fight with them. They seemed to ride well enough and they swore they had broken lances in Picardie and Paris. The damned whoresons barely spoke to me because they thought I was poor and landless.

Well, they were half right. Eva, my wife, said it was because they were afraid of me but then she said that about everybody.

Much of the noise, muffled already by my helm, faded away as the watching crowd fell into hushed anticipation. That meant they had seen the order given and were watching the trumpets raised.

My horse stamped a foot and quivered.

The trumpets sounded.

Across the field, the line of knights contracted as each man tensed into hunch behind his shield and raked his spurs into his horse's flanks. I did the same, urging my destrier forward. The magnificent beast sighed with relief as he could at last give way to his instinct. Still, I held him to the trot and he would only reach a full charge as we met the enemy. He was a fine horse.

Beside me, the mounted knights leapt forward, pulling ahead as the men forgot everything we had discussed and urged their horses from dead standing straight into the charge.

If we did not meet the enemy line as one, then the most advanced of our knights would perhaps face two lances instead of one. My side would lose men to the initial charge and make my own fight all the harder.

And yet I made no attempt to keep up with them. I looked left and right, my view through the eye slits bouncing around. Already, our entire line was ragged. The centre, other than myself, was pulling ahead and the sides were lagging behind, but it was not a spearheaded charge.

Ahead, beyond the two Bretons, the knights against us lowered their lances and couched them. Both sides picked their

3

final targets.

Mine was the man I had lined up against at the start. A knight of France named Bertrand de Cardaillac. A truly massive man in green and gold, newly arrived in Constantinople. Sir Bertrand was said to be a great knight with a reputation for brutality and no other wanted to face him, leaving me free to take the key position in the centre. I wanted his wealth. I wanted his horse and his purse.

And I wanted to see how good he truly was.

Two knights of Aragon flanked him, and they had together formed a temporary company for the tourney. As long as no other interfered, it would be my Bretons and me against Sir Bertrand and his Aragonese.

But the Bretons wanted his wealth, too, and they forgot their duty and aimed at him rather than the Aragonese on his flanks. In so doing, they narrowed the gap between their two horses and blocked my line of approach. What were they hoping to achieve? They had made it into a charge of three against two.

Stupid bloody fools.

My horse was annoyed and confused but I urged him on, faster, and lowered my lance. The crashing of lances on shields began to ring out up and down the line.

The Bretons in front smashed into the knights of Aragon. My supposed comrades were a mere lance length beyond me but even had they not deserved it, I could have done nothing to save them from their fate. It was three knights against the two impetuous Bretons.

And both Bretons were struck, hard.

4

I held my course as the crashing of dozens of wooden shields and lances echoed across the field, horses, and men crying out in triumph or fear.

Bertrand, the French knight, smashed through one of my Bretons, unhorsing him. Even through all the noise and the steel of my helm, I heard Bertrand shouting in triumph at his strike. His voice was as throaty as a bull's and as he roared he half-turned to watch the Breton tumbling sideways from his saddle.

As the proverb says, pride goes before destruction, and I thanked God for prideful knights.

The blunted tip of my lance caught Bertrand de Cardaillac on the side of his helm. It was a hard strike, though of course the man's head was knocked away at once, reducing the force compared to a hit to the chest or shield. But the blow knocked the knight from his horse, all sense gone. His arms stiffened and jutted up in front of him as he fell, dropping his lance and throwing his shield arm up and to the side. His helm, too, was ripped from his head. I heard but did not see him crash into the hard earth and I prayed he would not die.

A knight from Aragon lunged at me with his lance as we passed but I saw it coming and leaned away, making a show of my lack of concern. Still, it was closer than I had expected and scratched the paint on my shield. I prayed he would be disconcerted by my bravery rather than encouraged by my incompetence.

By then the lines were through each other and the knights of both sides wheeled about to reform. Dust thrown up by the galloping hooves drifted across the field. A few men were down in the middle of the field. Bertrand de Cardaillac was on the ground, unmoving. I searched for another target and found both Aragonese knights already moving their horses toward me with intent displayed in their movements. The enemy line opposite was unformed and yet already they were charging. The knights of my side were not content to wait either.

Already, the tourney would be every man for himself. Every man and his fellows, if they stuck by each other.

"With me," I shouted to the remaining Breton knight, while he raked his spurs into his horse's flanks and the beast jumped into movement.

"God, give me strength," I muttered and urged my destrier into the fray. The noise of battle sounded once again, with shouts and the clattering of wood rising above the pounding of hooves on the hard ground.

My Breton clashed awkwardly with the Aragonese and both fell in a jumble, dragging their horses down with them.

Steady beneath me, my horse ignored the wildly kicking hooves and kept on toward the mounted knight aiming at me. As his blunted war lance thumped on my shield, my lance point bounced low and connected with his thigh and then his hip, knocking the lance from my grasp. My shield blocked my view but I continued past and drew my sword, turning about as swiftly as I could.

Few knights had made it through the melee in the centre and most were positioning themselves to fight from horseback with swords or other weapons. Broken and forgotten lances lay strewn about the dusty ground where the horses stomped and turned as groups of fighters formed. Sweat dripped into my eyes and my breath sounded like bellows in my ears. Already it was becoming difficult to know who was fighting for what side and the dust flew up, obscuring the men.

I pushed my way between two groups as the Aragonese knights, all on foot, came together with their swords drawn, one shield between the three of them. Bertrand de Cardaillac, massive as he was, looked dazed, blinking about him as though he had no idea how he had come to be here, with powdery pale earth caked to his big sweating face. The Aragonese knights, unlike my idiot Bretons, were doing their duty by holding him upright and guarding him while he recovered his senses. They were looking for a horse or at least a way out and away from the clashing men and kicking destriers around them.

I rode straight towards the three of them.

With cries of warning, the two knights tried to drag Bertrand away in two different directions, one on each arm, and so succeeded only in holding him steady and right in my path. My dear old horse reared his head but his powerful chest collided with Bertrand and knocked him down with more force than I intended. Thanks to God, he fell to one side and my horse avoided stamping on him.

I pulled up just beyond and dismounted while the other two ran back to protect him. Robust fellow that he was, he was already trying to get up.

"Yield," I shouted as I approached on foot. I held my shield low and my sword point down.

The Aragonese came at me, circling to either side in an

attempt to surround me and attack.

I charged the one without a shield, deflected his thrust on my shield and barged him to the ground faster than he could retreat. While he was stunned I banged the edge of my blade across the eye slits on his helmet.

"You are mine," I yelled at him.

I turned at the sound of approaching feet and my sword point caught the charging knight on his mailed knee. The man screamed and went down, whimpering, all the fight gone out of him.

All around me, the tourney field was slowing down as men yielded. My side was victorious, despite my useless Bretons falling at the first charge and a ragged cheer went up from the exhausted knights and the crowd on their stand at the side of the field.

The knights from Aragon and the French giant gave up their swords to me, hilt first. I would have their horses and armour or the value of them.

And that was good because I needed gold and silver.

I needed it to help me to travel to the North, across the Black Sea, into the lands of the Tartars.

My immortal enemy, William, was there. And I was going to kill him.

* * *

Later that day, as the sun rolled its way down to the west across the tourney field, I sat in the shade of my tent with all four sides open and pinned well back so that the breeze could cool my skin. There was plenty of space around my tent and the other knights and squires ignored me, other than an occasional polite wave. Somewhere out of sight behind the tents, a smith tapped away on steel, reducing dents from helms and straightening blades. A gaggle of little pages ran by me, laughing and shouting abuse at each other in language so vulgar it would have made a Flemish mercenary blush. The smell of roasting meat wafted from somewhere and it made me salivate, even though I had already eaten my fill.

In the shade of my tent, with the sweat scrubbed from my body, dressed in a thin cotton tunic, and wine in my belly, my body was comfortable.

But my mind was troubled.

"You will never be content," Eva said, sitting opposite me across the small, square table. She was dressed like a man and acting as my squire. She had learned over the years to control the swaying of her narrow hips when she walked and could mimic the swaying-armed strut of a young man. It would fool most men, from a distance, at least. "You will never be content as long as you live."

"I am content," I said, which was not true. "Those knights were just too poor. I should have collected more."

"More what?"

"More silver from them," I said. "More knights on the field. It was all over too quickly."

"You always want more," she said, shaking her head. "More fighting, more silver."

"More wine?" I said and refilled her cup from the jug.

"We have enough silver now," Eva pointed out.

"We should have more," I said, feeling the anger build. "I should have taken everything from them."

The squires of the two Aragonese knights had, to their credit, brought their masters' horses and armour to my tent immediately after the tourney had been declared. Both of the young men wept before me like women as they begged to buy back their horses and armour from me there and then. Of course, coin was what I wanted anyway, so I agreed.

Two of the destriers were ancient and worth little enough. One was of particularly good breeding but it was close to lame.

"I could sell them to a butcher and get more than what you beggars are offering," I shouted at them. "And when were these helms made? Were they worn at the Battle of Hastings? And the rings on the mail are thin and flat as a blade of grass. Are you certain that you serve knights and not paupers?" The squires cringed and wept harder. Blubbing about needing the armour for crusading. They begged, on their knees, for me to accept the paltry sums in silver that their masters offered and swore, upon the hands of God in Heaven, that it was all they had.

After accepting their modest bags of coins, the pair had wiped their eyes and strolled off talking about where to get some wine before returning to their masters. I swear they were laughing as they went and I was sorely tempted to give them both a brutal thrashing. But they were just doing their duty, the little sods.

"If you wanted more," Eva said to me over her cup, "you should not be so susceptible to tears."

"It was not the tears," I said. "All Aragonese are like that, bawling at the slightest hint of strife. How could I take their horses and end those men's Crusade? Now, they may continue on into the Holy Land."

Eva nodded. "And sit in Acre drinking wine for a year before going home to tell stories for the rest of their mediocre lives about how they stuck it to the Saracens."

I could not argue with that.

"Where is the damned French squire?" I asked, for the tenth time. "The day grows long."

"The word is that this Sir Bertrand is an arrogant lord," Eva said. "He will not take kindly to being carried off the field after his first charge. We know he was newly arrived from Acre and is on his way elsewhere, only delaying his departure to take part in that sad little tourney. Perhaps he will neglect to pay his debt."

"I would go and take it from him."

She wiped her lips. "Is it worth the trouble? We have what we need, now. Unless you would rather stay here or go elsewhere rather than North?"

"It is the principle of the thing."

"Oh?" she said, tilting her head. "You are principled now?"

"The principle is that the big bastard has wealth," I said, "and I want it."

Eva nodded over my shoulder, sat forward and lowered her voice. "Someone approaches."

"A squire?"

"The squire of Methuselah, perhaps."

"What?" I asked, confused, as I reached for my sword that was leaning against the table. Eva shook her head, pulled her hood close about her face and ducked away to make herself busy with our gear. I left my sword where it was, within arm's reach.

"Sir, God give you good day." A man's voice called out as he approached.

I watched Eva. She made a show of wiping down the good saddle but tilted her head so that she could keep one beady eye on the man.

Slowly, I sipped my wine and I watched her. She watched him from beneath her hood, and I made ready to grab my sword if Eva gave me warning.

The man strode by the table, into my view and stopped across from me, standing behind the chair.

An older man, with noble bearing. His face was long and narrow but his jaw was square and his bones were big. No fat on his belly. A Templar and a knight, that much was clear, for he wore the white robe of a knighted member of that order and a sword hung at his side. Square shouldered and straight backed in spite of his advanced years, the old Templar looked me in the eye and held my gaze.

"You are the English knight Sir Richard, I am told?"

I said nothing, which was remarkably rude.

"My name is Sir Thomas de Vimory," he said. "I should say, sir, that you fought very well today."

I scoffed. "Hardly a fight."

He inclined his head. "It was a rather brief tourney, somewhat unconventionally contested."

I smiled at that. "This is not France. And no great lords wished to try their skill. It was a scrap between the dregs and the desperate as a brief diversion before they head east or west." I lifted my cup. "Speaking as one of the dregs, of course." I downed my wine.

My uncouthness made him uncomfortable. "Nevertheless, you came out of it quite well, did you not?"

I shrugged. "I defeated the poorest knights in Christendom and a coward who has not paid his due."

Sir Thomas the Templar pretended to be amused by my words as if I had been witty, but he was in fact disturbed. "May I speak with you about a most pressing matter?"

I indicated that he was welcome to take the other chair and I filled the cup sitting before him on the table while he did so and then filled my own cup.

"They tell me you are seeking to journey to the lands of the tartars," the old Templar said, taking a sip. The man sat as stiff as a board, with his hands flat on the table.

"Is that what they tell you?" I said, sipping my wine and feigning mild disinterest. The wine was very good.

For months, I had desired to travel north from Constantinople into the lands of the tartars but the merchants would not take me. Word of my intentions had spread, clearly, because it was considered a strange thing for a knight to want. And it was.

"And why, may I ask, are you unable to do so?" the Templar said. "It would appear that you have the means." He flattered me by indicating the quality of my clothing and my equipment.

I hesitated. "No trader will take me, for they fear the wrath of the tartars and those that are subject to them. I have no conceivable business in their lands. I am no merchant. I am no envoy. As far as the tartars would be concerned, a Frankish knight could only be assessing their military strength."

"And they would kill you for that."

"Most certainly," I said. "Without hesitation. They are barbarians, with little enough law between them and none at all for Christians."

Thomas nodded. "And so, you have no way forward."

In fact, I did have a way forward. I had spent weeks persuading one of the merchants to sell to me his boat, his contacts, and his merchandise. The man's two sons had died a year ago and his heart was broken. He was rather old already and with no heirs, he wanted no more of his trade. And so, I would dress myself in the garb of a merchant, hire on his small crew and take iron tools and sacks of grain north up the Black Sea, and bring back furs for sale in the markets of Constantinople. Once in Pontus in the north, I could journey into the interior, with the pretence of wanting to trade directly with the tartars themselves.

That was my way forward.

I took a sip of wine and looked closer at the knight. He was certainly well beyond his best years as his long face was deeply lined and his hair was grey. But his eyes were a clear and bright blue and his body was straight, wiry and strong. His hands looked like they could throttle the life from a man half his age.

Clever, too. I could tell, by the way he looked deep into my eyes, searching for the truth within me. Searching out dishonesty. Even a fool knows one should never trust a clever man. So, I said nothing of my plans.

14

"Perhaps," I allowed. "But I will go north, by one means or another."

I was sure that he would then, finally, ask me why. Why would any man wish to head into the lands of the vile and murderous heathens who had so thoroughly defeated every army who ever stood against them?

Yet he did not.

Instead, the Templar poured himself another cup of wine from the jug, as if we were friends, and looked me in the eyes once more. "I, myself, am journeying into the lands of the tartars," he said. "And I should like another knight to accompany us."

I nodded.

"I have heard talk of you," I said, putting it together at last, recalling a soused Burgundian squire gossiping about it a few nights before. I had not believed him at the time. "You arrived in Constantinople mere days ago. You are escorting a monk? Who comes from the King of France."

Irritation passed over the old knight's face but he composed himself. "Yes, indeed. William of Rubruck, a Flemish friar from the Order of Saint Francis, is entrusted with a letter from the King of France intended for a lord of the Tartars."

"What is in the letter?" I cut in.

He cleared his throat. "I do not know. Neither does Friar William. And yet, I believe it to be a simple courtesy, one king to another. Or whatever passes for a king amongst them." His face darkened and he trailed off.

"It is a large party, is it not?" I said.

"No." Thomas collected himself. "Indeed, no. Myself and my

squire. A French knight and his squire. Then Friar William has his companions, Friar Bartholomew of Cremona. Another brother, a young Englishman like you, named Stephen Gosset."

It was the first time I ever heard of Stephen Gosset. It was not a moment that held any significance for me at the time, of course. How could it have done?

Only much, much later would I curse the man's name. Curse it repeatedly and with fervour, despite all the things that he did for me and for England over the centuries.

"No servants?" I asked, surprised.

He nodded. "The Friar has purchased for himself a young boy, named Nikolas, from here in Constantinople. And we obtained a dragoman in Acre, who knows the tongue of the tartars and, indeed, a great many others. But no others. We wish to keep our numbers down, for we know not how the Tartars will welcome us. We will be relying on their hospitality through our journey, both there and back, and also when we are guests of their prince at our destination."

"And what makes you believe you will be admitted into their lands?"

"It is known that the tartars allow free passage to envoys," Thomas said. "And we have already sent word and have heard that we would be welcomed."

"Forgive my confusion," I said. "But are you this envoy? Or is it the monk?"

Thomas pressed his lips together before replying. "Friar William wishes only to proselytise to the heathens. You see, he has heard from another monk that some among the tartars are

Christians. In fact, he has heard how the son of the local prince is a follower of the Christ and so he wishes to go to them and beg to be allowed to preach amongst them and so bring more of the heathens the word of God."

I could not help but scoff.

Thomas the Templar tilted his head. "I do not altogether disagree. I would sooner the tartars be scoured from the Earth and sent to Hell." He took a breath. "But that is a base desire. The friar will be doing God's work."

"That may be," I said. "But it may also be that God wants them all dead. Not baptized."

The look on Thomas' face suggested his own desires would align with God's will if that were indeed the case. I was not curious as to why the old Templar would have strong feelings about the tartars. They were terrifying brutes. Savages who had emerged from nowhere, from the nothingness in the east decades ago. Wherever they met the armies and cities of Christendom, our brothers in Christ had been slaughtered, most terribly. Towns and cities reduced to rubble and the peoples slaughtered or enslaved.

The tartars had pulled back from conquest of all the kingdoms of Europe but no one I had spoken to really knew why. It is God's will, they would say. A phrase which has ever been no more than an admission of profound ignorance.

"So," I said, unwilling to let myself be deflected from my enquiry, "why are you accompanying the friar and his holy companions?"

"The King of France asked me to do so." Thomas said no

more.

King Louis of France. A king whose grand Crusade had ended in disaster. His army defeated, utterly, by the Egyptians and he himself captured. The great king who almost shit himself to death and had to pay a fortune to the enemies he had come to vanquish. King Louis now squatted in Acre, one of the last cities held by the Franks in the Holy Land.

"Are you not too great a man to be sent on such an errand?"

"I am no great man," Thomas said, wrinkling his nose at the suggestion. "I am a humble knight in the service of God. No more. And this is no errand. My order protects pilgrims, does it not? I can think of no more appropriate duty than to escort these men in their own duty to spread the word of God to the heathen barbarians. And I was with the King on his crusade and he made a request of me, which I accepted. It is really no more than that."

"Of course," I said. It was a nonsense that he was spouting. A yard of yarn he was spinning. A Templar had no business heading into the wild north.

What his true intentions were, I had no idea. All I did know, was that he was a lying old bastard.

But then, so was I.

He had to ask it, finally. "And why," Thomas said, "if I may ask, are you seeking to journey north of the Black Sea?"

I leaned back on my ancient chair, which creaked beneath me as though it were in pain. I drank my wine, looking across the table at the old man. I tried to think. Never my forte. "You want me to come with you. That much is clear. You would not be here, wasting your time with me, if you did not. But why?"

"I witnessed your victories on the tourney field today. I asked about who you were, I was surprised to discover this rumour that you wished to head north. And, truth be told, we would be safer with another knight, and his squire, to protect us."

"And why ask me? There must be a thousand men-at-arms you could ask."

"None of your obvious ability, nor your renown, and your stature. They tell me you fought in a number of tourneys. I must confess, I am surprised at your youth. In fact, I was told that you fought in the crusade of King Theobald and Richard of Cornwall but that was clearly a mistake, considering it has been fifteen years and you are scarcely old enough."

I could not resist smiling at that. The first time I had fought the Saracens had been sixty years before.

Not that I could admit such a thing to the Templar. "I started young. And flattery will not deflect my question. I know of a dozen men more noteworthy than I. A hundred." I wagged a finger at him, still smiling. "Allow me to guess. No one else that you asked before me would consider going into the lands of the tartars. Only a madman would do so."

He returned my faint smile and leaned back. "Many men would have gladly joined us, in return for payment upon our return. Yet, I could never trust a man so desperate for silver that he would make such a journey."

"Why, then, do you go?"

"The King of France asked me to."

"You are a knight of the Order of the Temple. You are not subject to him."

"I said that he asked me. He made a request, which was granted by the Grand Master of my order."

"And, when you return to him, what will you ask for in return?"

"That is not your concern."

I nodded. "And your other man? The French knight. What of him? What is his name?"

The Templar's face clouded. "He was once highly favoured by King Louis. A favour he no longer holds."

I smiled at that. "Must have done something bloody awful to get this for punishment."

Instead of being offended, the Templar nodded slowly. "Nothing that could be proven. But have no doubt, Bertrand is a magnificent knight who won his name and fortune through the pursuit of war. Rich men surrendered to him on sight rather than cross swords with him."

At the mention of the knight's name, the realisation gripped me.

"What did you say his name, was?" I said, grasping the edge of the table. "Bertrand? Bertrand de Cardaillac? The coward I defeated on the field? He is one of yours?"

Thomas clenched his jaw. "We both travel with Friar William of Rubruck into the lands of the Tartars, yes."

I laughed in disbelief.

"Did he send you here?" I said. "Is this all some ruse in order to avoid paying his forfeit to me?"

The Templar spread his hands in the air. "I swear, that is not the case. When you performed so admirably in the tourney, your intentions for travelling north were mentioned to me as a rumour. I come here in truth to ask if our ambitions perhaps aligned. We could each help the other, and travel together. That is all. He will still have to pay you his forfeit, it is not about that. Indeed, Bertrand does not know that I am here at all and if he did then he would be dismayed, to say the least. Also, he does not believe we need any additional men. And yet, he has no say over who joins us."

"Sounds like more trouble than it is worth," I said. "It seemed as though, even though he was so newly arrived here, he brought with him a reputation for arrogance."

"Bertrand was well favoured at one time and won a number of victories in tourneys. I am surprised you have not heard of him."

"I have not been to France for a long time."

He smiled to himself at that. What he saw, sitting across from him, was a young man. I died when I was twenty-two years' old. I had found that if I claimed to be older than thirty years, men would be surprised, or disbelieve me. Thomas assumed that, for me, a long time was a year or two. As much as five years, perhaps. A fair assessment, for young men often feel that way regarding the passage of their own years.

In truth, I had been born eighty-two years before. Older than the ageing knight before me, certainly.

"Say I was to join your company," I said. "You have yourself and your squire. And you have another knight and his squire. How many men do you mean to take with you? It seems to me that your small party, as you call it, is not so small after all."

"You and your own man there would complete our company to my satisfaction." He paused. "As soon as you reveal your reasons for seeking the tartars."

What reasons would he believe? Not the whole truth, certainly. But he may accept a partial truth.

"There is a man," I said. "An Englishman. His name is William. Once, he was a knight. A lord. But he committed murders. Then he fled. For quite some time now, I have been seeking his whereabouts. I have heard that a man named William is living amongst the Tartars. Is favoured by them. From what I know of this man, I believe these stories tell of William."

Thomas' face creased in concern. "Vengeance? You want to wreak vengeance on this man?"

I could sense my opportunity fading.

"Justice," I said. "All I seek is justice."

The Templar radiated disappointment. "In the lands of the tartars? A man who, if he exists, can only be there on the sufferance of the tartar lords? No, no. Impossible. You would risk our entire company with your act of vengeance, should you carry it out. You, sir, shall not be welcome in my company."

I held up my hand until he allowed me to respond. "May I provide you with my intentions? I have heard how the tartars allow no foreign man through their lands, unless that man is a known trader or envoy, with express leave to travel. Any other man may be murdered with impunity, for the Tartars reason that such men can only be spying for their enemies. When I discover the location of this man William, I shall send word to him and to the local lord that I am present and that I wish to discuss his crimes. My request shall be a simple one. William has committed a number of specific crimes that I can list. If the tartars consent, I ask only for single combat with William. A trial by combat. If I win, or if I lose, there must be no revenge upon my fellow Christians and we should be allowed to leave, as freely as we arrived in that land."

"And if the Tartar lords decline your proposal?"

I held my arms out to either side. "What could I possibly do but accept their decision? I am no Assassin, seeking to murder a man in plain sight. Nor would I murder a man in his bed. I would leave, and wait for the day that he leaves the protection of the tartars."

"What did this man do to you, that would drive you to this... this risk?"

"He murdered my brother, my brother's wife and their children," I said. "And I swore an oath to see William brought to justice."

And he killed my wife and he killed my wife's son, who was also my dearest friend. William poisoned King John to death, as well as William's own father. And he killed hundreds of others, men, women, children. From England to the Holy Land, he had bathed in the blood of an uncounted multitude.

My brother, William de Ferrers. The evilest man who walked the Earth. And no man but I had the strength to end his life.

Of course, I could say none of this to Thomas. The Templar would think me a madman.

"I have seen men drunk on vengeance before," Thomas said, fixing me with his blue eyes.

"Justice," I said, before finishing my cup of wine and carefully placing it down. "And I am not drunk on anything. But if you believe I will be a detriment to your company, then I accept your wisdom with a good heart. I shall make my own way. Perhaps we shall see each other there?"

The Templar drummed his fingers on the bone-dry table top. "So, you do wish to join us?"

He said no more and waited for me to make my decision.

"When Bertrand de Cardaillac sends me the value of his forfeit," I said, "and swears that he will cause me no trouble on the journey, then I will join you." Behind me, Eva coughed. "Myself and my squire."

Thomas the Templar smiled and we agreed our terms.

The Sun was setting as he walked away between the tents on the field, heading back to the city.

"This is precisely what we wanted," I said to Eva. "Official leave to travel into the Tartar lands, with the concealment and protection of a monk and his party."

"Yes, indeed," she said, standing by my side.

"So why do I feel as though I have just been swindled?"

She snorted. "How do you think they will feel when they meet me?"

* * *

It was another two weeks, on the Nones of May 1253, that the party was due to set off from Constantinople by ship. We would cross the Black Sea for Pontus, in the North across that great body of water.

Before we could set off, however, I had two hurdles to cross. The most important task was to convince Thomas and the others to accept a woman in their party. The other was to avoid coming to blows with Sir Bertrand and, if possible, establish a peaceable rapport with him.

"What is the meaning of this?" Thomas said, staring at Eva as she and I arrived together at the Neorian Harbour.

On the north side of the city, the harbour was the centre of trade for the Venetian, Pisan, and Genoese, all of whom hated the other with greater fervour than any had for the Saracens. They all traded in taking furs, amber, and slaves, to the east and bringing silks, spices, and jewellery back to the city, and from there into the Mediterranean. The harbour was heaving with cogs and galleys, a forest of masts sticking up toward the cerulean sky. Everywhere, men loaded and unloaded cargo and the shouted mix of Italian dialects, Greek and French was interspersed with barks of laughter and cries of warning. It stank of the salt sea, rotting fish, and the exotic mixture of spice and strange perfumes. Wealthy merchants in fine clothes stood in groups here and there, arguing with ship owners and ignoring the sweating men who toiled in the sun repairing the vessels or carrying heavy loads.

Thomas was garbed in the clean, white robe and red cross of his order, and had been engaged in a heated discussion with a member of the ship's crew.

But he broke off the moment he clapped eyes on Eva. She was garbed much the same as I was. That is to say, in a tunic and wore a close-fitting cap with her dark hair tucked tight into it. A sword in its plain scabbard hung at her hip. With her breasts wrapped as tightly as she could stand, and her lithe, square-shouldered frame, she did not present an overly-ladylike figure and yet Thomas had spotted her at twenty paces. Then again, the Templars were supposed to be celibate so perhaps it was no wonder he had noticed.

"What is the meaning of this?" Thomas asked again.

"Thomas," I said, pretending to be somewhat slow on the uptake, "we have come in good time for the tide, I take it?"

The knight gestured at Eva. "Why is this woman here?"

"Oh, this woman?" I asked, innocently. "She is coming with me."

Colour drained from his skin. "She is not. Absolutely not. You will leave her here. By the docks, where she belongs."

I sighed. "You may never speak to her like that again, Thomas. Do you understand? And she is certainly coming with us. Without her, I could not possibly join in your endeavour."

He stared at me, then at Eva and back to me. Finally, he spoke to the crewman without taking his eyes off me. "If you please, Guido, could you board the ship and ask Friar William to join me here? Soon as you can."

The crew member stepped back, bobbed his head and hurried off.

Thomas seemed stunned, so I spoke into the silence.

"May I introduce my wife, Eva? Eva, this is Thomas, of the Templars." The old knight stared at me in confusion. "Thomas, Eva is my wife and my squire. She squires for me in battle. She attends to my every whim, both on and off the battlefield." I risked a glance at Eva and saw that she was irritated by my minor exaggeration where her obedience was concerned.

"You have lost your wits," Thomas said, after a long pause. He quite rudely ignored my wife. "You cannot take a woman into the lands of Tartary. Did you take a blow to the head in that tourney? Or were you never blessed with wits in the first instance?"

"I do not—"

"A woman?" Thomas cut me off. "A woman? As a squire? A woman squire?"

"I will grant that it is somewhat of an unusual—"

He placed his hand over his forehead in anguish. "You cannot believe I would allow a woman to join us? No matter how you garb the creature, no matter if you call her your wife."

Eva and I had known that it would be difficult to persuade Thomas to accept. In our time serving in various mercenary forces in Spain and the Holy Land in the previous decades, Eva had acted as my squire. Often, we pretended she was a young man and most of those who noticed that she was not, chose to say nothing. Indeed, it often became a shared secret within the company we served with. Sometimes, the men adopted her and protected her. They would share in jests at the expense of our superiors and delighted in assisting us in the deception. But someone important would find out. I would anger someone, generate some resentment or suspicion, and she would be turned in and no matter the good will I had built up, we would invariably be required to flee.

Fleeing from Thomas the Templar and Friar William when

we were in the lands of the Tartars would not be possible. A lone man with a woman crossing the grasslands of the north, and no permission or reason to travel, would be a death sentence. And so, we had to drop any pretence from the start. By arriving to the ship as late as was possible, we hoped to give them little time to make a decision. Take us or leave us, I would say.

It was a slim chance, but our best chance. If it failed, I would have to become a merchant, as originally planned. I did not want that. One may as well attempt to make a horse into a duck.

"She is my wife," I said, turning to Eva.

She nodded at Thomas. "It is the truth. I am also his squire." Eva glanced at me. "And I can fight."

Thomas scoffed. "I think you had best take your leave," he said, addressing me alone.

Perhaps I should have considered who Thomas was before taking such a direct approach. He was no poverty-stricken man-at-arms, signing up to fight for one lord in a local land dispute with another in Castile. Thomas was a senior knight of the Order of the Temple, a man who had taken a vow of celibacy. Perhaps taken the vow as a young man. I had the impression that Thomas was a man who tended to keep the vows that he took and so it was likely that he knew very little of women. Perhaps had never known a woman. And what we do not know, we often fear.

"Our belongings are already on board the ship," I pointed out, as I had sent them along the day before.

"I shall see that all you own is removed from the ship and placed on the dockside," Thomas said. "You may wait here while that is done."

"It would be easier if Eva and I took our places on the ship," I said. "As agreed."

"Agreed?" Thomas said, his voice rising as he spoke. "Agreed, you say? We never agreed to you bringing this... this..."

"Squire," I said.

Thomas took a deep breath but before he could unleash it upon me, he was interrupted by the approach of a young man in the grey robes of a brother of the Order of St Francis, along with two more Franciscans. The young man in front was aged about thirty years. He was a big, burly fellow, with a clean shaved, red face and light brown hair. Fat beneath his robes and with a wide face now creased in concern as he approached.

At his shoulder, half a step behind was an even younger monk with fair hair and an old one trailed behind.

"What is the meaning of this commotion, my lord?" the fat monk called out as he approached. His French was excellent but surely this was William of Rubruck, the Flemish leader of the embassy heading north to the Tartars. If Thomas was a lost cause, perhaps I could persuade Friar William to accept a woman in the company?

Some monks were fair-minded, kind men. Others were lovers of reason who delighted in being convinced of this or that through clear argumentation. Others still were lecherous sinners. If William of Rubruck were any of these, it would be simple to have him take Eva and I both.

"Friar William," Thomas said, his good manners overcoming his anger so that he could make a formal introduction. "This is Richard, the knight who—"

"Of course it is," Friar William said, coming to a stop before me and planting his feet wide. The monk was only a little shorter than I. His barrel of a belly was close enough for me to reach out and poke. "But what is the argument regarding? Perhaps you have decided that you will not be accompanying us after all, Sir Richard?"

His disregard for formality gave me hope. "I would like very much to join you, Friar William," I said. "We were merely discussing a practical matter regarding my squire."

"Your squire?" William turned to Eva, who was of a height with him. She looked him square in the face. William looked her up and down and found nothing to be remarked upon. "What practical matter?" he asked me and Thomas.

The rest of us looked at Thomas, who cleared his throat before replying. "Friar William, his squire is a woman."

William of Rubruck was at first confused but he looked at her again with this new knowledge and became somewhat flabbergasted.

Eva was tall, square shouldered and slender. Her face was perfectly womanish, her mouth was wide and her cheekbones high and sharp. But her hair was hidden beneath her cap and her substantial breasts were wrapped beneath her tunic, and anyway, we see what we expect to see. And she was dressed as a squire.

"A woman?" William said, utterly confused. "Is this a jest?"

"She has served dutifully as my squire for many a year," I said. "And what is more, she is my wife."

William struggled to comprehend. The fair-haired young monk at his shoulder grinned from ear to ear while the elderly one wore an expression of pure horror.

The friar's powers of reason won out over his emotion. "I am sure that this sort of thing may seem... permissible in the Holy Land. But there are practical considerations. We simply cannot bring a woman. Where would she pass water, for example? How would she bathe?" He paused while he searched for other things that women do.

I grinned at him. "She will piss on the ground, like everyone else. How much bathing do you expect to do on the journey, Friar William? If she needs to wash, you can bloody well avert your eyes, like a decent man would. Can't you, Friar? Are you suggesting that you would look upon a woman's nakedness?"

"What? No, I most certainly would not. But that is—"

"Well then, there you go, Friar William, nothing to be concerned about at all, is there."

Our small gathering was attracting some attention from the people around the dockside, with workers slowing their toiling while they threw glances our way. Other men stared at us from a distance.

Thomas lowered his voice and addressed Friar William. "Perhaps you could leave the question of whether we need additional men-at-arms to me," he said. "While you and your brothers wait on the ship."

William frowned. "I seem to recall that it was you who argued you needed another man."

"That is true, however—"

"I would rather none of you accompanied me at all," Friar William said, lifting his fat chin in the air. "There is no requirement for impoverished brothers to bring guards into Tartary. To do so may indeed risk—"

"The King himself commanded—"

"I know full well what the King commanded, Sir Thomas, as it was to me directly that he addressed himself. I do not—"

This time it was the young monk at his shoulder who interrupted. "Friar William, if I may?"

William sighed. "What is it, Stephen?"

The young man smiled, as if unconcerned with the irritation he had caused his brother monk. "It is known that the barbarian Tartar welcomes women as fellow soldiers. Indeed, they say that when the men go off to war and to raid, it is the womenfolk who defend the homestead. The women fight with bow and lance, from horse and on foot. They say that the women are quite savage. That they fight almost as well as the men do."

William scowled. The elderly monk behind shook with indignation at the idea of it.

"Why do you tell me this thing, Stephen?" William said.

The young monk, still smiling, gestured at Eva. "Perhaps the Tartars will look favourably upon us if we have a woman who displays a similar martial inclination?"

"I have no desire to emulate their barbarian, heathen practises, Stephen."

"Of course not. Of course. And yet, if there was a chance such a thing were to ultimately help our cause, would not such a thing have value? For the greater good of spreading the word of the Christ?"

William nodded, almost to himself. "You may be right,

Stephen. I do not like it. Not one bit. But you may be right."

The young monk grinned at me, very pleased with himself. I found his attempt at ingratiation to be profoundly irritating.

"Wonderful," I said, forcing a smile onto my face. "Shall we board now?"

Thomas held up a hand in protest but another voice cried out from across the dock, a loud hail from a deep voice, and Thomas' face fell even further. "Ah. Well, this should resolve the debacle. Here comes Bertrand."

The monks all sank, their shoulders rounding and both the young and old ones gathered closer to the bulky form of William, like goslings round a goose.

Sir Bertrand strode toward us, along with two squires. Even out of his armour, Bertrand was a huge man, taller than me by half a head. Half a massive, bullock-like head. In those days long past, I was often the tallest man out of a hundred. Tallest out of a thousand, perhaps. But, of course, there were many who overtopped me. Sometimes they would be a yeoman or townsman but often such men are dragged into the profession of war and most commonly of all they would be men of good breeding. Men with the healthy blood and good food of the nobility or knightly classes.

Most men-at-arms, of all heights, would be of relatively slender build. There was rarely enough food and wine to make an active man fat, even if he be wealthy. Those of us who were strong enough to fight for half a day from horseback and with sword and shield almost never had large muscles.

But every now and then, you would get a man like Bertrand

de Cardaillac.

A man who towered over every other and also had shoulders like hams and a chest like a hogshead. Big boned all over, with blocks for knuckles and a wide face and a jaw like a ploughshare. The man's eyes were small and dark, darting about across all of us as if searching for a threat.

One of the two squires trailing him was almost as tall, though younger and not so large of stature.

"What is the meaning of this?" Bertrand said as he arrived. His voice was louder than a docker's mother but he spoke with the fine, haughty French of the nobility. "Is it true?" He squinted down at Eva. "Is this truly a woman? Or was your saintly little squire telling me lies, Thomas? Does not look much like a woman. Are you a woman, boy?"

I pushed myself in front of her. "How joyous it is to see you again, Sir Bertrand. I am Richard of Ashbury. Perhaps you recall our meeting on the field? Or perhaps not, you took a rather nasty blow or two, did you not? This is my squire, Eva."

He ground his teeth, his massive jaw working while he forced himself into a contemptuous, false jollity.

"Ah, yes. The lucky little Englishman. Thomas complained ceaselessly that he needed more men." Bertrand grinned while he puffed out his chest. "As if any other knight would be needed when you have Bertrand de Cardaillac?" He turned and grabbed his squire and pulled him in, throwing a massive arm around the younger man's shoulders. "And my dear cousin Hugues, of course."

It was obvious that the squire, Hughues, shared de

Cardaillac's blood. He was somewhat of a younger, shorter, slimmer version of the bigger man. His expression was just as smug, though his eyes did not exhibit the shrewd, penetrating glare of his cousin's.

"Yes, indeed, what a fine young squire you have. And let me just say, sir, it was very good of you to eventually send me your tourney forfeit by way of Thomas," I said, fixing Bertrand with a stare.

"Ah, of course, I hold no grudges for a lucky blow from an inferior young soldier," Bertrand said, with a tight smile. His eyes told a very different story. "It was all merely a diversion in between doing my duty for the King."

"Indeed," I said. "Indeed, I heard you were with King Louis in Egypt. A sad business. Very sad. I praise God that the Egyptians released him so that he could raise his own ransom. Praise God, also, that you yourself survived the Crusade. You must be a lucky little Frenchman, indeed."

Bertrand shoved his squire away and jabbed a big meaty finger in front of my face. "And you? You are a jester, who calls a woman his squire. And I know why." He leered at Eva.

I had told Eva to hold her tongue. Impressed upon her the need for her to avoid angering Friar William and Thomas. She had argued that she should be allowed to speak for herself, as we would be persuading the pair that she could act just as a man would. Exasperated, I had told her for the tenth time that a true squire would know to hold his damned tongue.

Even so, I could never control her.

"Fight me," Eva said to Bertrand.

Every man, me included, turned to stare at her.

"Quiet," I said.

She glanced at me only briefly. "Bertrand de Cardaillac, if you doubt my abilities, you should fight me yourself. If you beat me, we will leave you be. But if I beat you, I join your journey to the Tartars with my husband, Richard. Right now. With swords. No armour. I am ready."

We had not agreed this. Bertrand was as large as a giant and a trained knight.

But Eva was very good with the sword.

And, of course, she was an immortal vampire with inhuman speed and strength.

The men arrayed about us stared at Eva in shock, until Bertrand laughed in her face. "You are both mad. Utterly mad."

His squire laughed like a donkey but the monks and the old Templar and his young squire were apprehensive.

"You are afraid," Eva said, her goading shutting the man up. "You fear losing to a woman."

He sneered. "I would never use a blade on a woman, even one as shameless as this one."

"Go on," I said, warming to the idea. "What are you afraid of?"

The others were in a state of surprise and confusion and struggled to give word to their outrage.

"I would slay you with a single blow," Bertrand said, although he seemed somewhat perturbed by her confidence, or by the very notion itself.

"Practice swords then," I said. "Blunted wasters. We have

dulled, old blades and wooden cudgels with our belongings on the ship, if your squire will fetch them for us."

"That is it," Bertrand said, his lip curling in contempt. "You call yourself a squire. And so you can fight my squire. Yes, yes. Come on, Hughes. Fetch a pair of wasters, one for you. And one for this woman. You may then humiliate her."

He glared at me, expecting that I would put a stop to the madness. Little did he know that the madness was only just beginning, for him and for all of us. I simply smiled pleasantly up at him.

A space was made by the monks, knights, and spectators standing in a rough circle on the dockside.

"Get back," I said to those gathering. "Make room, there, you damned fools, unless you want to get your bellies cut open by a reeling squire."

Eva fastened her cap beneath her chin, handed me the sword and scabbard from her hip, and tightened her belt. "If these fools do not disperse, we shall be arrested for breaching the peace."

"Do not finish him too swiftly, they must see your ability," I said. "But do not toy with him too long, or the authorities may detain us. And do not kill him."

She gave me a look.

"Yes, yes, I know," I said, "but he will attempt to humiliate you. Do you recall what happened in Castile?"

"That was twenty years ago."

"So, you do remember."

"The boy was incompetent," she said. "I can hardly be held accountable."

"What about that knight in Aleppo?" I reminded her. "We had to run all the way to—"

She scowled. "Why do you nag at me like an old maid? Stop your prattling. Here comes the squire."

When they faced off from each other, the size disparity between the two of them was startling. The squire Hughues was a huge young man, with broad shoulders and a big head. He must have weighed half Eva's weight again. He was smirking as he advanced toward her.

Eva stood straight and held her blunted sword lightly, resting the blade on her shoulder as she slid forward in a most casual manner. A man finds it difficult to see an attack that comes straight toward him. One cannot effectively judge the distance.

She brought her sword back as she moved and then exploded forward with a thrust to his face. Hughues jerked back and managed to get his own blade up to parry the thrust away. But Eva had him on the back foot and she pushed cuts at him, low and high, while he circled away. The squire's face went from swaggering confidence to shock to utter confusion as he found himself desperately flailing and outclassed with every blow.

Eva whipped her blade onto his wrist, hard enough to cause him to drop his sword with a clatter upon the paved stone underfoot. In quick succession, she struck his knee, chest, upper arm and knee again. Hughues' leg buckled and she slapped the flat of the blade against the side of his unarmoured head. The squire fell, whimpering and clutching his head.

"Yield, I yield, for the love of God."

Eva stood back from the downed man and nodded at the

crowd. Some were shocked, others laughed. Many were scowling as they filed away.

Thomas and Friar William were shocked but both held my gaze. The young monk Stephen grinned from ear to ear. The old monk was horrified.

Bertrand glared at me with open hostility. Through our squires, I had humiliated him once again in front of a senior Templar and a monk acting as the ambassador for the King of France. A noble like Bertrand was obsessed with his own status. Indeed, he was only taking this journey in order to regain the favour of the King.

I knew Eva had won us our place on the embassy to the Tartars.

And, as I watched Bertrand drag his squire away, I knew I had made a dangerous enemy.

PART TWO
PONTIC STEPPE
1253

WE MADE SAIL ACROSS THE BLACK SEA for the province of Gazaria, a triangular peninsula at the north of the sea. On its west side was a city called Cherson. The region would later come to be known as the Crimea.

"Cherson is the city where Saint Clement was martyred," Friar William said to me on the deck of the Genoese galley that we sailed on.

"How interesting," I said, looking out from the side of the foremost part of the galley at the seemingly endless expanse of water. In the south of that vast inland sea, the air was often humid in the summer and under a deluge in the mild winters. Up in the north, the summers were blazing hot and dry, and the winters bitterly cold.

The friar and I were alone, other than the gruff but efficient sailors who adjusted the rigging constantly to best capture the strong but blustery, changeable winds in the sail above our heads. The great sheet of canvas rippled and cracked as the wind moved about its course, thrumming into life whenever the force caught it flush and the lines snapped taut as though a monstrous beast had been captured and fastened to the mast.

"Do you know of the lands to which we travel?" Friar William asked. "I am told that you know these parts, to some degree?"

I nodded. "I know some. A Venetian had agreed to sell me his cog and his contacts with the cities around this sea. I took the time to learn of who I would trade with."

"Hmm," he said, nodding. "A knight and soldier such as yourself becoming a trader. I believe that to be somewhat unusual." When I did not respond, he continued. "Do the Genoese and Venetians not guard their trade against outsiders?"

"If you have enough gold, you can buy acquiescence," I said. "Especially from those men for whom gold is everything."

"And you are wealthy enough to purchase a ship of such size? And to provision and crew it? And purchase goods to trade with it?" The friar, I would discover, genuinely embraced the chief madness of his order. The Franciscans were ostentatious with their vow of poverty and William of Rubruck lived what his order commanded. "You must have won a great many tourneys, sir."

"I have been accumulating wealth for a very long time," I said, shrugging. "Wealth enables any man, even a knight, to do what he will."

"I do hope you have not brought a great deal of coin or gold with you, sir," Rubruck said, fretting. "Such wealth would only confuse the Tartars as to its purpose."

"It would not confuse them," I said. "If they knew one of us had gold, the first barbarian we come across would try to steal it. Do not be concerned. I may sometimes act foolishly, Friar William, but I am not a fool. My wealth is kept safely with the various Italian houses, and indeed, with the Templars."

"Good, good," William said, waving away consideration of my fortune with his fat fingers. "And you say you studied what goods you should trade with the Tartars? And what the key cities of the region are?"

The Flemish idiot was beginning to annoy me. "What do you want to know, Friar?"

He turned away from the sea to look at me. His smile dropped from his face. "Why are you here?"

I said nothing.

He pressed me further. "It is clearly not for the payment, as Thomas claimed."

"No. Not for the payment. I was going north alone, with my wife, as a trader. But you already have leave to travel through the barbarian lands. And I know a man who serves the Tartars, or at least lives in their lands."

Friar William scowled. "A man? What man?"

"A man who committed crimes all across Christendom and Outremer."

He was silent for some time then turned to glare out at the horizon instead of at me.

"And you mean to punish him?" There was an edge to the Friar's voice. He was controlling himself.

"All I wish," I said, "is to request a trial by combat. If the Tartars who shelter him grant it, we shall fight. If I win, it is over. Finally."

Rubruck squeezed his fat fists as he struggled to control his outrage.

"And should you lose this fight?"

I laughed. "Eva will return with you to Christendom and find another husband, I hope."

"What of us, then?" He was certainly angry but pretending quite well that he was not. "What evil will your hatred and your vengeance cause for us and our efforts to convert the pagans?"

"Evil? Vengeance?" I shook my head, sadly. "No, no, dear Friar. There is no hatred in my heart." I was far from certain that was the truth but I was not feeling hatred in that moment. "I will do everything that the Tartars require to stay within whatever barbaric laws and customs they have. If they do not grant me the trial by combat, I shall acquiesce. I would not force the matter. I shall say to him that I will see him again one day in Christendom and there bring him to justice." I shrugged. "It shall be as God wills."

Whether I was lying to the monk or lying to myself, I do not know. Either way, my words seemed to mollify him somewhat. "I shall not allow you to endanger our mission."

"I understand," I said to him, for monks and priests can be placated as if they were women. "You are right. God comes first, always."

44

"God and the Church," he said, looking down his nose at me.

"Of course."

"And the Pope."

His order had only grown into such power due to their fanatical devotion to orthodoxy and their willingness to be the aggressive right hand of a pope who used the Franciscans to keep the perverted, wine-sozzled, acquisitive priesthood in line.

"Yes, Friar William," I said, grinding my teeth. "I assure you I am thoroughly conventional in every way."

He stood, bringing himself to his full height and full girth. "I shall be watching you very closely. Both you and that woman. If you threaten our mission, I shall be forced to expel you. For the greater good."

How very Christian of you.

I fought the urge to slash open his gigantic belly and tip him into the sea and instead grinned at him like a lunatic.

"You do not need to worry about me, Friar. I shall cause you no trouble whatsoever."

* * *

The cabins were tiny, fetid and dark. I could not stand up straight, not even close to it and Eva and I had to share a bunk that was not large enough even for her alone. Upon the deck, by the bunk, we had a single chest for our belongings and some hooks for a lamp and clothing. The cabins ran down on either side of the ship at the prow end, with the stern to midships taken up with cargo.

For privacy, we each had a canvas curtain threaded through a rope that pulled almost closed across the small space. The walls of each tiny cabin were boards that were little thicker than parchment.

At least it gave us a modicum of privacy and so she could drink blood from my wrist every other night and thus remain in good health. Without drinking blood regularly, every three days at the most, her skin would progress from rude health into a pallid green, and her sharp mind would descend into savage madness. We had managed to avoid her going without blood for decades, other than a few times, now and then, when we had kept such close company that it was difficult.

Once, we were arrested attempting to leave Obidos after a fight in the street that was categorically not my fault. For a while, it appeared they were going to sell us into slavery and they left us chained up in a tower room given over to the purpose of holding undesirables like us. That little makeshift gaol was full of prisoners destined to be slaves. It was always well lit, and there was always at least one man staring at Eva, and often it was all of them. Lest we be further accused of practicing some evilness, she held off for three days, becoming sick and twitchy, sweating and groaning in her sleep. Once, I had starved a vampire monk named Tuck of blood, and my dear wife began to resemble that vile beast. Although I knew not to mention that to her at the time. When one of the prisoners saw her drinking blood from my wrist in the night, he woke up the rest with his outraged accusations. I beat him unconscious and warned the rest of them to mind their own business.

They stopped staring at her after that and we were released a couple of days later.

Outside Obidos, I swore to Eva that I would never allow her to be taken prisoner again as long as we lived.

Another oath that I would soon break. Another way that I would fail in my duty to protect my wife in the pursuit of my vengeance. For such a thing is so very easy to swear, and yet not so easy to avoid in the face of a hostile world. Taking Eva into the wilderness, into a land ruled by violent savages, and in the company of men who would happily do her harm, was contradictory to my duty. I should have foreseen how such a contradiction would end, but I did not, and so I brought her into the confined space of a galley sailing across a foreign sea.

Our company on that Genoese galley on the Black Sea was metaphysically divided into two distinct social tiers. Thomas, Bertrand and myself were knights and the friars William and Bartholomew were spoken to as if they were equals.

The two squires, the young monk Stephen Gosset, the friar's servant boy Nikolas and the dragoman, who was called Abdul, we never conversed with unless it was to issue them commands.

Eva did not fit in either station. She was a squire but also the wife of a knight. The monks and the knights, I am sure, thought of her as a woman merely playing at being a squire, in spite of her skill with the sword. And any woman who would do such a thing was not a true lady. The squires and servants, she made uncomfortable with her presence. For all of our company, she was a conundrum seemingly impossible to resolve.

But both Eva and I had encountered such difficulties before and the only way to deal with these things is to pretend outwardly that they concern you not at all.

Either way, we shared a bunk which was closer to the centre of the ship, closer to the hatch through which came the fresh air. The squires came next, then the dragoman, Abdullah and the boy Nikolas. Both of whom were as miserable and sick as otherwise healthy young men could be. But we needed no interpreters on the ship, so they were welcome to lay in their bunks, located hard under the prow. Their ceaseless groaning and vomiting was, however, most unwelcome and by far the healthiest place to be on the ship was up on deck.

"You deceived me," Thomas the Templar said as we leaned on the rail late on the second day. "With regards to the nature of your squire."

We were as alone as one could be on the galley, which was to say, surrounded by the ceaseless bustling of the crew but not within earshot of anyone important. A warm wind tugged constantly at us and the mist sprayed up from the ship's prow smashing through the choppy waves. To the west, the fertile lands shone green in the summer sun.

"I did not tell you my squire was a woman, that is true," I said. "And I apologise for putting you in that situation with the monk."

"Bertrand is angered."

"She thrashed his squire without breaking a sweat," I said, not bothering to hide my smile. "I am sure that he will come to terms with it, in time."

Thomas sighed. "You do not know the man."

I nodded, for that was true. But I was sure I knew the type of man that Bertrand was.

"Tell me, sir," I asked Thomas. "What did he do?"

The Templar hesitated. "What do you mean by that?"

I leaned further out, looking down at the white froth running in a torrent where the hull smashed through the water. "I mean, what hideous crimes did Bertrand commit for the King of France to send him on this God-forsaken lunatic's quest."

Thomas bristled at that and I thought I had pushed him too far. But he ground his teeth for a moment then sighed. "Do you know his family? He is the second son but the family has two castles and Bertrand has one for himself. Somewhere near Cahors. Good land. Rich land. Bertrand brought twelve knights and their followers with him on the crusade. All dead now."

"Bertrand was at fault?"

"For his lost men? The King was at fault. He threw away his army." Thomas spoke with deep bitterness. As well he might, for the catastrophe of Louis' crusade was agonising and fresh. "No, Bertrand escaped death or capture and has served the King in Acre since. That is where he lost the King's favour. Bertrand is not a man who does well in the close confines of a court. Give him a horse and an enemy and he will do God's work but when required to be Godly, he is unable to control his passions. He is full of sin."

"Which sin of Bertrand's did Louis take umbrage with?"

"Lust. Bertrand lay with a wealthy widow of Acre. She claimed that he forced himself upon her and yet a child was placed in her womb, so her word was disbelieved. However, the child was lost and the lady almost perished herself. Some said it was God's proof that the lady had been raped after all."

"She probably drank too much pennyroyal," I said. "Why was he not tried and convicted?"

"The local lords clamoured for it. Louis would not submit one of his men to their authority so he sent him away." Thomas rubbed his eyes while screwing up his face. "And I had been pressing the King for more knights to accompany me on the embassy so when he insisted upon Bertrand, I could do nothing but accept. Which he knew. What a fool I was."

In fact, it was I, Richard, who was the fool.

Because I saw it then, striking me as suddenly as a slap in the face. Thomas was old. Strong, and perhaps even skilled at arms, but of middling height and with a slender build. His Templar squire was young and so humble as to be invisible. Friar William was a big lump of a monk but monk he was. The other two Franciscans were either old and frail on the one hand, or full of little more than the idiotically mirthful joy of youth.

"You only wanted me to join you," I said, as realisation dawned, "so that I would help you to control Bertrand."

I laughed heartedly at my own dim-wittedness for not seeing it earlier.

Thomas scowled at my uncouth laughter. "I always wanted more men, within reason, but yes. When I saw your ability, your strength, and your stature at that sad little tourney, I believed that you could act as a force to temper Bertrand's passions. And that is one reason I am so displeased at your deceit." He cleared his throat. "She should not be left alone."

"You don't need to worry about Eva," I said. I had left her snoring away down on our bunk. I grinned at Thomas, hoping to put him at ease. "If anything, it is they who should be afraid of her."

Sheer bravado, on my part. I claimed that I was not worried about danger on the ship and yet I wore my sword at my side so I felt threatened on some level, even though I denied it. Despite my general caution, I did not know then quite how dangerous Bertrand could be. And God was listening to my dismissive arrogance.

"Your lack of shame is unbecoming," Thomas said.

I scoffed. "She is my wife. I need feel no shame."

"Not for laying with her," he snapped. "For your deception."

"Ah, yes," I said. "You regret my presence, then?"

"Yours? No. Your wife's? I fear it will only add to my burdens." He looked me in the eye. "Yet, on the whole, I believe I shall be glad to have you." A smile twitched on his lips. "If not merely for the chance to have courteous conversation."

"I have been called many things in my long life," I said. "But never before has my conversation been called courteous."

"Your long life?" he said, smirking at what he thought to be my youthful perspective. "When you get to my age, you may speak in such a manner."

I was unsure how he would react if I told him that I was eighty-four years old.

"It seems like a long time," I said.

"You speak of your quest for vengeance," Thomas said.

"I suppose I do," I admitted. "William has eluded me for years."

"What has led you to believe he is with the Tartars?"

I wished I could explain how I trawled the edges of Christendom for traces of William's evil. How I had been drawn to the holy wars with the Moors and Saracens and pursued tales of his particular brand of messianic, blood-fuelled violence. All to no avail. Nothing but faint echoes of William. Stories of an English, or Norman, or French knight who had drunk the blood of an enemy on the battlefield, or a townsperson in an alleyway. Tales of a spree of grisly murders in a region that remained unexplained, other than by the blaming of witchcraft, demons, Jews, or foreigners.

Decades of frustration while Eva and I had earned our daily bread by fighting for one lord or another.

And then there had come the tales of the Tartars. The barbarian horsemen from the East, raiding and doing battle with the Rus and Hungarians in the north and the Christian kingdoms of Armenia and Georgia in the Caucasus. The reports were confused and confusing. Some said it was little more than the usual raiding from those lawless people of the steppe. Others said that great armies numbering in the tens of thousands or hundreds of thousands had crushed Christian forces. Stories of cities being razed and people enslaved were not unusual, yet they told also of entire populations being slaughtered beneath their own walls. Lurid tales told of the Tartars killing in creative fashion, torturing defeated lords by crushing them beneath a table supported by writhing bodies while the victors feasted and drank upon it.

It sounded like William. If he was not involved already, I reasoned, he would be drawn to them sure as a lion is drawn to the stench of death.

"I knew William would seek them out," I said to Thomas. "He is himself a bloodthirsty heathen barbarian at heart and yet he believes himself to be in God's protection. And so, when I came once again to Constantinople, I asked the Venetians and Genoese to listen for tales of such a man in the company of the Tartars. It did not take long."

"And what did you hear?"

"That the Tartar prince, Batu, has a foreign Christian with him. A man named William."

Thomas nodded. "Many of the Tartars are Christian, so they say. We know that the great Batu is said to be considering a conversion to Christianity. And Batu's son, Sartak, is himself a Christian." He paused. "A Nestorian Christian, of course. So they say."

"So they say," I agreed.

Thomas' eyes flicked over my shoulder to something behind me.

I whipped around with my hand on the hilt of the dagger on my belt.

"All is well, sir," Thomas said, placing a hand on my arm.

Before he had spoken, I was already relaxed. For it was only the junior Franciscan, Stephen Gosset. The fair-haired young man lurked a few paces aft, glancing in our direction.

"What in the name of God's hands does that little turd want?"

Thomas coughed at my blasphemy. "I fear he wants to speak to me."

"Well, why does he not approach?" I turned and raised my voice. "Come here, then, lad. What in the name of God are you lurking about for?"

The monk hitched up his habit and ran down the hatch to the lower deck.

"I ask you, Thomas," I said. "Are monks the most useless creatures to ever crawl upon the Earth?"

"I believe he is somewhat afraid of you."

"Of me?" I said, in a voice raised due to my incredulity. "Why would he be afraid of me?"

Thomas sighed. "Truly, I could not say."

"Well, so, why did he want to speak to you?" I said. Although I could not say precisely why, I did feel somewhat rejected by the pathetic young English monk.

"I suspected he was hoping to leave the Franciscans and join my order, perhaps because he seeks excitement that the poor brothers lack. Stephen is quite fascinated with my tales. He has been hounding me for these months since we left Acre."

"Your tales?" I was confused. "Are you a secret troubadour?"

"Tales of my battles with the Saracens and the northern pagans," Thomas said, smiling. "And particularly of my battles with the Tartars."

"You fought the Tartars?" I was astonished. "Where? When?"

He opened his mouth but before he could answer, a muffled shriek split the air. I was already moving toward the source of the sound when the shouting started. An eruption of angry voices down below yelling with full-throated vitriol.

Eva.

I leapt through the hatch and down the steps to the lower deck. I pushed forward through the cramped, stinking crew quarters and then ran sideways between stacked chests of cargo with my head lowered under the crossbeams. My heart hammered from fear, from the knowledge that my wife was in danger, from the rising panic and rage that filled me, body and soul.

Right forward, in our passenger section, the narrow space between the cabins was filled with shouting men. Between them and me was the forward ladder up to the hatch above. It was dim, light filtering down from the daylight above and from lanterns hung in the cabins.

Bertrand was roaring, venting his spleen about something of enormous importance, while Hughues was shouting also. Another voice cut through; a high, unmanly voice.

I swung around the ladder and half-tripped over young Stephen, who was crouching in the shadows and watching the commotion from a safe distance. I swore and shoved him aside with my shoe, causing him to fall very roughly. I did not cease my forward momentum and instead leapt forward into the fray.

The large men had their backs to me, hunched over in the confined space. Hughues, the squire, had his dagger in hand while Bertrand had one meaty hand on the squire's shoulder and the other braced upon the beams above. What they were shouting at, forward under the prow, I could not see.

Moving with the rolling of the ship, I charged between the two men. Stamping my foot into the back of Hughues' knee, I pulled him back off his feet with one hand. At the same time, I drove my other fist into Bertrand's lower back. And then pushed against him with both hands. The huge knight fell against the cabin partition, cracking his head on a beam and cursing even as he fell.

I moved forward between them.

There was Eva. Facing me, standing with her back to the prow, gripping a dagger in one hand.

She was angry but appeared unhurt.

The servant boy Nikolas that Rubruck had purchased in Constantinople stood in front of her, little more than half her height.

"Get back," he snarled at me, speaking in heavily-accented French and brandishing a small, rusted eating knife. He had vomit on his chin and on the front of his tunic. "Stay back from the lady."

"All is well," Eva said to me, with a nod. She placed a hand on the boy's shoulder. "All is well, Nikolas." She patted him.

Friar William and Friar Bartholomew stood in the open doorways of their own cabins, canvas curtains pulled back, looking out at the scene with expressions of complete shock on their faces.

I turned as Bertrand began roaring in protestation.

"Your woman is mad, Englishman." The massive knight and lord dragged himself to his feet, his big face as red as a slapped arse. "She needs to be locked away. She needs to be taught a lesson. By God, I will teach it to her."

He jabbed his finger in the air while he held on to the ship as it rolled. Behind him, the squire Hughues got to his feet, clutching his face. Blood welled through his fingers and his tunic was already soaked at the top. I did not recall injuring him so but that is often the way.

"Did you hear me?" Bertrand said. He shuffled forward and

placed a hand upon the hilt of his sword.

He drew a third of it as he approached.

My own sword was at my hip.

I did not draw it.

"Stop," I said. I forced as much volume, authority, and contempt as I could into the single word.

Bertrand paused.

"What kind of man are you to threaten a woman with a weapon?" I said, sneering. "Put your sword away."

"She is no woman, she—"

I roared him down. "Put your sword away, sir."

He shoved it back into his scabbard. "She must be punished," he said, in a more civilised tone.

"Tell me what you think happened," I said.

"Are you blind?" Hughues the squire wailed. "She has cut my face, you fool. She has cut off my damned face."

Bertrand growled at him to be silent and then turned to me. "My squire has been assaulted. There must be restitution."

"Why did she cut him?" I asked Bertrand.

Hughues stuttered. "All I did was—"

"Silence," Bertrand shouted at his squire. "Another word from you unbidden and I truly will slice off your face." He turned to me. "Hughues wished to make an apology to your woman. However, she attacked him with a blade, as you can see for yourself."

I sidled over so I could turn to Eva while also keeping an eye on Bertrand. "And what do you say happened, Eva?"

Her face was grim but her voice loud, clear and steady as a

rock. "I was asleep in my bunk. I awoke to find Hughues leaning over me, his breath hot on my face and his hand on my shoulder, holding me down. He whispered at me to be silent as he placed the hand over my mouth while holding a dagger in front of my face. I took up my own dagger from beneath my blanket and lashed out. I decided not to slit his throat and instead pushed him from the cabin. Then he began to wail like an old woman and here we all are."

I looked around at the monks. "Are there any witnesses?"

They shook their heads and avoided my eye. Monks are men who are paralysed by violence. That is why they become monks.

Bertrand spluttered. "This is not a trial. You have no authority to judge guilt or declare innocence and my squire has been grievously harmed with no cause by that—"

"You are lucky, sir," I said, raising my voice so that it filled the ship. Then I waited while he frowned in confusion. "You are lucky, sir, that I do not cut off your squire's head and throw it and the rest of him into the sea this very moment." He began to object once more but I did not give him the chance. "You will take your squire up onto the deck and explain to him that ravishing a woman is against the law. And wash out that wound with sea water, lest it becomes corrupted and rots his head from the inside. Go now."

I turned my back on him and went to Eva. It was a risk to do so but I knew that such blustering men were, as a rule, cowardly in their hearts. And a coward loves nothing more than being given instructions to follow. Perhaps Bertrand understood my gibe about ravishing a woman was aimed at his own transgression in

Acre and that served to confound his indignation. Whatever the reason, they stomped up the ladder, blocking the light for a moment and then they were gone, their shoes stomping away on the upper deck.

I glanced over my shoulder to ensure we were indeed safe, for the time being and noticed that behind the ladder, Thomas lurked in the shadows amongst a group of grinning crewmen. Catching my eye, the old Templar nodded once and moved away forward on the lower deck.

I asked Eva, with a look, whether she was well. She rolled her eyes and shoved her dagger into her belt.

The little slave Nikolas was still standing in front of my wife, between the two of us, staring at me with distrust in his eyes.

"Why did you place yourself in harm's way, boy?" I asked him.

He frowned and looked down. "I am sorry, lord," he said. His Greek accent was very thick but his use of French was perfectly fine.

"You have done nothing wrong. But what did you think you could do against two such men?"

He shrugged, still looking down. "Protect the lady, sir."

"And who taught you to do that?"

He was confused. "Taught me, sir?"

"Who trained you, instructed you, that it was a man's duty to protect women?"

The slave kept staring at his toes. "I am sorry but I do not understand, sir."

I looked up at Eva who merely shrugged.

Reaching down, I took hold of his besmirched chin and tilted his head up. "How many years have you, boy?"

He frowned. "Mad Alex said I was ten when he sold me to master William."

I had no idea who Mad Alex was but presumably a slave trader or former master.

"Show me that knife," I commanded.

He handed it up and I took it from him. It was perhaps two inches long, the edge on it as blunt as the handle, which was poorly wrapped in an ancient strip of leather that was coming apart.

I handed it back to him. "You have the heart of a knight, young Nikolas and you should have a knight's weapon. But you are too small for a sword. Until you get taller, you must use this."

From my belt, I took my dagger in its decorated leather sheath and held it out to him.

The blade was an excellent steel that held a wicked edge for months. But the real beauty of the thing was the ivory hilt. There was a glorious and deep carving on both sides of Saint George at full charge, driving his lance into the body of the dragon while it writhed around the wound in a most lifelike fashion. As if the dragon was snarling at the knight and about to bite his head off. As if the outcome of the battle between the man and the beast was far from a foregone conclusion. It had cost me more than I could spare twenty years earlier from a master smith in Antioch.

Nikolas reached up, slowly, hands shaking all the way and then clutched the sheathed blade to his filthy, narrow little chest.

Eva clipped him across the head, but softly. "What do you say, boy?" she said.

60

"Thank you, sir," Nikolas said and he ran off to his bunk.

I saw the dragoman, our interpreter Abdullah laying on his bunk and staring out at me. "Bloody Saracens," I said. "Where were you, eh? Grown man, laying there and doing nothing?"

Abdullah simply turned over in his bunk, facing away from me.

The two older monks were clucking over Stephen and examining his arm by probing it with their fingers while the young man winced. I recalled how I had injured Stephen in my haste to rescue Eva. All three of them at once caught my eye and scowled before turning away from me.

"Tell me, my love. Why do I make enemies everywhere I go?" I wondered aloud.

"We all reap what we sow," Eva said. "We will take turns sleeping from now on. While the other stands watch."

* * *

We arrived then in Soldaia in late May. The city stood at the apex of the triangle that is the Crimean Peninsula, on the south side, and it looked across towards Sinopolis. It was a trading centre at the extreme borders of dozens of lands. Thither came all the merchants arriving from Russia and the northern countries who wished to pass into Turkia. The latter carried vair and minever, and other costly furs. Others carried cloths of cotton or bombax, silk stuffs, and sweet-smelling spices.

The city was subject to the Tartars and every year had to pay a great tribute to Prince Batu, else their thriving city would be destroyed by the barbarians. However, they paid that tribute with false but prompt enthusiasm and so were left alone to do their trade, and to become wealthy even in spite of the payments they provided to their overlords. As far as I knew, the city prefects were more than pleased with the arrangement, despite being Christians under the rule of pagan savages.

Although some citizens were Genoese, others were their enemies the Venetians, and many more still were Rus and the like, those unpleasant folk with squashed features and cold-ravaged skin. There were Greeks in their hundreds or thousands for all I know, and Bulgars and other people from the diverse lands all about us. Who the natives were I have no idea, although it was probably the Greeks, as they had founded so many places on the Black Sea just as they had on the shores of the Mediterranean.

Others there, living as well as trading, were the Saracens. Chiefly, those that were Turks but also those from Syria and other far-off lands. And amongst them, and over them too, were the peoples who were from the steppe. Advising, guarding, and taking stock of all that went on there, with their cunning eyes and their tails of bowing scribes who made certain that the Tartar lords were not being cheated or plotted against.

"This is a strange land," I said to Eva as the ship bobbed outside the port. "Strange people."

"This is what you want," Eva pointed out. "Always seeking what is over the horizon, never settled in one place. You revel in strangeness."

I shrugged, uncomfortable with her accusations. "I go where William's trail leads."

She scoffed. "You go where your heart leads."

Reaching along the rail, I took her hand and peered into her suspicious eyes. "My heart leads only to you."

"I know what part of you leads to me," she said, lowering her voice. "And it is not your heart."

Nevertheless, she held on to my hand.

Looking around, I saw the man I wanted. "Abdullah," I cried. "Come here."

The scrawny man came forward along the deck, his bony shoulders bent inward. He was a young man, or young enough, but it had taken me days to realise the fact. He had the appearance of an ancient creature, beaten down by the regular blows of disappointment. Thomas had purchased him in Acre and claimed that, for all the man's obvious misery, his ability with languages was second to none. He was said to have detailed knowledge of the lands of the Tartars, their languages, and their customs. He also claimed to have once been a famed scholar at a great house of learning so he was likewise clearly a great liar.

"Abdullah," I said. "Why are you dawdling so, man?"

He cringed with every word and Eva leaned in close to me. "Speak softly, Richard. He is close to being a broken man."

"Oh, for the love of God," I muttered. But you should always obey your wife, other than those times when you do not wish to. I spoke to him with a courteous tone. "Abdullah, you wise young Saracen, come here and converse with me."

He shuffled over, looking out from under his long black

eyelashes like a coy princess. "How may I serve you, lord?"

"They tell me you have knowledge of the lands here about. I hear that some of the cities and kingdoms resist the Tartars and are not subjected to their rule. Will there be people from those lands in this city of Soldaia which lays before us?"

He frowned, unsure of why I was asking. I did not explain it to him but, in truth, it was simple. You never know who might one day be your allies, and who may be your enemies. And my main reason was that I wanted already to plan my escape from the Tartars.

Should it ever come to that.

"Yes, lord. Beyond this city, unseen to the east, is Zikuia, which does not obey the Tartars. And to the east of there are the Suevi and Hiberi, who also do not obey the Tartars. After that, further around the coast of the sea but to the south, is Trebizond, which has its own lord, Guido by name, who is of the family of the emperors of Constantinople, and he obeys the Tartars."

I waved my hand. "I know about Trebizond," I said. "That is on the other side of the sea from us entirely, you bloody fool. What about the other way?" I pointed to the west. "Who in the north and the west is there who is not subject to the Tartar rule?"

Instead, Abdullah pointed to the northeast. "From the city of Tanais," he said, and began to sweep his hand across from east to west. "All the way to the Danube, all are subject to the Tartars. Even beyond the Danube, lord, towards Constantinople. Do you know of Wallachia, which is the land of the Assan and Minor Bulgaria as far as Sclavonia? All of them pay tribute, lord. All. Even more, they say that the Tartars, as you call them, have taken in the past years from each house one axe and all the iron which they found unwrought."

I had heard that the Tartars had subjected many lands but hearing it again when I was on the edge of their territory, was greatly disturbing. A barbarian, savage people, who had conquered and subdued so many. Wherever we ran to, should Eva and I need to run, we would be travelling amongst people who would hand us over to the Tartars in order to save themselves from their wrath.

Eva intruded into my thoughts with a question for Abdullah. "What do you mean when you say, as you call them?"

"My lady?" Abdullah asked.

"You said the Tartars, as we call them," Eva said. "We call them Tartars, yes indeed we do. But what do you call them?"

He bobbed his head, eyes wide. "A simple slip of the tongue, my lady. My lord. My French is truly woeful. I beg your pardons for my stupidity and ignorance."

"Your French is bloody disgusting," I said. "And your false obsequiousness is revolting, I command you to stop that nonsense. But if you do not tell me the truth about the Tartars, I shall be forced to rip out your tongue entirely and toss it to the dogs." Saracens have an almost spiritual terror of dogs. I have no idea why. But it often does the trick.

Bobbing his head, he explained. "The Franks and Latins call them Tartars. They name themselves Mongols."

"Mongols?"

"Mongols, lord."

"Then, who in the name of God are the Tartars?"

"Some other tribe, lord. Barbarians, like the Mongols. In fact, there are a great number of tribes from the grasslands, stretching back into Asia and all of them have been subjugated by those that call themselves Mongols." The young Saracen grew ever more confident as he spoke. His voice became clearer and louder until it was almost as though he was preaching. "The Cumans are now the westernmost people who we call Tartars and these are the lands of the Cumans who we must cross to reach Batu, in the north beyond them. The Cumans fled the Mongols, and the Hungarians gave them sanctuary. But something went bad. It was all a trick, perhaps. The Cumans attacked the Hungarians, and the Mongols subjugated the Cumans. Further into the east, tribe after tribe is subject to the Mongols. One subject tribe is the Uighurs, whose script the Mongols use for writing in their own language. They do this because the Mongols are the most barbarian people of all the tribes of the East and were so ignorant that they had no form of writing of their own."

I stopped his babbling, confused by everything he said but that last, most of all. "Do you mean to say the Mongols were the most barbaric of all these savages and yet they conquered them all?"

He smirked. "The Mongols, so it is said, were so impoverished, lord, that they lived in the worst land in all Tartary, in the harsh mountains. And they had to sew together the skins of field mice to make their cloaks. But there was one amongst them, many years ago, named Chinggis, who became the leader. A giant, so they say. And he was so strong in the art of war that he conquered all, and none could conquer him in turn. And now they rule from Cathay, in the east, to Hungary in the west. All the tribes fight as one, now. They have armies of tens of thousands and even a hundred thousand or two hundred thousand horsemen."

I burst out laughing. "What utter nonsense."

He frowned and winced, and began to protest. But I cut him off and sent him on his way.

Eva was displeased. "You should listen to him."

"He is a fool," I said. "But I am the bigger fool for asking him. If we need to run, we will simply go west. Back into Christian lands. To the Kingdom of Hungary or the Kingdom of Poland."

Thomas' voice spoke over mine. "You mean to run, do you, Richard?"

The sneaky old bastard had crept up on me like a cat.

"Of course not," I said, not attempting to hide my irritation. "Yet it never hurts to make preparations for any eventuality."

"Unless I release you," Thomas said, "there shall be no running anywhere, at any time. Do you understand me, Richard?"

Eva placed a hand on my forearm.

She was right, and I swallowed my anger.

"I swore no oath to you, Thomas," I said, with as much calmness as I could muster. "Nor to Friar William. Not even to the King of France. But I shall do as I have said, which is to travel with you to the court of Prince Batu and there challenge William to a trial by combat. Between now and then, I shall protect you. From the Tartars. And also from other threats." I nodded over the Templar's shoulder.

We watched as Bertrand and then Hughues climbed over the side, down into the little barge which would convey all of us in turn to the busy shore while our ship awaited its berth in the harbour.

"He means to be first ashore," said Thomas. "Even though Friar William and Friar Bartholomew are the ones who demanded the barge so that they could arrange our onward transport without delay."

"Aye," I said. "That Bertrand is a strutting bloody old cockscomb. His arrogance will make further trouble in the north."

"His arrogance, yes." Thomas cleared his throat, managing to convey disapproval with the sound. "I trust that you will both remain on your finest, most courteous behaviour from now onwards."

I looked across the shimmering water at the city of Soldaia. It was the last outpost of civilisation before we crossed into the steppe and placed ourselves under the rule of the savages.

"Bertrand may be a prideful brute," I said, "yet he is a wealthy lord and a Christian. And yes, you are right that I also am arrogant, Thomas. And my sins are many. I am filled with wrath. But we stand here at the edge of the world and what lies beyond is all darkness. Bertrand is not my enemy. My enemy is out there, and he is the greatest sinner that ever walked the Earth."

* * *

We were not long in the small city itself. There had preceded us certain merchants of Constantinople who had said that envoys from the Holy Land were coming who wished to go to Prince

Batu. This man Batu was the ruler of the Mongols' northern and western forces and was one of the most powerful and richest men in the entire world.

"But I am no envoy," Friar William said, to the group of Genoese merchants and prefects of the city who had prepared our way.

All of our party sat at a long table with those merchants in a very pleasant courtyard in the richest quarter of Soldaia, eating fresh fish cooked in olive oil. It was warm, both the food and the people smelled good and clean, and I was comfortable and happy. Eva, the other two squires, and the servants were somewhere in the back. Eva had returned to pretending to be a young man and strutted around with her head down beneath an oversized hood. I concentrated on shoving as much food as I could into myself while I could, and I knew Eva would be doing the same with whatever slop she had been served. We had years of experience with travelling and we knew to make the most of fresh, hot food and sweet wine while we could.

"You say you are no envoy?" The chief amongst the Genoese merchants was startled. "Yet, we have sent word to the Cumans that you are an envoy, Friar William."

William was inexplicably outraged, his cheeks quivering as he responded. "I publicly preached on Palm Sunday in Saint Sophia that I was not an envoy. Neither the King's nor anyone's, but that I was going among the unbelievers according to the rule of my order."

The Genoese and the prefects all stirred, exchanging meaningful looks. The leader shifted in his seat. "If you please,

Friar William, may I caution you to speak guardedly, for we have said that you are an envoy. What is more, if you now say that you are not an envoy, you will none of you be allowed to pass with safe conduct through the Mongol lands."

Before the Franciscans could raise further objections, Thomas spoke up. "Of course, my friends. We understand perfectly."

Bertrand and I nodded our sincere agreement.

"We do not understand, sir," William said, his big face flushing red. "You say I must deceive our hosts with regards to our intentions? How can I do such a thing?"

"So, say nothing," I said, speaking with my mouth full of oil, fish, and bread. "Eat your supper, Friar. Try the olives."

"My lords," William of Rubruck said, heeding not a word. "It is imperative that we are not seen as envoys. For I do not wish to discuss matters of earthly power but to spread the true word of God and of the Pope in Rome. We have heard say in the Holy Land that your lord Batu may become a Christian, and greatly were the Christians of the Holy Land rejoiced thereat. And chiefly so the most Christian lord the King of the French, who has come to that land on a pilgrimage and is fighting against the Saracens to wrench the holy places from out of their hands. It is for this I wish to go to Batu, and also carry to him the letters of the lord king, in which he admonishes him of the weal of all Christendom."

"Letters," I said, and slammed my palm against the table with much force and the loud bang cut William off from his babbling. "Letters from the King of France to the Prince Batu. I ask you, my lords, does that not make us envoys, after all?" I looked around at

70

everyone while nodding my head, and focused my attention on Friar William. "Yes, indeed it does, my lords, quite right, yes."

Thomas picked up from me, speaking over William's protestations. "You have our thanks, lords, for sending word ahead on our behalf, to your overlord. Our sincerest thanks. We shall say prayers for you, will we not, Friar William?"

And when they knew that we would not cause them diplomatic difficulties, the prefects did receive us right favourably and gave the three friars lodgings in the episcopal church. The rest of us were given use of rooms in the villa of an old Genoese merchant who bowed repeatedly and told us how honoured he was to have us as his guests, even while his servants removed the valuable decorations from our rooms behind him.

For the journey into the wilderness, they gave us the choice whether we would have carts with oxen to carry our effects or sumpter horses. The merchants of Constantinople advised William of Rubruck to take carts, and that he should buy the regular covered carts such as the Rus carry their furs in, and in these we could put such of our things as we would not wish to unload every day. They said that oxen would be the best choice.

"Oxen are so very slow," I said, to William and to Thomas. "With those lumbering beasts, we shall not reach Batu before the Day of Judgement."

Even Bertrand agreed with me, as he was eager to complete his task with as much haste as possible so he could return to his king that much sooner and so return to his favour. Ideally, Bertrand wished to get back to Acre before King Louis left the Holy Land or else he risked being forgotten by the court, and his ambition would be thwarted for years and perhaps forever.

But William of Rubruck, the incompetent great oaf, did not wish to insult our hosts by going against their recommendations. "Should we take horses it will be necessary to unload them at each stopping place and to load other horses," he said, "because you see my lords, horses are so much weaker than oxen."

We took the oxen, and so doubled the travelling time for that part of our journey. Eva cautioned patience and so I did my best to accommodate the slothfulness of that gluttonous heap of pompous dogmatism, William of Rubruck.

For all his many faults, he was not a stupid man. Naive, of course, in the worst possible way. But not stupid. He had brought with him from Constantinople, on the advice of canny merchants, fruits, muscadel wine and dainty biscuits to present to the captains of the Tartars that we met so that our way might be made easier.

"For, among these Tartars," Friar William told me, "no man is looked upon in a proper way who comes into their land with empty hands."

We set out on our journey from Soldaia about the calends of June 1253 with our six covered carts in which was carried our supplies, belongings, and bedding to sleep on at night. And they gave us horses to ride, one for each of us. They gave us also two gruff men who drove the carts and looked after the oxen and horses.

And so arrayed, we set off into the wilderness.

The path north across the landscape was wide, and well-trod and the weather dry, and hot. Our horses were not good. They were short and sturdy enough, but they could manage only a slow pace and had to be nurtured less they tire themselves into standstill before the day was over. Bertrand had immediately seized the best horse for himself, that is to say, the largest and strongest. Thomas had taken the next best due to his status, and Friar William, arguing that he required a sizeable mount due to his own bulk, took the next best.

Eva had given me a probing look on the first day.

"It is not worth the conflict that would result from arguing," I had muttered.

"And yet, if we must flee..." she then began, indicating our tired old nags.

I had lowered my voice. "Then we kill them and take their good horses."

Eva had relaxed. "Fair enough."

Through each day, we rode upon our horses while the six wagons—which were sturdy, four-wheeled things pulled by a pair of oxen each—trundled along behind us. Each wagon was tied to the one before it so that the two moody servants the merchants had provided simply had to drive the first pair and the others followed in turn. The wagons carried our supplies for the journey and also the many gifts that we had been strongly advised to bring for the Mongol lords, as such things were expected.

Riding on poor horses is tiring and we spoke little as we travelled. When we stopped to make camp, we drew up the wagons all close together and used them to corral the horses and to partly shelter against the wind. We made small fires for as long as it took to boil fresh water collected in the day to make it safe for drinking, and sat to eat the food we had brought from the city. There was no reason to stay awake for longer than necessary, so we each retired to our bedrolls. It was still warm at night, so sleeping wrapped in our blankets upon the grass was perfectly comfortable. Bertrand demanded that he sleep upon the bundles of furs we had brought as gifts on the back of one of the wagons. None challenged him, yet he appeared pleased with his petty victory over us.

Every other night, Eva would drink her fill of blood from a cut I would make across the veins of my wrist. Decades before it had felt strange, to be drunk from in such fashion but by then, our final years together, I paid it little heed. Her drinking of me gave me great thirst, for blood, water, or wine that I would need to satiate as soon as I was able. Yet, any weakness was not long lasting and she needed it.

Together, we lay entwined, her head resting upon my shoulder, or she would sprawl her upper body across my chest so that the good weight of the woman held me down. With her in my arms, I stayed awake for as long as I could every night to be alert for assault from without or from within. When I felt myself falling asleep, I would wake my wife and she would pinch herself into alertness and take over the watch.

What a remarkable land it was. Good land for farming but it was not defensible and yet it seemed to be peopled with groups from everywhere on the Earth. There were forty hamlets between Soldaia and the land bridge of the peninsula and nearly every one had its own language. All these places were subject to the Mongols, of course, and none of them mixed with each other.

Among them were many Goths, whose language was Teutonic. I was told that there were Saxons thereabout, descended from men who had fled from the Norman conquest hundreds of years earlier. I greatly wished to meet these Saxons but no one knew where their villages were and I grew to suspect either they had all been killed or the entire story was a fabrication.

The guides were barely willing to exchange words with me but with much cajoling and with their words translated by the slave boy Nikolas, I winkled the knowledge of the wild land out of them. They told me that from Soldaia all the way along the coast to the city of Tanais to the east there were high promontories along the sea. And beyond the mountains to the north was a most beautiful forest, in a plain full of springs and rivulets. And beyond that forest was a mighty plain which stretched out to the border of the peninsula to the north, where it narrows greatly into a land bridge, having the sea to the east and the west. Once we were beyond that border we would be on the endless steppe, the grassland that ran from Hungary in the west to the ends of the Earth in the east.

Each time we stopped at sundown, I would ask Abdullah more about the people who populated the steppe and he would explain while some of us listened to his words, sitting upon the grass or on the backs of the wagons, while we ate what food we had in the moments before retiring for the night. The young Saracen slave grew somewhat confident when he spoke of such things, seeming almost wise at times, although we had to watch he did not get hold of the wine because he was a terrible sot.

"In the plain beyond us used to live Cumans before the

Mongols came from the east," Abdullah said. "Once, it was the Cumans that forced the cities and villages hereabout to pay them tribute. The Cumans were once from the east, and there they were subject to the Mongols but had fled here to escape their subjugation. But when the Mongols came, the Cumans feared their retribution and they fled down into this peninsula for the first time. Such a multitude of Cumans entered this province that the people of the villages fled to the shore of the sea. But there was nowhere further to flee, and no food to be eaten, for the Cumans had taken it all. And so all these people ate one another. The living ate the dying, as was told me in Damascus by a merchant who saw it. Saw the living devouring and tearing with their teeth the raw flesh of the dead, as dogs do corpses."

None of us had anything to say to that. Bertrand scoffed as if he disbelieved it, but his big face showed he was as disturbed as any of us.

"What happened to the Cumans?" I asked.

Abdullah shrugged. "They were subjugated by the Mongols once again." He squirted a stream of wine into his mouth from a skin. The ancient, frail Friar Bartholomew leapt to his feet, hitched up his robes as he scurried over and slapped Abdullah about the head before yanking the wineskin from him.

Toward the end of the province were many large lakes, on whose shores were brine springs which the locals used for the making of salt. And from these brine springs, Prince Batu derived great revenues, for from all Rus they came to that place for salt, also many ships came by sea. The young Franciscan lad, Stephen, was most intrigued by the notion that a fortune could be made from salt and expressed that curiosity that evening at camp.

"Your interest in worldly wealth is unseemly," Friar Bartholomew said to chastise him, while Friar William nodded.

"It is not my own personal wealth that interests me," Stephen said, innocently, "I simply wish to cultivate a clearer understanding of the world."

Friar William scoffed. "Cultivate your need to practice simplicity and detach yourself from materiality instead."

"And not only that," Friar Bartholomew said, in a nagging tone while Stephen hung his head. "You must become more charitable."

I burst out laughing. No one else laughed with me but I thought I could see a hint of a smile on Stephen's face before he hid it behind a biscuit.

And so, three days after leaving Soldaia, we came across the Mongols.

When I found myself among them, they were so strange, so repulsive, and backward that it seemed to me that I had been transported into another century far into the past, or to another world entirely.

How long they had been tracking us, I could not say. That country was alien to me, and I could not read the land, could not see it, in the way that I have always been able to read the land of England, France and the rest of Christendom. Even so, late on that third morning, we saw riders on the horizon. We stopped our wagons and waited where we were, as was the proper procedure. A group of ten men approached on stocky little horses the size of ponies, with a few more riderless horses following behind.

It was early summer and the day was hot, the wind warm and full of the smell of grass, and fragrant herbs. As the sun was so high, most of our party sat beneath the wagons as it was the only shade anywhere in sight.

I wore only a cotton tunic, hose, shoes and a wide-brimmed hat and, despite the heat, I badly wished to put on my armour. When facing an enemy, I always wanted to be wearing my long mail hauberk, with a coif for my head, neck, and throat and then an enclosed helm to protect my head. Ideally, I would wear chausses, which were mail armour for my legs. And yet we three knights; Bertrand, Thomas and I, had agreed that appearing before the Mongols while dressed for war would be provocative and may cause us more problems than it would solve. I had argued hard for wearing our gambesons at least, with a loose tabard over the top to disguise the armour. Bertrand was ready to agree but Thomas insisted that it would be just the same, or nearly so, as wearing mail and that a tabard would fool no man, not even a savage.

"We will at least wear our swords, will we not, Thomas?" I had said.

"Even that may provoke them into some evil action," Thomas had countered.

"We cannot be defenceless," Bertrand had blustered.

"Put your faith in God, sir," Thomas had said, with a certainty that brooked no argument.

Bertrand had nodded his monstrous great head, scowling. "I do, Thomas," he said, a sound that was more growl than words. "I shall. But a knight should have his sword at his hip."

Even though I agreed with Bertrand, I was honour bound to side with Thomas and so we stood, wearing no more than light clothing, waiting for a group of brutal savages whose intentions were unknown. If I had been wearing my gambeson, the thick layers of linen would have made me sweat profusely under such a sun, but that was the price we paid for protection against sword and arrow. Without it, I was vulnerable to the arrows that I knew all Tartars carried.

While they were still some way off, I strolled as if I had not a care in the world to the side of the wagon where I had stashed my gear, and I leaned against the side. Eva strutted over and leaned by me, pulling her own hat down over her face. She hated the bright sunlight and kept her skin covered when out of doors, even if not attempting to pass as a man.

Nodding to her, I climbed up and reached over the side boards into the wagon and pulled my stashed sword up slightly so that I would be able to draw it swiftly, should I need to. Getting down again, I leaned my arm on the side of the wagon, ready to move. I watched the riders approach.

All of us were quiet.

"Remember to breathe," Eva muttered.

I let out a huge sigh. "I was not holding my breath," I said.

We had all been apprehensive about our first meeting with the Mongols since we had set out from the city. Even the brash Bertrand had grown ever quieter the further north we had gone. The friars especially so. The elderly Bartholomew was so terrified that I could see him shaking beneath his robes from twenty-feet away.

The servants clustered together behind us, beneath two of the wagons farthest from the riders' approach.

"Do nothing to anger them," Friar William called to us all from beside the foremost wagon as the riders approached. "I shall speak for us. Do not overrule me or we will appear divided to them."

Before even leaving the city of Soldaia, we had agreed exactly that. In fact, it was my recommendation that we maintain a united front. The friar was doing no more than betraying his nervousness by speaking so to us, which was understandable. The Tartars were conquering devils.

I had seen many strange peoples from far off lands during my travels in Iberia and Outremer over the decades. I had seen tall, dark men from the highlands of Ethiopia, who worshipped Christ with as much reverence as any priest. I had seen even darker men from beyond Ethiopia, brought to the Holy Land as slaves by the Saracens, who despised the black men and whipped them most brutally.

But no people I had ever seen were as hideous and vile as the Mongols. Their stink greeted us, even when they were a long bow-shot away and the smell grew overwhelming as they approached. A sour, foul smell such as a man gets when he has not washed his body for a year or more. A cloying, oppressive stench as foul as brewed piss, like a tanner's yard, but with an animal breadth and depth that filled one's nose like a poison.

They were all clothed in thick, long, light brown overcoats. The belts wrapped about their middles were decorated in brass, with slightly curved swords suspended from them, bouncing as they rode. Each man also had a short, curved bow and a huge quiver absolutely packed with arrows. Even in that summer heat, they wore trousers and thick, long boots. Most wore a sort of quilted hood with fur on the inside. A couple of them were bare-headed and they had the most bizarre hair. The entire scalp was shaved to stubble, other than the front and back, where the jet-black hair was tightly braided into thin, ratty strands longer than their faces.

All ten of them rode with a swagger the like of which I had rarely seen from the most arrogant of Christian lords. They spread themselves in a wide arc as they ambled up to us. Their other horses, twenty or more, trailed behind without ropes tying them together. The ten men spread out and those in front pulled to a stop a few paces from our wagons, while the others kept their horses walking.

Friar William stood and went to greet them, and young Stephen went at his shoulder. Old Bartholomew hung farther back but shuffled after them, as did Abdullah, like one of the Mongol remounts.

The riders on the flanks continued to ride slowly, surrounding us on their horses, staring at us with sneering contempt upon their faces.

And what faces they were. Wide, round faces, as though they had been stretched by a mighty hand. Eyes narrow and filled with animal cunning, and thin black moustaches twitching beneath squashed noses. Their complexion was swarthy from the sun and yet wind-ravaged about the cheeks. Each man wore an expression of the haughtiest contempt and scathing viciousness. These were men who had done evil things, and who had suffered evil things done to them in turn.

One of them spoke, suddenly. Barking his barbaric language in a harsh, throaty voice like a broken trumpet.

Abdullah bowed and turned to Friar William. "He demands to know whether we have ever been among them before."

William half-turned to Abdullah. "Tell him that we have not ever been amongst them. Tell them that this is indeed our first time here in these lands, yes. Tell him so."

Abdullah babbled his response back to the four Mongols who had reign in right before us.

I watched as the savages rode slowly by me, three on my side. On the other side of our group, three more rode around. Bertrand and Hughues were on the other side. Bertrand had one meaty hand clamped down on his squire's shoulder. That was good.

In the centre, Thomas and his squire stood straight and tall, as if he had done such a thing a thousand times. Such is the strength that faith can give to a man.

Eva looked down, hiding her face with the brim of her hat. I stared at the riders, half-willing them to attack me. The one nearest to me sneered and muttered something to the fellow behind him, and they both laughed. A savage, hacking noise.

My heart's desire was to leap at the man, run him down and smash his hideous face into pulp.

Instead, I stayed still and watched them position themselves around us. We were badly outnumbered, for there were six fighters on our side and ten on theirs. Also, they were mounted and had bows and swords ready, while we stood unarmoured and unarmed.

On the other hand, we had the wagons drawn up somewhat together, which would impede their charge or provide cover from arrows. Our horses were saddled and ready to ride, but I would not fight from the back of a horse who was not trained to it. You may as well save yourself the trouble of climbing on and instead throw yourself onto your spine and smash your face with a hammer.

"What is he saying, Abdullah?" William said, as the lead Mongol babbled on and on, whilst gesticulating wildly.

"He is asking for some of our provisions, lord," Abdullah said, his voice shaking.

"That seems fair," William said, turning to us. "A small gift, a token from us. That we might share bread. Yes, yes, that is perfectly right and proper enough. Stephen? Would you mind gathering together a piece of biscuit for each man, and I think one of the skins of wine. Yes, a whole skin, why not, let us be generous."

Stephen called over the boy Nikolas and together they rooted out a basket with ten or fifteen of the small biscuits, which were wheat breads baked twice so that they were as hard as rock and had to be soaked in water or wine or milk before they were edible. The large skin of wine sloshed loudly as Stephen manhandled it back to the Mongols. They took the wine very roughly, with no manners nor sign of gratitude at all, and drank with gusto, passing the skin between them. The biscuits they crunched with their teeth, biting pieces off and chewing with their mouths hanging open. After only a few moments, one of the men tossed the wineskin to the grass, empty.

The Mongols before William began gesturing wildly again while they babbled at William, jutting their outstretched hands to the wagons behind us.

"What is he saying?" William said, backing up against the onslaught of heathenish language.

"He insists that we give them more," Abdullah said. "Apologies, lord, he says we must give them more wine. Another skin."

"I am not sure that we have enough," William said. "Tell them we do not have enough."

The Mongols did not like what Abdullah said, and the lead man rode his horse slowly, right at William. As he rode, he spoke in a low voice.

"He says, lord," Abdullah said, "that a man enters a house not with one foot only."

"Well, he can keep both feet out of my house, if that is his attitude," William said, puffing up his big belly. "The impudence of the man."

Abdullah began to jabber away but William cut him off.

"Wait, wait," William said, holding up his palms as the Mongol bore down on him. "Stephen, please would you find another skin of wine for our guests."

I was already moving before I made the decision to do so. I covered the distance quickly but walked with as casual an air as was possible. I was unarmed and had no wish to alarm the heathens.

Clapping my palm down on Stephen's shoulder as he turned,

I stopped him from moving away. Stephen tried to shake me off but I held him firm then pushed him back to where William stood gaping at me.

"What are you doing?" he hissed at me, eyes wide.

I planted my other hand on William's big shoulder and squeezed it, so I stood between and slightly behind the two monks, making a wall out of our bodies. I grinned up at the Mongol rider.

He scowled down at me and babbled some of his disgusting language.

"No," I said, shaking my head and still grinning like an idiot while the monks shook.

Our interpreter began to explain but I cut him off.

"I understand him, Abdullah," I said, looking up at the agitated Mongol. From the corner of my eye, I watched as others moved their horses closer. "And you understand me, don't you, you heathen bastard." I dropped my smile and raised my voice. "No more wine. No more food. Take us to your master."

He rode right up to us and turned his horse sideways with no instruction that I could see. With excellent horsemanship, he somehow got the creature to sidle into us so that its flanks were pressing against the monks. The beast was short but well-muscled, with a round belly. The stinking Mongol grimaced while he harangued us, and the monks quivered and tried to step back.

"Abdullah," I said without looking away. "Tell him to take us to his master so that we may give our gifts to him."

The interpreter jabbered away and I saw the Mongol's resolve fade. The heathen did not dwell upon his decision, but instead moved away, barking commands at his fellows.

When I turned around, I saw how Bertrand, Thomas, and their squires had taken positions between the wagons, a few paces behind me, ready to take action. That was a good thing to see. Friar William was angry at me for a while but the man had the intelligence and the humility to let it fade. Young Stephen, I fear, looked upon me with open wonder and admiration. I felt pity for him, for it is a small thing to stand your ground against those that you hold in contempt, but he was still naive, even then. Innocent to the darkness of the world.

He would not be for very much longer.

* * *

The Mongols asked whence we came and where we wanted to go. Friar William told them that we had heard that their lord Prince Batu was considering becoming a Christian and that we wanted to go to him. Also, that we had letters from the King of the French to deliver to him.

Then they asked what was in the carts, whether it was gold or silver or costly clothing that we were taking to Batu. I answered that Batu would see for himself what we were bringing to him when we reached him and that it was none of their business to ask. They made a big show of being offended but it seemed to me to be almost mere convention, and they accepted easily enough.

In the morning we came across the carts of a captain of the Mongols who was called Scatay. His carts were carrying the dwellings, and it seemed that a city was coming towards me across the wide plain.

Huge wagons, pulled by teams of oxen, rumbled over the grassland. More astonishing, however, was that every other wagon had a large, round tent on the back of it. It took me quite some time to come to terms with the fact that they dragged their empty homes up onto the flat backs of these enormous wagons and pulled them down to the ground again when they reached their new destination. The Mongols would move to new pastures for their herds, move from a river to a woodland, or from the plain to the hills, as the need takes them. Each lord had his own domain, however, these domains were so large that they could move regularly throughout a year and not camp in the same place more than once. They would usually spend winter in a single, sheltered place, near a woodland if they could, but would move with ease throughout the rest of the year. When the camp—which was called an ordus—was assembled, they would also erect pens and tethers for special animals and poles and lines for drying clothes, meat, and skins.

Some of their tents, called gers, were disassembled for transport and rebuilt at the new location. And that was how I saw the manner of their construction. The centre of the roof was a wooden ring, held up at a height of eight or ten feet or even higher by two posts. The circular wall was a lattice of wood, with long poles joining the centre ring with the wall. Over the top was pulled great sheets of whitened felt. And each building had a surprisingly strong wooden door. When complete, they were remarkably sturdy structures.

I was also astonished at the size of the herds of oxen and horses and flocks of sheep, though we saw but few men to manage them.

"Who is this captain?" I asked the Mongols, through Abdullah. "Is he some great lord?"

They were amused by my ignorance.

"Scatay has nothing," they said. "He has only five hundred men. There are ten thousand Mongol lords greater than he."

I felt the first inkling of the potential might of these terrible people. Still, I could never have imagined the true scale of their power until I saw it for myself, months and years later.

It seemed that there were many more than that, for each man had his own tent, and each tent had its own great wagon, with oxen to pull it. And each man had dozens or hundreds of horses. And some of the men had more than one wife, and she had her own tent, and her own horses and servants, and stocky children working as hard as a slave. So, five hundred men meant over a thousand people and more animals than I could count, roaming out of sight over miles and beyond the horizon.

We followed that mass of oxen and wagons and tents all day, moving through them at the edges toward the head of the procession where their leader's tents were. Late in the afternoon, the Mongols set down their dwellings near a muddy, wide lake. Their and Scatay's men came to us, and as soon as they learnt that we had never been among them before they begged of our provisions. Abdullah said to us that we must give something to Scatay.

The Mongols poked and prodded at us, asking for clothing

and other items. I insisted that nothing be handed over to these heathens. Our dragoman explained again that we could in no way go to the captain, Scatay, without gifts and so we got a flagon of wine and filled a small basket with biscuits and a plate with apples and other fruit.

The Mongols were angry with our meagre gifts. Again, they demanded some costly cloth. We went with this in fear that they would take offense and turn us back, or worse but we could not give up all our presents to some lowly provincial captain or we would have nothing left for Lord Batu.

While the servants waited with the wagons, the monks, with Thomas, Bertrand and I, were invited into the chief Mongol's tent.

This was the largest ger in the camp, and it was located right in the centre of the others. We were warned to not step on the threshold when we entered, as this was a terrible taboo, and after I ducked inside I was impressed by the comfort within. Rugs covered the floor, other than a large hearth in the centre. On the far side, opposite the door, was a low couch where the chief man and lord of the ger sat. We were directed to one side and bade to sit. Opposite us were a gaggle of Mongol women and girls who were rather subdued but who also pottered about in a relaxed, domestic manner.

The captain, Scatay, was seated on his couch, with a little musical instrument in his hand, and his chief wife was beside him. What a hideous creature she was. In truth, it seemed to me that her whole nose had been cut off, for she was so snub-nosed that she seemed to have no nose at all. What is more, she had greased this part of her face with some black unguent, and also her eyebrows, so that she appeared most vile.

Then William begged him to accept the trifling gifts, explaining how he was not allowed by his order to own gold or silver or costly robes. That was why we had no riches to give him, only food to offer for a blessing. Scatay made a show of being displeased and yet he immediately distributed our gifts among his men who had gathered there to drink.

He asked us if we would drink kumis or mare's milk; for the Christians, Ruthenians, Greeks, and Alans who live among them, and who wish to follow strictly their religion, drink it not. They consider themselves to be no longer Christians if they drink it, and the priests have to bring them back into the fold as if they had denied the faith of Christ.

"Abdullah," William said. "You must have translated that incorrectly."

Stephen interrupted. "What he says is true, brother. I have read such a thing in the records of the Church of Santa Anna. The Christians of these lands have many unorthodox beliefs, due to the corrupting influence of the heathens and from not being one with the true Church."

William glanced between Thomas and Stephen before lowering his voice to answer. "You will explain to me later what you were doing in the records of a Templar church but in the meantime, you shall hold your tongue, do you hear me?"

A chastened Stephen lowered his head, cheeks flushing red.

"Tell him that we have enough of our own drink so far," William said. "But that if that should give out, we would happily drink whatever he gave us."

This seemed to satisfy the Mongol captain and he asked another question of us.

"What says the letter from your king, the King of the French?" Abdullah translated.

"Those letters are sealed," William said, stiffly. "And meant for Prince Batu only. But he can be assured that there is naught in them but good and friendly words."

He then asked, through Abdullah, what we would say to Batu with our own voices when we reached him.

William answered. "Words of the Christian faith."

The Mongol asked what these words were, since he was eager to hear them for himself.

Friar William expounded to him as well as he could through Abdullah, who seemed neither over intelligent nor fluent in the creed of the faith, he being but an ignorant heathen and follower of Mohammed. When the Mongol had heard William's pious drivel, he remained silent but wagged his head, entirely unconvinced.

"Ask him if Prince Batu has a Christian man who serves him," I said. "A man from France, or England. A man named William."

The monks grew agitated at my interjection and also Thomas hissed at Abdullah to say nothing. While the Mongols stared at us in confusion at our agitation, I grinned at everyone and nodded at those who would meet my eye.

"Let us maintain a friendly demeanour, shall we, my friends?" I said, smiling and nodding. "And, Abdullah, you will ask the Mongol my question for if you do not, I shall hurt you very badly by breaking your thumb and forefinger on both hands the moment we leave the company of these charming people."

Abdullah was a coward and so he did as I had requested.

"The Lord Scatay says that, yes, there was a man like that serving Batu Khan."

My heart was in my throat as I pushed for more. "And his name? Is it William? Did he look like me?"

The Mongol captain tilted his head and looked hard at me while he babbled.

"He says that William was the man's name but as for you men from Christendom, he cannot tell one apart from the other."

Thomas scowled, even as I grinned like a madman. "If you are quite finished with disrupting our royal business for your personal quest, sir?" Thomas said.

Then William and Thomas spoke to Scatay in the terms previously used, for it was essential that we should everywhere say the same thing. This we had been well cautioned by those who had been among them, never to change what we said.

The Mongols were wary to the point of paranoia about enemy agents observing their numbers, positions and internal political divisions, lest any and all these things be used against them. A particular worry for them, because that was precisely how they themselves operated. No other people, not even the devious Syrians, nor the ancient and corrupt Persians, had such an extensive intelligence network. And we Christians had almost no concept of such things, certainly not in such a widespread and formal strategic fashion.

Finally, the Mongols agreed to do as we asked, supplying us

with new horses and oxen, and two men to guide us onward to Lord Batu. The servants from Soldaia who had brought us went back with their beasts.

Before giving us all this, they kept us waiting for a long time, begging of our bread for their little ones, admiring everything they saw on our servants, knives, gloves, purses, and belts, and wanting everything. We refused, over and over, every day while we waited to be sent onward, saying to every grasping heathen that we had a long journey before us and that we could not at the start deprive ourselves of necessary things. The monks explained with words, through Abdullah, while Eva and I explained by wrenching their hands and shoving them away.

It is true that they took nothing by force but they begged in the most importunate and impudent way for whatever they saw, and if a person gave anything to them, it was so much lost, for they were ungrateful. The Mongols considered themselves the masters of the world, and it seemed to them that there was nothing that anyone had the right to refuse. If one refused to give, and after that had need of their service, they served him badly.

No matter how much I explained to the servants to give nothing up, they were intimidated and I could not be everywhere at once. Thomas and Bertrand were determined to keep the peace, subject as we were to the mercy of the Mongols. Even Bertrand controlled his temper, for he knew he had to complete his embassy in order to return to the favour of his king.

While we waited with them, in their camp, they at least gave us to drink of their cow's milk, from which the butter had been taken. It was very sour. They called it aira. I did not like it but the

Mongols valued it, so it was their way of offering us something, however small, as a token of acceptance.

Finally, we left this captain, and it seemed to me that we had escaped from the clutches of demons.

In fact, we had barely begun our descent into Hell.

* * *

For two months, from the time we left Soldaia to when we came to Prince Batu's ordus, we never slept in a house or tent, but always in the open air or under our carts. Travelling north and then east, we never saw a city, but only Cuman tombs in very great numbers.

In the evenings, our guide us gave us kumis to drink. Even though it is fermented mare's milk - an intoxicating version of the foul, sour aira - it was quite palatable. The Mongols loved that drink, indeed, they drunk it every day and took much sustenance from it. They loved alcohol in all forms, for life on those endless grasslands, exposed to constant wind and sun and rain, was dismal indeed and like the life of an animal and so they sought comfort, warmth, and distraction in their inebriation.

"Why do the Christians here fear this drink?" I asked Stephen, as I was fairly taken with the stuff, and the young monk seemed wise beyond his years. Whereas I have always had years beyond my wisdom.

"They are ignorant of the true tenets of the faith," Stephen replied, shrugging beneath his dirty robe. "And their blood is inferior to ours, which makes them stupid despite being saved." He giggled because he was drunk on kumis.

We hopped from one Mongol camp to the next, often at intervals of five days or so, as the oxen travels. Some Mongol captains were wealthy, where others were impoverished. And when we came among one particularly destitute ordus, which was confined to a barren and diseased territory, they were such horrible looking creatures that they seemed like lepers. There were no children running about as in other camps.

"Why in the name of God are they like this?" I asked Abdullah.

"Their lord displeased Batu."

During our journey to the royal camp of Batu, the Mongols rarely gave us food, only very sour and bad-smelling cow's milk. Our own wine was quickly exhausted, and the water was so muddy from the horses that it was not drinkable even with boiling. Had it not been for the barrels of travel biscuits we had, and God's mercy, we should probably have perished.

Not only that, the men who conducted us began robbing the monks in a most audacious manner, for they saw that the holy brothers took but little care with their belongings. Finally, after losing a number of things, vexation made the monks wise to the Mongols' ways and all precious things they kept on their person, as the rest of us had done for some time. Not only that, we none of us went anywhere alone, even to shit, else we would be mugged by our guides.

I was warned by Thomas and William never to hurt the Mongols who guided us, even in retribution for their uncouth, savage behaviour, because then we would likely be killed or abandoned¬, which amounted to the same thing. They spoke as if I was a child who had no self-control and I was greatly offended by their words of warning. Still, it was true enough that at times I found it difficult to resist murdering those arrogant bastards. I would happily have feasted on their blood, for they were miserable, thieving heathens with no honour amongst them.

They would never leave us alone, for in their minds they were the masters and we were outsiders. When we were seated in the shade under our carts, for the heat was intense at that season, they pushed in most importunately among us, to the point of crushing the weaker members of our party, such as Friar Bartholomew, who was frail and a poor traveller.

Filthy creatures that they were, whenever they were seized with the need to void their bowels, they did not go away from us farther than one can throw a bean. They did their filthiness right beside us while talking together, and much more they did which was vexatious beyond measure. I grew to hate them and hold them in deep contempt and disgust.

Still, I swallowed my disgust and even attempted to learn their hideous language. After many days, I began to understand pieces of what they said. One of my few gifts outside of the marshal traits is an affinity for languages, thanks to God, for if it were not so I would have died centuries ago.

Bertrand and Hugues were surly but subdued. The entire time, I made sure to never turn my back on them and watched them closely, especially whenever Eva moved apart from the group for momentary privacy. She dressed always in mannish clothing, was hooded or sheltered beneath a wide-brimmed hat and she reeked as much as a man, or a boy at least. Still, the men in our party eyed her in hunger. All other than William of Rubruck who, for all his faults, was an honourable and strong-willed man and old Bartholomew who either hated women or had no interest in women, on account of his advanced years perhaps or because he was that way inclined. Young Nikolas was at her side so much that anyone would think he was her slave rather than Rubruck's and though I am sure he sought her company from a need to feel mothered, he was also approaching an age where his thoughts may not be so innocent. On occasion, I would catch the filthy bloody Mongols discussing her while casting looks in her direction from a distance and those men, along with Bertrand, were the ones I feared attacking in the night. How she was able to withstand such ceaseless attention, I do not know, because it was enough to drive me to a state of heightened anxiety. I slept little and was ever ready to draw a dagger in defence of my wife.

"Any woman who ever leaves her home grows used to such things," she said one time, shrugging. "Their endless gazing means nothing. But any man who lays a finger upon me will lose his hand, his balls, and then his life."

"What a true English lady you are," I said in jest but I also meant it. However, my remark did not appear to amuse her one bit.

We crossed the great River Don, which was called the Tanais back then, ferried across on small boats. That river at that point was as broad as the Seine at Paris and the Russians had a village there, an outpost subject to the Mongols. It was the season when they were cutting the rye. Wheat thrived not there but they had great abundance of millet. The Ruthenian women arranged their heads like my own people did back in England and France, but their outside gowns they trimmed from the feet to the knee with vair or minever. The men wore capes like Germans and wore felt caps, pointed and very high.

The country beyond the Tanais was most beautiful, with rivers and forests. To the south, we had very high mountains, inhabited, on the side facing this desert, by the Kerkis and the Alans, who are Christians and still fought to resist the Mongols. Beyond them was the Caspian Sea.

At the end of every day, we ate quickly and retired early, sleeping beneath the wagons when it was still warm enough to do so. On the easier days, we would perhaps stay awake and talk. Once in a while, we would camp near to a lake or river and there would invariably be scrub on the banks. Enough to make small campfires for a little warmth and light either side of the long sunsets. On those nights with fires, we would drink more kumis than usual and would stay awake longer.

"Tell us of the battle again, sir, I beg you," the monk Stephen Gosset asked Thomas on one such night.

"Again?" Thomas said, warily. "I have never spoken of it. Not to you, brother."

We sat in a rough circle on the grass. The ground was still warm after a baking hot day, and the herbaceous smells of the dry grass wafted up from beneath us. A small fire flickered in the middle of us, providing almost no warmth but plenty of light. Without it, there would have been enough light from the cascade of stars sprayed onto the blanket of night above us. I sat beside Eva and chewed on the dried goat meat. It took all evening to chew through enough to feel even half a belly full. Eva scrubbed the hints of rust from her second-best sword.

"What battle?" I asked, speaking around my food.

Thomas waved a hand. "Young Stephen has an interest in war."

"An unseemly interest," Friar William growled from the shadows. "Most unseemly."

Stephen opened his palms in front of him. "Brother, I wish only to know more of the Tartars. My lord Thomas is the only man I ever met who has fought against them."

When a dribble of brown spit ran down my chin, I realised my mouth was hanging open.

"You fought the bloody Tartars?" I said. "When?"

Thomas took a deep breath. "Twelve years past."

"The second invasion of the Tartars," I said. "You were there when they smashed the Hungarians?"

"No, not there. I was in the Kingdom of Poland. There was another battle. A series of battles, in fact." He surprised me with a question. "Where were you twelve years ago?"

"Acre, I think?" I looked at Eva. She returned my gaze with no expression, or confirmation, while she rubbed at her blade.

"And no doubt a mere page at the time," Thomas said. "Bertrand?"

"Twelve years past?" he said, pausing to take a mouthful of kumis. "Chasing the girls in my father's castle. That was a year or two before he gave me a castle of my own, you see. By then I had already taken up my sword and won many—"

"What happened in Poland?" I asked while Bertrand scowled at me. "What series of battles? Against the Tartars? Why was your order up there?"

"Our order is everywhere that there are Christians. My brothers and I were stationed there to plan a crusade against the pagan Lithuanians. There was an important leader there, a great lord named Duke Henry the Pious. It was when the Tartars were attacking the Rus, once again, as they had done in 1223. Long time ago. Thirty years, almost."

"I remember it well," I said. Eva stared at me. "That is, I remember hearing of it. Please, go on."

"This Lord Batu led them. He conquered the Rus, all their cities by 1240. Tartar riders were seen everywhere across Poland, in the Kingdom of Hungary, even into the Duchy of Austria. Sometimes in groups of dozens, even hundreds. Not fighting. Rarely even raiding. Just watching. Learning the land, prior to the invasions."

"Clever," I said, for that was far from standard practice. We Christians had no tradition of that kind of preparation, as hard as it may be to believe.

"They gathered a vast army and led it against King Bela of Hungary."

"The battle at the River Sajo," I said, nodding. "King Bela led the largest Christian army ever assembled, so I heard. And they were destroyed by the Tartars."

Bertrand belched. "A hundred thousand Christians," he said. "A hundred thousand fools."

I scoffed, for that was an absurd number.

"Fewer than that," Thomas said, glancing at me. "But yes, it was a great many. I was not there but I spoke to men who were. Fifty thousand, perhaps. But they were not fools. They fought well, so it is said."

"Who says?" Bertrand demanded. "They were all killed."

"Almost. Not all. Some of my order were there, supporting, observing. The Tartars were led by Prince Batu, a most cunning and brutal commander. He battered, then surrounded all the forces, other than a few here and there. Some small number of my brothers watched the battle unfold across the plain, and so escaped the encirclement and related the tale."

"But you were in Poland," I said.

"I was. With seventy brothers from my order, as well as many sergeants and five hundred bondmen from our lands there. It took us time to assemble and gather to protect the great cities. Krakow, in particular. Duke Henry the Pious brought his army. It was a vast force. Twenty or thirty thousand but most of them villeins armed with little more than sharp sticks and the foulness of their breath. But there were thousands of men-at-arms, also. Five thousand mounted and armoured, at least, so they said."

"I did not know the lands there could field so many knights," I said.

"They are a good people. Strong in arms. Strong in faith. Worth protecting against the heathens."

"I do not doubt it."

"The Tartars sacked a town named Sandomierz. Then, in the month of March, they defeated an army of Poles at Tursko. It was extremely bloody, for both sides, but the Tartars won the field. A fortnight later, another battle, this time at Chmielnik, where the Tartars won again. Not only that, almost the entire nobility of Lesser Poland was killed in that battle. The Tartars sacked Krakow. We advanced with Duke Henry with his thirty thousand men. We were confident, for we knew that King Wenceslaus of Bohemia was coming to join his forces to Henry's and the Bohemians had forty thousand, so they said. Together, our armies would be sixty thousand men, perhaps more."

"How many were the Tartars?" I asked, before correcting myself. "The Mongols."

Thomas sighed. "After the battle, men were saying the enemy numbered a hundred thousand strong." He gave a snort of derision. "I doubt it could have been much more than a tenth of that. But whatever their numbers, they were all mounted. And that was why they were able to force the Poles to battle before the Bohemians could arrive. Duke Henry should have withdrawn, should have pulled back, denied battle. Should have allowed them to do whatever they wanted to his cities and the people. But he could not. A ruler cannot do such things. His lords would never have allowed him to do so. In any case, he had ten thousand mounted men, well equipped and on good horses."

"So the Poles had perhaps an equal number of mounted men as the Mongols," I asked. "Plus ten or twenty thousand on foot? Little wonder he was confident. Were the heathens mounted on these stocky little horses or did they have true war horses?"

Thomas took a deep breath. "I was like you, back then. We all were. We saw those small horses and the riders on their backs.

Some of them were so close to the ground, I swear their toes brushed the grass as they rode. And many were mounted archers, with these short bows. And no matter the stories we had heard, how they would shower us with arrows while we advanced, we trusted our armour to protect us."

"What went wrong?" I asked.

"Nothing," Thomas said. "We were held in reserve, my brothers and our mounted sergeants and our bondmen soldiers. I had rather a good view from the right of the battle, on a rise, looking out across the fields of the plain. It was a cold day, and we had to keep our horses warm. Tartars roamed and wheeled about, coming close and pulling away again. It was difficult to discern their positions, where they were strong or weak. It was clear they had some sort of order to them but my brothers were convinced the heathens were a disorganised rabble. The Poles sent their levies forward while the thousands of knights waited for a chance to charge. But the levies came under attack from the mounted archers, who simply withdrew as the levies advanced with their spears. Of course, Duke Henry sent his archers and crossbowmen to engage with the horsemen but the Tartars did surprisingly well, riding in and out from all directions to pour their own arrows down on the Poles. Somehow, we lost hundreds or even thousands and yet the Tartars seemed almost untouched. And then, amongst all the wheeling of horse archers, their lancers appeared through a sudden gap."

"Lancers?" Bertrand said, his voice almost a growl. "They do not have lancers, Thomas. Have you seen a single lance amongst them?"

I silently agreed with the Frenchman.

The Templar ignored him. "There must have been a thousand of them, formed up in ranks and riding knee to knee. Their horses were larger than the others we had seen. The men wore mail and steel helms. They smashed into the ranks of the levies and crossbowmen from the flank and routed them immediately. Exactly what the knights were waiting for and they descended on the Tartar lancers. The Poles were elated. Finally, the heathens would pay for the destruction they had wrought. But the heathen lancers turned and fled at the sight."

"They did not stand?" I said, interested that the terrifying Mongols would be so cowardly.

"Ha!" Bertrand said. "They could not stand against the Poles. They would certainly die under the hooves of the French, am I correct, Thomas? Not the English, though."

Thomas was not amused. "The Poles are as fine as any knights in Christendom, and they were well led that day. But the Tartars fled, seemingly in panic. The mounted Poles charged until they were stretched out and separated into groups, the horse archers shooting into the knights and their horses which killed them and disrupted their communication. Further and further, they retreated and our army became disorganised as the lords of Poland tasted victory and charged again and again, but their lances found few targets."

"What were the Templars doing?" I asked.

"We were on the right, pushing forward in an attempt to keep pace with the greater body of the army. Pushing our levies along with us. Many of my brethren believed that the Tartars were about to be crushed, and they rode on, eager to be part of this great victory. None would listen to councils of caution."

Stephen Gosset spoke up. "You knew it was a trap?"

"Knew? No. Suspected. I felt only dread."

"Why?" Stephen asked.

"You are not a knight, Stephen," Thomas said. "You have not seen a battlefield. You cannot comprehend the disorder. Trumpets are used to sound a unified advance, or sometimes to initiate a more complicated manoeuvre. But men do not often obey, for one reason or another. And battles are loud. Louder than you could imagine. Chaos reigns. But the Tartars, for all their wheeling about and dashing hither and thither, were not disorganised. Their commanding lord sat far to the rear and never once approached the fighting. Instead, his men waved flags upon enormously long poles and the companies of Tartars would discern meaning in those flags. It seemed to me that they differed by shape and colour, and the height or distance from the top of the pole. Orders could thus be relayed immediately across the entire field of battle."

I could scarcely believe it. "These heathens? These men who cannot build a simple stone wall or a solid timber house? These men with their stinking, meagre food? They are utterly witless folk."

"My brothers felt then as you do now and urged our men on so that we could slay some heathens ourselves before they all ran away or were killed by the Polish." Thomas tilted his head back and looked to the darkness above. "Their retreat had been carefully planned in advance of the battle, for there was suddenly a huge cloud of dense smoke drifting across the field. The Tartars had lit enormous fires, with many green branches and pine leaves so as to make a thick smoke. Riders galloped across our front dragging piles of burning brush so that fires burned everywhere. Quickly, we could no longer discern the other side of our army. Soon after, was when they attacked."

"They turned around and charged?" I asked.

"From the front, yes. But also from the flanks. Thousands more of their forces had lain in wait. That part of the field, many miles from the first clashes, had been chosen by them and they had led us straight into it. By that time of the day, our horses were exhausted from charging. You know destriers and war horses have no legs for a prolonged pursuit. Knights were strung out over miles, even separated from their squires and friends."

"But man to man," Bertrand said, outraged. "Man to man, our knights would destroy theirs. Our weapons and armour are vastly superior. And our skill at arms is unmatched in all the world. Look at the Saracens, and they are far richer than these impoverished raiders."

"We were slaughtered," Thomas said. "Thousands of men at arms killed. Knights and great lords. Duke Henry himself was killed. Our defeat was total."

"Bad luck, that is all," Bertrand said. "Anyone can lose a battle like that. The important thing is that our knights are bigger, stronger and fight better, man to man."

Stephen, showing signs of arrogance even then when he was so young and naive, spoke up, his voice rising in pitch with indignation. "But they were outmanoeuvred by the heathens. The enemy fought with intelligence and wisdom and—"

"You know nothing, monk," Bertrand said, shouting him down. "What do you know? Nothing, you know nothing."

The dying fire cracked and popped as the lit branches collapsed into the coals.

Thomas said nothing for a while. "Have you ever seen a knight train a young page in the sword? The page will swing and thrust while the knight presents his unguarded chest or head only to dance aside, parry the blow and send the sword flying. Perhaps kicking the page in the rump while the other boys roar with laughter."

I snorted. "I have been both the page and the knight in that situation. Many a time."

Thomas nodded, slowly, staring at nothing. "We Christians were the page, against the Tartars. They toyed with us. I tell you this, as a knight who has been fighting at the frontiers of Christendom my entire life. I tell you, these Tartars. They are masters of war. And we are children."

* * *

And so we came to the ordus of Batu Khan.

After seeing a number of Mongol camps, I assumed Batu's would be simply a larger version. And it was. But it was much more besides.

It was a city, only one unlike any I had ever seen or even conceived of before. It was a city of tents. The great white tents of the Mongols, their gers. And what is more, it was a city that moved. Hundreds of enormous gers on the backs of wagons so big that their axles were the size of ships masts. Mongol women stood on their own wagon, in the doorway of their ger, holding the reins of the teams of oxen that pulled the massive wagons so that it was like seeing fleets of ships sailing across the great grass sea.

Each ger belonged to a woman, and she belonged to a man. One man may have many wives, but each wife controls her own household, with her children and her servants tending to their home and to the animals that the household owned. And there were many animals. Mostly horses. Hundreds and thousands of horses, everywhere one looked. But cattle, too, and other creatures. It reeked worse than any city in Christendom, worse even than Jerusalem or Paris, and possibly even Rome. A hot, shit-stench that filled one's throat so thoroughly that the fear was you would never get it out.

Batu Khan's ordus covered the land from horizon to horizon. And it seemed at first sight to be chaos and disorder. But, like Thomas' battle, that was deceptive. It was because I could not see what the Mongols saw. I could not understand their organisation, their hierarchies. But when their city stopped moving, each ger was set down in its proper place, to east and west. All doors faced south, as that was the holy direction for those people, and the Khan's ger had no other to obscure the view in that way. Their homes were set down by order of seniority but more than that, I could not understand, no matter how much Abdullah explained it to me. I suspect that he did not know himself but a scholar would rather lie and invent falsehoods than admit to his own ignorance.

The ger of Batu was not large enough to contain his court. The man was perhaps the greatest lord of the Mongols, other than the Great Khan Mongke. He was of the oldest generation and had proved his mettle by leading countless battles. And Batu was the eldest son of the eldest son of the legendary Genghis Khan, the first and greatest Mongol Khan. We were not the only visitors to the court. There were ambassadors from almost every kingdom and city from Central Asia to the Danube and so the Mongols were not impressed by us in the slightest and they made no special efforts for us.

We were made to wait, half-ignored, for two days, for the ordus to set itself down in its new location and then for the court to assemble. Not simply for the attendants and petitioners to gather but for the structure itself to be strung up.

In place of a ger, they erected a tent the size of a cathedral. Not in height, but certainly in length, made from poles taller than any tree and ropes as thick as any on the most massive of ships. It was large enough to hold a thousand people at least beneath the vast canopy overhead, and, at the head of all the assembled masses, sat Batu Khan.

Eva waited at where our wagons were parked, with the other two squires and Nikolas. She was under guard by the men who had guided us but still, I had no wish to leave her alone amongst thousands of barbarians.

"If they try anything," I said to her, "do whatever you must to resist them and scream bloody murder. Send the boy to find me."

She looked me square in the eye. "I will kill as many as I need to."

"Try to avoid killing them," I said. "If you possibly can."

"I promise nothing."

She made quips only when she was nervous.

I bent to Nikolas. "Are you well, lad?"

His eyes were wide and his mouth hung open. He had spent his short life inside Constantinople and the wonders of that place were like nothing to him. But the wide plains and vast sky had cowed him and now the city of tents, peopled by strange barbarians were more than he could comprehend.

"I am well, sir," he said.

"Listen, Nikolas," I said, and took a knee in front of him, placing one hand on his shoulder. "I must leave you and my lady, now. I will be going to see this Tartar prince. Can you keep a look out? Look for any trouble and should any trouble happen, you run and find me." I pointed north. "I shall be in or around that giant tent in the centre of the camp. The heathens may try to stop you, may shout at you. But you will not stop for anything, will you, Nikolas?"

Eyes wide, he shook his head and his hand drifted to the white, ivory dagger I had given him, which he now wore suspended from his belt so it hung on his hip like a tiny sword. I could see the beautiful carving of Saint George with his lance running the dragon through as it writhed in coiled agony.

He swallowed and spoke solemnly in his thick Greek accent. "I shall protect her with my life, sir."

I kept a straight face. "Do not fight anyone, Nikolas. You have the heart of a knight but not yet do you have the stature of one. You come find me instead, understand?"

Eva was afraid by the masses around us. She felt as trapped as I did, only now I was leaving her alone. I would not be far, as the crow flies, but we had rarely faced danger apart from the other for thirty-five years. I took her hand in both of mine for a moment. Her eyes spoke of their love and concern for me, and I felt the same.

We brought Abdullah with us to translate our words.

"They say to not step upon the ropes of the structure," Abdullah said, as our guides gesticulated wildly and babbled at us. "The ropes surrounding the entranceway represent the doorway and threshold of a typical ger. If any of us tread on the ropes, we will be removed from the camp, and banished forever. Another one of these men is disagreeing with his colleague, and claims that we would at once be executed in a most terrible fashion."

I shoved away the hands that pawed at me. "Tell them to cease their damned fool gibbering, Abdullah."

He said nothing of the sort. Mongols were everywhere around us. Hundreds of them, thousands. Some staring, others talking at us, many seemed to me to wish to do violence. With all my will, I remained outwardly calm. As well as I could.

We were all checked for weapons once again, and led in and seated together on the left side, sitting upon the patterned carpets laid thickly upon the ground. The monks were the ambassadors and sat in front of us, who were seen as the attendants. A hearth was at the centre of the tent, and a raised dais with benches to the north, opposite the entrance.

On the bench, sat Batu. A large man, broad-shouldered with a wide face and a massive forehead. His complexion was truly awful, grey and with terrible pimples and pockmarks. He looked to be in his later middle age, fifty or so, perhaps. Dressed just as any Mongol would be, in a voluminous tunic, and thick belt and trousers. Yet the cloth was shimmering, dark silk and embroidered with swirling patterns.

"Lord Batu," Friar William muttered.

"Prince Batu," Thomas corrected.

"Batu Khan," Abdullah said.

Friar William looked around at me, eyes wide. "He is of a size with my lord John de Beaumont, would you not say?"

"I would indeed," I said. To this day, I have no idea who he was talking about.

There were so many men within the vast space. Even though the sides of the huge tent structure were open, the air beneath the fabric roof hung heavy and stank of sour sweat. Across from us, were a small group of women, and some children were there.

We were given kumis to drink, and very gratefully did we receive it. Abdullah drank an unseemly amount until I squeezed his shoulder and whispered in his ear.

"Consume no more, you drunken heathen, else I shall gut you from beard to stones when we leave this place. Do you understand?"

William turned over his shoulder and scowled at me. "You shall do nothing of the sort," he said. "Not without my express permission. Nevertheless, Abdullah, if you do not control yourself, I shall be forced to abandon you here amongst the heathens when we return to the Holy Land."

"No, lord, no," Abdullah wailed, quietly.

Stephen hissed. "People are looking at us."

Many people were brought forward, close to Batu and there was much talking, and back and forth. Men from many kingdoms, in many modes of dress, speaking many tongues. Some went away happy. Others were grim-faced as they were escorted out from Batu's presence.

In time, it was our turn and they called us forward.

A herald or some such functionary asked us, through Abdullah, what we had brought in gifts for Batu Khan.

"We are but poor monks," Friar William explained. "Who have taken vows of poverty. All we can offer is some wine, and some foodstuffs, not as gifts but as blessings. Tokens of our good intentions."

The Mongol herald was horrified. "But you have many furs in your wagons. This will be your gift to the Khan."

"Those furs are for trading with," William said. "We are a long way from our own lands and all we wish is to survive through exchanging those furs, piece by piece, for food and other necessary items."

The herald was unmoved. "Those furs belong to Batu Khan, now. Come forward and speak your purpose here."

We were all required to take a knee, and then Friar William unleashed his holy nonsense upon the Khan. How he wished only to preach the word of Christ to the Tartars, and how him and his two brothers were praying they could meet Batu's son, Sartak who was a Christian himself.

Batu's face, already hideous and devoid of civilised niceties, darkened further when William's words were translated.

"The Khan says that his son is no Christian," Abdullah said, voice shaking. The Saracen was hunched over, his shoulder's rounded, like the cowering slave he was. "His son Sartak takes an interest in all gods, all religions, as is right and proper."

William was angry. "Tell him that there is only one God, and He is the God of the Christians."

Whatever Abdullah said to Batu, it was certainly not William's words, nor even his sentiment.

Batu Khan replied. "Do you wish to go? Or do you wish still to speak of your Frankish Christian words to the Mongol people?"

"We wish to spread the word of God, my lord," William said. "But there are many—"

Thomas stepped forward, in front of William, and bowed. "My lord," Thomas said. "We are also ambassadors from the King of the French. I carry with me a letter from him, to you." From within his tunic, William produced the parcel I had seen him hoarding for months and handed it to the herald. "The words are repeated in Latin, Greek, Arabic, and Persian."

It caused quite a fuss with the Mongols, and they busied themselves right there and then, with a group of squabbling scribes jostling to make a translation into their own version of written language. We were ignored while they did so and our group turned in on itself for a time.

William looked physically wounded by the shock. By the impropriety or the subsuming of his authority. "What are you doing?" he whispered.

"I pray you will stay calm, brother William," Thomas said. Bertrand stood with a smug expression on his face.

"That is why you are here?" I said to Thomas. "You came, not to protect these monks on their fool's errand but to deliver a message to Batu? Why not be open about it? These people accept ambassadors from everywhere."

"Quiet," Bertrand said. "You are no more than a hired sword. It is none of your concern."

I have always been slow on the uptake. But then, time does tend to be on my side.

"You are seeking an alliance," I said, astonished I had not realised earlier. "King Louis wants Batu's men to attack the Saracens? Is it to be a surprise assault, is that why this deception?"

Stephen Gosset, clever little bastard that he was, saw through to the heart of it. "The King's peace treaty with the Saracens," Stephen said. "If the Saracens knew about Louis seeking a pact with the Mongols, the Saracens would fall upon Acre at once, fearing to be trapped between two united enemies. And if you had travelled as an ambassador through Constantinople and Soldaia, word would have got back before we ever arrived to make the proposal."

"What do you mean, we?" Friar William said. "Are you on his side, now, Stephen? Are you renouncing your vows and joining the Templars, Stephen, is that what you and Thomas have been conspiring about? Ever since Acre?"

Stephen made no attempt to defend himself. William was dismayed and the monk shook with the hurt of it.

"Oathbreaker," Bartholomew said, looking down his nose.

After a good while, we were brought back before the Khan.

"Your proposal from your king is too important for me to decide," Batu said. "Your letter must go to the Great Khan, in Karakorum. Mongke Khan will hear your petition, and he will give me orders, which I will follow. For that is the proper way. And you must all go with this letter, so that the Great Khan may question you further, so he may make the best decision."

He nodded to the herald to signal that our audience was over.

Abdullah wailed and fell to his knees, muttering something. He was already so homesick that he had aged and grown frail, body and mind. I understood that Karakorum was a good deal further away but I had no true conception of the distance.

"Get up," I ordered, and dragged him to his feet.

"Batu Khan," I said, stepping forward with my arms held out.

This set them off. A dozen men took a half step forward and the herald grabbed the top of my arms from behind.

Batu looked confused and barked something at me.

Abdullah relayed it, between his sobs. "The Khan's decision has been made. If you argue, he will have you killed outside the tent. You do not know our ways and so he makes allowance for this. Otherwise, you would certainly be dead by now."

I knew I could survive terrible, otherwise-mortal wounds. But I knew I would not survive having my head cut off. Still, I had one chance to speak, to take action while I could before I was removed from Batu's ordus. If my brother was anywhere in Batu's lands, I could not be sent to some other city, nor could I return to Christendom.

"I am looking for a Christian knight," I said, undeterred. "A

Christian knight, from England but he may say he is from France. He looks like me. His name is William de Ferrers. He is your man, so they say."

Abdullah was still translating when six men came forward and seized me by the arms and shoulders. While they heaved and yanked me, I allowed myself to be drawn forward and forced to my knees.

A heavily calloused hand grabbed my jaw and yanked it up. I looked into the face of Batu. It was his hand under my chin, and I shook it off by jerking my head back. He was lucky that I was blessed with self-control because I had a powerful urge to tear his throat out for touching me in such a fashion. When he spoke, his breath reeked of onions and the fumes of strong wine.

"You serve him?" Batu said, through the sobbing Saracen. "This Frankish knight William?"

"Never," I said, sneering at the thought.

Batu peered closely at me with his beady eyes. "Why do you seek him?"

"He has committed many crimes," I said. "Done murder. Killed a king, and a bishop, and countless others besides. Women, children."

Batu nodded as this was relayed to him. "I will ask you one more time. Why do you seek him?"

My life hung in the balance. The wrong answer would result in my execution.

"To kill him."

The Khan let go of my chin. His men dragged me to my feet while he peered at me. "You have the look of the man you seek.

Why is this?" Batu asked me.

He had seen William with his own eyes. My heart, already racing, skipped a beat.

"He is my brother. It is my duty to bring him to justice. A trial by combat. That is all I ask of you, my lord."

Batu sneered, amused by something. He walked away, slowly, and took his seat while the others held me fast. "Your brother William is evil," Batu said raising his chin. "And that is why I sent him away. To the Great Khan."

"He is not here?" I said, almost wailing like Abdullah had done.

"He was. No longer. He is wreaking his evil somewhere in the east. At Karakorum. You monks can warm the Great Khan's ear with your droning prayers. You, old man, will bring the letter of your master. And you, brother of evil, will cut out the heart of the devil that is called William."

PART THREE

KARAKORUM

1254

BY GOD, IT WAS A HARD JOURNEY. One of the hardest, and longest I have ever undertaken.

On about the feast of the Elevation of the Holy Cross, in September, a rich Mongol came to us whose father was a chief of a thousand men. He spoke and Abdullah hurried to tell us what he was saying. "I am to take you to Mongke Khan. The journey is four months, and it will be so cold that stones and trees are burst apart by the cold. You should think over whether you can bear such a thing."

I answered him without hesitation. "We will bear what men such as you can bear."

He tilted his head as he looked up at me and babbled while Abdullah translated. "If you cannot bear it, I shall abandon you on the road."

"You will not," I said and I felt Eva's glare from across the ger. It was all I could do to control myself but I spoke again, this time with restraint. "That is not right. We are not going of ourselves, but are sent by your lord, Batu Khan. Being entrusted to your care means you should not abandon us, or you are going against the wishes of your lord. You are the son of a great chief, so I hear, but what would Batu Khan do to you if you failed in your duty?"

The rich Mongol scowled. "If you can keep up, all will be well."

"It had better be, or you shall have me to answer to."

I do not know if Abdullah translated my words accurately but I suspect he did not.

Friar William clucked about me. "Must you make an enemy of every man you meet?"

"You sound like my wife," I said, which nobody found amusing, Eva least of all.

After that the rich Mongol made us show him all our clothing, and what seemed to him of little use for the cold he made us leave with our host. The next day they brought each of us a sheepskin gown, breeches of the same material, boots according to their fashion, felt stockings, and hoods such as they use.

The day after, we started on our ride, with pack horses for each of us. We rode constantly eastward for three months.

In the first stage of our journey, to the north of us was Greater Bulgaria, and to the south the Caspian Sea.

The cold was paralysing and the distances we covered were astounding. Every day, I grew less concerned over the danger of

Bertrand's anger at me and lust for Eva and I thought that perhaps he had changed. Been cowed by fear of the Mongols, and weakened through hunger and exhaustion. And that was part of the truth. And then it slowly dawned on me that I had come to see that immense, hostile foreign land as my greatest enemy. And it was an enemy that could easily see us dead on the side of the road. If the Mongols abandoned us, or turned on us and forced us out, we could starve or die from thirst, encased in ice and buffeted by the relentless wind. And so I watched our guides like a hawk, day and night, wary of any sign that they meant us harm, or even if they meant us indifference.

After travelling twelve days from the Etilia, we found the Ural River, which flows into the Caspian Sea. The language of Pascatir was the same as that of the Hungarians, and they were shepherds without any towns whatever. In fact, from that country eastward, and also to the north, there were no more towns at all, all the way to the ends of the Earth, other than Karakorum.

One evening we sat huddled in a tight group in the lee of a little cliff. The soil of that part of the grassland had been blown away and the landscape was rocky with knolls rising up here and there, often with scrubby trees, all bent over from the wind. We indulged in the luxury of a fire but it was so cold we all sat almost on top of it, knee to knee and still shivering. Still, it gave us a few moments to speak.

Bertrand was angry at the world but all his anger was directed at his squire Hughues, who took it sullenly and then turned his own frustrations on Abdullah for his appallingly-feeble collection of firewood. Little Nikolas cringed away from their insults and harsh commands so I dragged him into my lap and wrapped my cloak around him. He felt as light as a bird.

Stephen seemed the happiest of us all. The world was a fine place to him. The young man had devoured the entire library at both of the monasteries he had spent his previous years in.

"It was from this country of Pascatir that went forth the Huns," Stephen said, excited and smiling, even though his words were terrifying to me. "Isidorus says that with their fleet horses the Huns crossed the barriers which Alexander had built among the rocks of the Caucasus to confine the savage tribes and that as far as Egypt all the country paid the Huns tribute. They ravaged all the world as far as France so that they were a greater power than are now the Tartars. With the Huns also came the Blacs, the Bulgars, and the Vandals."

"They conquered France?" I said. "The Huns were horsemen who conquered from here, all the way to France? And defeated the Romans?"

"And the Romans were a united people," Thomas said, looking very grave, his eyes full of meaning. "And Christendom now is not. What is to stop the Tartars from doing the very same thing, should they decide upon it?"

His squire, Martin, looked at him with his eyes wide. "Would our order not resist them?"

"We would unify against such a threat, should it come to that," I said. "Look at the Crusades."

"Yes," Thomas said. "Let us look to the Crusades. How successful have we been at winning back the Holy Land from the Saracen conquerors? There has been little enough unity there, not for a hundred years or more. No, we must find another way."

A gust of icy wind howled around the rock and the flames of our fire were flatted for a long moment. Our horses gathered closer together. I looked up at the top of the cliff above us, where one of our guides sat looking out at the horizon. He was fully exposed to the elements, and bare-headed, and yet seemed perfectly comfortable. I hoped he was simply idling at the end of the day, rather than plotting violence against us.

Stephen spoke up once the wind died down again. "What other way is there to protect Christendom from the Mongols, if not unity under the Pope?"

"A treaty," Eva said.

Thomas shifted on his arse, as Eva always made him nervous but never more so than when she spoke.

"That is why you agreed to be the envoy for King Louis," I said. "You have seen the Tartars in battle. You wish to facilitate an alliance with them, to turn their attention to the Saracens and save Christendom from attack. That is why a Templar is acting for the King of France." From the corner of my eye, I saw Stephen staring at me, a faint smile on his lips. "Turn your dim-witted gaze elsewhere, Stephen or I shall turn it with my fist."

Friar William became annoyed whenever he was reminded that far from being the leader of the group, he and his brothers were being used as a disguise for Thomas' mission for Louis.

"If we can but turn their leaders and enough of their people to Christ," Friar William said, scowling, "then they would never make war on Christendom."

No one bothered to respond.

Soon, we curled up for another long, cold night, listening to the howling of the wind. Praying for the night to end and dreading the coming of the morning.

We rode through that country from the Feast of the Holy Cross in September to the feast of All Saints in November. It was a blistering pace. Nearly every day we travelled, as well as I could estimate, about the distance from London to Dover, and sometimes even more, according to the supply of horses. Sometimes we changed horses two or three times in a day, while at others we went for two or three days without finding anyone and we had to go slower. Out of thirty or forty horses we, as foreigners, always got the worst, for they invariably took their pick of horses before us. They tended to give Bertrand and Friar William each a strong horse, on account of their great weight; but those horses rarely rode well. The monk did not venture to complain and tended to bear it all with good grace but Bertrand grumbled when he was tired and raged when his belly was full. The squires and servants were morose and silent, as they were experiencing the toughest challenge they had ever faced. I expected at least one of them to break under the strain.

Indeed, we all had to endure extreme hardships. Oft times the horses were tired out before we had reached the staging place and we had to beat and whip them, change our saddle horses for pack horses, and sometimes even two of us would ride one horse.

Times out of number we were hungered and athirst, cold and wearied. They only gave us real food in the evening. In the morning we had something to drink or millet gruel while in the evening they gave us meat, a shoulder and ribs of mutton, and some pot liquor. When we had our fill of such meat broth, we felt greatly invigorated, for it seemed to me a most delicious drink and most nourishing.

On Fridays the monks fasted without drinking anything till evening when they were obliged, though it distressed them sorely, to eat meat. Sometimes we had to eat half-cooked or nearly raw meat, not having fuel to cook it. This happened when we reached camp after dark, and we could not see to pick up ox or horse dung for the fires. We rarely found any other fuel, save occasionally a few briars. In a few spots along the banks of some of the streams were woods, but such spots were rare.

At first, our guide showed profound contempt for us and was disgusted at having to guide such poor folk but after a while, when he began to know us better, he would every so often take us to the gers of rich Mongols along the way, where the monks had to pray for them. The Mongols were never Christian themselves but sought out and accepted blessings from any and all religions.

Their great king Chinggis, the first Khan, had four sons, whose descendants were very numerous and all of them had a strong ordus. More than this, these offspring multiplied daily and were scattered all over that vast sea-like desert. Our guide took us to many of these, and they would wonder greatly at us and where we had come from. They enquired also of the great Pope; if he were as old as they had heard.

"What does he mean, as old as he has heard?" I asked Abdullah when this question was relayed to us within the shelter of the chief's ger.

"He has heard that the Pope is five hundred years old."

I laughed and received very hard looks in turn, so I controlled myself.

"I believe," Stephen said, because he could not help to impose his opinion at every opportunity, "that they are confusing the immortal title with the name of a single man. Tell them, Abdullah, that the man we call the Pope is a temporary bearer of that title. Just as their own leader is always the Great Khan."

They babbled back and forth for an age and I am certain they went away convinced we were ruled by an immortal king named Pope Khan.

These descendants of Chinggis probed us with endless questions about our countries, such as if there were many sheep, cattle, and horses. How many men could fight. Whether the women were strong.

"If you tell them anything about Christendom," I said to Abdullah the first time, "I will cut out your tongue."

"We must not offend them," Friar William had said, fretting.

"Tell them our lands are nothing but mountains, woodland, and swamp," I said. "Horses die there. And our women are dreadfully thin and worthless."

When we told them that beyond our lands was the Ocean, they were quite unable to understand that it was endless and without bounds. Their refusal to accept the truth that there was nothing to the west of Christendom was a clear sign of both their immense arrogance and their profound ignorance. It was more than two centuries before I discovered that they were, in fact, quite correct in their assertions but that was pure luck on their part and I give them no credit for that whatsoever.

After travelling east for three months, we left that road to turn due south and made our way over mountains that were like the alps continually for eight days. In that desert, I saw many asses called culam, and they greatly resemble mules. Our guides chased the creatures a great deal but without getting one, on account of their prodigious fleetness. The seventh day we began to see to the south some very high mountains, and we entered a plain irrigated like a garden, and here we found cultivated land. After that, we entered a town of damned Saracens called Kenjek, and its governor came out of the town to meet our guides with a false smile on his face bearing ale and cups, for they were subject to Mongke Khan. If the Saracens did not make a show of hospitality, they would surely be punished with extermination, for the Mongols would happily cut off a source of riches in order to make a point. And that was a lucky thing for us because the Saracens in that town looked at us Christians with murder in their eyes from the moment we arrived until we disappeared over the horizon.

I could see why they had settled there. In all that harsh land, that plain where the city lay was sheltered by the mountains around them. And there came a big river down from the mountains which irrigated the whole country wherever they wanted to lead the water, and it flowed not into any sea but was absorbed in the ground, forming many marshes. There at Kenjek, I saw vines, and twice we drank real wine, though it was sharp as vinegar.

We heard that there was a village of Teutons out there in the vastness, six days or so through the mountains out of our way so we never came across them in person but I was assured they were indeed there. It was a startling thought and only later did I learn that Mongke had transported these Teutons, with Batu's permission, so very far from their homeland. I should have known that they were not there of their own free will. The Mongols had no arts of their own, save those concerning the horse and other animals, so they pressed civilised men into service for them. And so it was with those poor Teutons, who were set to work digging for gold and manufacturing arms for their masters. Friar William did everything he could to persuade our guides to divert to them for a time so that he could pray with them, administer rites and do whatever else he could for their souls and so ease their hearts while they delved and travailed in a hollow existence. The monk was greatly anguished when they denied him, and he drew into himself further for many days as his mind dwelled on the suffering Teutons so close by.

From there on, we went eastward again staying close to the mountains. We had entered the lands of the direct subjects of Mongke Khan, who everywhere sang and clapped their hands before our guides because they were envoys of the great lord Batu, who was considered second only to Mongke in all the world. A few days later we entered more alp-like mountains and there we found a great river which we had to pass in a boat.

"They say that if any of us should fall in," Abdullah said, "the water is so cold that we will die immediately, even if we were pulled to the bank downstream."

I gripped the side of the boat so hard I swear my fingers marked the wood.

After that, we entered a valley where we saw a ruined fort

whose walls were nothing but mud but the soil was cultivated there. No doubt the people had fallen foul of the Mongols and all their efforts to tame that land was slowly being undone by the elements. Days later we found a goodly town, called Equius, in which were Saracens speaking Persian, though they were a very long way off from Persia. Unlike the village of Teutons, these people were there by choice because they were all merchants who profited from the goods moving up to the royal road from their own lands in Persia. The Mongols were greedy for Saracen goods, and the merchants of Equius lived in relative luxury despite the harshness of the jagged landscape all about them.

Descending from the mountains we entered a beautiful plain with high mountains to the right, and a sea or lake which was twenty-five days in circumference. All of the plain was well watered by the streams which came down from the mountains, and all of which flowed into that sea.

Such a fruitful land was like an island of fertility in the desert. In that plain, there used to be many towns but they were destroyed so that the Mongols could graze there, for there were most excellent pasturages in that country. They had allowed a single town called Qayaligh to survive under the yoke because the Mongols valued the market there and many traders frequented it to take advantage of the Mongol's wealth.

Here we rested twelve days, waiting for a certain secretary of Batu, who was to be associated with our guide in the matters to be settled at Mongke's ordus. It was there that I first saw idolaters, who were properly called Buddhists, of whom I was told there were many sects in the east.

Even amongst such a diversity of people, our company was very much outside of the norm in those parts and we were regarded with suspicion and hostility.

"We must stay all together," I said to my people. "All of the time."

Bertrand scoffed. "I am not afraid of these weaklings. They are no more than dogs. I could slay a dozen at once."

"And how many dogs does it take to bring down a bear?" I asked. "No matter how strong you are, sir, we are outnumbered more than a hundred to one. If they decided to rob us of our belongings, who would we go to for justice? Our guides?" He had no answer. "We stay together, in pairs at the least, and in as large a group as possible. And keep your hands on your valuables. Weapons and armour especially. Nikolas, you will not leave my sight, do you hear me? Any one of these Saracens would snatch you up and take you home as soon as look at you."

There was never a restful moment, for me at least, as I stood watch over the company and turned away many a hostile ne'er-do-well and would-be pilferer with no more than my gaze and an occasional kick to the guts.

In November we left the city, passing after three days a vast sea, which was called Lake Ala Kol, east of Lake Balkhash, which seemed as tempestuous as the Ocean beyond Bordeaux in winter, though they swore it was indeed a lake. I stomped down to the shore across the frozen mud and moistened a cloth in it to taste the water, which was brackish though drinkable. And it was as cold as ice.

The cold in those regions was savagely penetrating, and from the time it began freezing in the fall, it never thawed until after the month of May. And even then, there was frost every morning, though during the day the sun's rays melted it. But in winter it never thawed, and with every wind it continued to freeze further, covering everything with an ever-increasing thickness of ice as hard as rock. And with the ceaseless wind, nothing could live there and we barely survived wrapped in furs and carrying all our food and fuel with us as we rode. Every once in a while, a terrible gale arises and blows hard enough to stagger a man, if he be unbraced or weakened. Bartholomew was blown from his horse and fell on the ice so that his arm needed splinting and he grew a lump over his eye as large as a goose egg. Little Nikolas was once blown a hundred yards down a slight hill and so I tied him to his horse for a while and later I took to holding him before me as I rode. His bones were so sharp that I had to feed him from my own rations to fatten him up, for the sake of my own comfort.

"You cannot fatten a boy's elbows," Eva said when she caught me as if she had not been secretly feeding him also, which she had and far more than I.

We crossed a valley heading north towards great mountains covered with deep snow, which soon covered the ground on which we travelled. In December we began greatly accelerating our speed for we already found no one other than those Mongol men who are stationed a day apart to look after ambassadors. In many places in the mountains the road was narrow and the grazing very bad, so that from dawn to night we would cover the distance of two stages, thus making two days' distance in one and we travelled more by the light of the moon than by day. I thought I had known bitter cold before but I was wrong. We would all certainly have perished had the Mongols not cared for us as if we were children or fools and they allowed us the use of their sheepskins and furs, which we all took most gratefully.

One evening we passed through a certain place amidst most terrible rocks. The pass we climbed had grown narrower and sharper, even as it grew colder, and the jagged rocks, dark but streaked with red, stretched up like walls sculpted by the hands of a vengeful God. Our guides stopped, though there was a wind that howled through us like a storm of ghosts tugging at our clothes, and they sent word through Abdullah, begging the monks to say some prayers by which the devils of that cursed place could be put to flight.

"What heathen nonsense is this?" Friar William said, his teeth gritted against the cold.

Abdullah had always been as thin as a spear shaft but he had shrunk on the journey so that he appeared to be a skeleton with skin stretched across it and when he spoke, his voice was flat. The dead voice, I always called it, the voice of a man who has no hope in his heart. "They say that in this gorge there are devils. The devils will suddenly bear men off. You will turn to speak to the man behind you and he will be gone."

"What do you mean, gone?" William said, warily. He had lost much of his fat by that time and looked like a different man.

The Mongols babbled, their eyes darting about, and Abdullah related it to us while the wind tugged at his words. "Sometimes they seize the horse and leave the rider. Sometimes they tear out the man's bowels and leave the body on the horse. These things happen on every journey through. They say we should expect to lose at least one man."

"They cannot give us commands," Bertrand said, bundled up in the best furs, which he had claimed for himself. His bulk had reduced but he had coped with the hardships with surprising determination. Then again, the man had been to war before. And it felt very much as though we were at war with the land all around, and with the sky above.

Friar Bartholomew roused himself enough to provide us with his learned opinion. "Heathen fools. God will protect us. Onward with you."

He was ignored.

"It may be a ruse," Stephen Gosset called out. The young monk had never faced such difficulties, nor anything approaching it. He had withdrawn into himself and his rosy cheeks had faded first into grey and then into a wind and cold-blasted rawness. He did not look so young as he had. "A ruse, so that they may kill one of us and then blame it on the demons."

None knew what to think about that. When one is cold, thinking clearly is a great challenge and brave men become cowards. Energetic men grow idle.

"For the love of God," I said, raising my voice above the wind and their prattling so that the sound echoed off the rocks and made the Mongols wince. "Will you monks just chant some prayers so we may get moving again."

We proceeded through the pass while the monks all chanted, in loud voice, Credo in Unum Deum. The three monks, frozen as they were, gave full-throated conviction to their singing. It lacked the finesse of monks raising their voices to God in their own chapels but our three had to contend with the howling wind and the echoes of the iron-hard rocks all around. That far-off, God-forsaken heathen pass resounded to the beautiful, clear voices of those men of Christ. For the Mongols, it was no more than a spell of protection, and they would have been as contented with Buddhists, Mohammedans, or their own shamans. Yet it seemed to me that Christendom had conquered that pass. That we had left a mark upon it, though the voices echoed into nothingness. My companions were confused by my joy, for it was a terrible place, but the voices of those monks warmed my heart, and my body, too.

By the mercy of God, the whole of our company passed through.

Again, we ascended mountains, going always in a northerly direction. Finally, at the end of December we entered a plain vast as a sea, in which there was seen no hillock, and the following day, we arrived at the ordus of the great emperor, Mongke Khan, lord of all Asia from the ocean of the east, to the Black Sea in the west, king of all Tartar devils that rode upon the Earth. It may be true to say that there was no man richer than he in all the world at that time, for his armies and those of his grandfather, had stolen the wealth of uncounted millions and brought it back home so that even the lowliest in Karakorum wore silk from head to toe beneath his furs.

I was far from impressed.

"What town is this?" I asked our guides, through chattering teeth, when I saw it with my own eyes, looking down on it from the hills.

Abdullah was horrified. "This is Karakorum, lord."

"Dear God," I said. "What a pigsty."

* * *

Perhaps I was overly quick to judgement. But after such a journey, I was deeply disappointed by the place. Of the city of Karakorum, other than the palace quarter of the Khan, it was not even as big as the village of Saint-Denis outside Paris. And the monastery of Saint-Denis was ten times larger than the Khan's palace.

There was a rectangular wall enclosing it, with two roads running right through to make a cross in the centre where most buildings were, and one corner was taken up by the palace and associated buildings. Dotted here and there about the city were a number of smaller enclosures, each surrounding a temple of some kind.

The important buildings, such as palaces and holy places, were of stone and timber and the houses in the centre, clustered along the crossroads, were two-storey homes for the most eminent inhabitants. But the majority of the people, and the visitors of a lower standing, lived in gers packed very close together within one quarter where all the ground was churned mud, frozen into rock-hardness.

There were two non-Mongol quarters in the city, one of which was inhabited by the Saracens, where all the markets were. I was full of contempt for the steppe nomads' inability to learn to operate something so simple as a marketplace. A great many Tartars of all sorts gathered in the Saracen quarter to do business, as the Great Khan was never far from the city and so it was always full with ambassadors from every place on Earth. These visitors frequented the Saracen markets in huge numbers, buying and selling goods from everywhere that there were people.

The other quarter was that of the Cathays, which is what we called the Chinese, all of whom were artisans making a great many useful things in iron, silver, and gold, and in timber and stone, also. For the Mongols were utterly ignorant of all civilised things and could make nothing for themselves. I assumed that they were all too stupid to learn such things.

"Yet they are not stupid in war," Stephen pointed out when I made my judgement of their failures in mercantile activities and skilled crafts.

"A man may be stupid in one way but not another," Bertrand pointed out, and he was living proof of his own statement.

"Please pardon my presumption, my lords, but would you yourself seek to become a silversmith or a merchant?" Stephen said.

"Of course I bloody well would not stoop so low as that, you impudent little monk."

Stephen bobbed his head as his cheeks flushed. "Quite so, my lord, yes indeed. And each Mongol man, whether he be lowly or wealthy, considers himself to be something like a knight, in that his trade is war, and so none of them would become anything lesser, just as you would not."

"How dare you!" Bertrand had roared. "These little fat shits are not knights, you ignorant villein."

Stephen had hitched up his robes and fled from Bertrand's presence while the man shouted after him. I had laughed at the sight of it but I did believe Stephen was quite right about the Mongols. Still, it made their one city a very strange place, cobbled together as it was from the skills and cultures of alien peoples so that it felt like no other town I had ever seen. The closest thing I could liken it to was, perhaps, a busy port in the Holy Land.

Besides these foreign quarters and the Mongol ger quarter, there were the great palaces set about Mongke's own, though what were called palaces would have been grand townhouses in any leading city of Christendom. The palace quarter was home and workplace for the leading administrators of the court and the entire empire of the Mongols.

There were twelve idol temples of different nations all over the city, two mosques in which was cried the law of Mohammed, and one church of Nestorian Christians in the extreme end of the city. Karakorum was surrounded by a mud wall about ten feet high that did little more than keep out wandering animals and, I suppose, provided the Mongols with a means of controlling the entry of people. The four gates in the wall were guarded at all hours of the day and night by hard-looking men.

At the eastern gate was sold millet and other kinds of grain, although there was rarely any to be brought there. At the western one, sheep and goats were sold. At the southern, oxen and carts were sold. And at the northern gate were the horse markets.

Even though it was so small, and even though every surface was covered in ice and the ground was so hard that a pick could never be hammered into it, the city of Karakorum stank. It was surrounded by herd after herd of horses and oxen, clustered together in tight groups against the winds and shivering in the bitter cold. Every morning, more would be dead. Frozen to the ground. But the Mongols seemed not to care overly much, for there were always more animals to be had and the ones that died were eaten.

The animal smell surrounded the city but within the streets, such as they were, it reeked from the dung-fuelled fires that burned in every hearth. And, God forbid, when you were inside a ger that was warm enough to thaw out the people within and heat their clothing. For then the stench of months of sweat and filth would fill the air like a cloud of pestilence so foul that I saw children vomiting from it. And the food and the drink that they consumed was always sour and bitter. The iron-hard ground was too solid to bury night-soil or absorb urine, so it was collected in buckets and thrown into great mounds here and there all across the city, within and outside the walls. Those frozen mounds grew all through the winter and I wondered what would happen when summer thawed those mountains of shit.

This, then, was the capital city of the great Mongol Empire.

Yes indeed, I was far from impressed.

But I was not there to be awed.

From the moment we were led in through the gate, I looked everywhere for William, or for any sign of him. The city was so small and there were so few men who could conceivably be from Christendom that I was certain I would clap eyes upon him from across a marketplace or along a street.

But William was nowhere to be seen.

Our guides, who had brought us from Batu, housed us all together in a single ger on the edge of the city near to the church, which pleased the monks mightily. They told us to wait in the city and that the Khan would send for us. Every day, someone would bring food and fresh water. It was never enough but it kept us alive.

And we were free to explore the city at will. No one guarded us.

After so many months of hard travelling, our company was suffering from terrible ailments. Feet were rotten, skin was raw. All of them had sores and weeping blisters. I was astonished that Friar Bartholomew had survived the journey and I was certain that he would die at any moment. Abdullah, for the first few days, seemed as though he had already died but he was young and recovered quite rapidly. All they wanted was to stay inside the ger, away from the wind and by the fire.

Myself, I could not wait to explore the city.

William was there somewhere, so close now. And I was determined to find him. Someone would know. Someone would talk.

Eva, of course, came with me. And young Nikolas would not leave her side, as he had become besotted with her. He had only fared well because Eva and I had taken rather good care of the lad, I suppose, but he was still on shaky legs and would have been better off resting like the others. Then again, knowing how bad-tempered most of our company was, I thought the boy might be safer out with us in the city.

Stephen Gosset decided that he would also accompany us and though he still irritated me, there was something about the young man. Some force within him that intrigued me as much as it maddened me. Though he suffered physically, he claimed that his heart was lifted at the sight of the Tartar city and he could not wait to speak to the peoples of the world.

"And how will you speak to them, Stephen?" I asked, not wanting him trailing around after me and getting in the way of my vengeance. "You should save your breath."

"God will provide," he said, grinning. "Between Nikolas and I, we will get by."

"Let him come," Eva said. "For he is indeed learned about the ways of strange people and may help us."

Stephen stood to one side, smiling at me like the village idiot.

"Say nothing to anyone," I said, sticking my finger in his face. "Lest you get yourself killed by these heathens."

"Oh, yes, they are heathens, sir, but there is the rule of law here," Stephen said, earnestly.

"There is the rule of law everywhere," I said. "And everywhere men are murdered."

I felt profoundly alien, wandering in that city. And I felt exposed and vulnerable and expected an attack at any moment. For months, we had been amongst Mongols almost exclusively, other than crossing paths with occasional surviving local peoples, or fellow travellers on the road, coming or going to Karakorum. Often, these were Saracens, who the Mongols loved to use for their experience with trade, and with money and transactions of all kinds.

But the road was sparsely populated, where Karakorum was full to bursting with arrogant Mongols of all stations, from lowly slaves to powerful men. All were bundled up in their heavy coats but one can always tell by a man's gait and by the quality of the cloth he wears on which rung he stands on the ladder of his society.

There were women, also. Dressed the same as the men, wrapped up so thickly that they waddled when they trudged through the streets.

"Such strange faces," I said to my wife as we watched a group of four Mongol women walking by us. "Their eyes, and the width of their cheeks. I will never fail to be amazed by their strangeness. Utterly unlike women from civilised lands, are they not?"

"When they are naked," Eva said to me, "they will look just the same as a Christian woman."

I blinked at Eva, unsure how to respond.

"You were wondering about their naked form," she said, helpfully.

"I most certainly was not," I said.

She needed only to shake her head, for she knew me well.

Stephen lurked behind us. "Your pardon," he said, stammering. "But how do you know about their nakedness?"

Eva threw him a look over her shoulder. "I saw our guides and other Mongol men stripped and showing their bodies to the open air, on a number of occasions during our journey. Despite the difference of their faces, their bodies were like any other man's."

"Ah," Stephen said, staring at Eva in wonder. "You are applying logos to the question, in order to come up with a reasoned conclusion."

"No, no, I disagree entirely," I said, while Eva rolled her eyes at Stephen's condescension. "The men are soft. Barrel-chested and strong but somewhat pudgy. Their legs are short and bowed. Eva, they are not like us at all. Who knows what the women's bodies are like?"

"Well," Eva said, sighing. "Why do we not find a desperate Mongol woman and offer her a few coins to disrobe before us?"

I nodded. "Stephen, how much do you have in your purse?"

He begged us not to make trouble with our hosts, and so we agreed to temporarily postpone our investigation.

"They are making mock of you," I heard Nikolas whisper to Stephen.

I swatted the young Greek lad on his furred hood. "You are too kind-hearted by far, Nikolas," I said. "But what makes you think I was making mock of Stephen? Anyway, keep an eye out for any harlots, will you, son?"

Our young monk prided himself on his wits and, as he could not divine whether we were indeed serious, he stopped speaking to us all the way across the city until we reached the Nestorian church. It was small and simple, no more than a rectangle and had no tower. Built from plain stone, plastered, and with a low wall all around making a small enclosure, it was not much to look at. The roof was a sweeping gable in the Chinese style, so it looked halfway to becoming a temple.

"Do you wish to enter, and pray?" I asked Stephen.

"I do not like this place," Stephen said, glancing around at the crowds heading this way and that behind us. "It seems to me that the people are watching us."

"Nonsense," I said. "Our strangeness is unremarkable here. Half the people you see likely feel the same way as you do."

He was quite right, of course, but I wanted him to remain calm.

We had in fact been followed by a group of men from our ger, across the city. By taking many fleeting glances, I had determined that they were, to a man, competent warriors. Too arrogant to truly blend into the masses.

But whose men were they? Did they report to Mongke Khan?

Or were they followers of William de Ferrers?

"Stephen," I said. "I need you to find out where my brother William is."

His face dropped. "Me?"

"Speak to the Christians. They will trust you, as you are a monk. Would you not like to find out why we are being kept waiting? If there is some reason that they tell us nothing about our status amongst them?"

"Is it not simply the bureaucracy of the Mongol state? Is it not as we were told, that we must wait our turn to be seen?"

"I do not know, Stephen. Is it?"

He lowered his voice, looking around. "Are we in danger?"

He stared up at me in alarm. I paused, waiting to see if he was serious, then laughed. "Try to make a friend or two at the church. See what they have to say."

"About us?"

"No, no. Do not ask them about us directly. Men love to talk. All you have to do is smile and nod your head and listen."

Stephen nodded, then his face lit up. "Perhaps Abdullah can do the same in the Mohammedan temples?"

I sighed. "Not a bad idea but we cannot trust him. The man is a drunkard, and when he is sober he is a miserable cur. Who knows what he would say or do for a skin of wine, especially for his own people. No, you will find out plenty from the Nestorians."

Stephen chewed his lip. "My brothers will not like me speaking to anyone without them present."

"Why did you come here, Stephen?" I asked.

"To Karakorum?"

"You followed Friar William because you believe you will rise in importance with your order once you return, is that it?" He did not respond to my question. "Is that all that you seek for yourself?"

His obsequious façade dropped for a moment. "And what do you have to offer me instead, Richard? An empty, dead-end mission of familial vengeance? Or is there something more to the two of you?"

I clapped him on the arm, hard enough to stagger him and leaned in. "You have only one way to find out, Stephen."

Most places excluded us, but where I could speak to people, I tried my best. Without a huge amount of gold, or the ability to bestow favours, I had little to bargain with. All my questions about William were met with indifference or denials. Occasionally, I would see hint of a knowing smile and I knew that if I could take that man into a dark alley and beat him bloody, I could make him tell me where my brother was hiding.

But I could not do such a thing and hope to live.

144

Stephen reported that the Nestorians knew of my brother and they believed he was not in the city.

"I could have bloody-well guessed that by now," I said when he told me. "Where is he?"

"No man will say."

All the time that we waited in the city through that winter for the Khan to grant us an audience, I was alert to the danger all around us. It chafed my nerves so that I grew evermore short-tempered and everyone avoided me.

"Just as I need blood, you need a fight every few days," Eva said one night. "Else you will make one with someone."

"I dare not make a fight here," I said. "It would mean death for all of us."

Residing in such a place, where every man was a possible enemy, is no way to live. Whether Saracen or Cathay or Rus, all other foreigners were still more at home than we were, and they were a danger also. Not just the people but the bleakness of the landscape wore me thin. The madness that the Mongols would erect a city in the face of such barrenness was an affront to me.

Most of all, my frustration at not finding William, nor knowing what to do about it, was driving me into madness.

There was a particular cold after midwinter that came on with a wind which killed an uncountable number of animals about Karakorum. Little snow fell in the city during the winter until that bitter wind when there fell so much that all the streets were full of great mounds of it and they had to carry it off in carts. Even in our ger, wearing all our clothes at once, we still shivered beneath blankets while the dung fire smouldered and gave off more foul smoke than warmth. Little Nikolas had already grown as thin as a bird that winter, and through the sudden cold spell Eva and I held him between us beneath our blanket so that he did not expire.

Without prompting, young Stephen wrapped himself in strips of cloth, tunnelled out of the ger and struggled out through the great drifts and howling wind to beg at the palace for succour, claiming that elsewise his fellow holy men would surely perish. His cleverness and courage brought us from the ordus of Mongke's first wife sheepskin and fur gowns and breeches and shoes, which we all took most gratefully. I would not say that Stephen saved all our lives, but he may have saved the life of Nikolas, for which I was most grateful, and also the life of ancient Bartholomew, for which I forgave him.

There was no thaw in all the time we were there, yet the wind blew all the snow away in time and the cold became somewhat less deadly. Just in time, too, because I felt certain it would be only days before I murdered someone and drank his blood in public. I was almost beyond caring.

It was in January 1254, as I was pondering whether killing Bertrand or Bartholomew would give me greater satisfaction, that we were summoned to court.

Finally, we would be presented to Mongke Khan.

And there I would demand to be told where he was hiding my brother.

* * *

"You will be silent," Friar William said to me before we left the warmth of the ger on the way to the court. "Say nothing of this vengeance of yours. Do you hear me? Nothing. We were blessed by God in the court of Batu when we were all forgiven by the prince after you spoke out of turn. The Great Khan will never be so generous should you break with etiquette in such fashion once more. Do not think of yourself, Richard, but think of the all the harm that you would do to us, should you cause us to be expelled, or worse. We could bring many of the Tartar lords into the Church if we have the opportunity. Think of why Thomas and Bertrand are here. If Louis the King of France can make an alliance or even an understanding with the Great Khan then think what could be done in the Holy Land against the—"

"I do not serve you," I said. "And I value neither your greater good nor your advice. So save your breath."

He was outraged but I had spent months listening to his prattle, and he still did not realise that he had only ever been sent to Batu as a cover for Thomas' true mission. And even after so long living amongst the Mongols, he failed to see that they believed in everything, every God as it suited them, and so they ultimately believed in nothing. For the Mongols, Christianity was already available to them through the Nestorian Church and they had no need of Franciscans, let alone some distant Pope Khan.

Still, my irritation at his ignorance had been expressed only because I was dying to find my brother. It had been decades since I had seen him last, in the Forest of Sherwood. He was so close now, I could almost smell him.

After being officially ignored for weeks on end, our party was escorted most reverentially to the palace, such was the significance of the royal invitation.

Entering the walls of the palace compound, I strained to see the famous silver tree that a Parisian silversmith had wrought for Mongke. It stood in a courtyard at the entrance to the palace and it was a lovely thing to look upon. At first, it appeared to be a magnificent sculpture, dripping with fruits made of gold, the branches reaching into the upper windows of the palace. Yet it was more than that. The tree was also a device in the form of a fountain that dispensed different kinds of wine from its metal vines into basins below. At the top, a silver angel held a trumpet aloft that would play a sweet note and golden serpents wound about the trunk. Little birds and other creatures would bend and trill when the device was set in motion, which I saw only briefly that one time.

"It is a marvel, is it not?" Friar William said, breathily as we were ushered past it. "You see how it moves so, from some cunning mechanism within?"

"A little slave boy is encased within the trunk," I said. "Yanking on pulleys."

He thought I was being contemptuous to anger him but that was the truth, as I had heard it. It was still a marvellous sight to behold, even if it should have by rights been erected in Paris, if anywhere.

In an antechamber, the door-keeper searched our legs and breasts and arms to see if we had knives upon us, which we had already been told not to bring.

Then we were brought within the great hall of the Khan's

palace.

The palace inside was all covered inside with cloth of gold, and there was a fire of briars and wormwood roots, and of cattle dung, in a grate in the centre of the hall. It was set out just as if we were in a Mongol tent, only the walls were stone and square rather than felt and circular. There were hundreds of people within, men and women of all stations, though mostly it was richly-dressed men. Some sat in silence, others carried on whispered conversations so that there was a steady hum of quiet muttering filling the air.

Mongke was seated on a couch and was dressed in a skin spotted and glossy, like a seal's skin. He was a little man, of medium height, aged about forty-five years, and a young wife sat beside him. And a very ugly, full-grown girl, with other children sat on a couch after them.

They made us sit down on a bench to the side of the dais, just as if we were in a ger.

Mongke Khan had us asked what we wanted to drink, grape wine or cervisia, which was rice wine, or carakumiss, which was clarified mare's milk, or bal, which was honey mead. For in winter they make use of these four kinds of drinks. It seemed at first to be rather courtly, and quite peaceful, and I was apprehensive about the coming moments. I knew I would have to force the issue and by so doing I risked my own death and that of my wife and the other men who were in my company.

But I had set myself on a path and I knew no other way to fulfil my oath to kill William.

While we awaited our audience, a series of other suppliants

were brought forward to plead with the Khan. Mongols and men of other races. I dragged Abdullah to my side and made him speak in a low voice into my ear. All I wanted was the general gist of what was said by the Khan and by those brought before him.

The first few were discussions of disputes between the Khan's subjects, and also between his subjects and the kingdoms on the edges of the Mongol lands. Men sought guidance on whether to raid into neighbouring countries and the Khan appeared to tell each of them to maintain their own territories, to keep to treaty boundaries and to settle disputes with diplomacy rather than force.

It is fair to say I was shocked by the civility. Both that of the Khan and his honouring of treaties and that each man, many of them clearly great lords in their own right, took the Khan's judgements with not a hint of ire.

Until a young man was brought forward, along with a young woman.

The sight of the girl made me sit up as straight as an arrow.

She was remarkably beautiful. Most of the Mongol women were quite unpleasant to look upon. Their bodies were wrapped from chin to ankle in thick woollen coats, or great bundles of silk. And their heads were often crowned with elaborate headdresses made from lacquered wood and silks. For some reason, the Mongols found the forehead to be a most attractive feature, in both men and women, and so they shaved the front part of their hair. In the men, it made them appear rather savage and intimidating. In the women, it made them appear the same. And their countenances were often round and flat, and quite alien to me.

Some of them, though, were very fine to look upon. Their eyes could be astonishingly alluring, especially over high and prominent cheekbones. Many of those women had lips as soft and pink as a ripe apple.

But the young woman brought forward into the hall was something else altogether. She looked almost like a Christian, perhaps like one you might see in the lands north of Constantinople. Certainly, her skin was pale enough. And her face was narrow, not round, yet her cheeks were high and sharp and she had the flat face and narrow eyes of a Mongol. Her hair was as shiny and as black as any woman of the east. In her clothing, she was also like a Mongol, wearing a coat wrapped at her waist with a belt and on her legs, she wore trousers.

The man at her side was young, also, and a most strikingly handsome man he was. Not pale, like the girl, and his face was wider but his features were arranged in some particular combination of proportions that held one's gaze. A well-built fellow, too, broad at the shoulder like many a young Mongol warrior. It was no wonder that he had managed to win over such a wife as the girl by his side.

Neither was happy. Both held their handsome features still as they approached the Khan but it was clear that they were there against their will. Behind them, as they walked came a row of four sturdy fellows. Like a wall, warding against escape. I knew guards when I saw them, and they were certainly guarding the young couple.

While heralds made announcements regarding the couple, I

turned and whispered to Abdullah. "What is this all about?"

Through the centuries, I have seen many a man deeply in love. A man profoundly smitten with a woman. But on only a few occasions have I been witness to the very moment that a man lost his mind to love.

Abdullah was staring at the young Mongol girl with his mouth hanging open wide enough to insert the rim of a goblet. His eyes were about ready to pop from his skull. His dark cheeks and neck were as flushed as a Syrian can manage. The man was breathing rapidly, with shallow breaths.

I elbowed his ribs, hard. "Cease your panting, you dog."

He recoiled, wincing and then glared at me. Calling a Mohammedan a dog is a very grave insult.

"Why are these young lovers here, Abdullah? What are they charged with?"

He pressed his lips together and rubbed his flank, but dragged his resentful, dark eyes away from me and watched the back and forth between the young man and the court functionaries. Mongke watched and drank more wine.

"He stole her," Abdullah said, after a few moments. "She was married. But the husband mistreated her, the foul creature. Beat her, perhaps. How could a man do such a thing? And then this one stole her away from her ger in the night. They escaped for many days. Months, it was. Riding across country from somewhere. But they were captured and brought here."

A tragic tale, no doubt. "But what case is the young man pleading? He broke a law, I presume?"

"He is saying that the woman wished to leave her husband but he would not let her and that she never agreed to the marriage in the first place. So, she should be allowed to return to her mother's ordus, no matter what happens to the young man, here."

"And?"

I felt somehow invested in the young couple's fate. Not only because of their beauty but I was mightily impressed by their stoicism as they listened to what would be their doom.

Abdullah jerked as if he had been shot by a bolt and his thin hand shot out to grasp mine. I shook him off.

"What do you think you're doing?" I said.

"They are both to be killed," Abdullah said, tears in his eyes.

"That is a great shame," I said. "A great shame. But why? The man, I can believe but surely the husband wants his wife back?"

Abdullah wiped his cheeks and whispered. "She was the newest wife of Hulegu. He is the brother of the Great Khan."

"Ah," I said. A powerful man had been wronged and shamed, and so the crown had to make an example.

"Hulegu is on his way here. Those men," Abdullah gestured at the slab-faced guards. "They are Hulegu's men. They chased the girl across the mountains and the plains and they brought her to here many days ago, knowing their master would arrive in this season. And Hulegu is coming now. Mongke Khan has pronounced his judgement but will allow his brother Hulegu to carry out the sentence, as the poor woman is Hulegu's wife."

Some of those great Mongol lords had four or five or ten or even more wives. I suppose this Hulegu took it as a challenge to his authority that had to be repaid. Or perhaps his heart was so crushed by the rejection that he had lost his mind in a murderous

153

rage. But Mongols did not think about things in the same way as we Christians did and attempting to understand their behaviour would ever be beyond me.

The young couple were led out, their heads held high but their eyes shining and full of deep despair. Abdullah sobbed once as they went by us.

Next, came an official embassy by a small group of Saracens. The hall fell silent and the Mongols all around us grew very still. It seemed to me that they all edged closer to the Khan and all eyes were fixed upon the leader of the Saracens.

He was richly dressed in a green robe, with some embroidered pattern in yellow and a conical hat wrapped on his head. The man was tall, broad-shouldered, with a well-oiled beard. By his bearing, he demonstrated his nobility.

"Who are these fellows?" I whispered to Abdullah.

The translator scowled. "They are Nizari Ismailis."

"Saracens, yes?"

Abdullah sneered. "They are rejecters of the true faith. Heretics."

I had no idea what he meant. "Heretics? They look like Mohammedans. Persian ones."

He was filled with contempt. "You know them as Assassins."

I was shocked. Even when I had first arrived in Outremer, decades before, the name of the Assassins had been whispered in fearful tones by the crusaders. I knew they were a sect that had strongholds in the mountains of Syria and Persia and that all the other Saracens hated and feared them. Were at war with them, in fact. Because they were so few in number, they could not wage war against the Caliphate in Syria, nor against the Persians, or anyone else. Not in a traditional sense. So, they resorted to the judicious murdering of the leaders of their enemies to further their political aims. They were said to follow their leader, the Old Man of the Mountain, with complete and utter devotion. Willing to throw their own lives away, without hesitation, without question, for their lord. They were said to be willing to leap to their deaths from a cliff, at the mere click of the fingers from the Old Man of the Mountain.

So, I had heard, anyway.

"Why are they here?"

"The Mongols accuse this Nizari envoy of sending four hundred fedayin to kill the Great Khan."

"What word is that? What is fedayin in French?"

"I do not know how to translate this word. It means a man who gives up his life. A sacrifice. But for the Nizari Ismailis, the Assassins, the fedayin are the men who carry out the secret murders. They are caught and killed. Sacrificed."

"Martyred."

"Yes, that is it, yes. Fedayin. The martyred."

"This envoy must be facing a terrible death, no?" I asked. "If he sent four hundred martyrs to murder Mongke, they must have something exquisite in mind for this fine fellow."

"He is to be sent back to his people," Abdullah explained. "To persuade them to submit to the Mongols, before they are destroyed by the army of Hulegu."

That name again.

Hulegu.

I would come to know it well.

I would come to hate it.

"I thought no one could defeat the Assassins," I whispered. "Due to their great fortresses in the mountains."

"That is what the Nizarite lord here is arguing," Abdullah said. "But Mongke Khan says his brother Hulegu will march with an army of three hundred thousand men and crush every fortress and put every Assassin to the sword."

I chuckled to myself. They certainly seemed to like throwing numbers like that around but three hundred thousand was ten times bigger than any army was likely to be. "Absurd," I muttered, shaking my head.

The magnificent looking lord of Assassins was dismissed, along with his attendees. As he passed by us, he turned and looked us over. His black eyes held my gaze for a long moment, and it was a look full of meaning.

What the meaning was, sadly, I had no idea.

And then, finally, it was our turn to come before the Great Khan.

"Come forward, refill your cups," Mongke said, indicating his benches so laden with intoxicating liquids and the servants who would pour any of them for us.

Friar William was still the nominal leader of our party and yet he was a man so filled with the traits of deference and agreeableness that he had become a monk. Instead of simply saying what he wanted, he aroused the Great Khan's confusion and contempt.

"My lord," Friar William said, grandly, "we are not men who

seek to satisfy our fancies about drinks. Whatever pleases you will suit us."

I hung my head and held my hand over my mouth, lest I speak out of turn. All this time and the monk had not realised that the Mongols respected strength and assertiveness while they found excessive humility contemptible.

The Khan sneered and had us given cups of the rice drink, which was clear and flavoured like white wine. I sipped only a little, eager as I was for the audience to move on. However, while we sipped our drinks before him, the Khan had some falcons and other birds brought out to him which he took on his hand and looked at. It was a way of showing his contempt for us, and after a long while, he bade us speak.

Friar William stood once more, approached before the Khan and bent to one knee. Abdullah lurked at the side and translated his words.

"You it is to whom God has given great power in the world," William said, raising his voice as if addressing an army. "We pray then your mightiness to give us permission to remain in your dominion, to perform the service of God for you, for your wives and your children. We have neither gold, nor silver nor precious stones to present to you, but only ourselves to offer to you to serve God, and to pray to God for you."

Mongke stared for a long while before he answered, and Abdullah turned to us and related the words.

"As the Sun sends its rays everywhere, likewise my sway and that of Batu reach everywhere, so we do not want your gold or silver." Mongke slurred as he spoke, clearly suffering from too much drink. He seemed displeased that we had come to him at all, and he waved a hand and barked orders at a secretary or some other servant. This man came forward and handed the Khan a curling square of parchment. The Khan gripped it in his fist, rather than reading from it, and waved the crumpled document at us while he growled his words.

"My cousin Batu has sent to me a copy of the letter you sent to him, begging for his support in your war against the Syrians. It is wrong that your King of the French did this thing. Batu is a great and powerful lord of the west but he is subject to me. I am the Great Khan and Batu will not make war without my orders. Just as your King would take great offence at some foreign lord seeking alliance with one of the King's princes without his authority, so have you offended me."

"My lord," Thomas said, standing up with a look of determination on his face. "My lord, if you please." He stepped forward and stood beside. "King Louis wishes only—"

Mongke snarled a response and slashed a hand down. Be silent.

Thomas squeezed his mouth shut.

And then, Mongke Khan turned and looked right at me.

It was no accident. It was obvious that he already knew where I was seated. It was me he wanted to see.

And Mongke himself spoke my name.

"Richard."

He mangled it horribly on account of his foreign tongue and his inebriation but it was unmistakably my name.

One by one, everyone turned to stare at me.

I stood up and stepped forward. "Where is William?" I said.

Mongke laughed at me, even before Abdullah interpreted.

"My cousin Batu sent word to me. I know why you are here. You are another one, like him. Another man who cannot die. That is true, is it not? You cannot be killed? Like your brother, you will never grow old. Answer me."

I took a deep breath and tried not to look at any of the others. It was silent in the great palace hall. "The years do not mark me, that is true."

Mongke nodded and sat up straighter. "You are a hundred years old, yes?"

Again, I hesitated. The Khan was testing me. It would confuse the others but I did not need them anymore.

Or so I thought.

"I am eighty-four years old," I said.

The monks and the knights, my companions, stirred in disapproval.

But the Khan nodded and asked further questions. Abdullah was confused and hesitant but he translated all the same.

"You must drink blood, yes? To give you life, and strength. You must kill many slaves to make such magic."

If anything, I was relieved. I had been on the right trail after all. William was known to the Khan and so Mongke would know where my brother could be found. Was he a prisoner? Was William off at the edges of the kingdom, huddled in a cave with dozens of followers? Or had Mongke given William an ordus of his own?

To get any answers for myself I would have to give the right

159

ones to the Khan.

How much should I admit, I wondered? Was he testing me with his questions about blood drinking and killing slaves, or was he searching for answers for himself? How much had William told him? And what lies had been amongst the words of truth? I knew I could myself speak the whole truth about us and yet still end up dead at the end of the audience.

"I kill no slaves," I said. "And drink blood only when I need to."

Mongke found that amusing. "And when do you need to, Richard?"

I was never good at battles of wits. Many men would have found a way to appear to speak openly but in fact to tell the Khan nothing. Other men might have extracted information from the Khan with clever trading of information.

But I had no patience for that, and no head for it either.

"Drinking blood helps to heal me," I admitted. "When wounded."

Mongke Khan nodded again as Abdullah translated my words as if the Khan knew already. Or was pretending to know.

He waved at my companions. "And have you made all these men into blood drinkers like you?"

I was surprised. Friar William and Stephen, and Thomas and Bertrand were thoroughly confused but also outraged at the suggestion.

"None of them," I said. "They have no idea what I am."

The Khan did not seem to believe me. "And what are you?" he asked.

160

"In truth," I said. "I do not know. Only that my brother and I are the only ones in all the world."

He became angry as he listened to my words. "The only what, in all the world? What are you?"

"I am a man," I said. "With some gift given by God. Or a curse, perhaps. Just like my brother. You know why I came to you? All I wish is to be granted the chance to duel with my brother and so I beg that you summon him to your court from wherever it is that he is hiding. He is a criminal. Through a trial by combat, to the death, God will grant justice."

The Khan had his cup of wine refilled, and he drank it down in a few gulps before cuffing his mouth with a silk sleeve.

"I already sent for your brother. Months ago." Mongke's ugly face screwed up as if he had detected a foul smell. "Your brother now serves my own brother, who is called Hulegu. They are camped outside the city. Both of our brothers will be in Karakorum tomorrow. And then your brother will kill you."

"Thank you, Great Khan," I said. "But my God will surely grant me victory in our duel."

The Khan laughed aloud. "There will be no duel, Richard. You will be executed."

* * *

They were angry with me. Inside our ger, Friar William ranted and raved at my deceit and manipulation of him. Bartholomew, of course, railed at me with what little strength he had.

161

I ignored them while I gathered my weapons, armour, and equipment. Eva did the same. We would put on our armour and throw the rest of our gear and supplies over at least two horses that we would steal.

Neither of us needed to speak of it to the other. We knew that, whatever happened, no matter how unlikely it was we would ever get away, we needed to prepare to run.

Before we made a break for wild flight, however, I had other plans to enact.

"Your underhanded plotting has quite ruined our hopes for converting the pagans," Friar William said, quivering with rage. "You are a liar, and a traitor, and entirely unchivalrous, sir. Entirely!"

"The Khan has given you leave to stay and preach the Gospel and spread the teachings of the true Church," I pointed out, speaking over my shoulder. "I am astonished at his generosity and you should be, too. I am the only one who will be killed."

Even the fact of my imminent death did little to mollify the monks. But that was monks for you.

After we were dismissed from the palace, we had been escorted back to our ger with just as much respect as we had been given on the way there. It is likely that the Mongols were not concerned about letting me loose within the city because they had no fear at all of me or what I might do. Such was their unparalleled arrogance, they no doubt believed I could not escape across the plains without being ridden down and rounded up. Nor would they have believed me capable of harming them, when every subject of the khan was a warrior. So little did they regard me as a threat, they did not disarm me or any of my companions nor take away our armour. As far as they were concerned, their city was a prison and each citizen a guard. Perhaps I was wrong but, as far as I could tell, we had been left to our own devices.

And devices were what I intended.

Unlike the others, Thomas seethed in silence. He felt that I had been most dishonourable, I am sure. Yet he looked at me with an odd glint in his eye and he did not rave at me.

"You endangered us all," Bertrand said, pacing back and forth behind me across the ger. "I should kill you myself for this affront."

"You are welcome to try," I said, without turning around.

Eva said nothing, merely packed our equipment with practiced efficiency.

"What will you do, Richard?" Thomas said when their anger had begun to subside. "Will you appeal for mercy?"

I snorted. "From the Tartars?"

"From your brother," Thomas said. "This William, who is arriving tomorrow."

I grinned and looked to Eva. She did not return my smile.

"The last time I saw William," I said, "I destroyed his home, killed all of his men, and one of my knights ran him through the chest with a lance. He will not grant me clemency."

Bertrand scoffed. "No man could survive such a wound."

The young monk, Stephen, had been silent since we had been led away from the palace and back to our tent. "Back there," Stephen said. "You claimed to be eighty-four years old. And the Khan said you drank blood. And you agreed that you did. I do not understand."

Bertrand jabbed a finger at me. "He claimed it because he is a deceiver and a liar. Do not trouble yourself what he claimed, brother."

"I heard stories," Stephen said, undeterred. "Of men who drink blood. Men returned from the dead."

"Stephen," Friar William said, full of rapprochement. "Do not speak of such nonsense."

Thomas was interested. "Where did you hear stories like that?"

"At the monastery," Stephen said.

"Nonsense," Friar Bartholomew said. "You are always gossiping with servants, like the jumped-up little villein that you are. Their tales are utter fancy."

"I heard a tale once," Thomas said, staring at me. "Of an English knight who fought with old King John. I heard it from a man who was there. Fifty years ago now, this would have been. Swore upon all that was holy that this English knight was caught drinking the blood of his enemies. That he had magic that healed his wounds when he drank blood. He was in league with the devil, they said."

I stood and turned around, my sheathed sword in my hand. "The Bloody Knight, they called me." I shrugged. "For a while, at least."

"Absurd!" Friar William shouted.

"I would hear your tale," Thomas said, "even if it is nonsense."

"As would I," Stephen said. "Please. I beg you, explain what is happening, sir. We must know it all."

Eva shook her head but I am a prideful man and I wanted to tell them.

Most settled onto the benches, while Bertrand, Hughues, and Friars William and Bartholomew paced and scoffed and poured scorn on my words, huffing and sighing as I spoke, shaking their heads and rolling their eyes at each other.

I ignored them, other than to raise my voice over their objections, while I told them all my tale. A rapid summary of my life, from the death of my half-brother and his family to the murder of my first wife. I told them of my searches for William, in Outremer and elsewhere, only to find him many years later in the dark woodland of Sherwood Forest.

I explained, as best as I was able, how William had given some of his strength to his followers by giving them his blood to drink. That it passed on a modicum of his speed, and his ability to heal, but only for round seven days or so, until they needed to drink.

In spite of their incredulity, I told them how he had discovered a method to imbue his followers with a permanent change. How he would drain a man of his blood, and then at the very point of death, have them drink the immortal blood.

"I knew it!" Stephen muttered a couple of times. The others tutted at him but he simply shrugged. "I mean, I knew it was something."

I did not tell them that William had done that very thing to Eva. That he had used my blood to turn her into an ageless immortal. And I did not tell them that she had to drink blood every few days or else she would grow sick and become raving mad.

"If this were true," Friar William said, scoffing. "and it is not true, of course. But if it was true, then it would certainly be the work of the devil himself. And so would you be, sir!"

"Hear him!" Bertrand said, inviting Hughues to share the monk's outrage.

"But how did it come to be?" Stephen asked. "How did you come to be as you are, sir? You and your brother? What did you do to become so powerful?"

"Do?" I said. "I did nothing. At first, I believed that it came from our father, my true father, the old Earl de Ferrers. When William poisoned him, he was said to have woken up before burial, only for my brother to murder him again with a blade. It sounded similar to how William and I both died and were reborn. And as both William and I grew from his seed, I believed it was that which made us as we were. As far as William was concerned, he always appeared convinced that his power was a gift from God. That he was a new incarnation of Christ or even of Adam."

This drew hisses from the monks. "Blasphemy," Rubruck growled.

"Indeed," I said, continuing. "The Archbishop of Jerusalem many years ago suggested that William was created by the Devil and thought it possible that God made me as I am so that I may stop him. What the truth of it is, I honestly do not know. All I know is that I am as I am. And William is the same. Many times, we have survived wounds that would have ended the life of a mortal man. And we go on, ageless."

Bartholomew sneered. "At least you are to be executed tomorrow," he said, with relish. His skeletal face pulled into a wicked grin.

"Not if I can help it," I said. Darkness was falling and it was time to act. Eva helped me into my mail hauberk while my companions objected, in anger and fear.

"What do you mean to do?" Friar William said, repeatedly. "Why would you need that armour? You cannot fight your way through an entire city, you raving lunatic. What are you planning? Your actions will have consequence for the rest of us so you must—"

"I mean to find my brother." My words stopped them all. I looked at my wife. "Before he finds me."

"Richard, no," she said, voice low and meant only for me. "We must flee. Now."

"Perhaps. Yet how far would we get on a pair of stolen horses? We are months away from any hint of safety."

"So that is it?" She was appalled. Angry. "We kill William, and are caught and killed? Or we are killed in the attempt?"

"We kill William," I said. "And capture Hulegu. I will hold a knife at his throat for a thousand miles and none will dare to attack us."

She simply stared at me.

"You have lost your mind," Bertrand said. "You will bring punishment down upon all of us. It is time to end your lunacy." He turned to his squire, then gestured at Eva. "Hughues, take her."

Before Bertrand had taken two steps, I rushed the huge knight and smashed my mailed fist into his nose, hooked my foot behind his knee and tripped him to the floor, falling heavily. I was armoured and he was not. He screamed and struggled beneath me but I hit him again and drove a knee into his guts. Still, he was strong and tough and I had to near-enough crack open his skull with my elbow before he was knocked senseless and groaning.

I rolled off, drawing my dagger as I did so as I expected Thomas and his squire to be following up behind. The squire had indeed moved to intervene but Thomas held him back, though both Templars glared at me with anger.

Eva had bested Hughues easily, ending up mounted on his chest, hammering punches into his face. Blood spattered over her fists.

"Eva," I called.

She climbed off of him, leaving the young man spitting blood and whimpering, tears streaming from his swelling eyes.

The monks were clustered together on the far side of the ger, with Abdullah and Nikolas, like a gaggle of hens.

Stephen Gosset alone was smiling, like the madman that he was. Grinning at Eva, his eyes shining with passion.

"Do not do this," Thomas said. "You have made a mistake by coming here, you know that now. Trusting these pagan monsters to help you do justice. Do not make your failure worse by giving them reason to take revenge on all of us, when you are caught. What is your strategy, anyway? How can you possibly think you could find and kill your brother when he is out there, beyond the city in that wasteland?"

"If they will be here in the city tomorrow then they must be close by," I said. "Camped just outside the city, perhaps only a short ride away. All their camps are the same. The lord's ger is in the centre of every ordus. I will go there, kill his guards and take this Hulegu Khan, brother of Mongke. He will tell me where William is. I will kill William and flee with Hulegu as hostage."

Thomas shook his head in disbelief. "You say you have strength and speed. And though you are quite mad, I believe in your abilities as I have seen them with my own eyes. But such a thing could never be done by one man alone."

"Not alone," I said, looking at my wife.

Stephen spoke up, the words spilling from his lips almost faster than he could form them. "But she is one of you, also, is she not? She must be. Surely, by God, she must be as he says. Do you not see, brothers? Eva is one of the immortals, such as Richard has described. You have seen her strength, seen it again just now, you see? It is the only way she could have defeated—"

Friar William strode forward and smacked Stephen on the back of the head with such force than the young monk fell to his knees, silently clutching his skull.

"It is true," I said, placing a hand on my wife's shoulder. "She is over sixty years old but she can kill better than any knight I ever knew. Together, we will do this. Come on, the sun will be setting soon. And Bertrand is coming to his senses. I would prefer not to kill him but I will do so to protect myself."

"Wait!" Stephen said from his knees, rubbing his head and climbing to his feet. "Wait, please, wait. What about the Assassins?"

* * *

I glanced through the door of the ger, the freezing air stinging my skin. The sun was low in the sky and the temperature was plummeting.

Thanks to God, there were still no guards outside our ger. I suspected that the Mongols of the city continued to keep watch on us wherever we went, trusting that I would never be able to get away. And I had no doubt that if we were seen fleeing for one of the four gates in the twilight, we would be arrested.

"It will be dark soon," I said as I closed the door and turned back into the ger. "Only then can we leave."

"I will take them a blessing," Stephen said, earnestly. "That is what we shall say to the guards outside the Assassins' quarters. You others shall be escorting me through the city."

"You cannot use God's name for deceit," Friar Bartholomew said, his voice tight and rising in pitch. "I will not allow it."

"We must remain on the side of truth, Stephen," Friar William said, with condescension. "If we are to do any good here, if we are to win any souls for Christ, we cannot jeopardise the trust the Great Khan has generously placed in us."

Stephen laughed in their faces. "Do you truly not see? Are you both so blind?" He waved an arm around to indicate the breadth of the city beyond the felt walls. "These barbarians hold every faith to be equal, and it is for each man and woman to choose which of these to follow. A man here may be a Mohammedan, with a Buddhist wife, and a Nestorian son. And none of them, nor any other soul they know, would find anything remarkable about it.

Any of them can already choose Christ but in the manner of the Nestorians. When you tell them there is a better way of worshipping, the true way, that of the Pope in Rome, not a soul here cares one jot. They will tolerate your presence only because they love all priests and wish for blessings from any man who will give them. You are wasting your time. You came here for nothing. They have no space in their hearts for the true Christ."

The monks stared at him, open-mouthed. Friar William began to speak but Stephen cut him off.

"And even if they did, neither you, William nor you, Bartholomew, would be the men to turn them into Christians of the Roman Church. I have watched you, listened to you, these many months. More than a year, now, have I listened to you droning on about minuscule points of doctrine that none of these people could ever hope to understand, and both of you are too stupid to see it for yourselves. You have no hope here, none. You should return to civilised lands and do what good work with whatever years God will grant you with people who will listen to you. In truth, Bartholomew, I doubt that you will survive the journey home. But you must try rather than remain here, useless and pitiable, in failure."

Bartholomew gripped William's sleeve and his face turned grey. Neither monk spoke a word in objection.

"Now, leave me alone," Stephen continued. "I have no interest in following your orders, nor in my oath to obey the doctrine of Saint Francis. And so, I will use deceit to help Richard. And, in return, he will give me what I want."

"I will?" I said, amazed by his recklessness in disavowing his order. "And what is it you want?"

"You know what I want," he said, glancing at Eva.

"Eva is already married," I said, deliberately misunderstanding him.

He swallowed, glancing at her again as his cheeks flushed. "Not that. I want—"

"You will help me," I said, stalking over to him. "You will gain entry to the quarters of the Assassins, on pretence of your blessing." He backed away, until he bumped into one of the roof posts, eyes darting left and right. "And in return, I will refrain from tearing out your throat and drinking all of the blood from your scrawny little body. Is that acceptable?"

In a few moments, I was ready to leave.

"Bartholomew," I said. "Give Eva your robe so that she may disguise herself."

"I shall not!" he said, quivering.

"No," Eva said. "I will stay here."

"We must not separate," I said. "This could all fall into pieces at any moment. We must stay together."

"And who will watch them?" she nodded at the monks, and then at Bertrand and Hughues, both tied up on the floor. Faces bloodied and full of anger. "We leave, they will raise the alarm. No, I will stay. You will return."

"I will," I swore, then raised my voice. "If any of them give you cause for fear, you should run them through, do you understand?"

"It would give me great pleasure."

"Thomas," I said. "You will do nothing to hinder my wife, will you."

He looked me in the eye. "I shall do as honour dictates."

I turned to Eva. "Run him through first, my love. Stephen, come on. Abdullah, you are coming with me to translate." He was terrified but he did as he was told. What is more, he had already discerned where in the city the Assassin envoy had been quartered. It was the centre of the new city, in one of the many mudbrick houses built there. Most were two storeys tall, and some higher than that.

With a final glance back at Eva, I ducked outside. The cold attacked me and I pulled my Mongol coat tighter and tied the fur-lined hat under my chin.

Men were in the streets, hurrying to complete the day's business before retiring for the freezing night. Few of them gave us even a glance but I was nervous. Ready to fight.

"The Assassins are not to be trusted, my lord Richard," Abdullah whispered as we walked through the dark main street. The Sun had only just set and the sky looked like a pale blue silken shroud soaking up a pool of blood.

"Truly, Abdullah?" I said. "You are advising me that I should not trust the Assassins?"

Abdullah explained to the pair of stony-faced Persian fellows inside the entrance to the Assassins' quarters that the young monk had come to perform a blessing for the men within, and that I was his escort and assistant. They were suspicious, and I told Abdullah to simply say we had come with gifts for their lord. They let us further inside, opening the sturdy door from the antechamber and calling out for their master while we entered the building proper behind them.

I stepped through into a large central room with doors to either side and steps at the far side leading to the floor above. The room was well-lit with lamps all around the walls.

A dozen or so Assassins were busy within, carrying and stacking boxes and sacks in neat piles about the room. All wore thick woollen clothing, with trousers and some wore coats even though they were indoors. Servants busied themselves all around, with footsteps and banging and dragging noises sounding on the floor over our heads.

Their leader was called over, the fine-looking man I had seen earlier in the palace hall. He was no longer dressed in silks like a Persian lord but wore similar sturdy travelling clothes, like his men.

"This is Hassan al-Din," Abdullah said, introducing us with a clumsy attempt at formality. "And this is Richard of Ashbury."

Hassan surprised me when he responded in superb French. "It is an honour to meet you, sir. Welcome. How may I be of service?"

"You are leaving," I said, for it was obvious they were making preparations for travel though I was surprised that they would be free to do so.

He inclined his head. "At first light. Our embassy is completed and now we return to our lands."

"To Alamut?" I said. Every man in the Holy Land knew of the home of the Assassins, and half the men in Christendom, too.

He smiled but there was steel behind his eyes. "Why have you come here?"

"To ask you what you know of my brother," I said, unwilling

to say too much right away.

He looked at me for a moment, his dark eyes glinting in the lamplight. Perhaps he was wondering whether to waste his time with me. "Your brother is William, yes? The Englishman who has bewitched Hulegu Khan."

"That is indeed my brother. In what way has he bewitched Hulegu?"

The elegant Saracen lord's mouth twitched beneath his glistening beard. "Your brother is a master of blood magic. This is well known. They say that he cannot be killed. And they also say that with his blood magic he has made Hulegu into an immortal with the strength of ten men."

I felt as though I had been kicked in the guts. But I should have known that William would use his blood to forge powerful alliances. He had done that very thing in England.

"He has made Hulegu into an immortal?" I said, half to myself.

"Well, sir," Hassan said, with a slight smile, "that is what people say."

"How do you know this?"

"We have ways to know. Hulegu is an enemy of my people, even more than the Great Khan Mongke. His brother Hulegu is set on turning his strength against us, to conquering all Persia and destroying our people. We were surprised when this Frankish knight William was welcomed into Hulegu's court and given so much power at the Khan's side until we discovered that he had promised everlasting life to Hulegu, his chief captains and his keshig. That is to say, his most elite bodyguards." ·

My own blood ran cold. "You say it is not just Hulegu who is immortal but other lords at his court also? How many others?"

"We have been unable to determine this precisely," Hassan said, apologetically. "His keshig bodyguards may number ten or so. And his chief captains may be half as many. But what does it matter how many? Unless you also believe in this blood magic?" He looked closely at me but continued when I gave him no response. "Our people have been meeting with increasing resistance from Hulegu's court for years. We have sent a number of men to kill Hulegu but all who have tried to carry out their mission have been killed. There is an inner circle of five or so senior captains around Hulegu, each a great lord of Mongols in his own right. The keshig bodyguards are great individual warriors, honoured with a place at Hulegu's side, night and day. With William a key figure at the court, we would expect his presence to be resented by the Mongols, and yet he is respected. Feared, even."

"They are right to fear him," I said.

I felt my plan crumbling beneath my feet. I felt confident that I could cut my way through a number of mortal men, even trained warriors such as Hulegu would have in his ordus, and protecting his ger. But a dozen or more with the power of our blood would be a terrible danger. I recalled with horror the efforts it took to bring down John Little the former bailiff of the Sheriff of Nottingham. He was a huge man but was not a trained fighter, and he had almost killed Eva, even though he had received a sword thrust to the hilt up into his guts from his rear end.

Hard to kill. Even harder to kill quickly.

What is more, the Mongols were on their guard against attacks by the Assassins. The precise method of attack that I intended to use to kill my brother was the one that they would be most prepared for. To infiltrate the camp in the night without being detected.

"I am deeply sorry. These were not the answers you wished to hear," Hassan said. "You are to be executed tomorrow, I believe. A very sad state of affairs." He spoke lightly, barely even attempting sincerity. "You wished to seek clemency from your brother?"

"I swore an oath to kill him. I cannot allow myself to be killed before I fulfil my oath."

"And how will you kill him, sir?" Hassan was amused but growing impatient. He and his men were ready to leave. "Even a hundred of our finest men could not reach Hulegu, nor any of his captains. Or, perhaps, you, in fact, claim to have the same blood magic as your brother?"

He knew. This Assassin lord knew, just as the Great Khan Mongke had known, that I was immortal, that I had the power that William my brother claimed.

The Assassin was sceptical, of course. But he wanted something from me, or else he would not have granted me so much of his time.

"I have no wealth," I said. "I cannot bring you men or fortresses. But, yes, I do have the blood magic, as you call it. I do not age. I am stronger than any mortal man. My body heals wounds that would kill any other man. Perhaps these things would be useful to you. After all, the Mongols have chosen your people for destruction, have they not? Surely, you could benefit from such power."

Hassan raised his black eyebrows. "You claim to have the strength of ten men?"

I shrugged. "I never truly tested the limits of my strength. Ten men? Two or three, certainly. Perhaps more."

He smiled. "In Acre, and in Tiberius, I have watched Frankish knights training in war. You have this contest which is called grappling, do you not?" As he spoke, he called out to his men and waved two of them forward.

The biggest two.

They dropped the loads they were carrying and strutted over. Both were well-built. One was thick-set and older and the other younger and wiry but with big hands and wide shoulders. Perhaps they were cousins or an uncle and nephew. Both listened while Hassan explained what he required of them.

"Grappling, yes," I said. "We engage without striking blows, and without weapons."

"As do we." He reeled off a few terse words at his men, who nodded and stepped forward. Hassan, smiling, stepped back. "No blows, no weapons."

Everyone else in the room hastily scrambled to the edges of the space.

The burly Assassins launched themselves at me with considerable enthusiasm. They each took a hold of me, one on each arm and shoulder, and tried to force me backwards, then the other way, and then they tried to throw me down to the floor. It took discipline to resist striking them both.

I planted my feet, bent my knees, and resisted. They held on and twisted and heaved against me, our shoes slipping on the tiled floor.

Pushing into their grasp, I snaked my hands up to the top of their arms, squeezed their shoulders with my fingers, digging them in hard, and heaved down. Both men gritted their teeth and the fat one growled but neither could resist my strength. One man after the other, their legs buckled beneath them and they fell to their knees.

They attempted to pull away and get up but I held them there and turned to Hassan. "I could demonstrate my strength further by tearing their arms from their shoulders?"

The Assassin lord was not pleased. "Release them, sir, if you please."

They glared at me as they stood but I smiled at them. "You have seen my strength. Now you must believe what they say about my brother and I."

Hassan pursed his lips. "Some men are born with great strength and perhaps you are one of those. And yet you claim also that your body heals wounds that would kill other men?"

I sighed, seeing where these tests were heading. "I am able to resist great wounds and heal quickly, yes. But the effect is far greater when I drink a man's blood after I am wounded, and that wound will heal so rapidly that one may witness the flesh restoring itself even as you look upon it."

"Well, this is something we must see with our eyes, is it not? This is a thing that would give credence to your words, no? We must cut you open." He drew a wickedly curved dagger from the sash about his waist. "And then, once you are dying, we will blood for you to drink?"

I am not taking a mortal wound for you, Saracen. I am desperate but not utterly witless.

"I will cut my flesh superficially, and you shall watch it heal."

"I have seen too many conjurors' tricks to allow you to administer a wound yourself," Hassan said, in an apologetic tone. "I shall do it, with my own knife, and then I shall know it to be true."

It was not so simple a thing to receive a wound anywhere other than my face, as I was bundled up in a coat and clad in my hauberk. But I stripped them off quickly and pulled up the sleeve of my gambeson and undershirt and indicated that he should perform a shallow cut into the meat of my forearm.

The Assassins all stopped their preparations and gathered around Hassan. I felt extremely vulnerable, and especially when turning my back on them to hand my sword to Stephen, who trembled so much he had trouble taking it from me.

One of the servants held a wooden bowl under my arm while Hassan held my wrist in one hand and placed the cold blade of his dagger against my bare skin with the other.

Then he paused, his face close to mine. The scented oils in his beard filled my nose.

"Do you feel pain?" he asked.

"Oh yes."

His cut was deep. Far deeper than I had indicated and his dagger sliced down, through the skin, and through the muscles, down almost to the bone. I winced, sucking air through my teeth and watched as my blood welled out and ran down my arm, dribbling into the bowl beneath. Hassan recoiled and let go of my wrist before any reached him.

Another of Hassan's men sliced open his own palm and squeezed his blood into a cup.

I glanced at Abdullah and Stephen, who were so close they were practically clutching at each other, united in their horror of what they were witnessing.

The smell of the Assassin's blood was intoxicating and when he passed it over I drank the contents of that cup like I was dying of thirst. It had been some years since I had consumed blood. It was like coming home after a long absence. Like embracing an old friend. It was fire in my stomach, dull ache and a burning warmth that spread and spread through my body, up my neck so my face flushed and down to my fingers and toes.

Hassan and the others around me muttered and stirred, staring at my forearm. A servant poured water over my wounded flesh and swiped away the blood with a cloth.

When the blood was cleaned off, the wound beneath was already closed, leaving just an ugly pink line.

"This scar will soon fade into nothing," I said, quickly pulling my hauberk back over my head and wriggling into it.

Hassan stared at me. "The reports of this William's blood magic. I had always thought it to be a conjurer's trick."

"Now you know," I said. "And this blood surely has value to you."

"How is this possible?" he asked. "What did you do to gain this power?"

I hesitated. "I did nothing that I am aware of. Certainly, I did not ask for it. Perhaps I was born this way. Whether it was through the seed of my father or by the hand of God, I know not."

He was suspicious, believing that I deceived him even though I spoke sincerely. The Saracens, and the Assassins most of all, were well versed in deceit and because it was in each of them, they saw it in everyone else, also.

Hassan pointed at the bowl of my blood that one of his servants held. "But if I drink this, I will become like you?"

"No. Not like me. And there is a cost."

"I will pay any price."

"Not that sort of cost. You must first be drained of much of your blood, and at the point of death, you must drink down a pint of mine. It takes half a day or so to bring you back from the brink of death and not all men survive. You may die. If you come back, you must yourself then drink the blood of men, or women, every two or three days, else you will become weakened, then ill, and then you will lose your mind in raving madness. And you will never be able to father a child, no matter how often you lay with a woman."

"A heavy price."

I nodded, taking my sword and other things back from Stephen.

"And you, Richard, you must drink blood every three days?"

I hesitated, for I was giving my secrets to an enemy. But if I did not take drastic action then William would seize me come morning and then I would be no more. Besides, all I would have to do to keep the secret would be to kill every man in the room.

"No. Not me and not William, either. We are different. We are stronger."

"Why? Tell me, good sir, what made you as you are?"

"I do not know," I said. He still thought I was lying. "Truly."

"The tasks that my men could achieve, if they had this power," he said, looking through me into a future only he could see. "We might even resist Hulegu's assault."

"I want you to help me kill my brother," I said.

He snapped back to me. "In exchange for your blood? We can do this. Yes."

"Tonight."

He gaped at me, then spoke to his men in a bust of rapid guttural words. They all laughed, and he allowed himself a smile.

"Tonight, truly, sir? It cannot be done."

"We could kill Hulegu, also."

"We certainly would. But such a thing is not possible."

"I will do it myself, then," I said.

Hassan al-Din, the Assassin lord, and emissary, hesitated. I could see that he was weighing up a series of choices. One of which was surely to simply kill me, and the two men with me. He could deliver me to Mongke or to Hulegu or William, in exchange for favours from those men.

"Perhaps I might suggest a different course of action? You should come with us, Sir Richard. Back to Alamut. We leave at sunrise."

"Mongke's men would bring me back and punish you all. Kill you all for such an affront."

"My men are all prepared for death. None of us truly expected to leave here with our lives and if we do not return then our master shall know the outcome of our embassy just as surely as if we told him with our mouths. But perhaps they would allow us to leave? The Mongols are truly evil and yet they value greatly the role of ambassador and seek always to deliver envoys safely through their lands, even if they are emissaries from mortal enemies. That is also why we are not closely guarded within Karakorum, even though my master has sent four hundred individual men to murder Mongke in any way that they can. I would gladly risk the lives of my men to bring you and your blood magic away from this place."

"No, that would not be successful. I have delivered myself into my brother's hands, like a fool, and he will not let me go."

"Emissaries are used to negotiating terms," Hassan said. "What do you have that William might want? Or do you have something that Hulegu may want?"

"Nothing," I said because it was true.

Hassan tilted his head. "Is there anything that you can get that William might want?"

"I have no idea what he wants," I said. "I have not seen him for decades, and I never knew him well. I have no way of knowing what he needs now. Neither him nor this Hulegu, who I have only heard of recently. How could I have anything that he would bargain for?"

Abdullah, standing against the wall, raised his voice. "You do." Every face in the room turned to him and he trembled, lowering his head. "Forgive me, my lord, your pardon, sir, your pardon."

"Spit out your words, Abdullah, for the love of God."

"The girl," he said. "The girl who was Hulegu's wife. The young woman we saw in the palace who ran away only to be captured. She is to be killed tomorrow, too. Hulegu wants her, does he not? And also, might she not know Hulegu's needs? And, if William and Hulegu are as close as they say, might she not know of your brother, too?"

Interesting.

"You just want to feast your eyes on her again," I said.

"Oh, no, my lord," Abdullah said. "I am thinking only of your interest, my lord."

I looked at Hassan, who was stroking his beard. "They are being held in a house on the southern road," he said. "Guarded, of course. We will not be allowed to see the prisoners."

"I will kill the guards," I said. "Seize her and force the girl to tell me Hulegu and William's secrets."

"Even if she does tell you something of use." Stephen stepped forward, lowering his voice. "You will not have time to act upon that knowledge before you yourself are seized. They let us go from the palace but only because they knew where you were. What if Mongke's men come for you at the ger tonight, and find you absent? A search of the city would not take them long. And even if Mongke washes his hands of it, you will be taken to Hulegu's men come tomorrow. You must secure an escape, and the only possible chance you have is with these Assassins. Then, you can take the girl when we flee and question her on the road. Hulegu will want her and will pursue her but you could throw her off your horse once you were done with her and Hulegu's men would find her again, then kill her as they intended."

"Impossible," I said. "There is nothing I have to offer the Mongols to stay their hand." I looked at the servant holding a bowl of my blood. One thing I could do was promise to stay at Mongke's court and turn him and a number of his own captains into immortals, as William had done for his brother. But the thought made me sick to my stomach. I would be making myself a slave in exchange for my life. "In exchange for letting us go free, I have nothing that I can offer them."

"But he does," Stephen said, pointing a finger at Hassan.

* * *

My breath frosted in the air. Night proper had fallen when I approached the door where the young Mongol woman was being held. It was a house, the same as the others around it, but the Assassin leading me—assigned by Hassan al-Din—pointed it out. Abdullah and Stephen followed behind.

The door was not barred. As I opened it and stepped through, the heat from inside poured past me out into the freezing night. A single large room filled with lamplight, with steep stairs up to the floor above on one side, and a door on each of the other walls. A small dung-fuelled fire smouldered in the central hearth, and the air was thick with smoke.

Hassan had suggested there would be a single guard inside, perhaps two.

Four men sat around the hearth, drinking together. They fell silent as I stood there in the doorway.

"Good evening, gentlemen," I said, cheerily, and clapping my hands together. "Is this the Karakorum brothel-house?"

They jumped to their feet, their hideous faces twisted in anger at my intrusion.

Quite suddenly, my own days and hours of frustration and fear rushed up to engulf me in a murderous rage. I was on the first man before he had time to recoil, and my dagger punched him in the neck, up to the hilt. Shoving him down before me, I leapt into the next man, who was caught between drawing his own blade and retreating. As he turned from me, I grabbed his long, greasy hair and stabbed the side of his throat. I thrust the blade out of the front of his neck in a shower of blood and the gristly mass of his severed windpipe slapped onto the floor.

I sensed an attack coming from behind and ducked as a sword blade was thrust toward the back of my neck. As I twisted away, it caught the back of my head and cut a gouge into my skull. The attacker might have expected me to retreat in panic, so I turned low enough to place my offhand on the tiled floor and leapt up at him, close enough to hug him while I slammed my dagger up beneath his chin. As I followed him down I drew the blade out and jammed it through his eye.

The fourth man had been expertly dispatched by Hassan's Assassin, who nodded at me while he wiped his curved blade on the Mongol's coat.

In the doorway, Abdullah and Stephen stood with their mouths open at the sudden horror before them.

The delicious smell of blood filled the air and my mouth

watered.

"You are injured, sir," Stephen said, raising a shaky hand at my head.

I felt it. It seemed to be pouring with hot blood over my fingers.

"How bad is it?" I asked Stephen.

His face was grey. "There is a gash and, beneath, a... a flap, of skin."

That would not do. I bent to the first man, who was still struggling for breath as his life pumped away onto the tiles beneath his body. Without a word, I bent to his neck and drank down the hot blood that welled up from the wound.

"Good God Almighty," Stephen said. "That flap of skin has knitted itself back together, Richard. I watched it happen. Did you see that, Abdullah?"

A silence descended and hung over the room like a shroud.

The young Mongol woman stood at the top of the stairs, looking down on us like a princess. By God, she was a beauty. She was bareheaded and her shining black hair tumbled down in braids and was not shorn on top

Abdullah drifted towards the bottom of the steps, mouth agape.

As he started to speak, the young Mongol man pushed past the girl, a low growl in his throat, bare hands raised and ready to fight to defend his woman to the death. His eyes were steely but edged with that madness that shows a man is prepared to die.

I stepped in front of him with my hands up and out. "Stop!"

He jabbed his finger at me and snarled a stream of angry

words.

"Tell him we're here to help," I said to Abdullah, and to the Assassin. "Tell him we are fleeing the city and we want them to come with us."

The two young Mongols exchanged a look. The man barked a question.

"He asks why."

"I want to kill Hulegu. And I want to kill my brother William, who serves Hulegu. And I want him and his woman to help me."

They did not hesitate.

* * *

We wrapped ourselves in Mongol garb and hurried back through the bitter darkness. Faint moonlight provided just barely enough light to see the edges of things, whenever the clouds and dung-smoke did not obscure the sky completely. Every crunching step on the iron-hard icy ground made me wince, and my head swivelled left and right as I strained to hear any approaching danger over the heavy breathing of my strange company. The city appeared deserted but all it would take to ruin us would be for a single alert Mongol to raise the alarm before I could silence him. Inside the houses and tents, voices and laughter spilled out into the night.

And I wondered whether I would return to our ger to find Eva safe and well, or whether the knights had overpowered her, or if the Mongols had come for us while I was away.

It was quiet as I approached, with the others behind me. Smoke rolled from the top of the ger.

I tapped on the door in the pattern that Eva would recognise.

The few moments before the door opened, my heart was in my mouth.

Thomas opened the door, his face blank. He nodded and stepped back. All was quiet within and Eva smiled, briefly. I was glad to see her, too.

Waving everyone in, I closed the door behind us.

"Quickly," I said to Eva. "We must make final preparations and be at the gate before sunrise."

"You will bring disaster down upon us," Friar William said, for the hundredth time.

"Save your breath," Stephen Gosset said as he helped me to pack our belongings, including some stale food, and speaking over his shoulder.

"These murderers breaking the law is one thing," Friar William said. "But you, Stephen, you are a brother of our order and you are bringing us into disrepute with your—"

"Be quiet, I said," Stephen snapped, turning on his brothers. "I have seen things this night that are bigger than your notions of reputation. Go home, tell the Pope that you failed to convert anyone, and leave me be."

The monks stared. Friar William recovered, shook his red face and took a deep breath ready to shout down the youngster.

"Quiet," I said. "Quiet, all of you. And listen."

They all broke off and turned to me.

"I am leaving tonight. Eva and I together. We are taking these

Mongols with us. We will flee with the Assassins of Alamut, and go to their lands with them. In that way, I shall be free from the sentence of the Khan. Free to return and to fight again."

"Why would the Assassins welcome you?" Thomas said. "And why would the Mongols let you go?"

I hesitated. "The Assassin envoy, Hassan al-Din, has gone this very night to the palace of the Great Khan. He will make a trade for my life and together we will ride to Alamut."

"What trade?" Thomas asked. "What could they possibly offer that would be worth your life?"

"It does not concern you," I said.

"He is giving the Assassins his blood," Stephen said as if he was too proud of the knowledge to hold on to it. "He will make them into immortals, just as his brother has done for Hulegu."

"Good God Almighty," Thomas said.

"We should thank God Almighty," Friar William said, "that this power of his blood is nothing but a nonsense."

"It is true," Stephen said. "I have witnessed it with my own eyes. As has Abdullah. The Assassins have seen it, and that is why they are risking everything to protect Richard."

"How can you trust these Saracens?" Bertrand said, glaring at the Assassin who stood quietly by the door. "You are betraying God."

I scoffed. "You are the least devout man here."

"And yet he is right," Thomas said. "You cannot go with the Assassins. You will make yourselves prisoners, to be used and exploited by these heathens. They will kill you whenever they are done with you. And you cannot give them this power of yours...

if it truly does exist."

"I need allies," I said. "I cannot defeat my brother, nor Hulegu and the other immortals that William has made, without men to assist me. Men with the strength to face William's evil." I pointed at the nameless Assassin in his Persian headwear. "They are the only men with such strength."

"It should be Christian men by your side," Thomas said.

"I wish it were so," I said. "But where are they? Will you join me, Thomas, and fight at my side? Would you bring Martin with you? Would you use the strength of your order to help me?"

Stephen stepped forward. "I will join you."

I laughed in his face. "I need knights, Stephen, not clerks."

He was deeply offended. "I have knowledge of the world that could help you. I gave you the means for your escape, did I not?"

I hesitated. The young monk had shown a certain gift for creative thinking. Something that I sorely lacked. "Very well, you will come."

"I will come also," Abdullah said, stepping forward and bowing his head. "With your permission, my lord."

"Why in the name of God would you want to come with me?" I asked, appalled.

He glanced at the Mongol girl, who sat by the entrance with the man's arm about her shoulder, next to the Assassin who watched us through his eyelashes. "I wish to be with my people," Abdullah said.

"The Assassins?" I said. "You are a Saracen, subject to the Caliph in Baghdad, are you not? The Assassins are the sworn enemies of your people."

Abdullah's eyes twinkled in the lamplight. "They follow the word of the Prophet. They are closer to me than the Christians, or the Mongols. And I can be useful to you. How will you speak with the Ismailis without me?"

I jerked my thumb over my shoulder. "Are you that smitten with the girl that you would risk death."

He lowered his head. "I simply no longer wish to be cold, sir."

"If you wish to serve me, I will not say no."

"He belongs to me," Friar William said, outraged. "He may not go with you."

"Try and stop him," I said. The monks cursed me but what else could they do?

Little Nikolas ran forward. "I, too, will join you, Sir Richard." He grinned up at me with his hand on the ivory dagger I had given him.

"No, son," I said. "It is not safe for you. Stay with the monks. Serve them well and in the Spring they will take you back to Constantinople."

His eyes filled with tears. "No, my lord, no, I will come with you. You and Eva. I will serve you well."

William and Bartholomew protested but I waved them into silence. "You are too young," I said to Nikolas.

Eva placed a hand on my arm. "Richard?"

I knew what she wanted but I did not want to have to look after the boy. He would be pestering us and slowing us down. And, absurd as it was, I found his obsession with Eva to be irritating. He was just of the age that his interest in her would not be purely a platonic one, and I felt like Eva was allowing herself to be exploited in some vague, ill-defined way. Perhaps it was as simple a thing as my feeling excluded, and that he took her attention away from me. Whatever the reason, I found myself relieved at the prospect of being rid of him.

"The boy stays with the monks," I said. "It is fair to the Franciscans, who I am already depriving of one interpreter. Nikolas can assist them in Abdullah's stead. And besides all that, it is not safe for you, Nikolas. We will be riding hard, riding in a fashion that you are too small to do. Stay safe. The monks have been promised safety by the Great Khan. It will please me to know you are safe."

He half-drew his white dagger, gripping it tightly around the carving of Saint George killing the dragon. "Please, sir. I will make a good knight. I will serve you and become a brave knight and fight the Saracens."

I saw then how I had wronged him. Patronised him and given him false hope for something that he could never be.

All I could do was ruffle his hair. "Serve your masters well," I said.

Thomas grabbed me by the shoulder before I left. "I beg you," he said. "Do not give your power to our enemies."

"Come with me," I said. "You and Martin, both. The Franciscans do not need your protection. They have Bertrand and Hughues, and they do not even need them. The Mongols, despite their savagery in every other way, keep all ambassadors safe and well. No harm will come to them."

"I must return to the Holy Land," he said. "And the Kingdom of Jerusalem. When I get to Acre, I must tell King Louis, and the

Master of my order, that the Mongols mean to make war on the kingdoms there. I must tell them how these Mongols may destroy our enemies, but they may take everything that we hold, too."

"Send Martin with the messages," I said. "Ride with us yourself. God knows I could use your wisdom. And your skill in battle."

"Yours is a personal quest," he said, glancing at the Assassin and the Mongol couple. "I serve higher powers."

"That is fair to say," I admitted, though I knew would miss him very dearly. "Then I wish you well. Perhaps, one day, we shall meet again."

"If your new friend Hassan al-Din is unable to make his deal with the Great Khan," Thomas said, "I will see you dragged back here to Karakorum before sundown."

* * *

We had to make haste, and our strange little group carried our gear, along with what supplies we could muster, to the south gate of Karakorum where the Assassins were already assembled in the pre-dawn light. It was intensely cold, and the ground was hard as iron and sheathed in frozen dew. After a nerve-wracking night and no sleep, we were all tired. And yet the fear of capture was so acute that I was jittery and ready to fight with a moment's warning.

As we approached the gate along the empty road, I was surprised to see wagons gathered by the gate, with the Assassins heaving their wares into the backs of them.

"I thought we were riding hard," I asked one of Hassan's captains, who had been watching for our approach. "To evade Mongke or Hulegu's men. These wagons will slow us terribly."

Abdullah translated for me. "They say that no matter how hard we ride, we could never evade pursuit, should the Mongols decide to launch one. All depends on Hassan's embassy."

"Do you think he will have been received by the Khan yet?" I asked, though I knew the answer.

The Assassin captain looked at me like I was a buffoon, though he was kind enough to explain. "Mongke makes himself insensible from excessive drink very early every night. And though he wakes early, it takes much time for him to bestir himself for the day's business."

I nodded, for I had known many man who lived lives taken over by drink. I had been one of them myself.

The Mongols who guarded the gate were well armed and armoured with mail and steel helms beneath their thick coats and furs. They watched us all very closely, holding lamps out and peering into the Assassin's wagons as they strolled through us all.

We would be caught, I was sure of it. The gate, such as it was, remained closed and I did not know how I could force it open. We had little chance of killing every guard before one of them raised a cry of warning that would bring hundreds or thousands more down upon us.

Not only was I not supposed to leave the city, I was harbouring criminals. The two young Mongols hid their faces beneath their fur hoods and held tight to each other.

I gathered the rest of my brood to me. Eva, Stephen, and

Abdullah. In outer appearance, we were dressed much the same as everyone else; our thick overcoats hiding our amour or our robes, and our hoods hiding our faces. We kept our voices low and spoke barely at all.

Around us, the Assassins busied themselves. Hassan's captain stood by my side, watching the Mongols all around us from the corner of his eyes.

A guard approached, lantern held high, and the Assassin directed us away from him while he went to intercept. Another Assassin took control of our group and directed us to one of the wagons, where he invited us to load our belongings.

While the sky lightened, and preparations continued, they moved us between them so to hide us from the Mongols in plain sight. I noticed how the Assassins formed another group like ours, with the same number, and one of them was tall, like me. This group was allowed to be inspected by a guard, and then we were swapped for their position. Not for nothing were the Assassins said to be cunning in the extreme.

We waited for the gate to be opened and I was gripped with a sudden, mad fear that William would be standing there as it did so, backed by a thousand battle-ready savages. No matter how much I told myself it was merely a weakness of my own heart, I could not shake the fear.

As the sun rose, finally the gate was opened.

William was not there.

It was the harsh and barren landscape with the silhouettes of groups of horses huddled together against the freezing night dawn. I breathed a short sigh of relief but remained tense and anxious as we mounted our horses all together, with us fugitives in the centre and the Assassins shielding us from view as well as they could. We kept our heads down, in shadow within our hoods.

Finally, we rode out through the gate into the freezing valley beyond. Our immediate route was to follow the frozen river southward as it wound along the valley, edged by the sharp hills.

We went slowly. The horses were hardy but it was so cold it was a wonder they were willing to walk at all. The oxen pulling the wagons were subdued as if they could sense our tension, our fear. I had heard often how the Assassins were joyfully willing to die for their lord, but they seemed fearful also to me. Perhaps it was concern not for themselves but for Hassan al-Din, who we left behind at the palace with only one attendant so that he could secure our safe passage.

If Hassan were killed, or his deal refused, we would be brought back and I would be executed by Hulegu, who was arriving on the other side of the city that day.

That freezing morning, facing my imminent death at the hands of my immortal enemy, it is fair to say that I ached for my home.

England.

I had felt cold there, but the deep, crisp snows of English winter were nothing like the bitter, dry, howling winds of the foothills and mountains at the edge of the great grassland plains. I hated it, suddenly, hated the strange land, that was so lifeless and miserable that I understood at once how it could create such a foul people as the Mongols and other tartar peoples. England was green, with thick, dark, rich soil that crumbled between one's fingers. Soil that was deep, and always moist, and grew tall, healthy crops.

The hills of my homeland in Derbyshire were beautiful, steep and hard in places but civilised and on a human scale. My dear hills were so unlike the savage grey and black giants that jutted up into the bleached skies in the distance, like dungeon walls. I knew, deep in my bones, that God had lovingly sculpted Derbyshire and all England with his own hand, and had set the climate to make civilised men, and good women. A land hard enough to make us strong, and courageous but generous enough to breed within us a fundamental decency and goodness of spirit.

That land of central Asia seemed to be scoured by the hand of some demon, bordered by mountains thrown up out of the bowels of the Earth. Even the low hills that hemmed us in were an unnatural shape, with peaks like the edge of a curved blade, or the backs of giant serpents undulating across the landscape in a grotesque parade. Hot enough to kill a man in summer, cold enough in winter that many a traveller never awoke in the morning but lay frozen to the ground, as if the land wanted to devour him. A brutal place that bred brutal men. A people without the luxury of civilisation.

A pale sun dragged itself halfway into the sky to our left, casting long shadows across the stony ground. From our right came the howling, bitter wind that could cut through half a dozen layers of clothing, including furs, to numb one side of your body and drive painful aches deep into your bones.

All the while, I felt the presence of Karakorum behind me.

Would it be a galloping army come to take me away? Would William himself lead them? Would I be killed here, in this God-forsaken nightmare land? What would happen to Eva? Had I led her into ruin, finally?

It was the end of the day, as the sun grew weak and rested for a moment on the distant mountains when I had my answer.

A shout went up and the procession of Ismailis halted and turned. I could see nothing behind us but more broken land and a sky turned pale as ice, with a sun falling away to the West as if it were glad for the shelter.

Riders.

My hand went to my sword, and Eva moved to my side so that we could fight together against the pursuing enemies.

Yet there were so few of them. Just three riders, in fact, with three more riderless horses following.

"It is Hassan," Eva said, squinting, for her eyes were far better in the half-light than any mortal's, and better than mine also. "With his attendant. The third man is... I cannot make him out, it is as though he is hiding."

"Thomas," I said, hardly believing my own words as I spoke them. "That is Thomas with them."

Stephen positioned his own horse behind mine and spoke up. "What in the name of God is he doing here?"

"Why is he hiding?" Eva asked. "Hunched so low as he rides?"

"He is cold," Stephen said.

"He is injured," I said.

And so it was.

I rode out to meet them, along with Eva and a group of

Hassan's men.

"What happened?" I shouted as we came together.

"Mongke Khan agreed to let us all go," Hassan said. "All of you included. In exchange for me agreeing to call off all of the four-hundred fedayin."

Thomas was slumped over, barely conscious, and tied to his saddle. The horse was skittish, tossing her head and stepping sideways.

"What happened to him?" I asked as we took his reins. "Thomas, can you hear me?"

"Is he dead?" Stephen said as he rode up behind me against my orders.

"Almost," Eva said. "Look."

Thomas' lower body and legs were saturated with blood, as were the flanks of his horse. He seemed dead but the Templar groaned and feebly tried to fight us off while we cut him down from his horse. We carried Thomas and placed him on the back of a wagon, removing his clothing.

"Who did this?" I demanded, though I dreaded the answer.

"Your brother," Hassan al-Din said. "Used a dagger to cut him, here. See?" Hassan mimed the cut, low on the abdomen, from hip to hip.

Upon examination, the cut was not so wide as that, but it was bad. It stank of foul blood and shit, and only the frigid wind stopped the stench from being totally overpowering. It smelled of death and I knew Thomas would not be long for the world. Still, the Assassins moved to help us and Stephen poured their offered wine over the wound to clean it, then wiped at and soaked up the blood. Thomas shivered and his skin, where it was not bloody, was as white as bleached bone.

"Make a fire," Stephen said. "We must warm him. Hurry."

No one made a move to do so. All of us knew that it would do no good. Thomas had only a short while to live.

"My brother did this?" I said to Hassan, my own body shaking now, not with cold but from a white-hot rage that grew with every moment. "Sent him to me like this, just to taunt me?"

Hassan grimaced. "Mongke Khan agreed to the terms, and Hulegu could not persuade him otherwise." He pointed at me. "Your brother William calmed Hulegu and demanded to see your monks."

"He killed them?"

"William harmed them, demanding to know where you were fleeing to. Of course, they told him everything, immediately. They will live. As will the large knight who looks like a bullock."

"Bertrand."

"Hulegu himself demanded Bertrand tell everything about the King of France and the land of France. Precisely how many towns are there, how many sheep, how many horses."

The Mongols had asked us similar questions before. "Absurd. How can any man know such things?"

Hassan shrugged. "This Sir Bertrand made a sincere attempt to give them answers. Hulegu said that he would make Bertrand a great lord when the Mongols conquer France."

"Dear God," Eva said, looking at me.

"When did William do this?" I said, pointing at the dying Thomas.

Hassan looked back at the dark horizon. "Night will fall soon. We should make camp here." He called orders to his men, who immediately began to corral the horses and circle the wagons on the bleak plain.

I grabbed him by the arm, which alarmed his captains enough that they drew their daggers and made ready to strike. But they were utterly obedient to their lord, and he restrained them with no more than a look.

"Tell me what happened," I said, in a low voice.

"Hulegu and your brother arrived and your companions were brought to the palace," Hassan said. "The monks, the knights, the Templars. Even the servants. Hulegu was angry that Mongke had agreed to free you, and his traitorous wife, in exchange for my word to stop the fedayin."

"First, he killed the young Templar. The squire of this man," Hassan said. "Crushed the skull with his bare hands and drank his blood from the neck. His keshig were there. Evil men. While the body yet twitched, they passed it between them as if it were a skin of wine, many drinking from it before tossing it aside. The old knight here shouted curses and Hulegu's keshig held him so that he would see it all."

Eva shook with rage. "We shall kill them," she promised me.

"William spoke into the ear of Sir Thomas," Hassan continued. "And then cut him, like you see. He told me to take him to you. Take this old man to my brother Richard, he said to me, and the old man will tell my brother my message. I said that I would do so but that the old man would die before he could speak it."

I hung my head, for I knew at once what William intended. "And he told you I would have to turn him into an immortal in order to save his life. In order to hear the message."

Eva and I looked at each other.

Around us on the back of the wagon, the Ismailis placed lamps that cast yellow light over Thomas' body.

"And then, there was a boy," Hassan said, speaking reluctantly. "While William cut this Templar across the body, a slave boy attacked your brother with a white dagger. Stabbed him low in the flank."

"Nikolas," Eva said, her eyes shining in the dusk. "What did he do to Nikolas?"

Hassan's nose wrinkled. "You do not wish to—"

"Tell me," Eva said.

"William laughed at the boy, pulled the blade from his body without pain, and asked the slave from where did he steal such a fine dagger? The boy said it was a gift from the greatest knight who ever lived, Sir Richard the Englishman. William found this to be highly amusing." Hassan looked away from us. "They held him. William peeled the boy's skin from his face and chest using the white dagger. Played games with his pain. All the time, they were laughing. When they tired of it, two of Hulegu's immortals took an arm each and pulled him apart. The keshig tore his arms from his body." Hassan shook his head. "It was a very bad thing. Very bad."

Eva stood, her body shaking, her face set in stone as she glared back at the north.

"We cannot go back," I said, softly.

She did not look at me when she replied, irritated. "I know."

"Here," Hassan said, taking an object from inside his overcoat. He handed it over. Small, wrapped in a square of silk, cut from robes. "Before I was dismissed, your brother approached with this. I thought he was going to defy the Great Khan and kill me but instead he told me to give this to you."

I unwrapped the object.

My white dagger.

While the blade had been wiped clean, the carving of Saint George lancing the dragon was crusted with dried blood. William's blood? Or had it come from Nikolas?

An ember of rage grew in me as I imagined the horror of the death of the boy. My hatred for William had burned low for decades but when I pictured Nikolas in his final moments, the agony and fear he must have felt, that hatred began to burn once more.

Thomas groaned and I kneeled by his side again. "What is the message, Thomas?" He muttered, begging for water. "

Stephen pulled a blanket over Thomas' body. "What if this is the message?" he said. "Just this, returning him in this condition?"

"I do not have a mind to listen to your nonsense, Stephen."

"Your brother, he is devious, you said so. You said he once sent men to attack your manor, knowing they would be killed, simply to draw you to him. A manipulation of your actions, do you see? He wants you to give your blood to Thomas, to turn him immortal. What if that is what he wants to tell you?"

"I do not understand. How would my actions be a message? And why would he want that?" I said. "That would only serve to make me stronger."

Stephen opened his mouth to reply but closed it again.

I sighed. "I will feed him my blood."

Stephen nodded, placing a hand on Thomas' pale, glistening head. "He will not wish it. He thinks you are an abomination." He glanced up at Eva. "Both of you, and your brother."

"Perhaps he is right," I said. "He told you that?"

"Last night, when we returned to the ger. He urged me to stay away from you."

It annoyed me. Thomas was not wrong, not at all, and yet it annoyed me greatly.

Using the white dagger, I sliced into my wrist and pressed the wound to Thomas' lips. They were cold. He tried to turn his head away, tried to raise an arm and force mine away. But he was so weak.

And he drank. Slowly, at first, and then he sucked and gulped at my wrist.

"He will not like this," Stephen muttered, looking ill.

"It may not work at all," I said, quietly. "And if he lives and does not wish to, I will simply cut off his head."

While the others ate, drank and pondered the long journey ahead of us, I sat beside Thomas on the wagon, inside the little pool of yellow light given off by the lamp set down by his head. The small flame glowed within the waxed parchment sides, safe from the wind howling down the valley. Eva came to sit by my side, leaning her body against me for a time before she moved away to sleep. She draped me in furs and kissed my cheek before she left me.

Once in a while, I felt the skin of Thomas' chest, slipping my hand beneath the furs covering him to see if his heart was yet beating and if he still breathed. An intimate gesture that set me wondering about the old man's life, and whether he had ever had tender moments with a woman. At the start of the night, his skin was cold as ice and clammy. Later, he developed a fever that radiated from him like an iron pulled from the fire, and a sweat broke out to soak him right through.

"It is a strange life," I said, to Thomas, wondering if he would live to see the dawn. "We have seen much of the world. Seen many wonders. We have done many glorious deeds. But we have done ill, also. I have done murder. Killed men who have wronged us, or wronged others. Doing justice, as I see it, but the laws of England would say it was murder. And we have no home. That is to say, we have homes only for a while before we must move on. But you have been a Templar, sir. And you have served with honour, I have no doubt. You have fought in the Holy Land, and you have fought across Christendom. Perhaps ours would be a life that would suit you." I bowed my head and rubbed my tired eyes. "I shall have to feed you blood, as I do for Eva. You will not like that. No more than I will. But I hope that you will live, Thomas. The truth of it is, I could use a knight such as you at my side. A knight of your skill, and your experience, with the strength of one of the Immortals…" I leaned in closer to his ear. "Live, Thomas. Live."

The lamp ran dry of oil during the night and I fell asleep sitting by the man who was suspended between life and death.

As the sky grew light, before the sun rose, the old knight

muttered through cracked lips and bestirred me from my fitful slumber.

"Thirst," he said. "Thirst."

"I know," I replied.

The old man seemed stunned by what had been done to him and sat subdued on the wagon rather than ride his horse, despite the way those carts bounced and juddered over the rough road. We were all of us well on the move as the sun dragged itself up above the horizon and I asked Thomas, finally, what William's message was.

Stressing that he could not recall the precise words, in between mouthfuls of wine he recited the message back to me.

"Tell him this, he said to me into my ear. I wished that you had forgotten me. He spoke it as if I were you, do you see? I wished that you had forgotten me and had decided to take a path of greatness for yourself." Thomas stared into nothing. "Brother, if you leave me be, so shall I leave you. But if you continue to oppose me..." Thomas squeezed wine into his mouth, so much that it spilled from his lips and he swiped it away. "Then he gutted me with a hooked dagger."

The words affected me deeply. There was so many barbs within it that I did not know which of them wounded me most deeply. Worst of all was the sense that, to me, William was my enemy, my sole purpose in life, my quest, my obsession. Yet to him, I was little more than an annoyance. If he spoke truly, it seemed as though he had forgotten me in the years since we had last clashed. All the while, I had dedicated every waking hour to finding him, reaching him. Killing him.

It cheapened it. Made my oath of vengeance seem small.

Thomas looked at me from under his hood with red-rimmed eyes.

"You have suffered terribly," I said to him. "And I ask forgiveness. If I had known that he would do this, I would have forced you to come with me."

"How can I forgive you? Why should I?" Thomas was silent for a while, shivering and white. "I listened to your stories about him but I did not believe. No, I did not understand. Not until I saw his madness with my own eyes. He killed Martin. A decent man, who deserved a good death, at the very least, not torture. Not mutilation. And little Nikolas, that poor lad. Do you know what they did to him?"

Terrorised, tortured and torn apart before he had even become a man. Another innocents' death on my conscience.

"He will die for what he has done," I said. "Call it what you will. Justice. Vengeance. I will kill my brother or die in the attempt."

"And the others?" Thomas said. "Hulegu, and the other Immortals that your brother has made?"

Hulegu was, to all intents and purposes, a king. Not just any king, but the most powerful man in the entire world save only, perhaps, for his brother Mongke, who was an alcoholic who had rarely strayed far from Karakorum. Whereas Hulegu was acting like a true conqueror like his grandfather, Genghis. His army was already the largest anywhere, it was the most well equipped, with the best artillery and the most professional system of organisation and logistics, and with the most experienced and talented officers of any force from the four corners of the Earth.

A man such as he, with the immortal blood of my brother in his veins, would be unstoppable.

"They will all die," I promised.

PART FOUR
ALAMUT
1256

I COULD BARELY CONCEIVE OF the distances we travelled. When we had first travelled from Constantinople, north almost to the lands of the Rus, it had taken months. Then, we went east. Day after day, month after month we had gone east all the way to Karakorum and through the entire journey, we had been official travellers. Taken from place to place, given fresh horses to ride, passed from stage to stage at an astonishing pace. Even then, I knew I had travelled further than I had believed possible.

For my entire life, all eighty-odd years of it, I had known the world as it was from England to Jerusalem. And that was right far. A pilgrimage by land and sea, so long that one would see many a man beside you die from disease or accident. Beyond Jerusalem, I knew, of course, was the land of Syria and beyond that, Persia. I had always imagined they were the size of England or France, and beyond that was a land of desert and barbarity and myth and legend. A land of fantastic monsters, dog-headed people, fabled kingdoms of Christians. But even then, I had not suspected that the land would stretch so far.

And returning, from that distant east to the known west, seemed to me to be farther still.

We travelled at a walking pace. Our horses had to be spared, for we could not find fresh ones except to purchase or trade for enormously disadvantageous terms. Provisions were our first priority, and though we all but starved ourselves, we had to seek all we could from people along the way.

Our route out had taken us north of the Black Sea, and north of the Caspian Sea and also the Aral Sea. The way back would take us to the south of those seas into the Iranian plateau, to Samarkand, Merv, Nishapur and then into the mountains of the Assassins.

I knew little of all that, though, during the journey. To me, it was relentless travel, along rivers, besides inhuman mountains that went on and on for weeks and months. Frozen highlands, bitter deserts, and the taste of dust blown by relentless winds that howled into your face, and through your clothing, day and night, steady or gusting and sounding in your ears like the groaning chants of a thousand monks singing from beyond the grave.

We were miserable. Eva suffered greatly, as did Thomas. Both were heart-sick with loss and resentment. But they had my blood to sustain them, take away some of their weariness every two or three days or so.

212

"I feel strong," Thomas said, on one of the first evenings before retiring. "Stronger than I have since I was a young man, and stronger even than that. I carried that casque of wine down from the wagon with such ease that I mistakenly believed for a moment that it was empty."

Eva nodded. "One of the more profound benefits."

He leaned in and lowered his voice. "The light of the day, even when the sky is grey, causes me to wince and hang my head due to the discomfort I feel behind my eyes. Is that the case with you, good lady?"

She nodded. "Wait until you experience summer in the Holy Land, Thomas. It is quite agonising. Any portion of exposed skin will almost immediately become red and blistered. Prolonged exposure will make it blister and crack before your eyes. Ever since I became an immortal, I have gone about shrouded and hooded whenever I am out of doors. Even in the shade of a hood, the light of a bright day is quite unpleasant."

"Dear God," Thomas muttered. "But then surely the Holy Land is the very worst place you could choose to be."

Eva glanced at me before responding. "You are not wrong, sir."

"I have often taken pleasure in the simple joy of the sun's warmth upon my skin. Do you mean to say this is something I shall never again feel?"

"You will welcome all cloudy days for the rest of your life," Eva said. "And have you noticed, Thomas, that your sight is very much improved in the darkness?"

"I thought it was perhaps some quality of the stars or the air here in these parts. So, there are indeed also benefits to this terrible affliction."

"The prime one, sir," I said with more of a growl than would have been courteous, "being that you are now alive when you would otherwise have been dead." You ungrateful old bastard.

I did not voice that final point because I was of course sympathetic with his situation.

The change in Thomas' demeanour was quite severe. He was morose and close to silent most of the time, his head hanging low as he rode. Though we did not discuss it overly much, I had vast stretches on which to dwell on how he must have been feeling.

He had dedicated his life to the Templars as a man of God and of the sword. Living by the principles of chastity, obedience and poverty from his youth to old age while travelling on the Order's business from Acre to Paris, and from Krakow to Cairo. This mission to Mongke Khan had been a desperate hope but he had undertaken it because his master commanded it and because it was his duty to protect the Christians of the Holy Land. An alliance between the Mongols and the Franks would have had a critical effect on the balance of power in the Holy Land and Thomas had believed in the potential worth of his task, despite the enormity of it.

But the man was not all duty and honour. It was clear he held the Mongols in distaste, even disgust, and I would venture that in his heart he both feared and hated them for what they had done to the Christian armies of Poland and to his brothers and the subjects of the Order who had been slain by the barbarians.

These Tartars. They are masters of war. And we are children.

214

His words kept echoing in my ears. They were full of bitter admiration and also deep despair. And he had spoken them before his dutiful squire Martin had been murdered in cold blood before him.

As well as the Mongols as a people, Thomas certainly felt anger and resentment at Hulegu and his men, also at my brother William.

And he resented me.

The old Templar must have cursed the day he had ever approached me in the field outside Constantinople. But we all make poor choices in our lives and it is how we learn to live with them, and ourselves, that determines whether we face the future as slaves to our failures or as masters of our destiny.

Stephen had none of my blood and he was beaten into submission by the travelling, his cheerfulness eroded by the winds, and his parched tongue shrivelled into silences that lasted for days. I watched him age, as the hunger shaved the last softness from his features and his face became stretched over the bones beneath, the soft skin turning to flaking leather.

None of us spoke much. Weariness and hunger get into you deep. All we knew was taking the next step, and the next, and so on. Weeks, months. Were there seasons flying by in those places, or did we just pass from lands of winter into vales of summer and back again, over and over?

Excitement came rarely, and it was far between each visit. Cities were wonders compared to the landscape outside, though they were often sad places with mudbrick walls designed more to keep out the wind than any attacker. Lonely monasteries would welcome us in, despite them being idolaters, and give us shelter and, if we were lucky, hot broths. There were other travellers, and sometimes they would challenge us but the Mongol laws at least prevented outright banditry. Still, barbarians that they were, they would attempt to poke their greedy fingers into everything that we had and begged gifts with such forcefulness that oftentimes the Assassins acquiesced in order to avoid murderous consequences, first for them, and then later down the road, for us.

Time passed strangely. At times, I would be astonished that it had been only that morning that some event had occurred when it seemed as though it was many moons before. While other moments would feel as though they had happened the day before when it had in fact been months.

As we barely spoke, and only rarely even looked at one another, I did not grow to know Thomas very much better, nor Stephen. And as leader of the group of Assassins, Hassan was preoccupied with driving them on, returning them home. It was clear as day that each of them was loyal, dedicated, and obedient to him. Never did I see a bitter glance thrown at Hassan's back, nor did I ever overhear dissatisfied mumblings when he was out of his men's earshot.

There was rarely wine to drink, and never enough to become inebriated. And so, Abdullah ceased with his nights of loquaciousness and days in misery. Instead, he reached an equilibrium of nothingness. On occasion, I would even find him staring at a distant vista, or squatting to examine a blade of grass, twisting it in his fingers.

"He is finding himself again," Eva explained. I did not

understand.

She always spent more time speaking to him, and all of them, than I ever did. I saw her place a hand on Stephen's shoulder, or arm, or hand, many times, to reassure him that his weariness would pass and that all would one day be well. Abdullah would stare at my wife with longing in his eyes, and yet it was clear he remained terrified of her.

The Mongol pair often seemed set to leave us. Her name, I discovered, was Khutulun. His name was Orus. They would on occasion argue in hushed voices, him full of passion and her cold as ice. Abdullah would come to me every now and then to speak for them.

"You swear you will kill Hulegu," Khutulun said.

"I have sworn it," I would say. "It will be done."

They found it difficult to believe but they stayed, for the time being. Where else could they go? Off from the road into the lands of the Mongols? They suggested they had potential allies here and there but they were hesitant to do so. No doubt any ally they could reach would be powerless should Hulegu turn his attention to them.

And, I soon discovered, they wanted something else.

"Will you give us your blood magic?" Orus, the man, asked. They both seemed hopeful.

"You do not want it," I said. "You would never father a child, young man. Nor could you bear one, young lady."

That silenced them for a while before the woman, Khutulun, responded. "I will take no husband. Ever."

Orus, on the other hand, continued to look disturbed by my

words. However, he said nothing further about it.

"Why do we flee with the Assassins?" Khutulun asked. "The people of Christ are the enemies of these people, no?"

"These people are our best hope," I said. "Hulegu comes to conquer their homeland, and they are the only strong people between here and Syria who will stand against him."

"They will not be strong enough," Khutulun said.

Bit by bit, over the days and months, I picked up the history of Khutulun and Orus. The first surprise to me was that they were not lovers. They were siblings, sharing the same father and different mothers.

Their father was a chief of some tribe from an isolated and mountainous corner of the vast Mongol territories that had resisted the authority of Hulegu and his brothers for some time before being conquered and subjugated. The mother of Khutulun was herself a prize of conquest from a raid on the Tajiki tribes, who were a people closer in look to Persians, or even to Greeks or Rus, than Mongols. And it was from her mother that Khutulun got her astonishing beauty and also her wildness.

For she grew up with a love of fighting, riding, and hunting that was considered excessive for a girl but she did not care. Her father only encouraged her, because he loved her and her mother so much. Even when she reached the age where she should have been married, and she told her father and mother that she would never marry, they indulged her and believed that she would come around eventually, perhaps when she met the right suitor.

Then Hulegu had come. Their ordus was defeated and Khutulun was the greatest prize of all and he took her as one of his many wives.

Orus was a dutiful son, skilled in battle and destined to become a chief like his father. But he could not live knowing how his beloved sister would be suffering in the far-off ordus of Hulegu and so he said farewell to his home and dedicated himself to the impossible task of rescuing Khutulun.

Even though they had eventually been cornered and recaptured, I was astonished that he had managed it at all. I began to think that both of them could be even better assets than I had first imagined when it came to assaulting the ordus of Hulegu.

Little did I know quite how dangerous both young Mongols could be.

Despite what Orus and Khutulun said, the Assassins seemed to be a strong people. They travelled well, certainly better than I did through that land. I harboured a desire to learn their language, and to learn about them as a people, and to understand why they were heretics to other Saracens in Baghdad, Damascus and Cairo, and whether the rumours about them were true. But, though it was so long I walked and rode amongst them, I learned almost nothing until we finally reached their homelands in the mountains to the north of the Iranian plateau.

We ascended, on and off, for days. Sometimes rapidly and other times so gradually you did not notice until you turned and looked back on the way you had come. The mountains grew taller and more jagged as we reached the lands of the Assassins. They had over a hundred fortified settlements, possibly many more, but he would not give me the true figure, being that they were a secretive people. Abdullah whispered that it was most probably two hundred castles but some men desire to be givers of knowledge, even if their words are nonsense, and I waved him away. A hundred or two hundred castles, the Ismaili Assassins were certainly a powerful and well-protected people, but they were a small one.

All through that mountain range between northern Persia and the Caspian Sea, Hassan would point to peaks that we passed, and valleys that we could see, and say that there was an Assassin castle there. We stopped at a number of them, and Hassan and his people were welcomed as if they were dear family, though he assured me that they were not direct blood relatives but had great love for each other, for they all followed the true inheritor of Mohammed.

We Christians and Mongols, who were of course heathens in their eyes, were treated with courtesy and respect. But that respect was for Hassan and was only extended to us through him. I have no doubt that without his protection, those generous people would have torn us limb from limb.

But we never stayed long in those castles, despite their protestations, and Hassan would move us along, with fresh horses and provisions, from place to place. He had a message for the Master of all Ismaili Assassins, and he had to give it to him.

"Hulegu is coming, finally," Hassan would say before we left each place. "Hulegu Khan is coming with vast armies and you must make ready."

The people of each castle were afraid by Hassan's warnings but they were committed to staying and holding their fortresses against the coming storm. I could not understand why they felt able to hold out against such overwhelming force in such small, isolated places with so few people in each place.

"What else can they do?" Hassan said when I asked him why they did not flee and gather in strength. "No other fortress is large enough to take them. Besides, this is their home."

"If the walls are stormed by thousands of Mongols, it will be home to no one."

Hassan could not find a way to explain it to me but he tried. "How could you call a place your home, if you were not willing to die to defend it?"

I had no answer to that. Wandering so far and so long, I had almost forgotten what it was to have a home.

We moved from mountain to mountain, through valleys and high passes by day, until, finally, after eight months of travelling, we reached our destination. The homeland of the Assassins.

"There it is," Hassan said to me as we crested a ridge and looked down into the plain beyond. "The Valley of Alamut."

All that time, all that way, listening to them talk about Alamut, I had expected a high and narrow gorge in the mountains. I heard talk of a river and lake and imagined it to be like valleys in Derbyshire, where one may stand upon the side of a vale and look across to the other, and see with perfect clarity the grazing sheep, and men and women moving about. Perhaps even a valley that, on a still day, a man might shout across from one side to the other and, though the meaning be lost, the call itself could be discerned and you might wave at each other.

Alamut was not like that.

It was vast. Wide, and flat along either side of the river, though surrounded by enormous and jagged peaks. We came in from the east and it curved away to the west until it faded into a haze of hills and peaks. In the lush lower valley were clusters of dark trees, scattered farmhouses, and well-ordered fields. Higher up on the sides, the vegetation was sparser, drier, lighter in colour. Steep pathways led up and along the uncounted jumble of slopes that undulated away along the complex valley, in between the giant, bleak peaks surrounding it all and in the far distance.

Hassan wore the expression of a man coming home. The others, too, stood and drank it in with reverence and solemnity.

I was jealous, and my heart ached for England.

Eva pressed herself against my side and slipped her hand into mine. I wondered if she felt the same sense of loss in that moment, or whether she was more apprehensive about what the end of our journey would entail. Whether we would face imprisonment, exploitation, violence.

I had dragged her all that way. And in my wake had come a Franciscan monk, a Syrian scholar, an immortal Templar, and two fugitive Mongols. Each of them looked wary of the sight before us. We were in no doubt we were all entering the heart of enemy territory.

"Will your lord truly let us stay?" I asked Hassan, for the thousandth and last time. "He will not have us all put to death for being unbelievers?"

He took a deep breath, sucking the air of his homeland into his lungs, and let it out with enormous satisfaction.

"We shall see."

* * *

While the valley of Alamut was lush and beautiful, bursting with orchards and livestock and green life, the castle of Alamut was perched atop a savage peak. As soon as I laid my eyes upon it, I understood why the Assassins yet had confidence that they could resist the might of the Mongol hordes.

The enormous defensive walls of the castle sat on colossal slabs of well-eroded rock. The narrow path up to the walls crossed back and forth up the side of the valley and the final sections of that path were within arrow range from the battlements and towers that bristled along the high lines of the defences. Spars and ropes jutted up here and there, silhouetted against the blisteringly blue sky, which I recognised as the arms of catapults mounted on the walls and the tops of the towers. The realisation caused a shiver to run down my spine, as I imagined the stones that they could throw from such a height. Projectiles that could surely reach halfway along the valley floor.

"How could an army of any size assault this place?" I asked Thomas when we had dragged ourselves all the way to the top and stood beneath the walls. The entrance was up even higher still, where the road curved up and around a corner of the rocks that the walls sat upon.

Thomas shook his head. "It would take an act of God."

"All of you should stay here," Hassan said. "Other than Richard."

Thomas stepped in front of me. "I do not like it, Richard.

Once they have you up there, they can do as they wish with you."

Hassan understood his fear. "I have given my word that no harm will come to him, or to any of you."

"Your word?" Thomas said. "Your word? You are a people who survive through acts of murder. How can we ever trust your word?"

Hassan pressed his lips together and his men puffed themselves up, sensing that their lord was being insulted, or at least disrespected. Men had died for less.

I steered Thomas further to one side. Hot wind gusted up from the valley floor, bringing the smell of juniper and creosote. The sky was a searing ice blue above the castle walls and Thomas squinted beneath the hood of his light robe.

"Thomas, these men could kill all of us, right now."

He glanced around at the Assassins surrounding us. "We could make a fight of it, Richard."

I nodded. "You and I might even be the last ones standing. Eva, too. Then what? How far is it to Acre? A thousand miles?"

"So that is it? You just submit to them?"

"It is not submission," I said, urging him to understand. To see it my way. "We are negotiating. It is a trade. We cannot expect to be given shelter without giving something in return."

He sighed and glanced up, wincing at the sky. "You cannot give them that. These damned Saracens. Our enemies. Mohammedans. God's enemies. What they could do with this power."

"They will help us to kill Hulegu, William, and the others."

"Will they? And then who will they kill? The King of

England?"

I hesitated. "We are a long way from such a thing, Thomas. In all likelihood, this Master of the Assassins will have us slaughtered to a man." I patted him on the shoulder and turned to Hassan. "Lead the way."

When I was finally led into the inner hall, deep within the castle, the Master of Assassins sat waiting for us on a low dais in an ornate but delicate throne. He was dressed in dark green robes of silk, with a sash about his waist. Over a dozen armed men stood at the ready, a handful behind the lord of Alamut, the rest arrayed about the hall. It smelled of incense and roasted spiced goat.

Still, he made us wait while he attended to some other business with clerks until, finally, Hassan was waved over. Silence fell over the hall while the leader of the Assassins glared at Hassan.

Rukn al-Din Khurshah had been the leader for a few months only. His father before him had lost his mind due to his great age, and so the respected lord, who was like a king and a pope to them all in one, was murdered. A murder committed from practical necessity, as the leadership has always passed from father to son upon the death of the elder.

Necessary and practical though it was, the new lord, Rukn al-Din Khurshah, had convicted the murderer and had him executed himself. It was likely that Rukn al-Din had ordered, or at the least encouraged, the regicide and everyone knew it. And yet the assassin still had to pay the price. It seemed strange to me, cold and improper, and yet it had secured for the Ismailis a secure succession during a time of great crisis.

Rukn al-Din was in the prime of his life, perhaps in his mid-thirties. His beard was thick and luxuriously oiled. He was not a tall man and his body looked soft; shoulders narrow and belly bulging.

Over the decades in the Holy Land, I had picked up fragments of Arabic, the language of the Saracens. Abdullah had grudgingly taught me a few phrases and the names for common items during our travel across the steppe and our stay in Karakorum. I had picked up a lot more during our return toward the west with the Assassins, listening to them work, joke, and argue when camp was made and struck.

Still, I struggled to make sense of the words that were traded by Hassan and Rukn al-Din. But with what little I did know, and by watching closely the gestures and expressions of the two men, it became clear that Hassan was angry. Furious, even. Yet, out of respect, he contained that fury.

Not only Hassan, but Rukn al-Din grew angry, too.

I was able to discern that much of it was directed at the foreigners Hassan had brought into their midst.

It was not long before Hassan turned to me.

"I have tried to explain to him," Hassan said. "What you are. What you can do. What you could do to us. He does not understand. And so he wishes to see your abilities demonstrated for himself."

I sighed and nodded. I had expected it and began to bare my arm so that I could cut myself, and so this Rukn al-Din could watch it heal.

"No, Richard," Hassan said. "Not those abilities."

Three of the bodyguards stepped forward from their positions

226

by Rukn al-Din, and drew their swords before me, well out of striking distance.

"My weapons and armour are outside," I said. "Down with my companions."

Hassan drew his own sword and handed it to me, hilt first. "I have seen you admiring this blade. Now, you may try it for yourself."

I felt a need to protest. Explain to him, to all of them, that I had never trained with one of those long-curved blades, only played with them. That I always trained to fight in armour, with helm and shield. Always, I favoured thrusting with the point of my blade and yet there I was, expected to fight, unarmoured, with a strange weapon.

Against three men.

Three of the feared fedayin Assassins, men who trained to kill without thought to their own lives, and these three young men were considered skilful and steady enough to serve as bodyguard to their king.

It was not possible, for almost any man, to fight alone against even two competent opponents. The obvious strategy is to strike with speed at one man, to drive him away from the other and to finish him before the other can bring his blade to bear.

What good strategy there was for a man to fight three others, without armour, I could not imagine.

But I did not voice my protest. It would have achieved nothing.

And anyway, I had been more than a man for some time.

"What are the rules of this bout?" I asked Hassan while I

looked along the blade to discern any sign of existing damage.

"If you die," he said, "you lose."

"Ah," I said, nodding while I flourished the blade to test the handling of it. "I have played this game before."

No signal, nor even any warning, was given.

They all three attacked at once.

Their blades slashed at me as I leapt back, swept my sword up and swatted away one of them with the flat of my blade. While Hassan fled to the edge of the hall, two circled quickly to either side of me while the third threatened to attack me head on.

The only sensible thing to do was to retreat back. Only, that would end with me cornered and attacked on three sides at once.

After feinting that retreat, I leapt forward, charging the man in front. Though I surely moved faster than any man he had ever faced before, he was not so surprised as I would have liked.

His blade slashed into my left shoulder. As he pulled the cut, he stepped back and to the side with well-practised footwork, and his blade sliced through the sleeves of my tunic, and my shirt, and deep into my flesh. Pain lanced through me, a sharp ache that took my breath away.

The clever move did not save him.

I sliced up and across his throat, pulling the edge across the front of his neck. He jerked back, so the cut was not as deep or as wide as I wanted but it was enough to cut into his windpipe and one of the great veins beside it. It would take him some time to die, and he was still dangerous. Using our momentum, I grabbed hold of his sword arm and twisted as I stepped by him, throwing him back at the men behind me.

Even as I did so, the tip of a blade sliced into the back of my skull, hitting bone but sheering off.

The swordsman was on me, following up with another blow. His cuts fast and precise, I parried with the strange curved sword in my hand and cursed my lack of a shield.

From the corner of my eye, I saw the other man leap over his falling comrade and come at me from the flank.

Both twirled their weapons, flashing and frightening by their display of mastery.

Why should I fear a blade?

Years of training had taught me how to defend. Any fool can learn to swing a sword, my old teachers had told us, but a great knight is one who can protect himself from harm. Any cut could be fatal, and often was, even if it was weeks later due to infection. Any blade thrust into gaps in your armour would very likely kill you quite quickly, assuming it severed an artery. Training that gets into you when you are young gets in deep. Old habits die hard.

And there was the fear of pain, of course. An animal fear, barely controllable, that says get away from harm, from injury, from some danger or other that you know, down to your bones, will be agonising. The pain from a sword cut will take your breath away, buckle your legs, cause you to weep and to shake in spite of your desire to be virtuous.

But I could heal my wounded flesh in mere moments. And I had already felt so much pain in my life that it was like an old friend.

I forced myself forward onto him and ground my teeth as his sword slashed me across the chest. Before he could retreat, I grabbed him by the upper arm, slashing at his groin while in close and butting his face. While he reeled, I stabbed my sword into his guts, twisting and tearing it out. The foul stench of hot shit filled the air as his intestines popped out through the gash.

Sometimes, your body takes an action before you realise it. And so it was as I turned, slid sideways and slashed behind me at the last man, whose own blade missed me by a hair's breadth. Mine caught him across the face, the impact from his skull jarring my arm. It was a poor cut, but it did the job and he retreated, wailing, his sword clattering on the tile floor. I had cut through one of his eyes and his nose was a bloody, flapping piece of gristle dangling from his face.

Someone in the hall shouted, perhaps a cry to let the man live.

But the smell of blood filled my head and I would not be denied.

I seized the man, though he flailed and attempted to flee, and slipped the curved point of my blade into his neck, slicing through the skin. While he still attempted to fight me off, I dropped my sword and grabbed him with both hands. I bent my head and placed my lips around the wound on his throat.

Oh, such sweet relief. That hot, rich blood pumped into my mouth and I gulped it down, mouthful after mouthful. It surged to fill my mouth, I swallowed, and another pulse flooded between my lips as I held him close, pressed to me like a lover. The man's black beard tickled my nose, and I could smell olive oil on his skin and garlic in his breath. His strong, young heart beat frantically, not yet knowing it was dead.

My belly felt good. Warm and heavy, the strength of it

spreading through me. It was not long before I had my fill, and I dropped the dying man. He was as limp as a rag doll, and his ruined face hideous to see.

The other two men lay dead also. Under my feet, the white tiled floor was smeared with blood and dark pools of it continued to spread from beneath the bodies.

Around the edges of the hall, the other bodyguards stood with their own blades drawn, staring at me, some with disgust, others wore a look of horror. All would have liked to kill me, I have no doubt.

Rukn al-Din held a cloth over his mouth and nose. His eyes were narrowed above them, glaring at me with malice. He muttered something and the guards around me advanced.

This is it, I thought. This is the place where I die.

I took a quick step and scooped up my sword.

They all froze.

"Drop your sword," Hassan shouted. "They will not kill you."

"I do not believe you," I said, turning and turning to keep an eye on all of them. Yet they did not advance.

Rukn al-Din shouted at me but my Arabic was not good enough to understand.

"He says you will come to no harm," Hassan explained, walking forward into the blood with his hands spread apart. "He wishes to see if your wounds have healed, as I told him they would."

It seemed plausible. Anyway, even if I killed every man in the room, I would never escape from Alamut alive.

I dropped my sword and held out my arms as they seized me.

Hands tore at my tunic and my undershirt, baring my shoulder and my chest to the Master of Assassins. Water was brought and they washed the dried blood away. My skin was marked with pink lines where the cuts had been. Even these seemed to fade while I watched. They turned me around and scrubbed the blood from my hair with their fingers.

Finally, they were waved away and I stood, naked from the waist up, wet and bloody. Rukn al-Din held the cloth over his mouth and nose while he stared at me, thinking. It felt as though I was being examined like livestock.

I decided that, should he order that I be led to the slaughter, I would be sure to kill him, Rukn al-Din, before they could do so.

But he muttered something to Hassan, leapt up and hurried from the stinking, filthy room, trailed by a handful of his men.

Hassan rushed forward, grabbed my elbow and dragged me from the room while the remaining men glared.

"What did he say?" I asked Hassan in the corridor. "What is happening now?"

When we reached the antechamber where his own men waited, Hassan paused and turned to me.

"I am allowed to hold you and your people at my castle, Firuzkuh. He orders me to use your blood to make thirty of my men into immortals. And with them, perhaps, he will allow us to infiltrate the Mongol army and kill Hulegu."

* * *

Hassan's Castle Firuzkuh was a journey of two days from Alamut. I was struck, time and again, by the beauty of the place. The lushness of the fields, the prosperity of the people who worked them.

"It will be very different in winter," Hassan explained when I spoke of it to him. "The snows will fill the passes. Travel will be impossible."

"Every winter?"

"It never fails. It is one of our greatest defences. Every settlement must be stocked with enough food and fuel every winter. We are well used to sieges here. God besieges us in our homes for months on end, every year."

"That is why you want the Mongols to make a concerted attack. You want the snow to kill them for you."

"The Mongols are hard people," Hassan said. "The hardest, perhaps. But if they are caught out in the mountains when the snows come, thousands of them will die while we sit content in our fortifications. It was always the plan of 'Alā' ad-Dīn Muḥammad, who was the lord of all Ismailis for my entire life, and who sent me on my embassy to Mongke Khan. He wished to delay and delay, to frustrate the Mongols for long enough that they would turn their attention elsewhere."

"Why would they do that?"

"Every time the Great Khan dies, a successor must be chosen. All campaigns are called off, all leaders return to their homeland to take part in the choosing. It has taken many years on previous choosings. It has saved Christendom when they turned back decades ago."

"And that was why your old king sent so many fedayin to kill Mongke. Not just for vengeance but because it could save your people. But you called them all off? So that you could leave with me and my companions. Why would you do that?"

"I swore that I would do it," Hassan said. "But it was not true. I could not call them off, even if I wished to. They are everywhere and I have no way to contact them all."

"You lied?"

He nodded. "Lying is a moral act if it leads to furthering the aims of our people."

Stephen was trailing close behind me, listening keenly as he often was. "This concept is known as taqiyya, is it not?"

Hassan turned to glance over his shoulder. "Where did you hear that word?"

Stephen nodded over to Abdullah, who was walking beside Khutulun, babbling away at her. "Abdullah told me about it. He said taqiyya means you can lie if there is a good reason for it, and by the law of the Mohammedans, it is no crime." Stephen smiled, as smug as always. He never discovered that the possession of knowledge was in itself worth very little.

"No," Hassan said, scowling. "It is much more complicated than that."

Thomas muttered in my ear. "These people have no honour."

Firuzkuh Castle and surrounding settlement supported a little over two hundred fighting men, and a little over five hundred people in total, including children. It was not on the highest peak, nor was it a massive fortification. But it was a remarkable place, with four towers. Two of them squat and square, and two taller and round. Like the other Ismaili castles I had seen, Firuzkuh was built expertly into the landscape. A steep and rather narrow approach from the front would confine an attacking force between a steep cliff and a jutting rock wall. To the rear, a bleak plateau that was only accessible via long and difficult paths across the jagged mountains.

Even though he had been away so long, and others had been in command of the place for years, the transition of power back to Hassan was seamless. More than that, it seemed to be a happy homecoming for the people and Hassan both. They loved him.

We were tolerated and welcomed with cold courtesy. Given fresh clothes, good food. They even had people move out of their rooms within the castle so that Eva and I could have private quarters within the walls. The others of our party shared rooms near ours.

"We are prisoners as much as guests," Thomas pointed out on our first night.

Stephen was simply amazed by the wonders that he saw. "What a place this is to be prisoners, though, is it not? Did you see the stores they have in place already to resist a siege? Rooms and rooms. That tank with the honey, it was big enough to swim in, I swear it was."

Eva rubbed her eyes. "Sometimes I wonder how you can know so much about the world and yet still be such a fool. But then I remember that you are very young."

Stephen did not like that. "In what way am I being foolish?"

"You do not seem to understand the danger that we are in," Eva said.

"Hassan loves Richard. He would not let anything happen to us."

Thomas scoffed. "He wishes to use Richard for his own purposes."

"Still then," Stephen said. "It is a fair trade. Sanctuary and support in exchange for... the Gift. Richard's Gift bestowed on thirty of the men here."

"And the Mongols," Eva said, smiling at him. "You are not concerned about the fact that a hundred thousand crazed barbarians are bearing down on us?"

"This castle is safe. Who could assault such a fortress?"

Thomas and I glanced at each other. He pinched the bridge of his nose. "This is a strong site. Sheer cliffs on two sides, steep approach from the front and a Godless wilderness to the rear. Good walls and sturdy towers. They have catapults. But do you think two hundred men could resist ten thousand, Stephen? We could kill five hundred, a thousand, five thousand. If they were determined, they could take us here."

Stephen shook his head. "They are marching into a trap, you heard what Hassan said. If they arrive soon, the winter snows will trap them in the mountains. If they arrive late, we will have months more to prepare. To make more men into Richard's immortals, if need be. More like you, Thomas. Make enough, perhaps, to defeat the Mongols?"

Thomas cleared his throat. It sounded as though he growled. "And that is what we wish to do, is it? These people are Saracens. Mohammedans. Do you wish for them to be made stronger? They are our enemy. Christ's enemy. We should do nothing to help them."

"But these Assassins are the enemy of all other Saracens. The kingdoms of Egypt, and of Syria especially. Mortal enemies. If we help to make the Assassins powerful, they could even help us defeat the Saracens in the Holy Land. With them attacking from the rear, with thousands of immortals, who knows, we could even take back Jerusalem."

We groaned and shouted him down.

"Your flights of fancy are of no help to us here," Thomas said to him.

We soon retired but I could not help but dwell on Stephen's words. It was the sheer ambition of it that struck me so powerfully. My brother seemed always to be putting into motion such grand plans, as evil as they were. He created for himself a religious sect in Palestine, preying on travellers and caravans to build his strength until he could do more, such as take over a town, then a city. Even the Holy Land itself.

And then he worked to crush the King of England, creating immortals from men like the Archbishop, and the sons of great lords. He poisoned King John and might have won control of the Crown, or at least a great part of the country for himself.

Now, he had made more immortals in the heart of the most barbaric and evil force the world had ever known. What is more, he had in some way turned them toward the Holy Land, and then meant to drive them on to conquer Christendom. If his plans succeeded, then William could end up as the King of France, or the Holy Roman Emperor, and he could rule and rule for centuries until the Second Coming of Christ.

The sheer audacity of it all. It was a sign of his madness, certainly, and his hubris.

And what was I doing? Wandering around from place to place, living the life of a mercenary, a freelancer, trying to shelter Eva from men who would do her harm. I was ever afraid of being separated from her so that she would be forced to drink the blood of another and risk being caught and killed. A restless life. It was not a vain one, I had a purpose. But William always felt so far away.

The rage I had felt for him in my youth had faded. My pursuit of him had long ago turned to duty over emotion. No doubt someone like Thomas would say that was only proper but it had come to feel like an empty existence. Or, if not empty, then a small one.

What Stephen had suggested, in his naive way, was to use my gift to do something grand. To use the Assassins to bring down the Saracen armies of Syria and Egypt.

But Thomas was right. Say I did make a hundred, or a thousand, or ten thousand blood drinking immortals and they conquered the enemies of Christendom. What then? How could I ever hope to control them? To bind them to me?

William intended to set the Mongols loose on Christendom and even he would not be able to control them. And so he must simply not care about the consequences. He wanted to sow chaos, he wanted wanton and random destruction, for then he could take more power for himself from the rubble and dust of the kingdoms that had fallen.

Was that ultimately what separated me from my brother? Not

a lack of imagination or ambition but a fear of chaos? A preference for law over anarchy?

Or was that simply another way of saying that I lacked imagination and ambition?

Was William committing the sins of greed and pride while I was consumed with envy, and mired in slothfulness?

Either way, I had sworn to Hassan that I would turn thirty of his men, and I was committed to that path for the time being.

We would begin in the morning.

* * *

And so it was that I began to turn a group of Hassan's fedayin into blood-drinking immortals, like Eva and Thomas. And like Hulegu and his men.

In the open interior courtyard, Hassan stood on the wall, looking down and explained it to all of them. I stood back and to one side, watching the sea of faces turned up to their lord.

That they would no longer be able to father children. That they would need to drink human blood, at least twice every week, to avoid turning raving mad. That bright sunlight would hurt their eyes and burn their skin more than it ever had before. But in return they would become faster, stronger, and, by drinking blood after battle, would be able to heal wounds rapidly.

The fedayin were men already committed to dying for their people and so Hassan had more volunteers than we needed.

"I am tempted to take more," Hassan said when the full count was made. "We will need men to father the children of the next generation so I cannot turn them all. And Rukn al-Din commanded that we make thirty but perhaps I shall make fifty, and report that we have made thirty."

"Is that taqiyya again?" I said. He did not like me using that word. "You and I agreed to thirty also. I swore to turn thirty, and that is what I shall do. Afterwards, perhaps I will make more. We shall see."

Now that Hassan was in his home again, he became ever more like the great lord he truly was. Already, he was unused to any resistance to his orders and while he looked calmly at me, his nostrils flared and I was sure he would argue.

But he nodded and we had our thirty men.

"Each man will need to be drained of blood, down to the point of unconsciousness," I explained. "But he shall need enough strength to swallow a pint of my blood."

"A pint?"

"An eighth of a gallon," I explained, though it did not make sense to him. "About this much," I said, making a shape with my hands to indicate the volume. "Roughly speaking, that seems to be what it takes."

"And it must happen at night?"

"I have only ever seen it done at night. I do not know if it will work during the day. Perhaps one of your men would like to take the risk, and then we may discover the truth of it?"

"We will do it at night. How many can you make in one night?"

"Losing blood weakens me. I would prefer to do no more than

one, but I suppose I could do two. If you supply me with blood to drink in between."

"Of course," he said.

For he had also requested volunteers from the women and non-combatants of his lands. These folk would supply our company of immortals with blood from their veins. There were over a hundred of them all told, each one bleeding into a bowl every few days.

Eva and Thomas too would no longer be reliant on small volumes from my veins. And though Thomas liked to pretend moral outrage and claimed that it turned his stomach to think he was drinking the unholy blood from the veins of a Saracen woman, he guzzled the stuff down keenly enough. Between drinking from me or from them, he knew it was the lesser of two evils.

That night, I pierced a vein in my wrist and filled a jug with it while an Ismaili fedayin lay on a table nearby, drained of much of his own. Lamplight filled the room, along with the smell of blood. Unground seed corn filled the spaces between the floor slabs. We were down in the depths of the castle by the storerooms, away from where people lived and worked, which felt appropriate to what we were doing. To what I was creating.

The man was named Jalal. He was in his forties and a leader and warrior of some standing who would be in command of the thirty men. He had insisted on being the first.

Jalal was as pale as chalk when I lifted his head and commanded him to drink. He barely had strength enough to swallow.

Hassan hovered at my shoulder. "Is this correct?" he asked. "To be so weak? This is how it is done?"

I ignored him, and tipped the cup up, emptying the last of it into the man's mouth. Jalal coughed with his throat full of blood and it seemed for a few moments that he would drown in it until I turned him on his side and some of the blood was coughed out onto the floor. He breathed easy again and I pushed him onto his back.

"Will that lost blood cause the ritual to fail?" Hassan asked.

"The ritual?" I asked. "I do not know. I am sure that all will be well."

"What is the next step?" he asked.

"Now we wait," I said.

We looked down at Jalal, who—pale and cold as he was—seemed to be dead but for the occasional flickering of his eyes beneath the lids.

He lived. Before morning, he opened his eyes and said he was thirsty.

We gave him blood to drink.

For a month, I turned one fedayin every night, and on some nights, I turned two of them. Out of the first thirty, we lost eight men. The first of the eight stopped breathing before I could get enough of my blood into them, and so we bled others less. And yet those ones who were not taken to the very edge of death were more likely to die from violent convulsions. They would thrash about in spasms, their skin hot to the touch until they moved no more. One man opened his eyes in the morning but remained otherwise insensible for days, and neither blood nor fresh air nor anything else could elicit a response. And so, Hassan cut his throat.

Despite all this, finding replacements for the eight failures was no problem. The fedayin did not hesitate.

Thomas urged me to leave the eight dead men, and argued that it was within the letter of my agreement with the Assassins, and yet it allowed us to limit the number of immortals. But that seemed petty to me and would create bad blood between me and Hassan, which I strived to avoid.

I did not like being so beholden to him, or to the Assassins in general. For the first time in many years, I thought back to Ashbury Manor, and my time as lord there. It was no grand place, certainly nothing like a castle, but it was mine and I had servants, and I had knights and squires, all looking to me to command them. And I thought how that place was nothing compared to what I could have, should I so choose. What if I could find men who would serve me, as Hassan had his fedayin? With a fortified home, with immortal followers, I could become a great lord and I would be secure, finally. All I needed was an overlord who would protect me, who would help me to fend off rumours of my agelessness, and of the blood drinking that would no doubt leak out.

But what Christian lord would do such a thing? Unless he was an unchristian man. Perhaps I could offer the gift of my blood to a king from distant yet civilised lands. Somewhere like Armenia, or Georgia, I thought. Or even the semi-barbaric lands of the Rus.

And yet, an immortal king would have more power than I would have. And such a man could have me killed whenever he wished, so what kind of freedom was that?

I could make myself into a king.

The thought popped into my head, clear as a bell. The obvious end of such a line of reasoning.

"If you did that," Eva whispered to me, on the night that I spoke my thoughts to her, "then how would you be different to William?"

"No, no," I said. We sat on stools beside a table in the corner of our quarters. "I would do it, not from hubris or love of power over others, but only for our safety, Eva." I lowered my voice and took one of her hands in both of mine. "Imagine us, sitting on thrones, in the hall of some castle. In a Christian land, perhaps one in the East. Or in the Thracian kingdoms. We could make a kingdom in those hills and dark forests. The Hungarian mountains, surrounded by wolves and bears. No one could touch us."

"I think all your bloodletting has drained the wits from your head," she said, patting my hands with her free one. "Even if we could take power somewhere, a king rules with the consent of his people, whether he knows it or not. Do you think they would still support you after fifty years on that throne? A hundred? How long before they rose up to dethrone you, in your own castle? And those lands you just mentioned, you think they are defensible? They have all been crushed by the Mongols. Is that who you would like as your overlords?"

I sighed. "Are you not tired of all this? Running from place to place? With no home?"

She looked at me and spoke softly. "For a long time."

"So what do we do?" I asked her.

Taking a deep breath, she hesitated. "I do not know if you have ever asked me that before."

"Of course I have."

"I understand that you do not wish to be beholden to any man who is not worthy of your loyalty. You are an English knight. You want to serve a good king, and a king of England, too. But we are where we are. And we must do what we have set out to do," she said.

"I think," I said, then stopped myself. I did not speak for a long time but Eva simply sat and waited. How well she knew me. "I think, that my hatred for William has faded. It used to burn inside me. Oft times, I feared the sin of wrath would consume me, as I wanted nothing other than to kill him. And that wrath has driven me, driven me to murder and sin. But now..."

"William has done incalculable evil. Murdered your first wife, your brother's family. Who knows how many other woman and children. He murdered my father. He murdered King John. He must be killed. And who can do it other than you? You have said the Archbishop of Jerusalem told you that God made you this way so that you can put an end to William's evil. You do not need to feel wrath to do this. All passion fades. Richard, you are a sinful man, that is true. But since the time I first met you, to this moment now, I could always see that your heart is ruled by justice. You do not need passion, or wrath, to fulfil your oath and deliver justice to William. You will do it because it is your duty."

"What about my duty to Christendom?" I asked. "I have made thirty immortals for our enemies. Surely, I should turn only men

245

such as Thomas. Knights, dedicated to preserving our lands, our people, against the Saracens and all other enemies. This is wrong, is it not?"

"Thomas has filled your heart with dread because he is a fearful old man who wants the world to stay the same as it ever was. And Stephen has filled your head with grand ambitions because he is young and wishes to remake the world with himself as some great part of it. They are both lesser men than you, and they will do as you say. They are followers of yours, Richard. Ignore their fretting and stay the course. We will use the Assassins to kill Hulegu and the other immortals. They cannot be allowed to live. Once that is done, and William is dead, we can find a place in this world."

"What would I do without you, Eva?" I asked.

I did not know it then but one day soon, I would find out.

* * *

The night air was cold but there was little wind. The waxing moon was half full and I could see across the rocks of the mountainside down to the faint shape of Firuzkuh Castle. Summer was all but over and winter was well on the way.

I could not see the men I was stalking but I could hear them, and I could smell their stink. They were down in the deep shadows under a steep cliff side. I could probably have climbed down it in the daylight, wearing light clothing. But at night, in my armour, I knew I would fall. So I began to work my way around, moving slowly and as quietly as I could.

My helm was back at the castle, as it would have blocked my hearing and sight too much. Instead, I wore my mail coif that covered my head and neck. My body was protected by my thick, padded linen gambeson and over that my mail hauberk. Over the mail, I had a cotton overcoat in the Persian style that fitted me perfectly, and I wore it to reduce the noise and cover any shine from my armour.

I had to move deliberately as I approached my prey, and yet still I kicked the occasional stone downhill or snagged myself on brittle bushes. No doubt the men below me could hear something of the noise, and I hoped that they would. If I made too much noise, surely they would think I was drawing them into a trap, and they would be wary. So I had to judge it right. They would expect a Christian knight to be a clumsy oaf, and so that was what I had to be.

In truth, it was not a difficult part to play. Put me in a damp woodland and I will slither through it like a wolf. I will slip from outcrop to boulder in the hills of Derbyshire but even after months of practice, in that stony land, with powdery sand underfoot I made for a poor Assassin.

And I knew that, in the dark, their eyesight would be better than mine.

They leapt out at me, striking fast and hard. Not with cries but with grunts of effort and hard breathing.

I fended them off as best I could, retreating back up the hill as they came at me. They were six, crowding themselves in an effort to be the one to strike the killing blow, and I backed myself against an outcrop of sandstone twice the height of a man. Cornered as I was, they attacked hesitantly, wary of my skill.

One rushed in and I cracked him on the head, just as the one behind lunged at me. I batted the weapon aside and stamped on his knee, breaking it. He cried out, the harsh throaty sound splitting the night.

They fell back a few steps to collect themselves, and the four that were uninjured took the lead, brandishing their clubs.

Finally, I heard a sound above on the rock, and Eva leapt from it. Her silhouette flitting above me like a bat. She landed behind the Assassins and smashed two of them before any could react. And Thomas rushed from the flank and crashed into another, bringing him down with the weight of himself and his armour. I jumped forward and brought my club down on the others.

We beat them down into submission, and they begged for us to stop. They lay whimpering in the shadows.

"You did well," I said to them in Arabic. "But you should not have left your position."

"We need blood, master," one of them said. "To heal."

"And this is why you must always win. Every fight, you can either get weaker or you can get stronger," I lectured. "When the Mongols surround us, you must drink the blood from those that you kill, and thus heal your wounds, and gain their strength. Do you understand?"

"Yes, master," they said, holding their heads and bodies.

"I think my leg is broken," one said.

"Well then," I said. "You should get yourself back to the castle and ask for blood, do you not think? Go, now."

After they scrambled to their feet, Thomas removed his helm. "What did you say to them?" he asked me.

"That they have a lot to learn before they can kill a thousand Mongols apiece."

Eva's shadow moved to my side. Her footsteps were as soft as a cat's. "Few of them are ready. And the Mongols are almost upon us. Perhaps you should turn more of Hassan's men."

Thomas scoffed. "Perhaps we should leave, while we still can."

"Come on," I said. "Let us go home."

Strange, to call it that. But that is what Firuzkuh Castle had become over those months. Gradually, the people had become less hostile and we had grown to see them, not as Saracens, or enemies, but as people. The men laughed and insulted each other as they worked and trained. The women laughed and gossiped as they did their work. Children ran and played, shouting always as if they were deaf, or they thought that all adults were.

Yet there was dread. The dread of the approach of the Mongol armies. Word came to us from the spies and scouts of the Assassins that Hulegu had brought the full might of his armies, over a hundred thousand Mongols, along with that many again of Turkomen and even Christian armies from the subject lands of Georgia and Armenia. Every day, the people talked of the snow that would come and save them, for another winter at least.

And there was something else. Some sense that I had, that many of us outsiders had, that the Assassins were hiding something from us. The feeling had grown over the weeks, and I saw less and less of Hassan. They often steered us away from the sacred parts of the castle, which was to be expected. None of us

249

was a Mohammedan. But even Abdullah was barred from entry to the place of worship, and despite being from Syria, he was a Shiite, which I understood was a doctrine not so far from the teachings of the Ismailis. It even seemed to me like fear, that they were afraid of us going there. Thomas suggested that they had some Christian captives there that they were torturing, but that was pure speculation.

That night, we had just reached our quarters when Stephen rapped on our door and begged entry. It was so late by then that it was almost early, but then Stephen had spent years living as a monk, and they loved to wake in the dark of night, like soldiers.

Eva was removing her armour and he stared at her with his mouth open.

"What do you want, Stephen?" I said.

He tore his eyes away and shut the door behind him.

"I think he means to spend the night," Eva said over her shoulder.

Stephen gulped and came over to me. "Richard, I have discovered what Hassan is hiding."

Eva stopped and turned. "Keep your voice down." She came over, wearing only her undershirt, which was very thin, very loose and quite soaked with sweat.

Stephen cleared his throat, lowered his head and stared at Eva's chest while he spoke. "I do not know the full story, and it has taken days to discover this much. But Hassan has created living quarters for a group of fedayin. Quite separate from our thirty. They train in secret. And the servants are afraid of them. A woman was hurt a few days ago, and one of the old men who brought them water was killed yesterday, although no one will admit it fully. And these men, this new group, they have blood brought to them. Lots of blood."

"What is this?" I said, feeling anger building. "How can this be?"

Eva put a hand on Stephen's shoulder. "Are you certain of this? Be sure that you are because it makes little sense. How have more been created, if Richard did not turn them himself?"

"I am sorry, I do not know," Stephen said.

"Where is Hassan?" I asked him. "In his quarters, asleep?"

Stephen shook his head. "I believe he is with these men now, in the jamatkhana."

I pulled my coif back onto my head and grabbed my sword.

"Ricard," Eva hissed. "Think. Think before you act, here. Our position is precarious."

"I will act now," I said, strapping the sword around my waist.

"At least wait for me to put my armour back on," she said. "I will come with you."

"Put it on but wait here," I said to her. "Get Thomas and the others ready, we may have to flee. Stephen, help Eva and do precisely as she orders, do you understand?"

He wanted to argue, I could see it on his face, and he wanted to come with me.

Eva grabbed his arm. "Help me put my gambeson back on," she said and winked at me over his head.

I nodded to her and strode out, heading across the castle grounds to the jamatkhana. It was their communal hall, the place where they did worship and had other sacred events. It was a place closed to me, but I would force my way inside.

The castle was never quiet, not even at night, and I was seen by a number of people before I was halfway there. Someone or other must have run ahead to raise the alarm, and I was met in the hallway outside a doorway that led to the jamatkhana by Hassan and four of his fedayin.

They were all armed, and armoured.

The four men all had their swords drawn.

"Stop," Hassan shouted. "Halt, stop. Stop, Richard."

"What are you doing here?" I shouted as I came to a stop before Hassan. The men loomed behind him, blocking the way.

"You cannot enter here," Hassan said. "Come, let us return to—"

I was already angry at the deceit, and I was angry at myself for being so naive. For allowing myself to be deceived.

So I drew my sword.

The four fedayin stepped forward and pulled Hassan back behind them.

"I could kill you all," I said in their language. "And go and find out for myself. Is that what you want, Hassan?"

He called for them to lower their swords, and to stand aside. "Come, Richard. I will show you. I do not wish there to be secrets between us. And, if the truth is to be told, I must admit that I may need your help with a large problem... It is best that I show you."

Even though I knew he was not to be trusted, I still went with him. It is right and proper to be wary and to consider that almost any situation in life could be a trap, designed to capture and kill you. But you cannot avoid walking into risk, else you would never take any action worth taking.

Keeping my sword in hand, but the blade tip lowered, I followed Hassan into the jamatkhana. His men surrounded me at all times. As we got closer, the sound of voices and clashing wooden weapons grew louder.

"This is it," Hassan said as we entered the hall. He seemed nervous. "This is the secret I have been hiding from you."

The jamatkhana was like a church for them, and also something like a manor's hall, or a court. But they had turned over that space into what amounted to a bunkhouse. A few lamps in alcoves in the walls cast pools of dim light and left lots in shadow. Two long rows of beds ran down one side, and the other half was open space. A side for sleeping, and a side for training.

Most startling of all was the fact it was filled with raucous fedayin. It was the end of the night, not long before dawn, and they were shouting and fighting. Some men lay on the beds, awake and talking to each other. One man jumped up and down on a bed, laughing while another shouted encouragement. Groups of others stood fighting in the open space. Some wrestled, stripped to the waist or naked, while others sparred with practice swords made from wood.

It smelled strongly of blood. I saw jugs, cups, and bowls on tables or tossed to the floor, which had held the stuff, and some dried stains showed on the floor and even on the walls.

"What have you done, Hassan?" I asked, watching the scene before me. "How have you done this?"

"Please, Richard, you must understand what a dire situation we are in. I have asked you to turn more men. I have all but begged you. You would give me no more than thirty, and I had to have more."

"But how?" I asked him, as much curious as outraged.

He looked apologetic. "We used one of the men you had turned. It was Jalal. And we used his blood to turn these."

I could not believe it. It had never occurred to me that such a thing would be possible.

"And it worked?" I said, my anger turning to horror.

Hassan hesitated. "The blood is not as strong. Almost half the men we tried to turn died. And these immortals are also weaker. Slower than the first generation. But still much stronger than an ordinary man." He scratched his beard. "They are extremely sensitive to sunlight. Even more so than those turned by your blood directly. And they need to drink blood more frequently than the men you turned. They... they never seem to get enough."

"These are not your best men, I take it?" I asked, looking at them acting like fools and madmen.

He shook his head. "These are fine men. I mean... they were. They are themselves when their bellies are full of blood but is not long before they begin to lose their minds. It is like when the men you turn go without for many days, and they become angry, and they lose their control and seek conflict. The only way I am able to maintain discipline is through controlling the supplies of the blood."

"They sound dangerous," I said.

"To our enemies, I hope."

Hassan's betrayal of our agreement was considerable but I should have expected underhand tactics from such a deceitful

254

people. The men slouched and grinned at each other and at me. The amused, smug expressions on their faces reminded me of children who had been caught breaking a petty rule.

They are themselves when their bellies are full of blood but is not long before they begin to lose their minds.

There were endless tales of strange peoples in those days, usually spoken of by ignorant common folk, soldiers, and gentlemen who were inebriated. One reoccurring notion was that the dead would rise from their graves to do harm to the living before returning to their tombs once more. It was said that these cursed people returned from the dead with barely any memory of their former selves, as they were in life. The word that these animated corpses were known by sprang at once into my mind.

Revenants.

Hassan's abominations brought to mind these revenants. Men who had died only to return as violent shadows of their former selves. The notion was so apt that it disturbed me quite profoundly.

I lowered my voice and grasped Hassan by the arm. "These men must be killed."

Hassan tried to pull away but I held him tight. He waved his own men back but they were at my back, ready to run me through. "I need to use every weapon that I have. Or we will all be killed anyway."

"We had an agreement. Thirty men, I said."

He lifted his bearded chin and looked me in the eye. "I must think of my people."

I nodded. "So, this is taqiyya, is it? You can break your oath with a man who has not broken his, and you may say to yourself that you have done it for the good of your people?" He began to reply but I spoke over him. "And how many people can you have left? You must have spent all of your men, now. What of their wives, and their children? Who will make more children in the years to come?"

"There are some men who remain mortal," Hassan said, though I could see it was weighing heavy on him. "But I fear that none of us will live to make more children anyway."

"You must take heart, Hassan. Your people look to you for their strength. Even if you do not feel it, you must show it so that they do not break when the time comes."

He shook his head. "You do not understand. Hulegu has come. The snows are late. Later than they have ever been, and nothing stands in his way. His armies have already besieged our castles to the east. His scouts are already in Alamut Valley."

"Why have you hidden this from me?" My fear made me angry.

He shook his head again, looking down. "We had a messenger from Alamut Castle before sundown." Hassan hesitated, drew me aside and lowered his voice even further. "Rukn al-Din has been summoned by Hulegu. The Mongols command our master to submit to Hulegu. And Rukn al-Din sent his son in his stead."

I was appalled. "He sent his son to the Mongols? Alone? What cowardice."

Hassan waved it away. "The messenger said that it was not truly his own son. I believe it was a bastard son of the last master, Rukn al-Din's father."

I laughed. "He sent a bastard brother of his to Hulegu, to pose as his son. Truly, you people have no honour."

That made Hassan angry. "It is simply a means to delay Hulegu." He took a deep, shaking breath. "As is the agreement that he made with him."

"Tell it, for God's sake."

"Rukn al-Din has agreed with Hulegu that he will submit to the Mongols, in exchange for the life of himself and the lives of his entire family. He has sent orders to all castles to dismantle the towers and battlements, as a symbol of our submission."

I stared, open-mouthed until I came to my senses. "That's more than a bloody symbol, Hassan. He has capitulated. It is over."

"No," he said, forcefully. "No, this is the true use of taqiyya, Richard. He lies to buy us time. There is still hope that the snows will come."

"So you will defy his order, and keep your towers and your battlements intact?"

"I will."

"How many other castles will do the same? And how many will follow his orders to the letter?"

"I do not know."

"So," I said. "The Assassins, feared throughout the world, have given up without a fight?"

"We will fight," Hassan said, raising his voice. "We will fight to the last man."

The men in the hall stopped to stare at us. Some grinned, others glared at me with murder in their eyes. Murder and madness.

"What good is that to me?" I asked. "We were here to kill Hulegu. Now you wish to go down fighting? Turn your men against Hulegu, now. Send away what women and children you can spare, save at least some of your people."

His lip curled, as if tasting bitterness. "Send them where? Every castle will be surrounded before long."

"Your people have castles in Syria."

"That is a thousand miles from here. It is too dangerous."

"More dangerous than being slaughtered by the Mongols when they take this place?"

The truth was, I cared very little for those Saracen women and children. At least, I would not allow myself to do so. But I wanted Hassan to focus on attack, not defence.

"They would never survive the journey. They could be taken by anyone before they reached Syria."

He was right. A group of women and children on foot would be snapped up by the first warband that came across them, whether Christian, Saracen or Mongol.

"But you must fight," I said. "Surely, you see that? If you submit, you are all dead anyway."

"Some of us would be made into slaves. We would survive."

"A few of your women, the youngest and prettiest perhaps, made into wives for those stinking barbarians? You call that survival?" I lowered my voice. "Send the first of the immortals with me and my people. We will make a break for Syria, fight our way through if we have to. We will come up with a way to get at Hulegu there."

He shook his head. "There is still hope. I believe that Master Rukn al-Din has a plan for our survival. He is playing for time. Why do such a thing unless there was a course of action that he has planned? No, none of us flee until there is no hope left."

I acquiesced. Likewise, I put aside my revulsion for his revenants for the time being and did not seek the conflict that would have arisen from slaughtering them, or for arguing further for their destruction. I chose the peaceful path for I would need guides to take me over the mountains when everything fell apart.

And I was increasingly certain that it would not be long before all hope for the Assassins was truly lost.

* * *

It was November 1256 when Hulegu finally lost patience with the delays and evasions from Rukn al-Din.

The Grand Master was given a final command to appear—in person, no proxies—, which he declined to do. And Hulegu's final message to Rukn al-Din stated that, despite the promises of submission, and the fact that towers and battlements at key castles were being dismantled, he did not believe that the master truly intended to submit.

The snows did not come. Even more than Rukn al-Din's pathetic and humiliating attempts at stalling for time did not dismay Hassan as much as the failure of the snows.

"God has forsaken us," he said, and many of his men said the same.

It was bitterly cold in the hills, despite the lack of heavy snows. Flurries would be whipped up by the biting winds and the icy flakes would slice into exposed skin from all angles, including from below. Mongol scouts roamed the hills, and we busied ourselves laying ambushes, day and night. Those few we captured alive we questioned thoroughly. Often, we encouraged them with the application of heated steel to delicate parts of their bodies, but they rarely knew very much that we could not discover through our own scouting, and through communication with other castles.

But one by one, those castles were cut off and surrounded.

The Assassin's castles were particularly well equipped to deal with sieges and most had at least one mangonel mounted upon a wall or tower so it could loose stones at attackers from a distance.

The biggest castles, at Alamut and the other regional centres, were equipped with the latest-style catapults, which were devices that Christendom called counterweight trebuchets. With such engines, we could throw massive boulders down onto the attackers to break up their assaults, harass their siege works and, ideally, smash their own trebuchets and engines, and break their assault towers.

By using those weapons, the Ismaili Assassins were employing the most powerful siege engines in the world. Even the siege masters of distant Cathay could not throw stones of such sizes as these were capable of. But the Mongols had something that no one else west of China had yet employed effectively in warfare.

Gunpowder.

From across the valley, well-hidden in the rocks, I watched the enemy mangonel throw something like a keg toward the castle of Nevizar. The small black shape tumbled slowly in the air as it hurtled up the hill from the Mongol siege lines. I lost sight of the object as it closed on the castle. Then, a flash of light and smoke and dust flew apart from the base of the wall. A few moments later, an almighty bang sounded, making us all jump in fright. The explosion echoed from the peaks. When the smoke cleared and the dust settled, the wall of the castle appeared unharmed.

"What in the name of God is that?" I said.

"I have heard of this," Stephen said beside me, for he had begged to journey with us to witness the Mongol forces that were pushing into Alamut Valley. "It is made with certain substances and creates an artificial fire that can be launched over long distances. A monk in Acre told me that by only using a very small quantity of this material, much light can be created, accompanied by that horrible fracas. He claimed it was possible with it to destroy a town or an army. But, see, it appears to do almost no damage to the walls. A simple stone launched from the same mangonel does more to wreak destruction upon the fortifications. I wonder why they use the artificial fire at all?"

Thomas scoffed. "Did you not hear the noise, young Stephen? Did it not stir your heart? Such a noise and us so far distant from the source of it. What do you think it would be like to be a man inside that castle? To be a man upon that wall?"

Eva's eyes shone as she stared down at the scene. "Imagine that fire, burning in that fashion, in the midst of us here. If one of those casks fell at our feet, how do you think we would fare, Richard?"

Over the decades, I had taken terrible wounds and healed them all. I feared decapitation, and I feared losing a limb. But such injuries were not very likely in the course of ordinary combat.

The sight of that Mongol bomb, however, awakened an old, mortal's fear of sudden death. More, it was a fear of the flesh and bone of my body being blown apart like the stones and twigs that weapon threw out across the mountainside with every detonation.

"I would prefer not to face such a thing, my dear, it is true. But we must attack all the same."

The detachment from the Mongol army was perhaps only five thousand strong, and yet that was a great many men more than we had. The most forward group encamped below us leading the attack numbered about a thousand and even that many would crush us easily.

Messages had flown back and forth across the free castles of the Alamut region and Hassan had urged his fellow leaders to make an attack on the Mongols while they could yet do so. As well as my own companions, I had brought the thirty immortals, who were steady men and Hassan had forced the thirty revenants on us also. Although they were dangerous, the immortal fedayin kept the revenants under control. And I kept my own people far away from them.

"Where are they?" Thomas muttered, looking up and down the valley. We were expecting a coordinated attack to begin but I was beginning to wonder whether any of the other castles had sent the detachments that they had promised.

"They should have been in position and ready to attack at first light," Eva said, looking up at the pale sun as a cloud passed across it. "If they are not here by now, why should we expect them to come at all?"

"Ever since I could remember," Thomas said, "the Assassins were spoken of in hushed tones. They were masters of death in the Holy Land. Men even feared their daggers in Rome and in Paris. And now I am witness to their complete lack of interest in fighting for their own survival."

"What can anyone do in the face of this?" Stephen said.

"Do you mean to say you would not fight to the death to protect England?" Thomas said, looking closely at him.

Stephen's eyes took on a faraway look. Above, clouds gathered quickly, as they often did in the mountains. Pale grey, swirling and thick, as though the sky was liquid lead.

"Well," I said, "if no one else shows then there is nothing we can do. Even with so many immortals, we would be too heavily outnumbered." Hard words to utter, for I was dying for a fight. I wanted to kill those Mongols and being abandoned by the other Assassins was infuriating.

"If there is no battle today," Eva said, and glanced over her shoulder, "then your immortals are going to be deeply disappointed."

"You too, no?" I said. "Thomas, also, I would wager you were looking forward to guzzling some Mongol blood." He ignored me, pretending that he was above such things. "But the immortals will accept it. It is the revenants, Hassan's mad blood drinkers, that we will have to contain. They will not listen to reason."

"When the blood hunger is upon you," Eva said, "reason is beyond your reach."

Thomas nodded to himself as she spoke.

And that hunger, that madness, meant they were almost as dangerous to our own side as to the enemy. It was as if they were no longer themselves, or not in their right minds, and the blood satiated them for so short a time. Whenever their bellies were not filled with blood, most of them delighted in petty violence and thrilled at the suffering of others. That was not so unusual in soldiers, but it was their lack of self-control that concerned me as their notional commander. In fact, the only thing that had kept them subdued and under the cover of the rocks and their cloaks was the sunlight, which they could not stand at all in midday and disliked intensely even on a grey winter morn.

It grew dark even as I pondered what to do about getting them all back to Hassan's castle without having to kill many of them. A light snow began to fall all across the valley.

"Oh, God," Eva said. "Richard."

The revenants had broken away and were descending the mountainside. Heading right toward the flank of the siege engines.

Down in the bottom of the valley, roaming Mongol patrols at the edge of the enemy formations spotted the approach of the group of Assassin fedayin. We watched from high on the side of the hill as Mongol horsemen moved to intercept. They did not move with haste. Why would they? They would have seen a group of around thirty men, on foot. And they were approaching a thousand.

"Should we flee?" Stephen asked. "When the Mongols are done with them, might they not search for others?"

"There is no rush," I said. "And I wish to see how long before they are slaughtered."

"At least we will be free from their madness now," Thomas said.

He hated the revenants more than anyone. I believe it was because he was unhappy with becoming a blood-drinking immortal. He had stayed as himself, but he feared the madness that he knew would come with the blood-starvation. Hassan's revenants, blood-mad and inhuman, reminded Thomas of what he could become, what he would certainly become, should he be deprived of blood. His resentment and fear were reflected onto the others. Also, their behaviour and conduct were objectively despicable.

The Assassin revenants advanced at a slow run, in three rough ranks, keeping a surprisingly disciplined spacing between each man, and the three ranks. A small group of nine horsemen drew near to them and loosed a volley of arrows.

A couple of the Assassins stumbled but their lines did not slow.

Two more volleys had no effect and the horsemen fell back at walking pace, where more of their comrades joined them. Quickly, a group of twenty, and then thirty or more horsemen milled across the line of attack. Most were the lightly-armoured kind, with the small horses, bows and light spears. But a handful were the Mongols in mail armour, steel helms, riding heavier horses and good swords and heavy lances.

The Mongols were in good spirits as they advanced to the charge. It would be little more than sport to them. A brief diversion from the boredom of a siege.

A moment before the first lines clashed, the revenants surged forward and swarmed the horsemen. They yanked the horsemen from their saddles and slashed at the horses, swords, and daggers flashing. Some tried to wheel about and ride away but the immortals chased them down on foot, accelerating faster than the horses, and pulled them to the ground.

"God's bones," Thomas muttered, standing up to get a better look over the rocks.

The revenants ran further toward the loose flank of the Mongol formation while the remaining horsemen scattered. It seemed as though few in the camp had yet noticed they were under attack, and they continued to mill about, busy with normal camp business. The artillery experts brought from distant Cathay continued to work their enormous devices, paying no attention. Even if they noticed, they would trust to their Mongol masters to keep them safe.

In fact, though, there were few soldiers between the revenants and the camp of the siege engineers.

"How far do you think they will get before they are surrounded and swamped?" Stephen asked.

I stood. "Stephen, you will stay here until we return."

"You are not going down there?" Stephen said, looking to Thomas to share his outrage.

Eva jumped up, grinning, and clambered across the rocks. She was already heading downhill when I turned to the leader of my immortals, squatting patiently in the shade behind the jagged boulders.

"Jalal," I said, speaking Arabic. "We will attempt to cut through to the Cathay engineers and kill them all. Then we will retreat."

He nodded and unfolded himself. The fedayin immortal was calm, and as icy as the sky above us, while he related the objective to the rest of his immortal men.

We hurried down the hill. The Assassins were ahead of us, spread out but staying together. Thomas was at my side. Eva in front, moving like a lioness. Orus and Khutulun moved by me and then pulled ahead as if they were racing each other. We slipped and stumbled and charged on.

"Are you," Thomas said, breathing heavily, "certain. About this?"

We both carried our helms in one hand, picking our way down the slope, sometimes using pathways that cut across our route, other times ploughing right through scrub and sliding down powdery scree. After so long feeling frozen, it was exhilarating to be moving.

Why had I ordered us to join an attack that was doomed to fail?

The most cunning course of action was certainly to allow the revenants to be surrounded and killed, as Thomas had earlier said.

There was an opportunity to kill some of the engineers, the experts from Cathay, but they would most likely flee before ever we reached them, and I was exposing myself and my people to great danger. We could kill five men apiece and still we could be swarmed.

Perhaps the only reason was that I was a killer. I loved nothing more than to fight and to kill, and I had been too long without. Far too long.

"We must keep watch on our route of flight," I said to Thomas. It was quite foolish to have such a climb back up a steep hill as our only direction to escape, but then an enemy in pursuit would have to contend with the climb, too.

I looked over my shoulder, to take note of the challenge, and there behind me I saw Stephen. He was a ways behind, stumbling and flailing his arms. Even as I watched he tripped and fell, rolling over in a cloud of dust.

Calling to Thomas, I ran back up to grab the young former monk.

"What in the name of God are you doing?" I said, shouting in his face as I yanked him to his feet.

He winced and cringed away from me.

"There were men up there," he said, breathing hard. "It was not safe to remain."

I looked up at the ridge. No movement.

"There is no one there, Stephen."

He was outraged. "There is. There was. I swear it."

"You saw them?"

He hesitated. "I heard them. Voices. Footsteps."

The hillside above was desolate and wild but nothing moved there.

I clipped Stephen on the head with my mailed hand and shoved my helm into his grasp.

"Hold this and stay by me. You bloody fool."

The others had pulled far ahead, though Thomas and Eva had held back so they would not be so separated from me. A riderless horse ran by me. A few steps away, a Mongol warrior dragged himself across the ground. Where he thought he was headed, I had no idea, and I ran over, drew my dagger and dispatched him.

"One cannot be too careful," I said to Stephen, then dragged and prodded him on toward the others.

A thousand Mongols were camped nearby, mostly further down to the valley to my right, and the siege engines and specialists were directly ahead. We were at the head of the encampment and they had not bothered to build any defences.

Perhaps they thought the farmland would be protection enough. Just moments before, looking down from a height, the crisscrossing walls and ditches had seemed trivial, but now I was amongst them I could see how they would slow us down. But the walls would obstruct the Mongols too.

The truth was, they simply believed the Assassins to be fully cowed, and did not expect an attack.

Still, small groups of the enemy massed on our flanks but we pushed further in toward the trebuchets. Those engines continued to be worked. Another bomb arced into the air and exploded against the castle wall.

We leapt over a stone wall and stomped through the remains of a vast orchard. The Mongols had cut down every tree in Alamut Valley, for fuel, and for their siege engines, and also to ensure the Assassins' destruction, come what may. Even if you beat us, such an act said, you will starve next year. Farmhouses and outhouses had been demolished and the stones used as ammunition for the mangonels, and the timbers for the engines themselves.

A thought unbidden flashed into my mind. I pictured the Mongols thoughtlessly demolishing Ashbury manor house and tearing up our apple trees. My home no longer, all men that knew me surely dead, but the thought was pure horror.

"Come on, Stephen," I said, as we caught up to the others. He was panting, sucking air in and wincing. It was impossible to keep with the pace of us immortals. I felt pity for him, then annoyed that he had ignored my command to stay safe on the hillside.

"Richard," Thomas called. "The Assassins have gone ahead. Making a run for the engines."

I nodded. "Let us not become separated from them, we are vulnerable here."

The shouting grew louder as the raised voices of friend and foe swelled in the valley.

"Here they come," Eva shouted. "Cavalry east." She pointed with her sword.

Hooves drummed the hard earth. Arrows whipped through the air, thudded into the ground, clattered against the tree stumps. I covered Stephen with my body and cursed my lack of a shield. At least I thought to grab my helm and pull it down over my head. Horsemen rode toward us, loosing more arrows.

Shoving Stephen down behind a meagre tree stump, Eva and I charged the horsemen. There were eight of them, and they did not retreat. In fact, I was sure I could hear them laughing as they rode to meet us and surround us.

I slashed the face of the nearest horse, cutting a gouge into its face as it reared in pain and terror, and grabbed the shaft of the rider's spear and pulled him from his saddle. As I stabbed down into his guts, something smacked into the back of my helm, the sound enormous in my ears. Only an arrow, but the disorientation allowed another pair of riders to close on me. One, I smacked with the butt end of the spear I still held, but it was an awkward backhanded blow and he held on to his seat and swerved away. I kept moving, circled around the second rider and slashed at his thigh, cutting his leg and his horse's shoulder.

Thomas appeared on the other side of him, stabbing his sword up into the Mongol's body. Orus and Khutulun swarmed another rider and dragged him down. While Orus killed the man, Khutulun leapt onto the horse in a single bound, yanked the beast's head around and charged at another rider with her sword in hand, screaming some challenge or curse.

Eva shouted something from nearby and I ducked and swerved as I ran to her, heart pounding in my chest.

But she was not in distress. She was calling my attention to something.

"There," she said, breathing heavily inside her helm. She pointed at the castle.

The besieged Assassins were breaking out from inside their fortification, riding and running down the pathway toward us in their hundreds, or possibly thousands.

Eva slapped me on the shoulder and turned me around, and around again. I pulled my helm from my head and looked up at the hills on the north and the south, from where we had come.

Assassins. From every hillside, the free fedayin came to join the attack in groups of dozens or even hundreds. Each formation presumably from a different castle.

"They came after all," I said. "There must be two thousand of the bastards."

Eva laughed at me. "They were here the whole time. Too afraid to attack at first light or make themselves known to us. They must have just been watching. Waiting."

Stephen ran over with a stupid smile on his face. "I told you," he said to me, sounding very young indeed. "I told you there were men up there."

"And you still should have stayed. You could have been killed, you fool." I clipped him around the ear again but I was too exhilarated to even feign displeasure.

Orus rode over, leading another horse, and offered it to me. I climbed on its back and looked out over the Mongol camp. They were stirring themselves in the face of the onslaught and preparing for a battle.

What followed was a disorganised scrap. It was a rather shameful display of a complete lack of any coordination or cohesion on the part of the Ismailis but they got the job done. All those months, cooped up, inactive, and afraid of the Mongols. Finally, they could unleash their fury on a small number of them.

Hundreds of Mongols were slaughtered, and the rest driven out of the valley through the eastern pass. My immortal Assassins murdered most of the siege experts from Cathay. A handful were captured by Jalal so that their secrets could be winkled out of them later. The enemy's tents were burnt, horses and equipment taken as booty. We spent the night around a big campfire, and it was half of the next day before we managed to round up all of

Hassan's blood-drunk immortals and headed back to Hassan's castle.

We lost two of Jalal's men, and one of those was murdered in an argument with one of the surviving revenants. Sixteen of them had lived through their suicidal attack, and those men were insanely pleased with themselves. They took credit for the success of the battle and seemed to think nothing at all of their fallen comrades. During the return journey, I entertained myself with imagining slaughtering those revenant survivors.

Instead, we returned home all together in good spirits, and all of them wanted to be the first to tell their lord the excellent news. Jalal felt proud that his men had performed so well in battle. They had killed a huge number of the enemy and had used their abilities to perform a tactical thrust into the enemy lines and deprive them of a key resource. Hassan and Jalal looked forward to using the immortals to punch through enemy formations on the battlefield in order to kill the enemy commanders.

Despite the enthusiasm of the Assassins, I felt a deep unease.

Two nights after our return, I gathered my people in a corner of the training hall. Some sat on the floor, others on benches against the wall. I stood in front of them and shared my concerns.

"The Assassins are not the force I had believed them to be," I said, keeping my voice low. "That much is clear now."

Abdullah was wound very tight, and he jumped in. "They have just won a great victory. Do you not believe they can defeat the Mongols?"

"It is the very fact they are claiming a minor skirmish as a great victory that has finally opened my eyes to what I have suspected for some time."

"They are effective at infiltration, and murders," Thomas said. "And their castles have no doubt served them well against their Saracen enemies in Persia and Syria. But they cannot fight."

Stephen spoke up. "They are too disparate. It is a strength of theirs, in some ways, but their military might is disbursed over too great a distance. An army of any size and competence can take each castle without facing the combined forces at any time."

I nodded, impressed that the young monk—or former monk—had the wisdom to see it.

"But the immortals," Abdullah said. "Can they not sway the balance?"

No one answered, and Abdullah slumped.

"The Mongols will be surrounding this place soon enough," I said. "These famous snows may never come. Either way, the Assassins can only slow the advance of the Mongols. They can never stop them."

"Can we take the immortals," Thomas said, "and cut through to Hulegu?"

"We should retreat," Stephen said.

I agreed. "But where can we go?"

"Is it not obvious?" Thomas said. "We return to Acre and prepare our people for the coming storm."

"That is a long journey," Eva said.

Thomas was not concerned. "It may take Hulegu another year to conquer all of these mountain lands. And then he must subdue Baghdad to the south of here so that his path and his supply lines are unchallenged. Surely that siege will last at least a year, perhaps even more. Then he will take Damascus and the rest of Syria before he comes for us. We have time."

Abdullah, who had been translating as usual for Orus and Khutulun had stopped at some point, and the Mongols were urging him to explain what we were speaking off. He stared at nothing. As if he was looking at something a thousand miles off. Khutulun turned to Stephen and asked him.

"We kill Hulegu," Stephen said in French, speaking slowly and using elaborate gestures. "We kill Hulegu in three years."

She jumped up, spoke to Orus, and both of them babbled at me.

"Yes, yes," I said, holding up my hands, "be silent, will you, you damned barbarians. You are quite right. That is too long to wait."

Stephen laughed. "But you will never die. You may live another century, at least. What is three years to you?"

"We will all die," I said. "We may not even survive this month if we do not flee before the Mongols encircle us. The longer we wait, the stronger Hulegu becomes. He is on the move with his army, he will be more vulnerable in such circumstances than if he is settled in a palace in Damascus."

"How, then?" Thomas asked. "How do we take him?"

No one had an answer.

"Armenia," Stephen said. "They have submitted to Mongol rule but they are good Christians and must chafe under the yoke. There must be men who would ally with us. Or Georgia, if not."

"I suppose that will have to do," I said. "Does anyone have any knowledge of those kingdoms? Or any possible allies there?

Thomas? No? Do you expect us to walk from place to place, asking strangers if they would spare some food, shelter, and some blood for a group set on murdering their overlords?"

Judging by the despair on their faces, I had them where I wanted them. All I had to do was to persuade them that attacking Hulegu and William in the mountains, there and then, was the only possible course of action.

But fate decided otherwise.

"Baghdad."

We all turned to the voice who had spoken into the silence I had crafted.

Abdullah stood to one side, a cup in his hand. While we stared at him, he poured himself another cup of wine and drank it off. He turned and looked at me.

"Baghdad. We should go to Baghdad."

Thomas laughed. "Why would we do that?"

"It is the strongest city in the world," Abdullah said. "If any place can resist the Mongols, it is there."

Thomas turned to me. "We would not get within a hundred miles before being killed."

Abdullah responded. "I could guide us to the city. Through the city. Get us an audience with the Vizier."

More of us laughed. I smiled to myself. "You would get us an audience with the most powerful man in the city, other than the caliph?" I said. "And how would you manage that, Abdullah?"

"Well, you see..." He poured another cup of wine and drank it. "The Vizier is my uncle."

* * *

Two young rafiqs escorted me through Firuzkuh Castle but turned away from Hassan's quarters and brought me out into the freezing pre-dawn courtyard. An old man guarded the door and he handed me a thick blanket that I wrapped around my shoulders. I nodded my thanks but he only sneered, full of contempt.

The rafiqs led me across to the front of the castle and there on the wall stood Hassan, wrapped in a cloak, staring out at the darkness. A bitter wind whipped at the fabric. The old men surrounding him fell into silence and backed away along the wall as I approached, and the rafiq announced my presence. To the east, the peaks were silhouetted against the rising sun beyond the horizon.

"They tell me that you are preparing to flee," Hassan said without turning around.

I went and stood beside him. There was little to see out there but shadow and a cold that stung my eyes. The icy wind filled my ears, making them ache in moments.

"I was coming to tell you," I said, speaking over the wind.

"Tell me?" he said. "You mean, to ask my permission."

I pursed my lips. "I have fulfilled my part of the bargain. It is unfortunate that your people were not stronger. Not as strong as I believed."

I expected him to berate me for that, for it was a grave insult, despite also being the truth.

Instead, he sagged and leaned his hands upon the crenellation in front of us. In one hand, he grasped something, crumpled up.

"Not as strong as I believed, either," he said. His hood masked his face.

"Have you had another communication?" I asked, pointing to his hand

He took a deep breath and growled out a great cloud. "Betrayed. We are betrayed by our own master."

A ball of apprehension formed in my guts. "What has he done?"

"You know that Rukn al-Din was besieged? He has surrendered and delivered himself and his family into the hands of Hulegu. He has ordered that all castles, all of us, submit also."

I leant on the crenellation and turned to look at Hassan. His eyes glistened in the shadow. It was no wonder that he wept, for it was as deep a betrayal as I had ever heard.

"What are the terms of the surrender?" I asked. "For us, I mean?"

He scoffed. "The terms are that his family gets to live, and the rest of us will be killed and enslaved. Our women will be taken. Everything we have, everything we are, destroyed."

"Good God," I muttered. "But you will not surrender." It was not a question.

"We shall make them pay with their lives," Hassan said. I saw, then, that he wept from the anguish but also due to the depths of his rage. "But we will fall. All will be lost."

"So," I said. "We will flee at first light. You would not believe it, but Abdullah, our Abdullah, is the nephew of the vizier of

Baghdad. He was banished, disowned, so it is certainly a risk returning with him. But we shall attempt to kill Hulegu there. When his armies surround Baghdad, it will take them months, perhaps years, to bring down those walls. While he is encamped, we shall slip through the lines and kill him, his men, and my brother." He did not respond. "What do you think, Hassan? It is the best course of action if we wish to avenge the dead, no? Who knows, perhaps Rukn al-Din will be with Hulegu in the camp and you can kill the man yourself."

"No," he said. "It is too late."

I could not believe what I was hearing. The defeatism had spread even to him.

"What do you mean, no? Come with us, Hassan. Bring Jalal and his men. Even your others, the savage immortals. Preserve your most powerful forces."

"Richard," he said, turning to look at me for the first time. "It is a fine plan. But you are too late."

He pointed out across the wall into the darkness beyond. Even as I looked, the first rays of morning light rose over a gap in the mountains, and I saw.

The other assassins on the walls gasped and exclaimed.

Men, horses. Mongols in their hundreds. I could even make out the beams and trusses of their great siege machines being assembled.

"But the southern gate," I said. "The route across the mountains. We must move, now."

Hassan stayed perfectly still. "My men have brought me reports all night. The Mongols are already in the hills. It is no use.

All we can do is make them pay dearly."

I grasped his shoulder and turned him to face me. I sensed his men all around us come forward, ready to strike me down.

"You must act, now," I said. "So there are Mongols in the hills. We can cut through them, Hassan. Think, man. Pull yourself together, for the love of God. Lead us out, Hassan."

He nodded, slowly. "The woman and children. I cannot abandon them to their fate."

"Their fate will be the same no matter where you chose to die," I said. "But you can still kill Hulegu. You can. But only if we take the best fighters and go. Now. Right now."

He stared at me. "Make your preparations. I must speak to my people."

While I ran back, he called everyone but the sentries to the jamatkhana. Standing ready by the southern gate, my people strained and fretted. Stephen suggested that I overpower the guards so that we could go before any more of the Mongols circled into our path.

Eventually, the assassins emerged, and Hassan himself came to us, along with Jalal.

"It has been decided. Jalal will lead the immortals and go with you to Baghdad. I will keep the others, my savages. I will turn them against the Mongols when the time comes."

"What will you do?" I asked him.

"They will send an envoy to negotiate terms," he said, his voice flat and his eyes distant. "I shall welcome them in and do everything in my power to prolong the negotiation. That should at least grant you a day, perhaps more."

Jalal could barely wait until his lord finished speaking. "All of us begged him to flee," he said to me. "We want him to leave. To avenge our families. It need not be you, why not allow—"

Hassan waved his hand. "Negotiation is a knife edge and—"

An almighty bang shook the castle around us. Dust fell down from the ceiling.

We ran through the corridors to the courtyard and up to the wall.

You have to give it to the Mongols. They were a horse people, from the steppe, from the endless grasslands. They had never built anything permanent, not even a timber hall, let alone a fortified settlement or a castle. And yet, in fifty years or so, they had become masters of siege warfare. Rather, they had kidnapped masters from Cathay and pressed them into service. But not only that, they had provided the necessary logistics so that these masters could ply their trade.

In less than half a day, they had dragged timbers the size of ship masts up the hillside, assembled the first of the massive engines, and launched the first missile. An A-frame crane perched over the second trebuchet and men covered the structure like ants. The first trebuchet was already being reset.

In front of the engines, dozens of Mongol troops stood in war gear, gesturing at the walls and towers of our castle.

Already planning their assault.

"They do not mean to assault us today?" Jalal asked.

While we watched, the trebuchet launched another stone projectile at us. The long arm moved in deliberate slowness through a vast curve, flinging the sling over at the top of its arc.

The massive stone rose into the sky. It seemed to be coming right for me, though I could not quite believe it. The fact that, out of the entire length of the defensive wall, the murderous boulder would be coming directly at me seemed absurd. I almost laughed.

"Is that—" Hassan began.

I dived to my side, shoving Hassan and Jalal down before me with all my strength, sending them sprawling.

The impact was so loud, so close, that I felt it resounding through my body and for a long moment I thought I was hit. Debris and dust filled the air and my ears rang.

It had clipped the crenellation right where we had been standing. The boulder had then crashed into the courtyard and obliterated an unlucky rafiq. Other than a great smear of blood of his body was gone, but a weeping relative or friend clutched the dead man's tattered clothing. Someone else held aloft one of his severed arms in a corner fifty feet away. After bouncing once, the massive rock had crashed into the wall of a workshop and stopped.

After a moment where we checked ourselves for injury, Hassan and Jalal began shouting orders. The castle's mangonel crews were ordered to take out the enemy's trebuchets. Every able-bodied man was ordered to take up their weapons. The fedayin began to arrive, dressed in their full panoplies.

I hurried through the courtyard to my people at the gate.

"We are too late," Thomas shouted from the wall above. "They are in the hills."

I climbed to the wall and looked out at the jumble of rocks and hills. My heart sank. "Those devious savages."

Dozens, perhaps hundreds of Mongol soldiers were busy setting up positions all across the hillside, their true number and activities obscured by the rises in the jagged landscape.

"Are they there to keep us in?" Thomas asked. "Or are they preparing to assault the walls?"

There were bundles of arrows being stacked with each group of ten Mongols. I could see no ladders or ropes but that did not mean they were not there.

"Either way, we must attack them now," I said. "Break through and flee before we are trapped."

Thomas looked at me as if I was mad. "Break through? How, Richard?"

In truth, I had no idea. "We must break through, and so we shall do it." I clapped him on his back. We ran down to the others at the gate, as the castle walls boomed from the impact of further strikes. Would the walls crumble in a day? Would the Mongols even wait, or would they attempt to scale the walls directly?

"We have a fight on our hands," I said. "A rare fight. Listen, we will go through the gate and we will stay together. Do you all hear me? We will stay together. Not only do we have to cut our way through the men outside, we must fight off all pursuit, and avoid or slaughter any patrols we meet, for days on end. Our provisions will be only what we can carry, and what we can take from our enemies. The passes over the peaks cannot be traversed by horses, and so we will be footsore for a long while. Then when we reach the foothills, we shall take the horses of the Mongols, and ride for Syria."

They stared at me, apprehensive and unsure.

"Take heart. We get to show God what we are made of today, my friends. Are your swords sharp? Straps tightened? Make your final preparations, and I shall see what assistance we will receive."

They turned to go over their equipment. I was most concerned with Stephen and Abdullah, who were neither warriors nor immortals. If Stephen died, it would make no difference but I needed Abdullah to get into Baghdad. They each had a helm to protect their head but no one would provide mail for a useless scholar. I could protect Abdullah from anyone who attacked with swords and even spears but we were all at terrible risk from those wicked Mongol bows.

"We need shields," I said to the Assassins who were helping to equip me for the breakout. "Bring us shields, enough for each of us." Of course, their home was under attack and they were understandably distracted, so I went to find Hassan or anyone senior enough who could order their men to find shields for my people.

The castle was in subdued chaos. Men ran across the courtyards and along the walls, carrying bundles of javelins. Most wore their mail, and many already had their conical helms.

A group of captains stood around Hassan up on the wall by the northwest tower, protected from the trebuchet by the mass of the tower itself. I pushed through the mass of men and called for Hassan. Before I could reach him, Jalal appeared and cut me off.

"Richard, listen. This is what will now happen. My men will leave first by the south gate. We will engage the enemy. You will break through, and my lord Hassan will go with you."

I had questions that I wished to ask. What if we all joined

together and routed the enemy on the south slope, perhaps we might lead a mass breakout from the castle and perhaps hundreds could escape into the hills. I wanted the immortals to come with me, to protect us on the road and to be used against Hulegu and William, so why not send the savage immortals, or even better, just the ordinary mortal fedayin?

"What about the immortals that you made with your blood, Jalal? Are they to stay?"

"They will replicate their success and charge the engineers. This may prolong our siege but either way should draw in the main forces to the front, hindering pursuit of you and Hassan, while my men tie down forces at the rear."

It was the best chance for me to escape, so I asked no more questions but one. "Can you find shields for my men?"

Time passes strangely in such moments. Did it take half a day to finish the preparations or was it almost an instant, as it seemed? Orders were shouted, advice and reminders passed along between us. My Arabic was very good but I found that I could understand not one word of the men around me, wound as tightly as they were. The stones kept pounding the wall on the other side of the castle and we stayed tight to the internal walls that we prayed would protect us from more overshooting stones or debris.

"What is taking so long?" I shouted to Jalal. "We must go, now."

"Not until my lord is here."

I threw down most of my gear and went hunting for the lord of the castle. I found him standing on the front wall, alone and exposed like a madman. Running to him, I saw what he looked at

285

beyond the wall. The savage revenants that he had made using Jalal's blood, were charging the enemy. If the plan truly had been to attack the trebuchets then it was doomed to failure, as the machines were far back from the front lines. Hundreds of men blocked their path. The revenants were outnumbered ten to one, if not more.

Still, the revenants cut through the Mongols with ease. I was strangely proud, even though I had not contributed to their skills and had never wanted them created with my blood once removed. Yet the damned revenants did feel like my grandchildren, in a way, and I could at least appreciate their work. The first fifty Mongols were killed, and the enemy sent another fifty or a hundred forward. Arrows filled the air and some of the vampire assassins fell. The Mongols clustered around the twenty or so revenants who remained fighting.

"We must go," I said to Hassan. "Make their sacrifice meaningful."

He shook me off, turned, and shouted orders at his men inside the castle. Those orders were relayed, and the two mangonels on the walls slammed into action moments apart, and their projectiles hurtled out over the combat.

Bright fire erupted. Both objects smashed into the massed, disorganised group of Mongols and burst into flames. The roar of the fire reached me and I saw men dancing in the fire. The sound of screams came next.

"By God," I said. "Is that naphtha?"

He ignored me and shouted more orders down into the yard below. The front gates were opened and the fedayin marched out.

Hassan was sending his troops out to take the fight to the Mongols rather than wait to be overrun.

The mangonels launched again, the fire bursting close to the immortals, surely engulfing and killing some of them, too.

"Hassan," I shouted. "I am leaving, now. You are coming with me."

He nodded, tearing his eyes away from the sight of his men dying in the flames. Bowstrings hummed as the assassin archers loosed a volley before advancing.

We fled back through the castle, his remaining men nodding to Hassan or offering a prayer or some other words. It was the end of their lives, their families, of their entire world. Their hopes for vengeance would be kept alive in Hassan, while they would achieve great holiness through their deaths, and spend eternity in Heaven with all the rewards that were due to them. Some were grim, others had the mad look that some men are filled with when they feel touched by God and have gone beyond the fear of death. I could only imagine what would happen to the women and children hiding deep within the castle. The best they could hope for would be a lifetime of slavery.

"Jalal," I shouted when we drew near. "He is here. Go, now."

Jalal's immortals were out of the gate like wolves after a deer. Sleek, swift despite their armour, they slipped through the gate and were gone.

"How long should we wait?" Thomas asked.

I pushed to the front, shoved Hassan at Thomas for him to take care of, and grabbed Abdullah. "You stay by my side at all times. Leave my side and die, understand?" He swallowed and nodded. The man shook all over like a newborn lamb.

Eva had Stephen by the upper arm, and he clutched his shield to his chest.

"We go now," I said to Thomas. "Orus, Khutulun. Go." I nodded out the gate and they slipped out. One by one I ordered my people out and counted them all to be sure no one was left behind.

Once clear of the protection of the castle, wind howled down from the peaks and icy dust whipped into my face. Ahead, Jalal and his men were cutting through the enemy and their shouts and clashing blades rang in the bitter air. I pulled on my helm, grabbed my shield and held it ready, placing Abdullah behind and on the flank opposite the enemy. Arrows flew but not toward us, yet. Ahead, my people stomped across the hilltop, heading across the enemy front at an oblique angle so we could get by them and off into the passes and secret ways through the mountains.

Hassan, Jalal, and his men knew them, and so I prayed to God that he would spare at least one of those Saracens so that we might find our way clear of the heathen Mongols.

We made good progress and the fighting was clear of us. A few arrows clattered on the stones around us but it seemed Jalal's men were keeping the enemy well occupied.

Then I heard—or rather, felt—the thing I dreaded most. A drumming on the hard ground, growing stronger.

"Cavalry!" I shouted, in French, English, Arabic. "Horsemen! Riders!"

I stopped to get a better look and saw a group of twenty horsemen charging into the flank of Jalal's men. They were lancers, on armoured horses. Madness that the Mongols had brought them up the mountainside for a castle assault. But the Mongols were nothing if not full of surprises. The Assassins were run over, speared, and broken up.

How I wished I had squires. Even one, who could pass me a spear or a polearm of some sort. Together with two squires, we could face a mounted attack with our flanks protected.

"Run to our people," I shouted at Abdullah and pushed him ahead while I followed, keeping an eye on the horsemen. "Come together," I shouted at the others. Stopping, I slung my shield and removed my helm. "Come together," I roared again.

Some of the horsemen turned to face our direction. One gestured at me with his bloodied lance.

Up ahead, my people were gathering in a group. The ones up ahead filing back, the ones nearest to me looking back for instruction.

"Keep moving," I shouted as I hurried to them. "Keep moving but stay together."

I reached them and Thomas turned his helmeted head to me. "By God, Richard. What I would not give for a horse."

I laughed, clapped him on the back and jammed my helm back on my head.

"On, on," I called, harrying them like a dog herding a flock. I searched in vain for a place where we could make a stand if we needed to.

The hillside curved away in all directions, and there were boulders and large stones, but nothing that would interrupt a cavalry charge.

"Richard!" Eva shouted from ahead. The ground thundered as the horsemen moved toward us.

I threw Abdullah at Hassan. "Keep him alive," I said.

Eva pushed Stephen at him too. "And look out for Stephen," she said. Eva was a warrior but she still had a woman's heart, filled with compassion for useless boys like Stephen, a weak English monk who was nothing more than a liability.

"Two lines," I shouted. "Thomas, Eva, you stay in front of Hassan. Work together. Orus, Khutulun, with me, understand? With me."

Orus looked wild, eyes bulging and filled with the madness for blood, and the lust for glory of combat, of death. Khutulun was calm as a mountain lake, holding a spear in one hand and her wicked curved blade in the other focused on the advancing cavalry.

Putting distance between my first and second lines, I edged forward, checking that my two Mongol rebels stayed with me. Six horsemen, their lances low, came on. Behind them, two more circled to my left so that they could take us in the flank. I would have to let Eva and Thomas take care of them.

The Mongols had no need to thunder at us in an almighty charge. Their horses were heavy, and horse and rider were weighed down with armour. So high in the mountains, the air was thin and the horses laboured mightily. I considered attempting to force them to chase me down and thus exhaust them. But I put that thought aside. They were too many, and even if I could outpace the horses, it would take too long.

"Come on," I shouted. And I ran at the nearest rider. His

armour was not mail but a kind of coat of plates, dozens or hundreds of small rectangular iron pieces covered his body and his legs to the knees. The horse had armour over its face and neck. He swerved to spear me but I was faster than he could have expected and I changed direction, ducked under his horse's nose and leapt up on the other side. My first thrust glanced off the armour covering his legs, jarring my arm. I swung my shield up and smacked it into him, hard, but he stayed in the saddle and swerved on, heading for Eva behind me.

Orus brought a horse down, somehow. Khutulun dragged a Mongol from his saddle.

I was letting myself down.

Another rider was almost on me. This one had no lance but held a single-edged curved sword raised in one hand while he shouted some barbarian scream at me. He was armoured like the others. Where were they weak? His helm had no protection over his face. His raised arm showed a very large gap in the armoured plates. His hands had no protection, not even gloves.

Charging at him, I twisted and cut across his front to his left side and swung a tight cut at the hand that held the reins, parried the blow that he aimed at my head and slipped the point of my sword up into a gap between his ribs. My blade caught, twisted between two ribs. I grabbed my sword with both hands and pulled. He screamed in anger and pain as he tumbled from his saddle and smacked hard into the ice-hard ground, his felt-booted left foot caught in the stirrup. Before I could finish him off, he was dragged away by his horse leaping ahead.

Eva and Thomas had brought down the rider I let through

and Eva stabbed at him on the ground. Two riders circled Khutulun, shouting at her as they cut at her with their blades. I ran at the nearest one, crunching across the hilltop with my breathing loud inside my helmet. The Mongol faced away from me, all focus on Khutulun who darted and slipped from their attacks. From behind him, I slipped my blade between the saddle and the leg protection from his long coat of plates, slicing a vicious, deep gash along the back of his thigh. He kicked his horse away from me automatically, leaving Khutulun and I to kill the other.

So quickly, the tide had been turned. We outnumbered them now, and we killed them all but one, who rode away, bleeding heavily.

Jalal's immortals had been hit hard, and half of them had been killed.

But their attack had been so powerful that the Mongols had retreated. Pulled back down the hill.

I rallied everyone to me, and we continued on with our escape. Jalal's surviving men were almost all wounded in some way but I ordered them to cover our flanks and the rear, while Jalal and Hassan took the lead to guide us through the hidden ways.

We were free.

But we were far from safe.

It was hard, those first few days. Very hard. There were Mongols everywhere, and even with the masters of stealth guiding us through their homeland, we had to spend a lot of time hiding, huddled together, shivering and waiting for enemy scouts to pass by. We were spotted many times. Sometimes, they must have decided that a few fugitives far across a valley or gorge were simply not worth pursuing. Other times we had Mongols hunting us through the hills.

Jalal's immortals, hungry and damaged though they were, saved us through laying ambushes for our pursuers, and by leading them away down blind gorges while the fedayin climbed up and out and met back up with us. One time, three men waited behind to spring an ambush. We heard the fighting. Despite Eva cursing me for my foolishness and selfishness, I crept back close enough to see the remains of my immortals being hacked to pieces by the Mongol survivors.

After such heroic actions, the Jalal's immortal fedayin were down to two men. Black-eyed killers named Radi and Raka, dangerous and violent even before the disaster that had befallen them. Hassan, Jalal, Radi and Raka had lost their home and their families, including women and children, had been slaughtered or taken as prisoners while they fled in the faint hope of exacting future revenge on those responsible. It was a wonder that they did not break entirely but still I watched them all closely, lest they turn on us Christians.

My chief fear was that they would be seized by their lust and attempt to take Eva in the night but it was not long before I was disabused of that notion. Whatever their natural inclination may have been, the harshness of the journey turned each of us into hunched, shuffling old men who lusted only after warmth, bread, and blood.

Still, I endeavoured always to sleep with one eye open.

It was hundreds of miles to Baghdad, away to the southwest.

Unimpeded and with enough supplies, we could have walked it in less than a month. But we could not walk straight there. Our route crisscrossed through the mountains and hills and later took us down from the highlands onto the vast Persian plateau before descending to the green plains of ancient Babylonia. First, we went northwest toward Armenia, driven away from Persia by the huge numbers of Mongols travelling in groups from place to place. They were everywhere. Soon, we discovered that they were many even in the north. We knew that Armenia and Georgia were in a state of formal submission but it was clear that the Mongols were a constant presence in those Christian lands, with horsemen carrying messages and even wagons carrying supplies through the winter. We spent many hours lying hidden on the bitter, hard ground in shallow depressions while we waited for groups of riders to pass.

If it had not been for the contacts that Hassan had in various small and scattered communities, we would certainly have perished. As it was, we barely made it. The journey was harder than any before, though it was far shorter in distance and in time than our previous crossings of central Asia.

It was not long before I had entirely forgotten what it was to be warm. My belly ached from hunger so severe that it was agony on occasion and many of us, myself included, woke ourselves in the darkness with involuntary wailing. We grew thin. The people who kept us for a night or more were themselves suffering in hunger. But even up on the plateau, it was not so cold as up in the mountains and so we could at least thaw ourselves a little.

One night, in a sheltered valley, we huddled in an

outbuilding. The farmer and his extended family were asleep inside, the women and girls unseen by us. The trees of their orchard had been cut down and carted off by a band of Turkomen soldiers while the family hid in the hills. While the father was sympathetic and treated Hassan with respect, he could offer us nothing but a draughty roof where his sheep used to live. During the night, a hushed argument amongst Jalal's two surviving fedayin welled up and broke out. Hassan and Jalal subdued Radi and Raka, physically pinning them until they relented, but the bitterness between the Assassins remained for days. When we bartered for strips of dried goat two days later, Radi and Raka were not allowed to eat so much as a bite.

"They wanted to eat the family," Hassan admitted to me later.

"You did right to punish them," I said, although I could not judge them too harshly, for I had momentarily considered the very same thing. Still, it did nothing to allay my fear of the desperate killers.

"If it comes to it," I whispered one day to Eva while we walked, far back behind the others. "We will kill the Assassins, drink their blood and eat them."

She screwed up her face but nodded. "Thomas will not like it," she said.

Even without speaking their language, I knew that Orus and Khutulun would have committed any atrocity if it meant getting their revenge on Hulegu and William. I did not care what Abdullah thought.

"Stephen will be trouble, too," I said.

"No," Eva said. "He will be first in line."

It was true that the monk had dealt with the hardship well, far better than I had expected. When his shoes wore away to pieces, he silently cut strips from his clothes and bandaged up his bleeding feet and continued on without a word. In response to my gaze, he merely nodded once and set his eyes on the horizon once more. Yes, he did rather well. Especially as he remained a mortal, as did Abdullah. Still, Eva's certainty about him surprised me.

"Have you not noticed?" she asked, incredulous at my naivety. "Stephen is a wolf in sheep's clothing. He would kill us all if it gave him what he wanted."

"And what does he want?"

"I do not know," she said.

"He wants the Gift," I said. "He wants to become one of us."

"Obviously," Eva said, rolling her eyes. "But that is only a stepping stone toward the shores of his ambition."

I should have heeded her words, and the sense of foreboding that they aroused in me.

Other than Stephen and Abdullah, Hassan was the only other mortal amongst us. He was a remarkable man. A warrior, a leader, and a diplomat. Yet, the fall of his people, the loss of his castle, the deaths and unknown fate of the men, women, and children who he had sworn to protect, all weighed heavy on him. The first few days he was so dejected that I expected him to turn back or go mad. But, like Stephen, there was some ember deep within him that did not go out. And, despite the privations, he started to come back to himself.

Hatred can be a powerful motivation.

Stephen and Abdullah helped me to feed Eva, Thomas, Orus and Khutulun with our blood. While Hassan allowed Jalal and the fedayin to drink from him.

The mortal men resented it, for it was degrading and uncomfortably intimate, but they did it all the same. With familiarity, it became less unpleasant for them and even at times seemed to be an almost ritualistic undertaking. A ritual, if one could call it that, which was as disturbing as it was comforting. What is more, the immortals made sure to take good care of the mortal providers of their sustenance and usually offered them the first of the food and water.

So, stage by stage, over weeks that turned to months, we crisscrossed the highland plateau and finally descended to the fertile plains fed by the Tigris and the Euphrates. It was there where Abdullah, finally, began to show his worth. For all his faults, and for all he cowered in fear at the sight of physical danger, he could talk the hind legs off of a donkey. Local people would challenge us with scowls on their faces and after only a few moments listening to Abdullah jabbering away at them, they would be leading him into their homes for refreshments and begging his pardon for the state of the place.

The land around Baghdad, stretching for fifty miles or more from the city, was something like paradise on Earth. After so long in the pale, dusty, frozen hills and uplands, I had almost forgotten what deep green looked like. It was a land of superbly ordered canals and irrigation ditches, dividing the land into perfectly arranged parcels. It was a balm for the soul, I do not mind admitting so, despite it being the Saracen heartland. I felt like I could breathe again. The people were wary but welcoming, and they were of a healthier stock than the desiccated folk just up over the hills in Persia.

They were aware that the Mongols were threatening the caliph and they were understandably concerned. And no matter what we said, they did not believe that the Mongols could come that very year to threaten their great city.

And finally, after months of walking, we were there. We were exhausted and dragging our feet along the road, looking like the desperate beggars that we were.

The city of Baghdad was on the horizon, her walls every bit as imposing as their legend had suggested even from a distance. Towers jutted up all along the lengths of the varied walls and behind them thrust the peaks of minarets, some glinting in the powerful sunlight. Coming as we were from the sparsely populated wilderness, running for cover at the sight of horsemen on the horizon and conversing with locals only rarely, the masses of people travelling to and fro along the roads into the city were quite overwhelming and we gathered close to each other like a clutch of newborn chicks.

"We cannot enter like this," I said, standing up straight and shaking Eva from my arm. Wincing in the sun, she pulled her robe tight over her face and muttered black curses at me. "Come, Abdullah, come to the front here. We must wash ourselves clean in the waters and comb our beards with sticks if we must."

On the city-side of the river, a wide sloping bank descended into the water on the inside of the lazy arc of a bend. There, hundreds of fishermen mended their nets while remarkably large coracles bobbed upon the sparkling, wide river. Strange vessels, circular with bowed sides coated in thick, black bitumen, large enough for a dozen men. Behind them were clustered a multitude of suburban houses on the outside of the grand walls that rose above it all and stretched away for miles to either side like the ramparts of fabled Troy. Our way across the river was a pontoon bridge with a sturdy roadway raised high over the anchored boats. Though the floating bridge was thronged with tramping feet, horses and camels, it hardly swayed at all.

"Abdullah," I said, dragging him by the arm as we crossed, "why are you dawdling so?"

His mouth gaped as he stared at the city and I believed first of all that he was overwhelmed by his homecoming.

In fact, he was staring in horror at the heavily armoured riders pushing their horses through the crowds.

They were coming right for us.

"Do not concern yourself," I said to my company as we clustered together once more, "they cannot possibly be coming for us."

We were promptly surrounded, seized, and thrown into gaol.

PART FIVE
BAGHDAD
1258

"YOU STILL WISH TO BECOME an immortal, Stephen?" I said into the darkness.

We were locked in a cell beneath the city. We Christians together in one cell, along with the two Mongols. Hassan, Jalal, and the two other fedayin were somewhere else. Whether they had been given better treatment as fellow Mohammedans or had been taken away and executed as Assassin heretics, I had no idea.

Abdullah had been taken away from us as soon as we were brought within the massive gateway through the grand outer walls. That wall was thicker even than the length of Ashbury manor house.

The riders from the city had surrounded us on the pontoon

road as we crossed to the far side of the Tigris. Magnificently-attired men, all big, fine-looking fellows with shining armour and glistening beards.

"Someone we spoke to along the way," Abdullah had said, "must have run on ahead and sent word that Franks and Assassins were coming."

"Bloody shitting bastard Saracens," I had cursed.

But there had been no point in fighting. We had lost most of our equipment during the journey, through one means or another. I had dropped my shield not far from the mountains and sold my precious mail hauberk weeks after that for a pittance. Even my helm, which I had been determined to keep, had been sold for the price of six scrawny chickens. All I had left of note was my sword and white dagger, and the Saracens of Baghdad had taken those from me, too.

It was not quite the arrival into the city I had been hoping for. Not by any means. Still, it did not dampen my astonishment at the sight of the city itself. All my life, I had heard of how the place was a wonder, was enormous, was beautiful. Soldiers in Outremer had spoken of the impenetrable walls and myriad towers, of how it would take an army from all Christendom to take the city. The Franciscans had spoken of it as something akin to Rome, in that it was the spiritual home of the Saracens, as Rome was to us.

Seeing it with my own eyes, though, demonstrated the limits of my imagination. It was vast. Far bigger than any city I had ever seen. The waters around it were wide and beautiful. The towers and spires jutted over it all like the masts in the ports of Constantinople, only far larger, more numerous and almost as lovely.

Our captors did not treat us with any malice. Perhaps that was Abdullah's doing, for he had jabbered at them so rapidly that I could understand barely one word in ten, and he had spoken incessantly. The leader of the guards had hardly responded at all, and I could not tell if we were being escorted directly to the Vizier himself, or to our deaths.

In the end, we were dragged through busy guard quarters and pushed into a series of cells. The Mohammedans into one cell, and the rest of us into another. Before I was impolitely propelled inside, I saw Abdullah being escorted back up the steps into the light.

"Why would I not want to become an immortal?" Stephen replied. "Surely, that is better for me than being your blood slave, is it not? What shall my fate be now? To be drunk dry by Eva and Thomas and these two heathens, prolonging their lives while ending my own? Perhaps I would rather lose myself in the blood hunger and become a savage like those Ismaili revenants."

I considered turning him, there and then. Giving Thomas and Eva and the Mongols one last drink by draining Stephen, then make him one of them.

But he was right, in a way. What if I was taken, and could not provide Eva with my blood? I had to keep him human so that she might not be driven mad by the hunger.

"If you want me to turn you," I said to him in the darkness, "you must have something to offer. Can you fight for me?"

"So, I am unwise in war. But as I have shown you, I have my mind and my knowledge. I could advise you on the course of action you might take, for example, drawing on the writings of..." He trailed off, perhaps realising he sounded absurd. "I would do whatever I could," he said, quietly.

"Which is nothing," I said. "Nothing of value."

Eva, beside me in the dark, spoke. "Richard."

It was all she said. By her tone, I knew that she was warning me that I was being unnecessarily antagonistic and that I should stop bullying Stephen. She was always the more sensible one. The more rational one, less fuelled by rage, more aware of what was in men's hearts.

One day, not too long after, Eva would be at my side no more and I would miss her presence in every way.

"But why, Stephen?" I asked, softening my tone. "Why would you want this? You know the price. You renounced your vows, did you not? You could yet take a wife. Make some sons."

Thomas cleared his throat but said nothing, while Stephen shuffled around on the cold floor before answering. "I already feel the years slipping through my fingers. There is so much that I could accomplish, yet I am so far from where I need to be."

"And where is that?"

"You speak often of England, Richard," Stephen said. "And that is where my heart lies, also."

"I do?" I asked.

Thomas, Eva, and Stephen chorused that it was, in fact, the case. Eva reached out and patted my leg.

"You said before," Stephen continued, "that you feared what Hulegu could achieve as an immortal king. And rightly so. But what if there was a king who was good?"

Not bullying the man was all very well but I was exhausted, starving and fretting and so had little patience remaining. "You do understand that the blood could never make you into a king, do you not, Stephen?"

He sighed, almost growling in frustration. "You could advise a king. You could advise an entire dynasty, king after king, and shape a kingdom into what it needs to be. Make England into what it could be."

"And what is that?"

"A great kingdom. The greatest kingdom. A kingdom greater even than France."

I burst out laughing. "Your hunger has made you delirious, Stephen." He began to protest but I spoke over him. "It is a laudable fantasy, I am sure. But you are dreaming about something so far away from where we are, that it is meaningless. Stephen, we sit in a gaol, confined in darkness. Show me your worth by freeing us from this place. You do remember why we are all here? We have each sworn to kill William, Hulegu, and the immortal Mongols who serve him. We are here in the hope that we can somehow help the Caliph's army defeat the Mongol hordes and so complete our quest. Even if the Saracens cannot defeat them, we can use the chaos of the siege to creep into Lord Hulegu's tents and execute him there."

"And to save the Christians of Baghdad from slaughter," Thomas said.

I sighed. "If such a thing is possible."

Stephen was hurt, I could hear it in his voice. "I know why we are here."

"Good. Now, we all know what we need to do. But, ignorant and uninspired as I am, I do not know how we might accomplish these things. Can you show me your worth and tell me what we should do, Stephen?"

He was silent.

"Perhaps you could begin by drawing on the wisdom of ancient sages to get us out of this gaol?"

His only answer was a wet sniff.

Thomas cleared his throat, then spoke very softly. His voice gruff with age. "There is no need for you to turn your frustration at your own failures on the young man, Richard."

I was about to turn my anger on the Templar but Stephen finally answered.

"Perhaps we could pray," he said.

"I shall pray with you," Thomas said.

"Ha!" I scoffed. "Do what you wish. I am going to get some sleep."

I do not know how long I slept for. It seemed but a moment before the bolts on the door slammed back and it was thrown open, flooding us in the painful glare of lamplight.

* * *

We were escorted with relative civility by the soldiers who came for us. They wore magnificent armour, all polished and shining. All their cloth was shimmering silk. These men were the personal guard of someone important. I hoped that the Caliph of Baghdad had ten thousand such men in addition to his other troops, but I doubted it.

It was with some considerable relief that I saw Hassan, Jalal, Radi and Raka waiting for us in the antechamber of the gaol, blinking and dishevelled from their incarceration but no worse for wear than we were. A strange thing, to feel so connected to Saracens, to Assassins, men who would have happily seen me and my loved ones dead, had we been strangers to one another. I tried to tell myself that my relief was a result purely of their utility to me as soldiers but going through such an ordeal as our journey across Persia together had helped to strengthen the bond formed in Alamut. What is more, three of them had been changed forever by their ingestion of my blood and I felt a faint sense of responsibility for them. Not as one might feel for their own child but perhaps reminiscent of the accountability one feels when one of your trusty old hounds suddenly mauls the face of a little servant girl.

The Saracen soldiers guarded us closely as they led us through the corridors, beneath covered walkways and across courtyards that resounded with the sound of tinkling fountains. It slowly dawned on me that we were weaving our way deep into a magnificent palace via the routes used by servants rather than guests. The guards barked orders at servants and functionaries we crossed along the way, demanding they stand aside for us. We climbed flights of steps and were finally ordered in through a rather magnificently gilded doorway and into a large audience chamber.

One side was open with a view onto a beautiful courtyard,

with bright green trees sculpted into perfect shapes surrounding a series of small pools. The high ceiling above was supported by slender pillars of pale red marble that arched together in scalloped carvings of intricate patterns. Beneath my filthy, half-rotten shoes, the floor was a gleaming cream and grey marble, polished so highly that it reflected everything above it with remarkable clarity.

A handful of men stood at the edges in small clusters. They had the demeanour of minor lords and senior functionaries but their clothing was very handsome indeed, and I felt utterly out of place in my tattered, Persian serf's robes. I was very aware of how we prisoners radiated a foul stench into that civilised beauty. Some of the Saracens glanced in our direction, disgust, and contempt on their faces.

In the centre, an angry Saracen lord was ruining the harmony of the space by ranting in a loud voice whilst pacing back and forth. His deep blue coat, worn over his patterned cream and white robes, flowed behind him and his huge sleeves flapped as he gesticulated. All of his clothing, including his red slippers, was trimmed in flashing gold. Over his neat, glistening beard and beneath his white and orange headdress, his dark eyes flashed and bulged.

The target of his ire was Abdullah.

Dressed as he was in fine robes, I hardly recognised him at first. And perhaps would not have done were it not for the way he bowed his head and curled his shoulders, withering under the verbal barrage from the older man.

"I assume that is Abdullah's uncle," I said under my breath to Eva. "The vizier."

The captain of the guard escort whipped around and snarled an order at me under his breath. I smiled and nodded, bobbing my head in what I hoped was a subservient manner. As I did so, I took note of how he wore his sword and where his dagger was beneath his sash. Probably I could snatch both of his weapons and cut his throat before he could raise a warning cry.

Our presence was noted by enough of the men in the room that the vizier must have sensed he was losing the attention of his audience and he broke off, turning to us.

The vizier pointed at us across the room and barked something I did not quite catch.

Nevertheless, I cleared my throat, preparing mentally for what arguments I would make when called upon to do so. During the journey to Baghdad, Abdullah, Hassan and I had thought up different points that might sway the vizier into taking immediate action to defend the city, such as describing the astonishing swiftness of the Mongol assaults on the Ismaili castles and stressing the expertise of the siege engines, and the vastness of the forces coming for his city. We had practised for months, refining our arguments with the most emotive examples we could think of, all for this one, vital meeting with the vizier.

So, I was quite astonished when one of the magnificently-attired Saracen lords strode across to Abdullah, seized him quite roughly, and dragged him through the audience chamber across where we stood. The vizier watched, hands on his hips, while his nephew was removed at his instruction, and then he gestured at us again.

This time, I did understand the orders he gave.

"Take them away. And kill them all."

The soldiers guarding us used their shields and weapons to herd us out of the audience chamber, following the lord who had taken Abdullah.

I knew that I would have to take the soldiers' weapons, kill them, and then flee. I thought it likely I could do that but escaping from the palace, and then from the centre of the biggest city in the world would be beyond me alone. If I could free Abdullah, then he could lead me and Eva out. Thomas, too, if possible. And perhaps even Stephen, seeing as he was an Englishman and all.

As a general rule, I have always found that it is better to take action immediately rather than to wait for potentially more favourable conditions. But in the circumstances, I wondered if we might be taken to the outer city, or even outside the outermost walls to some execution field. Eva could sense my tension, and she also began eyeing the soldier's weapons.

After a few turns through narrow and ornate corridors, our captors directed us into a walkway that had a dead end. They stopped behind us and propelled us forward. We were trapped. Cornered.

"Get ready," I said, in French and then in Arabic.

Thomas balled his fists and stepped in front of Eva as if she needed protecting. Hassan and his Assassins spread out along the wall at our backs.

"Wait."

It was the Saracen lord who spoke, in a powerful voice that echoed from the arched ceiling above. He pushed his way through the soldiers and stood between us and them.

"You will not be harmed," the lord said. "I am Feth-ud-Din. I will not kill you."

Thomas whispered. "What does he say?"

I ignored the old knight. My attention was wholly given over to the Saracen lord.

Most men that one meets in life are hiding behind layers of dishonesty. They lie to themselves about their abilities or what their station is in life and what they think it should be. Or they are confused about who they should be, what role in life they should fulfil the most fully. Many are deluded about how they are regarded by other men. Yet, once in a while, one will come into contact with a man who is totally self-possessed. A man who knows who he is, what his purpose in life is, what his true talents are and what he contributes to his society. These men may be a country priest, or the village blacksmith, secure in their position as shepherd for their flock, or father and contributor to their community.

As I laid eyes on the Saracen lord, I knew he was one of those. A man of robust build, with a rider's straight back and the shrewd eyes of a soldier. The stockiness of a strong man growing thicker in early middle age while yet radiating health. There was a stillness to him, a calm centre and a hard, steady gaze.

Though he was an enemy of mine due to his race and faith, and though he looked completely different, his presence brought to mind another man who I had known; William Marshal.

I think I understood the Saracen immediately. Understood who he was.

A moral man.

311

"You would disobey your master?" I asked.

He turned his eyes to me, took in my filth. If he was surprised by a Frank speaking Arabic, he gave no sign of it. Perhaps because I butchered his language so terribly.

"I serve Caliph Al-Musta'sim Billah," he said.

I fixed him with my gaze. "We have come to fight the Mongols. We have come to protect this city."

"Who do you serve?"

"I serve only my oath of vengeance," I said. "Against Hulegu Khan. And his keshig bodyguard and certain men of his court."

He glanced at the others. "And who do these others serve?"

"Me."

I caught Hassan whip his head in my direction but he had the sense not to argue. And anyway, it was not far from the truth, now.

"Why do you bring this one with you?" he pointed at Abdullah.

"He serves me, also," I said. "He served me in Karakorum, and he served me in Alamut. He wants only to save his city from the Mongols. We had word of them during our journey, as their riders ranged about all across these lands. One day, soon, sooner than any of you think, Hulegu Khan will bring his vast army down on you."

He looked at me. "We had word today. Hulegu has left Hamadan. They approach."

I asked Abdullah. "How far is that from here?"

The Saracen lord, this Feth-ud-Din, answered instead. "With so many men, with their wagons and siege weapons? We expect three or four months."

Hassan laughed without mirth. "Whatever you expect, you will be wrong. They will come sooner than that."

"Perhaps," Feth-ud-Din said, revealing only a little distaste at addressing a heretic. "There is another Mongol and allied army coming from the north. I believe they will seek to cut off armies coming to our aid from the west."

"You are expecting help?" I asked. "From the Mamluks in Egypt? From Damascus?"

"The Caliph has requested aid," Feth-ud-Din said.

"Will they come?"

His face alone told the story.

"Is that why you want us?" I asked him and glanced at Hassan. "You seek allies. Any allies, even heretics like the remaining Assassins in Syria." I almost laughed. "You are even willing to consider asking the Kingdom of Jerusalem for aid, through us?" I gestured at Thomas, who could not understand what we were saying.

"I will do anything, explore every path, pay any price, to save the City of Peace," Feth-ud-Din said.

"We will help you," I said at once. "If you swear to help us to kill Hulegu."

He looked at us, one after the other. He must have seen a strange group of people. Franks, heretics, Mongols, all thin and filthy.

Feth-ud-Din snapped his fingers at one of his men and commanded something too rapidly for me to catch. The man handed over a dagger and Feth-ud-Din held it up balanced on the fingers of one hand.

"Your weapons were taken. My men recovered this from a guardsman who was already attempting to sell it for a considerable price. It is fine work. Armenian, is it not?"

"It is mine," I said.

He pursed his lips at my impudence and his men stirred beside him but after a moment he inclined his head and held it out to me. "Indeed."

I took it, bowed, and thanked him, for it was truly a noble gesture. "If you return our weapons also, we shall all fight for this city, and we will cut off the head of the snake."

"I will keep you safe in my home," he said, shaking his head. "And you will begin drafting letters asking for aid."

He was desperate indeed.

Thomas and I knew that all Christian states would rejoice at the destruction of Baghdad and would find the notion of helping them in any way to be laughable. Indeed, the Christian kingdoms of Georgia and Armenia formed a large contingent of the army approaching from the north.

But we went through the motions while we regained our strength and health in the enormous, opulent home of the powerful general Feth-ud-Din, hidden away from Vizier Ibn al-Alqami. We wrote letters that were passed to messengers who were to rush to Acre, Antioch, Tripoli, and even Constantinople. Thomas was sincere in his pleas to the Templars, writing on behalf of the Christian population of Baghdad even though they were Syrians and other peoples.

"Will your brothers and the Master not be confused," I said

to him, "when they read both your letters and reports of your death?"

Thomas waved it away. "Like as not William of Rubruck is still in Karakorum. And if he has returned, I doubt his first concerns will be writing to the Master of the Order of my fate. Even if he has done so, it is likely his report of my death will be disbelieved when they read my letters."

More likely they will consider the letters a Saracen or Assassin trick and so ignore them.

But I said nothing and he sent off his letters to Castle Pilgrim, the White Castle, Tortosa, and further afield to Cyprus and beyond.

And in the end, it was all too late.

The great military minds of the caliphate confidently predicted that the Mongols would take four months to surround the city so that the siege would begin in early spring. In fact, it took less than six weeks. By late January 1258, the Mongol vanguard approached from the east.

* * *

Living in that great lord's home had chafed on me. The Saracens, even the soldiers and servants, considered themselves to be above me and all of us, because we were Christians, heathens or heretics, and their continued condescension for those six weeks had driven me into a tightly-woven ball of frustration. Thomas also had been driven close to mad by the continued proximity of his lifelong mortal enemies.

So it was with some excitement that I urged our host for news of the recent expedition of his forces. For Feth-ud-Din had returned from a few days away from the city and then summoned me to his private quarters even before he had washed or changed his clothes. There had been a steady, light rain for two days and his robes were spattered in mud thrown up by the hooves of galloping horses. He first wanted to know if any of us had received word from the messengers we had sent off just six weeks earlier. It was absurd to hope for such a thing and revealed the desperation of the man. I ignored his question and asked my own.

"You rode out to meet them?" I asked Feth-ud-Din. "What happened?"

"We were forbidden to take forces from the city," Feth-ud-Din said, in response to my question. He looked exhausted. His eyes wide and staring, rimmed with red and his household guards could not hide their concern for their master.

"Was that an order from the Caliph?" I asked. "Or the Vizier?"

He chose not to answer, which was confirmation in itself. The word in the household was that Feth-ud-Din and some other commanders had defied the order and taken a huge force out to stop the Mongols before they even reached the massive walls of Baghdad. I wondered if the man who sheltered us would now fall to internal politics before the battle itself began.

"You have done as I asked and written to your lords in Dar al-Harb," he said while his servants hovered around him. "Before the siege begins, you may take your people and go."

He turned away as if expecting me to hitch up my robes and

run from the room.

"We do not wish to go," I said. "We want to fight. Why do your people not?"

He turned on me, full of rage. I was sure he would draw his sword. "We did fight. At Ba'qubah. Two days ago. Our men won a victory against the Mongol vanguard. Twenty thousand of our men smashed them, drove them back."

I resisted scoffing at his supposed victory. I could well imagine it. The Mongols feigning retreat or simply withdrawing and the foolish Saracens calling it a triumph.

But it was far worse.

"Then why do you look as if you suffered a defeat, my lord?" I asked.

He did not turn away. "We took the position that they had held and fortified our camp for the night. Ba'qubah is low ground. Somehow, in the darkness, they destroyed the levees and dams. They massed their forces on the high ground and cut off our retreat. Most drowned in the flood waters."

I was astonished. The Mongols had somehow baited the Saracens into a trap set on their own home ground. I had never heard the like of it.

"How many men did you lose?"

Finally, his strength of will failed and he turned away. "Fifteen thousand. Perhaps more. Mostly cavalry. Some of our strongest forces. Survivors are yet trailing back but they are so few."

A true disaster. There was nothing to be said about it.

"What will now be the plan to defend the city?" I said.

"The Caliph has given orders that citizens be armed and

trained. Also, that the walls be repaired where they have been neglected."

I could barely believe it. The Mongols were a day or two away and there was no time for these orders to be enacted. It was farcical.

There was perhaps still time to flee but Hulegu and William were close, and I could not in good conscience run away from my oath yet again.

A city under siege was a dangerous place and that danger was not only from the enemy beyond the walls. The populous would be in the highest state of anxiety, full of well-founded fear and to be an obvious foreigner at such a time would invite attack. I knew from experience that a mob of angry citizens could be almost as deadly as a horde of Mongols.

"If my people leave your home," I said, "we will be set upon by the people of this city. Let my people fight for you. Equip us, as you would your own men, let us fight by their side when the assault comes."

General Feth-ud-Din agreed, ordered his secretary to organise our equipment, and then dismissed me. His servants led him away so that he could bathe, and he seemed already like he was broken. Every time the Mongols fought, their enemies were left stunned in this way. Disbelief, their world shattered by a foe that seemed centuries ahead of them.

I recalled something that Thomas had said to me, a long time before, on the steppe.

These Tartars. They are masters of war. And we are children.

Four columns of Mongols and their allies converged on Baghdad. In every direction to the horizon, enemy forces filled the fields and villages. The city of Baghdad may have been the largest in the world, but it had been surrounded by the largest armies on Earth.

One army occupied what had been a commercial quarter, on the west bank of the Tigris. Hulegu's force established itself in the Shiite suburbs beyond the eastern walls, and the Sunnis inside the city spoke in bitterness of their easy capitulation.

The rattling of their innumerable carts, the bellowing of camels and cattle, the neighing of horses, and the wild battle-cry, were so overwhelming as to render inaudible the conversation of the people inside the city. It was a sound like the continuous crashing of a vast wave against a rocky shore.

In less than two days, the enemy dug a ditch and rampart to protect their siege engines from attack by the Saracens within the walls. No such attack was forthcoming.

On 30th January 1258, the bombardment of the city began.

I gathered my people together on a section of the inner eastern walls just before it all started. There was a pause, a lull from both sides as if they were both taking a deep breath before plunging onward to death.

Thomas was remarkably unhappy. I know that he was cursing the day that he ever met me, that he ever asked me to accompany him on his quest to Batu.

"All that is left for us is to protect the Christians of this city," he said.

Hassan and his men, Abdulla, Orus and Khutulun all looked at me and I felt the pull between them and us. Eva and Stephen were aware of the gulf within our company, even as Thomas remained oblivious, staring out at the mass of forces.

"Our agreement," I said to Thomas, "between all of us here, was to work together to bring about the death of Hulegu, William my brother, and the immortals that they have made."

Thomas dragged his attention away from the cacophony beyond the walls. "I mean no offence when I say this. But how can we hope to carry that out, now? In the face of this." He gestured unnecessarily at the Mongols. "There is no chance of us reaching him."

Stephen, keen as ever to find a solution despite his fear, spoke up. "Perhaps Hulegu will enter the city when it falls?"

I looked to Khutulun. Her understanding of French had come on leaps and bounds. Still, she furrowed her brow as I rephrased the question.

"Hulegu never come here," she said, shaking her head. "Inside here? No, no."

Orus agreed with her, and I did, too.

"It will be madness when it happens," I said to Stephen. "A city of this size would take weeks to subdue." He stared at me, nodding slowly. "Do you understand what I mean when I say subdue, Stephen? I mean that they will kill every living soul."

"I know that," Stephen said, bristling.

"The only people who may just live through it," Thomas said, "is the Christians. We all know this. Does anyone deny it? Well, then, perhaps we should help to protect them in order to help bring that about. And, they may then even shelter our friends here who are not Christian."

Hassan rolled his eyes. "I will not hide amongst the Christians. Nor will my men. And neither would they protect us."

"I do not believe," Abdullah said, "that the Mongols will spare the Christians."

Thomas was about to argue but I had heard it from both sides a dozen times already for weeks, so I cut him off before they all started again.

"William may come into the city," I said.

They all looked at me.

"He loves death. He loves chaos. He creates it, and he is drawn to it. It is no accident that he is here." I nodded out at the masses of enemy. "He helped to make this happen, did he not? He would not be able to control himself while the blood flows within. Perhaps he will bring some of the immortals with him."

For the first time in months, Hassan smiled. "We can lay an ambush for them. These buildings all around are ideal. We can lay in wait upon the roofs, inside upper windows. Come at them from the front and rear, and from above."

His grin spread between all of us as we imagined catching our enemies in an enclosed space.

"This city has how many gates?" Eva said. "And how many breaches will they make with their stone throwers? There are hundreds of thousands of people within these walls, and a hundred thousand or even more outside. Richard, you know that I want to kill him as much as you do, but we will never find him amongst the chaos."

I growled and clenched my fists, and my teeth. Frustrated at every turn, for weeks and months and years now. "There must be a way."

"What about..." Stephen started, staring out at the Mongols. "No... never mind."

"Do not be so bloody coy, Stephen. Out with it."

"I was wondering if you could make a banner," he said. "Something that William might recognise. Something that would draw him to you. Or to where you wanted him to go. But I recall that you do not have any personal emblem that would be known to him, and any other possible symbol such as a cross would only serve to bring the soldiers of both sides down upon us in a rage."

His mind worked in ways that mine never could. So many times now, his suggestions had helped me, from Karakorum to Alamut and in a thousand ways ever since. It annoyed me that a man such as he had a wit so superior to my own but I could deny it to myself no longer. He was useful to have around.

And we were about to face an assault more terrible and more massive than anything I had ever known. Perhaps more than the world had ever known, for when before had such a force ever been assembled? We had done what we could to teach him the sword and how to use a shield but it was not his forte and in the face of even the most useless Mongol, Stephen would be instantly slaughtered.

There remained one way to grant him the speed, strength and heartiness that might just give him the chance to survive. It would also bind him to me, or so I believed, in a way that would allow me access to the wisdom and knowledge that I sorely lacked.

"Stephen," I said, placing my hand heavily on his shoulder. "Do you still wish to become an immortal?"

His mouth smiled but his eyes were filled with hunger. I wonder if it was the first flush of what he would become, or if I had simply seen his mask slip. He had told me his ambitions for England, for the English people, to make us into a great nation that would rival or exceed France. Such an ambition might be suitable for a king but for a lowly jumped up villain like Stephen it was gross pridefulness and certainly sinful in the extreme. Eva had told me Stephen was a wolf, that he would enthusiastically partake in cannibalism for the sake of ambition. All the warnings were there but out of selfishness, I ignored the unease that I felt.

Hassan stepped forward. "It is time for me, also."

I nodded. He had done well to last so long while maintaining his authority, being as he was so much weaker in body than Jalal, Radi and Raka, the men who he commanded. But then, the Assassins were a highly disciplined people who obeyed their superiors without question. An admirable trait in general but one which had helped enable their destruction.

As much as I did not wish to bring more blood-drinkers into the world, promising it to each of them came easy after I had already granted the Gift to so many. Not only that, as I looked out over the uncountable multitude of savages covering the plains all around, I did not expect all of us to survive the coming assault.

And so it was on that night that I turned Stephen and Hassan.

I made Stephen swear an oath to serve me for the rest of his life but even as he dutifully repeated my words, I recalled how easily he had thrown off his life as a brother of the Order of Saint Francis.

As for Hassan, I asked him only to follow my orders until Hulegu and the immortal Mongols were dead. He also agreed, and I remembered how he would draw on taqiyya, and promise me one thing while intending another. What a sad thing it was, I reflected, that I had ended up surrounded by such men so far from my homeland, a place where oaths were binding and held a sacred power.

For half the night, I sat watching their bodies fight the blood within them. For a time, Stephen appeared so pale and still and cold I thought he would not make it. But their hearts were strong and at sunrise they were welcomed into the strange brotherhood of the blood that I had created. The Assassins knelt before their lord, while Stephen was clapped on the back by all of us. Khutulun kissed him hard on the mouth and he blushed like a maid.

And the next day, the siege continued apace.

The Mongols demolished homes, farms, commercial buildings in the suburbs beyond the walls and used the stones as ammunition. They even uprooted the massive plantations of palm trees and flung entire tree trunks at the walls, and over them. The trebuchets were enormous. The largest machines I had ever seen, indeed, that any of us had ever seen.

The Saracen military response was appalling. The thousands of soldiers and militia inside the city were struck with inactivity or carried out ineffective training that only served to demonstrate their poor morale. We urged anyone who would listen to ride out and make assaults on the enemy positions. Burning the enemy equipment would slow them down, and we knew that the Saracens had naphtha and incendiary weapons. And many captains and soldiers would agree with us to our faces. Yet they would do nothing. Indeed, it seemed that the soldiers grew ever less visible on the walls and I suspected that they were either hiding in their quarters or even deserting within the city. That is, throwing off their armour and slipping away back to their families in the vain hope of avoiding violence.

It was a failure of leadership, of course. The Saracen soldiers were perfectly capable of mounting a sustained defence, if only they could be directed to do so. They claimed that there had been fifty thousand soldiers in the city, and the place was so vast that it was certainly possible that had been the case before up to twenty thousand of them were drowned north of the city. But the thirty thousand remaining could have formed a core, and with citizens armed and organised, they could have put up stout resistance even in the face of such a multitude of savages outside.

But there was not the will to do it.

For instance, for many days while under bombardment, the Mongol mounted archers rode in their hundreds to the walls and shot arrows over the tops of them into the streets. Tied to these arrows were tightly rolled pieces of paper, upon which messages had been written in good Arabic. These messages promised safety to the people of the city if only they would surrender.

In response, the Saracens loosed a few half-hearted volleys back at the horsemen each time but that was all. No one organised a force to seize these messages before they could be read.

"Give me a horse and I will ride out and fight them," I said, to the captains at the gates, not because I would actually do it but in the hope of shaming them into taking action. Of course, I was ignored, or driven off. I could see in their eyes that they had already lost the battle in their minds.

The city was battered, uninterrupted, day after day, for an entire week. A bombardment of stones, and explosives that shook the walls and the people to their roots. Those outer walls and buildings slowly crumbled, and so did the remnants of the people's will.

Escape from the city was impossible. The wide Tigris, flowing as it did through the outskirts of the city, appeared to present the best hope of slipping away. But everyone could see how the river was blocked upstream by the pontoons that the Mongols had built so their troops could flow between both sides of the city. Downstream, it was plain that the shores were patrolled by masses of horsemen who certainly watched closely for people to try to float away by one means or another.

Every day, the caliph or someone serving him sent messengers out from the gate. The rumour was that the caliph was now begging to be allowed to surrender the city. But every day, the messengers returned and the bombardment continued without let up. The caliph had left it too long. Hulegu, I was sure, would never now be turned from the blood-letting that awaited him once the machines of his enslaved Cathay engineers broke through the walls.

The focus of the bombardment was on the eastern wall.

That eastern portion of the city was quite distinct and

separated from the rest of Baghdad by the River Tigris that snaked in between in a pronounced curve. Although the walls were said to be over a hundred years old, they were three miles in length, massively built and studded with strong towers. It was not a weak point in the defences. For all their faults as a people, the Saracen builders had designed it well. Joining the eastern section of the city and the rest was three bridges. So even if the Mongols took the east, they would still have to fight across the river. No easy feat.

And the eastern part of the city would surely be fought for. It was newer than the core of the city and contained a beautiful royal palace, and their law college known as a madrassa, as well as the ubiquitous canals and holy buildings.

Masses of Mongol forces converged on that eastern side behind their massive counterweight trebuchets. The troops camped in good order, waiting, and waiting for the walls to crumble, for the towers to fall.

* * *

"What if all this focus on the eastern wall is merely to divert our attention away from the real direction of the assault?" Stephen suggested as we planned our ambush in the shade of a row of ornate low palms by a narrow canal.

It was a cold day for the lands of Babylon but perfectly comfortable for an Englishman. Indeed, it was warm enough to be comfortable sitting on the paved floor in no more than long

Saracen tunics. It would have been a peaceful place, but for the garrison troops sitting and standing in groups all around, just as we were, many in a state of high agitation.

There was also the regular resounding boom of projectiles smacking into the massive, thick walls out of sight to the northeast about a mile away from us.

"Why break a wall," Hassan said, "only to ignore the breach?"

"To concentrate the Saracen defences here, so the walls elsewhere can be scaled at will before the defenders can cross the city." Stephen was rightly suspicious of Mongol trickery. "Diversionary assaults are a common tactic, are they not?"

"That is true," I said, well aware that tens of thousands of men surrounded each side of the city. Any one of the enemy armies would be enough to overwhelm the Saracens within, if they did it correctly. "Let us take a look at it again, shall we?"

Abdullah unrolled the map of the city that he had procured for us and spread it on the floor between us. It was by no means a highly refined document and was seventy years old but it served its purpose well enough. The Tigris snaked and arched through the map, dividing the eastern quarter from the ancient Round City beyond the western bank of the river.

The Round City had three concentric walls, cut through by four roadways leading out from the centre, with gates in the walls. The gates and roads divided the city into quarters, and each gate pointed in the direction of the lands for which it was named. There was the Syrian Gate on the northwest, which led to Damascus. The Basra Gate opposite would lead a man along the route of the Tigris. Southwest was the Kufa Gate, named after the great city on the banks of the Euphrates. And northeast, closest to the river and the eastern quarter beyond, was the Khurasan Gate that led to Persia.

A man travelling into the Round City would proceed along a plumb-straight roadway, walled upon either side, all the way into the open centre. Along the road, he would pass through three gatehouses, in order to pass through the three concentric walls. These gates were like small forts in themselves. Like squat towers. Passing through them was like entering a cool, dark tunnel. There were doors at either ends of the tunnel, with an iron portcullis in the middle. An attacking army would have to fight through that corridor, while defenders above could shoot arrows and throw God-knows what else down on the poor bastards fighting their way along it, step-by-step.

No doubt the Mongols would do it, though. They might force their prisoners through first, then send their Turkomen and Georgians in. Hulegu had enough men to spend a thousand on each gatehouse.

The Round City was a marvel of a design, truly. A work of mathematical precision. Easy for an engineer to draw upon parchment, I suppose, but the Saracens had actually made the thing from stone. And the Round City was vast, filled with homes, mosques, palaces, gardens, pools.

"Where are we now?" I asked.

Abdullah tapped a point across the river in the eastern quarters. "Here. You see, this is the road to the bridge. On the other side is the Palace of Khuld, then the Round City via the Khurasan Gate."

"Stephen? Did you survey the bridges?"

"As they are pontoon bridges, they can be easily cut if the Mongols attempt to cross by them from the east and so we would find ourselves cut off. We should remain on the western side of the Tigris when the attack proper comes."

"The eastern city will almost certainly be attacked first," I said. "William will come. I believe it. Like a feral dog to a carcass, he will be drawn inward and then we shall draw him to us. They will breach the walls in one place or many on the east." I jabbed my finger into the eastern quarter, where we sat. "Where is the square where we lay our ambush?"

"It is here," Abdullah said, placing his finger between the outer and middle wall of the Round City.

Hassan let out a long sigh. "It is a wonderful place to lay an ambush, Richard. But getting away from there will surely be almost impossible."

"I am certain you have it right, Hassan," I said. "But how likely is it any of us can escape from this city with our lives?"

It was not something we had spoken of overly much, but we all knew it was the truth. Eva caught my eye for a moment with a look that was full of meaning. Fear, sadness. Perhaps even hope, or relief that we would at least die together.

Hassan coughed and stroked his beard. "As long as Hulegu Khan is dead, I shall die with peace in my heart."

"Fine, fine," I said. "Is the square close enough to the road that William or Hulegu could be drawn into it? Could they see a banner that we might hold aloft?"

Eva nodded. "A banner could be seen from there if the riders can see over the walls that run beside the road. We could make it more certain if the main road was blocked by something between the outer gatehouse and the middle one, then our square by the madrassa and the palace would be the most obvious route to ride through to go around the blockage."

"Why not go the other way around a barrier?" I asked, tracing it with my finger on the map.

She had thought of that, of course. "A man can get through on foot but the archways in the wall on that side of the road are too low for riders. And Hulegu and William would be mounted, would they not?"

Of course.

"We draw his company into the square between the palace and the madrasa, yes?" I asked. "Thomas, Abdullah, did you find a way to the roof of the palace?"

The Templar nodded, a smile forming on his lips. "You would not believe it but there are no great lords within, now. Just Saracen soldiers lounging about. A few captains challenged us but Abdullah shouted them down, saying we served Feth-ud-Din and he would have them castrated if they obstructed us."

"Good man," I said. "And it overlooks the courtyard?"

"A section of the wall, perhaps twelve or fifteen feet high. As high as that tree over there with the dead palm leaf. But with clear view down into the square, yes, good for archers and perfect for javelins."

"Could you jump down from that height?" I asked.

"I would rather not," he said.

"I could," Khutulun said. "So could Orus." She muttered a

translation to her brother, who nodded in confirmation.

"And it is possible to block the exits from the square?" I asked Eva.

"There are five ways in at ground level. Three pathways from the streets, and one leading into the madrasa."

"That makes four," I said.

She nodded. "A corner of the square overlooks a pool. There is a fence that I doubt any horse could jump."

I looked at Hassan as I spoke because he had described how his fedayin would carry out such a murder. "We let his first soldiers through, then block the exits behind them, trapping Hulegu, William, and the others within. We attack from all sides."

"Assuming Hulegu comes into the city," Thomas said. "Which he will likely not."

"Assuming William comes at all," Stephen said.

"And the other immortals of Hulegu's court," Eva pointed out.

"Indeed, all of it is based on the assumption that William and Hulegu's immortals will enter the Round City at all," Stephen said. "And if they do, that they will use the Khurasan Gate."

I snatched the map from the ground and rolled it up, growling at them. "We have thought it through as well as can be. Do not lose faith, you doubting fools. All will be well. Trust me, I have done such things many times. This plan will work perfectly."

In fact, it would be a disaster.

* * *

The trebuchets slammed ton after ton of rock into the high, thick eastern wall. Stones in the wall shook with the impacts, then cracks between them began to form. Chunks of mortar and sandstone were chipped away, piece by piece, and the base at points along the long wall began to accumulate piles of rubble.

Enemy formations continued to ride close to the city and rain their arrows down onto the defenders up on the walls.

The Abbasid soldiers fought back from the wall, shooting arrows and throwing javelins. But the Mongol's Turkomen infantry were sent forward to collect the massive piles of rubble and bring them back out beyond the suburbs to the irrigated fields where the trebuchets sat. Even though hundreds were killed in the process, the Turkomens were so numerous, and they worked so tirelessly, that they constructed a number of stone platforms out in the wet fields.

In less than a day, the trebuchets were brought forward onto these platforms. Hassan and Abdullah said it was to provide a solid base to spread the weight of the machines and stop them from sinking in the friable, fertile earth. Stephen suggested the extra height to which they were raised would increase the range and elevation of the projectiles the machines threw. I pretended to be unimpressed.

"Have you ever seen a siege progress this rapidly?" Thomas asked me on the third day.

"I have never seen anything like any of this," I admitted.

I had ordered that my people stick together at all times. The common inhabitants of the city were suffering incredible fear, and although we were all dressed as Abbasid soldiers and Baghdad housed people from all over the world, some of us were quite obviously foreigners. That was not a safe thing to be in such a situation and we had to deal with everything from angry glances to arguments that had to be diffused, to being cornered by garrison troops and forcing our way free. Eva and Khutulun kept their faces and bodies hidden but still they were subjected to hungry looks every time we were on the streets. While we could not be all together all the time, I felt safest when I had Abdullah with us, because giving the plebeians an aristocratic tongue-lashing turned out to be one of his greatest talents.

Beyond the wall, the barbarians swarmed amongst the partially ruined suburbs that lined the crisscrossing canals and channels. The conurbations thinned and became the homes of the agricultural people in the distance, where the thousands upon thousands of barbarians had dug their camps.

"The benighted bastards are in a rare hurry," Thomas said, shaking his head in wonder.

Enemy forces swarmed forward, under attack from the walls. A group of dozens and then hundreds began to form about half a mile along the wall from us. We could not see clearly, because of the towers and the buildings of the suburbs blocking the view. But we pointed out to each other the sight of ladders and ropes being brought forward.

"They're making an attempt at the walls," I said.

"Don't think much of the Saracens, do they," Eva muttered.

I knew what she meant. Chances of storming a well-manned

wall were very low unless the defenders were to break and give up the position.

"They are used to their enemies running in terror," I said. "The bloody bastards."

"We should rejoice," Thomas muttered very softly. "We should praise God that this, the greatest city of the Saracens, is destroyed."

I glanced along the wall to where Abdullah stood, watching the attack with a face full of anguish. He still had family within the city, and although they had disowned him, he must surely have felt the terror that we all feel when our loved ones are in danger. His mother was old and useless to the Mongols. His brothers were minor functionaries and would surely be slaughtered. His sisters' husbands would also be killed, and the women would be taken as slaves and forcibly married to some filthy barbarian, treated horribly and would be expected to bear him children until she died. If she was lucky.

"It is good that the city falls," I said to Thomas. "And we are thankful to God. But where will these demons be stopped? Do you believe that Damascus will stand where Baghdad falls? Will Acre withstand this army?" I gestured at the uncountable horde that camped in companies as far as eyes could see. "Or even a quarter of it?"

"God will not allow Christendom to fall," he said.

I nodded. "As He did not allow Jerusalem to fall? As He protected Spain?"

The Templar grew uncomfortable. "We must be worthy of His protection."

I sighed. Theology was beyond me. "I hope He can see we're doing our bloody best."

One of the towers far to the north along the wall flung a smoking projectile at the massed companies near the base of the wall. It slammed in amongst them and a great belch of flame bloomed to engulf dozens of men. It roared, like some demon. I imagined the agony, the screams. The survivors streamed away in panic, horses bolting. The Saracens on the wall cheered and Abdullah pounded a fist on the stonework.

"Can we not find a way to fight?" Abdullah asked, turning to me with tears in his eyes. "We could help fend them off, could we not?"

I felt a momentary urge to do just that. There was the smell of blood in the wind and then smoke with the mouth-watering scent of burning flesh. It would feel good to kill a few Mongols or their allies. Or Saracens, for that matter. But that was all a distraction.

"We have discussed this many a time," I said to Abdullah. "We must stay the course. Our revenge is close at hand. Come. Watching this does nothing for us. There is still much to prepare. Come, Abdullah, come away."

After less than a week, three breaches were created in the eastern walls and multiple towers fell.

The Mongols attacked the eastern walls by climbing up the rubble piles at the base of the breaches and the Abbasid garrison defended as best they could. Using their poorest troops first, the enemy sent hundreds at a time with ladders and ropes to scale the slopes and the standing walls at the sides of them, even while the trebuchets continued to send their stones crashing into the walls and towers. Most assaults were turned back with relative ease, with thousands of arrows pouring down on the Turkomens and Uyghurs. There were Saracens employed, also, many of them formerly of the Khwarazmian lands centred on Samarkand but also former allies from closer to Baghdad were employed. The Atabeg of Mosul and the Atabeg of Shiraz sent armies from their cities against the wall. Khorasani and Turanian troops threw themselves up the ladders, determined to break into the greatest city in the world and loot the caliph three ways from Sunday.

I never understood the enmity that the Sunnites and Shiites had for each other. At least, not until hundreds of years later when Christendom was engulfed in decades of warfare between the Catholic and Protestant nations. But it seemed Shiite cities in the province like Basra, Kufa, and Najaf had thrown open their gates to the Mongols and then sent detachments to join in the destruction of their overlord, the Caliph. This made it even more dangerous within Baghdad for Shiites like Abdullah and we kept off the streets as much as possible. Fights broke out all over the city, and looting had already begun, especially between the different sects and tribes. It had always been somewhat rare to see women in public but now we began to hear them, wailing in despair from behind the walls of their homes.

Thomas urged us to take shelter with the Christians, which we did after the fifth day of the bombardment. We made the move into the Christian quarter under the cover of darkness so that we would be less likely to be seen and challenged by a mob. Still, it was a tense night crossing the city with our belongings which we had begged and stolen from our former hosts.

Jews and Christians lived in the city as dhimmis, that is as second-class citizens who paid an excessive tax to demonstrate their utter subjugation to the Mohammedans. I found the very fact that they lived in such a state to be contemptible but my companions had great pity for the Christians. They were not proper Christians, following the Roman law. They were mostly Syriacs, supposedly subject to the Patriarch of Antioch, but there were also Coptics from Egypt and even some who followed the laws of the Church of Armenia.

Within the homes and churches of the Christians, the people were feeling quietly optimistic. Of the many thousands of messages shot over the walls of the city had been messages swearing the archons—that is, the priests—should feel comforted as they were not fighting against Hulegu and so would not be harmed when the city fell, nor would their families be harmed or their property damaged.

"You cannot believe his lies," I said to them when I heard this. "Hulegu would say and do anything in order to win."

"Do not frighten them, Richard," Thomas hissed at me. "They must have hope."

"A false hope is no hope at all, but self-deception," I said, grandly and loudly so that the priests who had welcomed us would hear me well.

"Who are you to say whether this hope or that is false?" Thomas pointed out.

He was right but I did not wish to concede the point in front of those people, who chose to live so utterly at the mercy of the Saracens. Mohammedans who wished to see all of Christ's

338

children dead, converted, or subjugated. Perhaps I was angry because I had put myself in precisely that very same condition.

"We shall see," I said.

Only a day later, a rumour spread that the Vizier had ordered the garrison to cease resisting, to cease their defence of the eastern wall and to return to their homes. Some said, no, the order was only that they should cease throwing stones down on the attackers because they would only be launched back up again.

Whether the order was real or not—and it certainly sounded like hysterical nonsense to me—it was believed by those men who wished to believe it. And so many hundreds or thousands abandoned their posts along the eastern wall.

"It will surely happen quickly now," I said, as we watched the troops file back across the pontoon bridges over the Tigris and into the Round City and to other parts.

There was so much more they could have done. So many more tactics they could have employed. But every soul in the city, and for a hundred miles all around, must surely have felt the inevitability of it all. Any civilian east of the Tigris with any sense in their head fled across the river, away from the coming danger.

And then, one morning, the bombardment ended. The Mongols had captured the entire eastern wall and the eastern quarter, filling it with their shouts of victory. We were miles away across the city by that point but I could imagine them pouring down the stairs of the wall, and over the piles of rubble where they had crumbled the tops of the walls, and into that beautiful quarter.

They sat there, poised to take the rest of Baghdad.

Across the river, the garrison manned the barricades between the beautiful buildings and waited for the hammer blow to fall. Waited for the thousands of barbarians to come streaming across the river to murder them all and seize their families.

And we waited, my people and I. Waited to lay our ambush and to spring our trap.

But there the Mongols and their allies waited, also, occupying the eastern quarter of the city as if their work was already done. And gradually, the city surrendered itself. The garrison, the nobility, and the scholars. They lost their backbones and their minds.

"The rest of the city is ready to fall, why do they not attack?" Stephen said, angry at what he saw as the savages' lack of reason. But it was just that Stephen did not understand. Brutal savages they may have been, but they were still men. No one wants to fight if he does not have to.

Almost no one.

"There is no doubt now," I said. "The city cannot resist. There is no hope left for the Saracens. The Mongols hope to draw them out without losing any more of their own men, which they certainly would if they forced a crossing of the river."

"So," Stephen said, with hope twinkling in his eyes, "so, the city may now fall peacefully?"

I laughed in his face. "No."

Hulegu sent messages to the commanders of the garrison troops in the city. The messages said to lay down their arms and abandon their posts. The captains could not believe their luck, and they pretended to be saddened to be leaving their home, and their families.

But I could see the relief on their faces.

"Do not go," I said to the soldiers near to the quarters that my company had taken over.

Hassan and the others urged them, too. Abdullah begged them, that they did not understand the Mongols. That they had no honour like civilised men had honour. That their promises meant nothing, that they had massacred entire cities before, many times.

It did no good. No man would listen to us. Why would they? We were all foreigners, and Abdullah was an exiled Shiite academician.

Besides, they did not want to believe it.

It was a false hope, I knew it. But it was all they had.

"God is punishing the Saracens," Stephen said. "It is the only reason they would march to their deaths like this."

"Praise God," Thomas said.

I suppose it was a good thing that the Mohammedans were going to be slaughtered but it did not feel like it. Their idiocy made me feel nauseated.

And so we watched from the eastern end of the southern wall, at the Tigris, as they marched out, unarmed, in their thousands. Perhaps thirty thousand men, a great army of men, taking hours to pass through the gates. They marched smartly in their companies and were escorted away from the city by the Mongols out to the fields in the west. Each company was divided up from the others and forced into tight groups by the Mongol forces.

"They handle groups of men with such ease," I muttered,

realising it for the first time as I looked out at the formations in the distance beyond the city.

"This is how it is when they fight on the field of battle," Thomas said.

Hassan nodded. "They are herders by profession, by nature. On the steppe, they manage animals from a very young age. There are many more animals than people out there in the grasslands. They round up sheep or horses. And they hunt, all together, riding out beyond the sight of each other before turning and driving all the game in an area into an ever-tighter circle. Like a noose tightening, do you see? And so they gather up a great multitude of beasts all together and there they slaughter them."

I felt sick as he said it, for that described how the Saracens were being herded, into small groups of a few hundred or a thousand. Surrounded on all sides by horsemen, and dismounted infantry with spears.

And then the killing started. Arrows first, in their many thousands, rising and falling in clouds. Then the survivors were speared and any remaining men were cut down with sword and dagger. Their screams and the jeering of the Mongols was like the crashing of some hellish ocean.

They made short work of it. Thirty thousand men killed in a single afternoon.

It was butchery, not war.

Thomas was quite right, and it was true that the Saracens were my enemy, and that they would have slaughtered a Christian city in just such a manner, given the opportunity. Still, it was difficult not to feel a great pity for their ignominious, pathetic end.

The groaning and wailing from inside the city was as loud as a hurricane, and people tore at their hair and clothing and they howled in despair. There was yet half a million men, women and children inside Baghdad, and the Mongols were still outside or perched high upon the eastern wall.

After another two days of negotiation, the Caliph was persuaded to come out himself, along with his three sons and three thousand courtiers. Along with them, thousands beyond counting of citizens attempted to surrender also.

The Caliph was taken prisoner by Hulegu, as they had agreed. As were his sons, and the members of the court, those great nobles and their families who stood shivering in their finery, subjugated before their new masters.

As for the ordinary citizens who had hoped and expected to receive the same mercy, they were rounded up just as the soldiers had been, and then they were slaughtered. Some of the women and girls were dragged away from the mass slaughter, but most were savagely murdered. The Mongol method for mass extermination was like some unholy device, an infernal machine that churned through people with all the relentless efficiency of a millstone grinding corn.

So much death.

And then, finally, on 13th February, the order was given to sack the city.

* * *

343

It was a risk. Staying inside the city as it was sacked. There would be thousands of Mongol and allied savages losing their minds in an orgy of destruction.

We staked out our territory inside the Round City, using for our fort the former home of a senior scholar of Mohammedan jurisprudence, located between the palace and the madrasa, and we fought to defend it. The scholar had fled weeks before and his home had already been quietly looted before the Mongols even attacked the walls. But we repaired the building, cleaning away the damage and fixing most of the doors and windows shut. Over a few days, we brought in what provisions we could barter and steal. I did not know how long we would have to wait to attract Hulegu or William but I knew that roaming the streets during the height of the destruction would be akin to murdering oneself.

The building had a narrow tower in one corner, as many of the prestigious buildings did. Inside, a steep stair around the inside edge of the tower led to a top floor with large arched windows. Abdullah claimed such structures, called minarets, were utilised for allowing hot air inside the home to rise up with the tower and escape, while Hassan said they served to allow cool winds to flow down from the sky. It hardly seemed to work in either capacity, but we used it as a watchtower and as the point to fix my banner.

No single symbol any of us could conceive of would be unique to me. We discussed variations of crosses, or perhaps the lion of King Richard.

Instead, we wrote a single, short word. Painted in black letters, on both sides of the white cotton fabric.

344

ASHBURY.

"It is hardly legible," I complained, looking up from a hundred yards away across the square when it was first erected. "And it can hardly be seen. There are so many towers and domes and bloody great buildings in this God-forsaken, pestilent heathen bastard city."

Eva punched me in the shoulder, a glint in her eye. "This was the best idea we could come up with."

I shook my head. "That is the worst aspect of this situation. I can feel that this will not work to attract our enemies. How could it? A man could spend a month walking back and forth across this city and never see that pathetic little banner. If William is not with them, even if Hulegu's men see it, they will not know its meaning."

"Then you should pray," she said.

If there is one thing I have learned over the centuries, it is that when someone suggests that prayer is your best chance, then you know that you have made a grave error.

"God help us," I said, praying all the same. "Come, let us get out of sight before the savages get here. I can hear them. They are close."

Hulegu wanted the people remaining in the city rooted out and killed. He wanted the food, wine, and other supplies dragged out from stores and from homes and consumed by his men. He wanted the wealth of the city plundered, for his men to take for themselves and so grow rich and be happy with him as their lord, and fight for him all the harder for the next city, and the next. But he did not throw all the gates open and send in a hundred thousand men. He knew, I am sure, that sending so many would only result in his men murdering each other in the orgy of violence, for there would not be enough of the populous to go around and so they would turn on each other. Still, there were many thousands in the city, moving in companies from quarter to quarter.

I have seen more cities sacked than I can remember, and they follow a similar pattern. The men who loved wealth most made first for the palaces and mosques and madrasas and any building that looked as though wealth may lay within. Other, lustful, hateful men, loved rape and murder, and they would swarm into the homes of the city folk, smashing through ceilings and floors to find the pathetic hiding places of the terrified people who had stayed, hoping for a better fate. Some men are gluttons first of all, and they sought wine with which to render themselves insensible. Most of these men, their most pressing passions sated, then seek other sins to surrender themselves to, over and over, for days on end until their energies are spent or their lords send in sober men to round them up and drag them out.

"They are like animals," Stephen muttered, aghast, as we looked down at the violence in the streets from our vantage point atop the minaret of our commandeered house. The screams of the victims could barely be heard over the roars of triumph and savagery.

Abdullah was also keeping watch from the upstairs rooms of the house somewhere below us, peering through peepholes in the shutters.

"No," Eva said. "No animal is capable of such depravity,

Stephen. Only man can be filled with evil."

"No Christian man," Stephen said, his eyes wide.

Eva and I exchanged a look, both thinking of the things we had seen Christian men do. And thinking of the things we had done ourselves.

"You have read more texts than I have ever seen, Stephen," I said. "But you have a lot to learn about the world."

"Well then," he bristled. "No true Christian."

A banging sounded far below.

"Is that our door?" Eva asked.

I nodded. "They are trying us again. We should go down."

"Should I stay, perhaps?" Stephan asked, innocently. "Someone should be responsible for keeping watch, no?"

"What a generous fellow you are, Stephen," I said as I descended the stairs behind Eva, who flowed down them like a cat.

We had cleared the entrance hall of any furniture that might hinder us and had reinforced the heavy doors with two mismatched table tops, held in place with boards pulled up from one of the floors. Still, the doors shook with the impacts from those men trying to get inside our temporary home. The looters clearly assumed that a building of such size, in such proximity to a palace and other grand structures, would contain riches of one kind or another. They could not have known the home had been emptied of riches and the fact that the door was barred would have seemed like a sign that breaking through it would be well worth the effort.

The floor of the entrance hall was already stained with blood from previous, brief incursions by unwanted guests.

"Is it them?" Thomas asked as Eva and I came down.

"Not that we could see," I replied. "Perhaps we should open the door and find out?"

"Same as before?" Orus asked, grinning like the maniac he was.

"As my old steward used to say, if your pail is not broken, then one repairs it not," I said. Orus stared blankly at me while the doors shook and men shouted outside. "Never mind. Just open the bloody doors, will you."

Orus and Hassan unbarred the doors and ran back to us as the doors were thrown inward. Eva and I hid from view in the doorway to the dining area, while Khutulun and Jalal hid around the other. Orus and Hassan ran straight ahead toward the inner courtyard with its lovely fountain and pool, and so they could be seen escaping by the Mongols who strode in through the front door behind them.

I could hear how they were full of madness and fury. One of them shouted and their footsteps stopped, while their voices immediately rose in argument as they clustered inside the entrance.

"Six?" Eva whispered.

I nodded. "Smells like six hundred. But yes, six or so. And they know it is a trap." I raised my sword and looked across the hall to the opposite doorway where Jalal and Khutulun crouched. The Mongol woman grinned from ear to ear. A savage's smile on an angel's face.

Even though they were wary, they were still not ready for my attack. Coming out of hiding at a run, I caught them unawares. It was not six, but nine men crammed into the entrance hall just inside the door. Not the finest Mongol troops, as they were clad in filthy coats and not mail or other armour. A few wore iron helms rather than leather caps or hats. Beyond, the courtyard was bathed in sunlight, the men somewhat silhouetted.

Two men were arguing, and the others were glaring or grinning. At a glance, I knew they were drunk. Most did not have a weapon drawn, and only two held their swords ready. Others gripped daggers. One man had a remarkably ornate mace with a steel shaft that he had no doubt looted from somewhere in the city.

My sword sliced him across the neck before he had time to flinch and I slashed at two more, roaring at them as I shouldered my way through. I was fast, and loud in the enclosed space, and they leapt back to let me through.

While they stood momentarily dumbfounded, I heaved one of the front doors shut.

That snapped them into action and they came at me, suddenly understanding I wanted to trap them inside with me.

I slashed wildly, back and forth, connecting with an arm, a helm. A thrown dagger bounced off the door beside my head and clanged on the paved, bloody floor.

And then my own followers crashed into the Mongols from behind. Eva's first cut took a man's head from his shoulders in a single blow. Khutulun, screaming in joy, sliced a man's face open from ear to ear, then shoved his falling body towards her brother to finish off while she leapt into the next enemy.

We made short work of them, and they were soon lying dead or dying in the darkness of the entrance hall.

"Do not finish that one," I said to Thomas, as he stalked over to a man crawling away. I called out to my people. "Drink what blood you need, then throw the bodies with the others into the storeroom."

"Bodies give bad smell," Orus said. "We throw from roof into alley, yes?"

He was a truly gifted fighter but, unlike his sister, he was not the sharpest tool in the box. "That would attract attention, Orus. The storeroom, please."

Orus shrugged, slung one filthy dead Mongol onto his shoulder with graceful ease, and strode off.

"Should we save the blood?" Thomas asked.

"No need. We will be seeing plenty more soon, I am certain."

"What do you want with him?" Hassan asked, coming up and pointing with his dagger at the prisoner.

"Get him to tell us where Hulegu is," I ordered Hassan.

The Assassin was sceptical. "This one is a nothing. He will not know where his lord is."

"Get him to tell you everything he has heard. How long were they given to sack the city? Tear it out of him."

Hassan's eyes were cold when he nodded and stalked toward the dazed Mongol.

A cry echoed from above.

"Richard!"

It was Stephen, shouting so loudly that his voice cracked. I took the steps up the inside of the minaret three at a time.

"What is it?" I called as I ran. "Is it Hulegu?"

Stephen had his face pressed against the ornate stonework carving in the corner, staring out at something, his hands planted on the stone either side.

"He is gone," Stephen said as I came up behind him.

"Who has gone?" I asked, dragging Stephen away from the window and pushing my face where his had just been. The city beyond thronged with Mongol troops. "Who, Stephen?"

"Well, I do not know for certain," he began. "I thought that I saw a knight—"

"Where?" I said. "Was it William? Did he look like me? What did he look like? Where, Stephen? Where?"

"Down by the path to the palace. I may well be wrong... in fact, it is quite likely that I am mistaken. It may be that I have been looking down for so long that my mind's eye has deceived me—"

I turned, grabbed him by the shoulders and jammed him against the wall. "Who did you see?" I snarled in his face.

He swallowed. "Sir Bertrand. Possibly. That is, Bertrand de Cardaillac, and possibly also Hughues, his squire. But, surely, that cannot be—"

I leapt away from him back down those damned steps. "Come on, you fool," I shouted over my shoulder. "Everyone, to me," I repeated my call to my men to assemble in the entrance hall.

The bodies of the Mongol troops and their weapons littered the floor.

Hassan looked up from where his prisoner was propped against the wall. "What is it?"

"Kill that one and take his coat," I said. "Get the coats from all of them, and their helms and the hats." My people filed in from all over the house, asking each other what was happening. "Everyone, clothe yourself in the enemy's garb. We are going to leave this place, seize one or two men, and bring them back here. Stephen, Abdullah, you close the doors behind us and guard the building."

Stephen was appalled. "What if the enemy break in again? If it is only Abdullah and I—"

"You are an immortal now, Stephen," I snapped. "Take up a weapon, use your strength, remember your training. Defend this place until we return."

"Why go and take another one?" Thomas asked, pointing at Hassan's now-dead prisoner. "We had a perfectly good one already."

They busied themselves stripping the bodies and trying on the stinking, blood-soaked clothes of the Mongol men.

"Stephen saw Bertrand de Cardaillac heading for the palace," I said.

He stammered. "I am not certain what I saw. It may be that—"

Thomas froze, his arm halfway into a Mongol coat. "Why in the name of God would he be here?"

"It makes perfect sense," I said. "My brother William has brought him. Him and his squire. He had him prisoner in Karakorum, did he not? The night he killed Nikolas and stabbed you, Thomas."

"I remember," Thomas said, his jaw set. "Hulegu promised to

let the monks go free, and Bertrand was their escort."

I shook my head. "William would never let a man like Bertrand go free. He would use him, make him a follower."

Eva spoke up. "He would turn him."

"By God," I said. "You are right. He would have turned him into an immortal. Given him the Gift. Hughues, too. Two more knights to follow him."

"It is too dangerous out there," Hassan said, stepping forward. He held a Mongol's hat and coat but made no move to clothe himself with them. "These disguises will never pass any inspection."

"We will not stop for any inspection, Hassan," I said, feeling the red anger burning. "We will go quickly, heads down. Ignore all who speak to us. Orus? If anyone seeks to obstruct us, shout that we are on important business for Hulegu or some other great lord whose name is feared, understand?"

"Bertrand may be a mile away by now," Thomas said. "We may never find him."

"We bloody well better find him," I said, letting my anger show. "Or else all this, everything we have done, will be in vain. He will lead me to William, do you not see it? And William will lead us to Hulegu. And all of them will die. You are all coming with me, and we will all have our vengeance. Agreed?" I stared at each of them in turn. "Agreed? Agreed?"

One by one, they acquiesced.

"We will stay together. We will keep moving. We will not allow ourselves to be cornered. And we will not allow ourselves to be distracted. Understand?"

When we were all cloaked in bloody, stinking Mongol clothing, I led them at a run from the house and into the square where we had hoped to lay our ambush. No enemies in sight but their shouts and the screams of their victims echoed from the walls. The sun was bright and my immortals flinched from it, shielding their eyes.

I sensed that my terrible plan was already falling to pieces but, despite what Thomas believed, God cares nothing for a man's intentions and hopes, and so we must accept disasters and respond swiftly to overcome them. We followed the wall of the house and crossed to the huge madrasa on the other side, heading for the path that led to the entrance of the palace. It would have been quicker to cross directly but I wanted to avoid detection from anyone for as long as was possible.

At the edge of the building, I peered around the corner at the pathway, lined with ornamental trees. A large band of soldiers filled the grand entrance, many lounging on the steps or against the walls. Others carried loot from inside the palace. A group carried piles of clothes and other silks to a row of carts in the open forecourt. A trail of dry blood stained the stones of the path and continued into the light dust of the courtyard. It led to a pile of bodies tossed against the wall of the palace. The building rose up three or four storeys high above, with window after window reaching up to the roof above, each one with intricately patterned stonework jutting over the arches.

Could Bertrand truly be within? Even if he was now one of William's men, how could he walk freely through a company of drunken, looting Mongols?

If he was within, he was certainly my best hope of finding William himself, for surely Bertrand would know where he was. But how could I storm such a place with so few men of my own? How many were inside? Twenty? Fifty?

Although there were dozens of palaces in Baghdad, and this was a small one, it was perhaps a madness that drove me to head into the palace, an enclosed space full of looting Mongol soldiers. Taking all my followers down that path and into the palace was likely to end in disaster, surely.

"Wait here," I said to my people. After all my talk of staying together at all costs, they stared at me in surprise. "I will draw Bertrand and Hughues out, and lead them here where we will take them. Disburse yourself about here and fall on them from all sides."

Eva moved in front of me. "We stay together. Do you recall the last time you went into an enemy force alone?"

"No," I admitted.

She punched me in the chest. "Forty years ago, you went into that village alone in Nottingham to rescue me. And you were captured, and I had my throat slit."

"But that was a trap, laid to lure me in."

She tilted her head. "What makes you think this is not?"

I froze, astonished that the thought had not even occurred to me.

Reaching my hand out, I stroked her cheek. "Truly, my love, I would be dead a dozen times over, if you were not at my side. What would I do without you?"

She did not smile at the compliment, as any other woman

would have done. Instead, she slapped my hand away. "You are a bloody fool, Richard."

I laughed, because the battle thirst was upon me, and she could tell that was so.

"Orus?" I called. "You will come with me. We will lure the enemy into the square. And the rest of you will cut them down, do you hear me? Kill them all. We want Bertrand or Hughues, and we want them to tell us where to find William, and Hulegu. Come, Orus."

We strode toward the Mongols, who had not yet noticed us.

"Kill them?" Orus asked, with a hand on his sword.

"Tell them that a gaggle of Saracen princesses are fleeing across the city and that you need help killing their guards. Do you understand? Tell them a dozen Saracen maidens are making a run for it, across the square, and they have their wealth with them. Do you see, Orus?"

A cunning smile stretched across his handsome face.

After a moment to compose himself, he ran forward raising his arms out at his side and began shouting at the men in an agitated voice. He jabbered and roared at them. The sharpest few came to him with their swords drawn but Orus did not respond to their threats, other than to beg and plead in the barbarian tongue for them to help him to take this great prize which was getting away, just out of sight, so close, so close.

I watched the hunger light up their eyes, and more and more jumped to their feet and dropped what they were carrying. A handful more came out from within the entranceway. I kept my head lowered so that my Mongol hat would shield my face from them. Some were wary, but they were overcome by the greed filled amongst them, who dragged them forward. Orus kept on at the stragglers, no doubt urging that they needed every man. The first moved by me and I backed away, making myself smaller and meeker. A few barked words at me and I bobbed my head and mimicked the gestures that I observed the Mongols making in my time at Karakorum and on the steppe. No one troubled me, for they were hurrying to seize their prize before it escaped.

I slid by them, sidling to the palace entrance where those too drunk or too lazy remained. Orus tried to rouse them but I clapped him on the back and told him to cease. The bulk of them were moving away and would soon feel the blades of my people cutting them down. But some would no doubt escape, and there were many more nearby and within, so we had to move quickly now.

Orus followed me and we ducked inside the decorated archway into the entrance hall. It was bright and airy and open, with clear lines and geometric designs in the stonework. The polished floor was littered with detritus and spattered with blood. Rooms led off through high arches in front and to either side. Above, two levels of balconies looked down on us. Two doorways led to stairways that wound up to other storeys above. Banging and crashing noises echoed through the building.

"It is too big," I said to Orus. "How will we find them??"

He nodded, cupped his hands around his mouth and mimed shouting.

"You bloody heathen madman," I said. "Why in the name of God would Bertrand come to me if I—" I paused, thinking.

He would not come to me.

I cupped my hands around my mouth and roared. "Bertrand!" My voice echoed from the walls. Did I sound enough like my brother to fool him? I had to hope so. "Bertrand! Hughues!"

Taking a breath, I was about to hurl insults at the man, as I imagined my brother might have done when I stopped myself. Thinking back on Palestine and Sherwood, it seemed as though his men worshipped him. He commanded depths of loyalty and devotion I had seen only in the followers of Richard the Lionheart. It was unseemly and quite profoundly un-English, but there it was. William treated his men with courtesy and addressed them with respect.

"Come down, brothers!" I roared. "I require your presence!"

Orus stared at me with a lopsided grin on his face, and I shoved him across the hall into the archway so that we would be hidden from view. The banging subsided somewhat but three Mongols wandered in from outside and stood together in a group, watching us. Orus raised a friendly hand at them and babbled something. Whatever it was he said, they appeared to be unconvinced and their hands remained on their weapons.

I sighed. "Nothing in this world ever goes according to plan, Orus. I suppose we can at least take comfort in that."

He smiled, nodding, not understanding me at all.

I pointed at the three Mongols, and then dragged my finger across my throat.

He grinned, drew his sword and charged at the Mongol soldiers. They scattered, but he caught the first one with a thrust to the unarmoured soldier's lower back, driving him to the steps.

It would have been visible to any others outside the palace.

Footsteps resounded on the stone floor behind me, echoing out of the stairway nearest to me. I slipped across the room to place my back against the wall beside the archway and drew my sword, ready to strike down the two or three armoured men who clattered down the steps.

The first man stepped out into the hall. A man dressed in the garb of a Frankish man-at-arms, with his straight-bladed sword at his side, and his helm tucked under his arm. His surcoat was faded, dirty and much-repaired but it was a familiar one.

In fact, I recognised him at once.

Hughues. Bertrand's squire and cousin.

The second man, which was surely Bertrand himself, stopped within the stairwell, out of my sight.

I willed him to step out also so that I could take them both.

But he did not.

I watched as Hughues peered through the archway and out into the entrance hall where Orus fought with the Mongol soldiers.

Hughues turned back to the stairwell and began to call out in French. "There are merely—"

His eyes widened when he saw me, and I am sure the sight confused him for a moment. Brandishing a curved sword, I wore a Saracen soldier's armour and clothing, from head to toe, and over the top wore the massive coat of a Mongol rider, with a fur-lined conical hat pulled over my Saracen helm. An ill-fitting ensemble, with my grimacing face staring out of it. No wonder, then, that the young man was struck by a momentary bafflement.

I leapt into his confusion, charging him with great speed and shouldering him in the chest. He was a big lump of a man and it hurt me, but it would have knocked the wind from him and he flew back off his feet toward the entrance, his helm clanging away. His skull smacked into the floor with a wet thud, like an apple being crushed, and he bounced into motionlessness. I had not intended to murder the man.

Footsteps behind me.

I ducked and twisted away from the blow that was surely coming, turning to face my attacker as I retreated away further into the palace.

Bertrand.

I had forgotten how big he was. His helm obscured his face but I could imagine the look upon it. His sword point danced in the air as he feinted his way closer to me. Neither of us had a shield but his armour was certainly better than mine, and I had a rather light blade with which to attack his. It would have to be my dagger, slipping it beneath his helm or through his eye slits, or up into his groin beneath his hauberk.

Then again, I needed the bastard alive.

He lunged at me to drive me back, then launched a series of rapid cuts at my unprotected face.

So fast.

Any doubt that he had been granted the Gift was now gone. He was certainly one of William's immortals.

And now that our strength and speed was closer to equal, I could truly appreciate his skill as a swordsman. Bertrand was an emotional, prideful man but he did not fight with emotion.

Instead, he attacked with controlled, precise cuts and thrusts, the point of his sword searching for gaps in my defence. My sword blade was shorter and was not designed for the thrust, and I parried and retreated. Even if I had been armed and armoured in my native style, I would likely still have been outmatched by his skill.

His point glanced off the top of my helm as I mistimed a lunging thrust at his lead knee and I shifted away as he followed up to keep me off-balance. Another cut struck me on the shoulder and I changed direction again to avoid being cornered. Frustration and fear began to surge inside me. A terror and anger that I would die an ignominious death at the hands of an arrogant Frenchman. That rage gave me strength to turn his sword and slip inside his guard to thrust my sword into the mail at his stomach. The force of it at least caused him to wince and grunt and suddenly he was on the backfoot. To get through his armour, I would have to grapple him to the floor and employ my dagger in a way that would disable but not kill him outright.

Across the hall, far behind Bertrand's back, I noted that Hughues climbed gingerly to his feet with one hand on the back of his head but the other hand already gripping his sword. His face was covered with blood that must have leaked from a wound on his skull, unseen beneath his aventail. The tough little bastard had surely also been turned by William and I would have to now deal with both of them, just as soon as Hughues could shake the wits back into his head. The younger man staggered toward us while we fought, before lurching over to lean one hand on the wall.

"Bertrand!" Hughues shouted. "I cannot see. Is that you?"

The knight attempted to break off from me but instead, I pressed my advantage while he was distracted by his cousin's wailing.

Behind Hughues, a dark shape darted and loomed up.

"No!" I shouted.

But it was too late.

Orus gabbed Hughues from behind and jabbed a dagger into his face and dragged him off his feet. Hughues screamed as he died.

While Bertrand was momentarily frozen in indecision, I hammered my sword into his helm, grabbed his arm and wrestled him off his feet. We crashed into the floor, and I struck him with powerful blows about his chest and body. Orus joined me, yanked Bertrand's helm from his head and bashed his face into a bloody mess. Together we subdued the massive knight, lashing his hands together behind his back.

"You have murdered him," Bertrand said, his lips split and oozing blood. His eyes fixed upon his young cousin's body.

"It was not my intention," I said, as I dragged him to his feet and propelled him rapidly from the palace and onto the path and into the orange sunlight. Dead Mongols lay on the steps, slain by Orus. The sun had moved far across the sky and was sinking low. It would not be long before evening came.

"There," Orus said, nodding at the approaching group.

It was my own people, coming from their ambush in the square to escort us quickly back to our safehouse. Quickly, I found Eva amongst them and saw that she was unhurt. All of my company had survived the ambush they had sprung.

"We all live," Eva said, falling in beside me with barely a glance at Bertrand. "A few injured. No Mongol escaped. But surely our combat was noted by others. We cannot remain long in this place before more come for us."

I nodded my thanks to my wife and then threw Bertrand down against the entrance hall wall just inside the doors to our home on the edge of the square.

"Where is William?" I asked him, while the others shut the doors and checked themselves and their equipment after their ambush of the Mongols.

"You murdered him," Bertrand said. "Your savage killed my dear Hughues. Killed him dead."

He was a knight and a lord but our survival in that place was precarious and would not suffer delay. I dragged the aventail from his head and punched him in the temple. "Where is William?"

Bertrand's eyes glazed over and he screwed up his face. "How did it come to this?" he said, almost in a wail. "You and your brother, you are an evil pair. You bastard. True evil."

I sighed and crouched in front of him.

"What happened in Karakorum?" I asked, lowering my voice. "You were free to return with the monks. Instead, you chose to follow my brother. Why?"

He laughed until his throat gargled and he spat a mouthful of clotted blood onto his surcoat. "I believed his lies."

"What lies were those?"

When Bertrand hesitated, I grabbed my dagger and reached down to hold the top of his head still. "I am going to cut off pieces of your face now, Bertrand. I will cease only when you speak to me of my brother."

"For the love of God," he said, eyes wide and staring at the blade point hovering an inch away from the tip of his nose. "I will speak, Richard, I will speak." When I did not withdraw the dagger, he quickly continued, swallowing hard. "William promised me a dukedom. In France."

"And how would he accomplish such a thing for you?"

"The Mongols would invade France, he said. He had urged them to do so for years now. And after the kingdom falls to Hulegu, it will be rebuilt and new lords chosen to rule. I would be one of them."

It was just as we had feared. After the Saracens were crushed, the Mongols would be turned against Christendom and the same horrors inflicted upon the people there.

Driven by fear, many questions leapt immediately to fill my mind. When would this happen? How many years would it take? What could we do to stop it?

But then I recalled what Bertrand had earlier said. "But now you believe his promises were lies? Why? What has happened since between you?"

"Between William and I? Nothing. But William and Hulegu?" Bertrand hesitated, glancing at my dagger.

"Come on, out with it," I said. "My brother is nothing if he is not a braggart. I have never known him to keep his grandiose plans from his men. Speak."

Bertrand licked his bloodied, cracked lips and looked away.

I sighed. The prideful ones always have to make it difficult.

364

"My hope, sir," I said, "is that once this unpleasant business is concluded, and you give me your word to do me and my people no harm, I will free you to do as you will. And I would rather you did so as a whole man, and not one lacking his ears or one of his eyes. Or some other part."

It was sad, how the hope filled his eyes when he turned them to me. He must surely have expected that I was lying about sparing his life, yet the hope that he could survive the encounter overcame his sense of reason. Such as it was.

"Hulegu and his men, they grow tired of William urging them to conquer Christendom. All in good time, they say. First, the Mohammedans and then, later they will finish their conquest of the remaining peoples of the Earth. The Khan and his retinue, those changed by William's blood, they speak now in terms of twenty years, or forty years, or even longer. They know that they will live forever, and are in no hurry."

"And William is impatient?" I asked. "Why?"

Bertrand glanced at my dagger again. "There are men like us. In France and throughout Christendom. William has given the Gift of his blood to many great lords and I believe he fears that these men will grow powerful in his absence and that they will challenge him when the time comes. Possibly, I do not know for certain, he does not speak clearly of such things." He trailed off, no doubt seeking to obscure the truth through vagaries. But I did not care about him, as my heart was gripped by a cold sense of dread.

I glanced around at Eva, who stood watching beside Thomas, Stephen, Hassan, and some of the others.

"William has made many Christian lords into immortals?" I said. "When? How many? Who are they?"

"I do not know, I swear it. He did not tell me. That is to say, he said he granted the Gift to many after he last fled England, and he journeyed through Christendom on his way east. It was many years, so he said, and he chose which men he could count on to do what he needed them to do."

"And what was that?"

Bertrand attempted to shrug. "Some he wished to accumulate power and wealth, so that he could take it from them when he returned. Others, he said were good only for sowing chaos and disorder. Criminals and outlaws, by law or by nature. Their deeds would weaken the kingdoms that William would then conquer."

"How many?" I asked.

"I do not know, I swear it."

Pushing the back of his head hard against the wall, I took the dagger and pressed the point against his cheek beneath his left eye. "I sincerely beg your pardon, Bertrand, but I am going to take your eye now."

"Wait!" Bertrand squirmed. "It was perhaps a dozen. A dozen."

I hesitated. "So few? That cannot be true, Bertrand."

"Forty, perhaps," Bertrand said. "Yes, a great many, perhaps. Or less."

"For God's sake," I said. "You truly have no idea of how many, do you."

He let out a shaky sigh. "No. He would not say. And I do not know."

"Where is William right now? Is he in the city?"

"Yes," Bertrand nodded. "We came in together, along with Hulegu's courtiers. The damned savages."

"Where are they now? Where is William, Bertrand, right at this moment?"

He breathed heavily, for he was betraying the lord he had sworn himself to, and it weighed on him. "William went to the house of learning near to here. He wished to find texts and maps on Cathay and the lands of the East."

"He is in the madrasa?" I said. I could feel Eva shifting behind me. "How many men with him?"

"Six of the Gifted, and a hundred or so royal troops loyal to Hulegu."

"And Hulegu wants maps of Cathay? Why?"

Bertrand shook his head. "No, no. It is William who wants such things. He told me in secret." Despite everything, there was pride in his voice that William had taken him into his confidence.

"Why does William want them?" I asked.

"I am sure he has his reasons," Bertrand said, grudgingly admitting his knowledge of my brother's plans went only so far.

"If all this is true, why were you and Hughues in that palace instead of by William's side?"

"It was the residence of the lord of the madrasa," Bertrand said. "We were to find him or his family, or his belongings and writings, and bring them back to William."

Abdullah came striding in behind me and mumbled something to Thomas before hurrying away again.

Thomas stepped close and bent to speak into my ear. "The

enemy are concentrating nearby. We must flee, immediately. Else we shall be surrounded and crushed."

I nodded my thanks as he retreated and turned my attention back to Bertrand.

He licked his lips again. His face was already healing.

"If I gave you fresh blood to drink," I said. "which would heal your wounds, and put a sword in your hand, would you serve me?"

I saw how the idea of it outraged him. He, a great lord, serving me, a landless, rootless knight. But he must have known that he could never go back to how he was and he marshalled his civility and nodded.

"You would take no revenge against Orus, the man who killed your cousin Hughues?"

Hatred crossed his face but again he nodded.

Thomas bent down beside me. "We will be hurrying across the city for a long time, avoiding patrols. One shout from him would condemn us all."

Bertrand glared at the old Templar before fixing me with what I am sure he believed was a sincere expression. "I would serve you faithfully." He swallowed. "My lord."

Outside, shouting filled the air, and my people gathered together in the hall behind me, ready to leave.

"You should pray now," I said.

"I swear, Richard, you can—"

I stabbed my knife into his head. He went down, bucking like a landed fish. He was an immortal and would have died hard from such a wound. For all that he had to die, I did not want him to suffer unduly. I pulled the blade from his skull and sawed it across his throat, worked it through the gristle and hacked through his spine.

Thomas was white as a ghost when I turned around. Stephen mumbled a prayer over the body.

"What do you think?" I said to them. "What is William doing here?"

"We must go," Stephen said. I ignored him.

Thomas growled. "It sounded to me as though William has fallen out with Hulegu and is attempting to flee from him. No?"

"Yes," I said. "Why send that damned fool and his squire into the palace at all?"

"That is it," Eva said. "William was sending him on a fool's errand. While Bertrand and Hughues were occupied elsewhere, William was going to flee."

"Leave by himself?" I said. "Yes, that is what he does. When his plans fail, he flees. Like a rat. He has lost control of Hulegu and he has fled."

"What was all that about immortal lords that William has made in France?" Thomas said.

"If we survive this city," I said. "We can think on it then. So, where is William? In the madrasa?"

"We believe William is fleeing, yes?" Stephen said. "So where is he fleeing to?"

"Anywhere," I said. "Away from Hulegu first, then he can go where he pleases. He has done so before."

"Abdullah?" Hassan said. "If you wished to flee to the west from the madrasa, which route would you take?"

The Saracen scholar needed no time to ponder it. "The Syrian

Gate leads northwest, and the Kufa Gate to the southwest."

"Word is that Kufa surrendered to Hulegu's armies," Hassan said.

I nodded. "And the Syria Gate road leads to Damascus. And from there, he could travel to Acre and back to Christendom." Looking around at my men, I was struck for a moment by the uniqueness of each of them. They were powerful, grave, reliable. Almost all of them wanted revenge on Hulegu and not William. "Are we agreed that we shall travel across the city and cut William off before he flees through the Syria Gate? If he has already left through it, we shall pursue. Once William is dead, we shall withdraw." I held up my hands at their protests. "We shall withdraw from this Hell and prepare for an assault on Hulegu when he moves against Damascus. It is too dangerous here, we have pushed our luck far enough already and now we must push it further, travelling across the city. If we stay and wait for Hulegu we shall be caught for sure. This way is best, is it not?"

Some were unhappy but they acquiesced.

Quickly, we collected everything we needed, wrapped our Mongol clothing tighter about us, and set out once more into the boiling chaos.

In spite of the thousands of men rampaging through the streets, we made it all the way across the city and were closing on the Syria Gate when we met with disaster.

* * *

It was growing late in the day and I prayed for the night to envelop us. We kept together as we moved through the smaller streets, heading north, then west, then south, and west again. The city was scarred and bloodied. The frenzied first days of the sacking was fading into exhaustion, as the easiest pickings had been plucked and countless thousands of the residents of the city had already been slaughtered. Most doors were thrown open and the rooms within dark and covered in debris and blood. We cut through the side streets and alleys until we came to the main road.

That roadway, leading from the centre of the round city to the edge through the three concentric walls, led right the way through all three gatehouses. The road was itself bordered by walls with open arches every few yards, leading to the streets to either side. Beside one of those arched entrances, we paused and my company gathered in a loose group, looking outward along the main road.

"We are now between the outer gatehouse and the centre gatehouse," Abdullah said, peeking out.

"Orus," I said, pointing up. "Climb the wall. Look for a Frankish man. Any man who looks like me."

The Mongol nodded, and Khutulun—always at his side—scrambled up beside him. After only a moment, Eva followed, pulling herself up the ornate stonework of the wall all the way to the flat top.

"We cannot go this way, Richard," Hassan said, pointing to the enclosed roadway. "We could be surrounded and trapped."

I did not bother to disguise my contempt. "That is why it is the perfect place to ambush William." He began to argue but I stepped up to him and lowered my voice. "Flee, then, if you are

371

so afraid."

He was gravely insulted but he did not have time to voice his protestations for a shout came from above my head.

"By God, Richard," Eva said from up on the wall. "He is there!" She pointed toward the outer gatehouse. "Dressed in Mongol attire."

My heart hammered in my chest and my people stirred all around me.

"You are certain?" I asked.

She glanced down at me and her eyes were cold as the winter winds of the steppe. Eva had been his prisoner. William had held her and he had cut her throat, bleeding her to the point of death. It had been decades but I could picture it in my mind's eye. Of course she was certain.

"How far?" I said as she and my two Mongols jumped down.

She grabbed me. "He is right there. Close enough to spit on. A hundred yards. He stood out as he is alone, on foot, walking swiftly."

I grinned. My quarry was about to be under my blade. "Come," I ordered my people.

"But if he is dressed as a Mongol and not even mounted," Stephen said, "how can we be sure it is William and not some—"

I shoved him aside and ran out into the roadway. It was wide enough for two wagons to pass each other and as straight as an arrow. Far ahead was the massive, squat, outer gatehouse with its shining cupola on top. Close behind me was another gatehouse. These structures turned the roadway into a tunnel, and I knew I had to reach William before he reached the outer one.

For there he was. A solitary man up ahead, dressed as a rich Mongol warrior—in mail armour and steel helm—but his tall frame, upright posture, and loping gait marked him out as an Englishman in a barbarian's clothing. At the pace he was making, he would be through the gatehouse and outside the round city walls in little time.

There were other men about. A group of three riders ambled in my direction. Behind, in the centre gatehouse, a dozen or more men joked and shouted, drunk and belligerent.

But William was alone. Without followers.

Without protection.

My feet pounded on the paved surface as I ran headlong at my brother. There was no thought of honour in my head, simply the urge to slay him. I would draw my sword and assault him without challenge, and then my companions would assist me in cutting him into pieces. There were so many of us, and so few of him.

It was so close that I felt that my task was already done. I could taste the victory on my lips.

But God is cruel.

He had given me that taste, had brought me and William together on that road from across a city of a million people as though it was fated that I would finally fulfil the destiny that He had set out for me.

Only to snatch it away.

Just behind William, a group of Mongol warriors streamed out of a row of archways in the side of the road on their horses. They came out quickly, a half dozen, then quickly more followed behind. They spilled out to fill the road from one wall to the other. They were not looting, they were a zuut of close to a hundred sober soldiers, mounted and armoured, clutching their lances and bows.

William was lost from view beyond them.

I wanted to push my way through but there was a wall of horse and metal in my way. Behind me, my companions drew to a stop and looked to me.

Eva, Thomas, Hassan, Orus, Khutulun, Jalal. Stephen and Abdullah.

We were outnumbered more than ten to one.

"Are they here for us?" Thomas said, his voice tight and anguished.

The enemy were indeed taking an interest in us, and many rode toward our position. We must have looked incredibly suspicious. A few of them already had their hands on their weapons.

Every moment we delayed, William was getting further from my grasp.

"It does not matter," I said, drawing my sword. "I am cutting my way through."

Would my people follow me? Eva would, and Thomas too. Would Stephen flee for his life? Would the Saracens and my Mongols turn tail and decide that Hulegu was their only target after all?

There was no time to discuss it or to force them into obedience.

One of the dozens of Mongols just ahead saw me for what I was. A foreign enemy with a drawn sword. He pointed with his spear and raised his voice to his fellows riding at his side and they were not the sort to hesitate.

Then again, neither was I.

So I charged them first.

The sturdy horses were mostly unarmoured and so I slashed my blade into the animals' faces and eyes and sent many reeling. I moved into the mass of enemies, laying about me at man or beast who ventured near. Some riders fought to hold on to their injured animals, but a few slid off their horses and came at me on foot. Spear thrusts and sword blades flashed, clanged against me. Something smacked into my helm, and I was struck hard on the shoulder. My armour held but my anger built. I cut at whatever flesh I could see, and punched and shoved, always moving forward.

Sounds of battle grew behind me, and I knew that at least some of my men were fighting.

But the enemy were too many. The horses were like mountains of flesh and the air grew close and the shouting loud. I could not find my way through and clear. Their number appeared endless. It was difficult to see in any direction but for a moment I had a glimpse through the chaos.

Behind me, my company was surrounded and attacked on all sides. Eva was swarmed by furious Mongols, their lances thrusting at her all from all directions as she twisted and danced in an ever-smaller space. Thomas thrashed at the spears that jabbed down at him. A blade flashed at Abdullah, who screamed as he fell, blood gushing from his neck, before an axe crashed into the top of his head.

My people needed me. And yet, with every moment, William's escape grew ever more certain.

Marshalling my strength, I threw down the men around me and climbed up onto a horse. It tried to throw me but the others were crowded so tight around it that the beast could not even turn. There was a half dozen mounted between me and the nearest wall. I struck down the men in my path, avoiding or turning their blows. A weak spear thrust from an overextended Mongol hit me on the chest, checking my progress. I seized the weapon and heaved. The foolish man attempted to hold on to the shaft of his spear and he fell from his horse amongst the stamping hooves. As he fell, I jumped over him to the back of the next horse. Those Mongols had never faced an enemy as strong and fast as me and as brave as they were, they were also afraid. I powered through them all the way to the wall and leapt up to the jutting stonework over the archway. My sword blade scraped against the plaster but I dragged myself up onto the top of the wall. It was flat and level and wider than shoulder width. On the other side, the street leading into the city was also packed with Mongol horsemen. I was wrong about it being a single zuut of a hundred men. It was two zuut at least, crowding the streets and ready to kill us when they got clear.

Glancing behind me, I saw my company engaged with the Mongols down on the road, making little headway. They were surrounded. Orus and Khutulun fought back to back. Thomas stabbed into the horses with a fury I had never seen in him before. Stephen crouched behind Eva, who ducked and slipped from the blows while striking back at the Mongols who tried to kill her.

Hassan, Jalal, Radi and Raka fought together and cut a swathe into the enemy at an oblique angle away from the others. But all four Assassins looked wounded already, Radi with a great gash across his crown, and Raka being supported by Jalal. The air reeked of blood. Writhing Mongol bodies littered the path and more fell with every moment. The shouts and screams echoed between the walls as they died. But there were so many. How long could my people survive against such odds?

Glancing the other way, I saw William still hurrying away, now almost at the massive gatehouse. Almost free. He seemed to half turn at that moment but I did not know if he saw me or not.

I had to kill him. It was my last chance.

But it meant sacrificing my people.

Losing Eva.

An arrow struck the wall at my feet and snapped, just as another slashed the air by my head.

I ran.

Along the wall, heading for William.

My leather shoes slapped on the stones that capped the top of the wall, and I raced along it faster than any mortal man. A Mongol archer can hit a bird on the wing but none of the arrows shot at me brought me down. In no time at all, I left the roaring mass of men behind me and the gatehouse loomed ahead. It was the size of a squat castle keep but was a simple structure. I considered climbing from the wall up onto the top of the gatehouse, running across the roof and then dropping down the other side to cut him off.

If only I had made that choice. I may have ended William's

life there and then and so saved the people of the world from centuries of his evil.

However, I saw men up there on the top of the gatehouse. Mongols or their allies had seized the building and I would have to avoid them or fight them. I was afraid that any delay on the roof would mean William escaping beneath me and so decided on the direct approach. Nearing the gatehouse entrance, I stepped down the stonework over the last archway in the sidewall and then dropped to the road, landing heavily in my Saracen armour. Ahead of me, the road became a dark tunnel. Inside the gatehouse, William fled.

Shouts behind me. It was the Mongol zuut. Of course, they were chasing me. Of course, they would never have simply watched me run away in full view and done nothing to follow. There were at least a dozen riders, perhaps many more.

I felt dread descending. A sense that, on that day and in all the years since I left Constantinople, I had always been making the worst choice in every moment.

But what could I do? I had to fight on along the path before me.

So I ran for William, ran into the chill darkness beneath the mass of the gatehouse.

"William!" I roared, in my battlefield voice. His name echoed from the black walls and the low ceiling above.

Ahead, halfway along and silhouetted against the square of light at the end of the tunnel, he stopped. He turned.

Despite the darkness, and his Mongol garb, I could see it was certainly my brother. His build, his stance and the outline of his features in the gloom. And he would have been in no doubt who it was that challenged him. Finally, after so many years in pursuit, we would face each other in combat, one man against the other, with God alone as our judge.

And William ran.

The coward turned back and ran away from me toward the outer city and freedom.

Even though I should have known, I was outraged by his cowardice. My anger gave my feet wings and I gained on him while I outpaced my mounted pursuers. William grew so close that I could hear his shoes slapping on the stone, could hear his breath heaving. He was in front of me, so close that I could almost reach him with the point of my sword.

And then there was a sound. At first, I thought it was the thundering of hooves closing on me. But it was instead a great clanging sound that came from all around and especially from above me. Instinct slowed me as I searched for the source of the danger. A metallic clashing of chains running and a rumbling sound that grew in volume and pitch as if some mighty armoured monster descended from the sky.

It came from above.

At the last moment, I looked up and saw something massive rushing toward me and so I checked my run and fell backwards. I scrambled away, terrified and confused by what it could be.

The huge portcullis crashed down with an almighty bang, closing off the tunnel. It had missed my outstretched feet by a few inches. For a long moment, the only sound was my panting breath and the blood pounding in my ears. Then, behind me, dozens of hooves echoed and I rolled and jumped to my feet.

On the other side, William rose and turned. He looked up at the thick timber and iron portcullis that divided us.

He laughed.

William looked through one of the square gaps at me and he laughed.

"Do you doubt that God is with me, brother?" he asked, smiling like the devil.

I was struck dumb. Stood there, breathing heavily, shaking with rage. After a moment, I dropped my sword, grabbed the portcullis and heaved upward. I was ready to jump back from him in case he attacked me through the square spaces but William simply watched me, an amused expression on his face.

Of course, I could not move it. Not even an inch. Not even with my great strength. I may as well have tried to lift a castle wall.

"Are they friends of yours, Richard?" he asked, pointing behind me. "Or should you be concerned?"

I snatched up my sword.

Mongol soldiers from the zuut filled the entrance of the tunnel from wall to wall. Gathering in a mass of horses and men and approaching slowly, cautiously. No doubt unsure about what was happening, and frozen in indecision by their race's unwillingness to be trapped in an enclosed space. Yet they still approached, and when they decided to attack, they would have me cornered and outnumbered at least twenty to one.

"Friends of mine?" I said. "Friends of yours, you heathen bastard."

He made a sound like a snort. "I do not know those barbarian filth. And they do not know me."

A mad, faint hope that he would be able to call them off died into nothing.

I looked back at him, keeping an eye on the Mongols. "Ah yes. You have fallen into conflict with Hulegu, your lord and master."

His grin fell from his face. "I have no master. Lords and princes serve me."

It was my turn to laugh. "You are a damned fool. You gave the gift of your blood to these barbarians and you expected them to stay subservient. You were always mad but now you have betrayed your people."

He scoffed. "My people are whoever I chose them to be. You cannot understand, Richard. You lack the wits to see it. You lack the courage of thought. My plans are beyond you."

"Your plans?" I said. "Like granting your gift to certain lords in France? Who are they, William? Who did you turn into an immortal?"

The Mongols argued with each other behind me.

William tilted his head, a frown creasing his forehead. "You have been speaking to Bertrand, I take it? How is our friend? Is he with you?"

"I cut off his head. As I will do to you."

He sighed, pinching the bridge of his nose. "Richard, that is the difference between us. You had him in your power. A knight, a lord. Immensely rich. Known to the King of France. You could have turned him into a follower, an acolyte, and strengthened yourself immensely. Instead, you destroyed him. You are a fool."

"Is that what you were doing in France, then?" I said. "Who

there did you turn into a follower?"

His eyes flicked to the Mongols and back to me. "Are you not concerned that you are about to be murdered, Richard? I hope you have a plan to escape? I would hate to witness your death."

"Save your jests. And do not tell me, then. It matters not. I will undo your plans, wherever you have laid them in France."

He waved a hand, casually. "I gave the Gift to many people, great and small, and not only in France but all over." William grinned at my shock. "But you should not be concerned about them. If you do return to Christendom, you should seek our grandfather. The Ancient One."

The Mongols edged closer. A small group dismounted and strutted toward me, spreading out as they approached. At least two clutched bows but they did not shoot at me.

"What are you blathering about?" I said over my shoulder. I assumed he meant our father's father. "The old lord de Ferrers was long dead when we were sired."

"The old Lord de Ferrers was not our father's true father." William laughed. "Our true grandfather lives, and he is thousands of years old, Richard. Thousands! The things he has seen. The power that he has. You would learn a lot from him, brother, if you would but go to him."

Before I could respond, eight of the Mongols moved quickly to surround and then attack me. Spear thrusts to keep me pinned against the portcullis, while others darted in with their swords.

I was too angry to fight intelligently. I cut down two of them and wounded three more before they retreated. But I took a hard blow on the helm, which hurt terribly and I had irrevocably bent my sword blade so I picked up one dropped by an attacker. The Mongols did not retreat far, and many more of them pushed their way closer inside the tunnel. Behind them, more still seemed to come from the road to block out the light and fill the tunnel with their stench. I wondered whether any of my company had survived. I wondered if I had sacrificed the life of Eva for nothing. William was so close but he may as well have been on the other side of the Earth for all the good it did me.

And I was growing ever more certain that I could not fight my way clear of so many. Dozens of Mongols now, many mounted, many with bows, spread themselves around me and prepared to attack once again.

I was going to die in that tunnel, and I would die alone, and without honour. Dishonoured and unremembered.

"Here they come again, brother," William said.

"Waiting to see me die?" I said over my shoulder, bitterly.

"I would prefer it if you lived," he said.

The Mongols rushed me again, coming in a group of ten. A full arban, ten men who lived and fought together as one. They fought well, but they had never trained to fight just one man all at the same time, and they had never faced any man like me. When one grappled me, I threw him into another. I grabbed a spear swung at my head, ripped it from the wielder's grasp, flipped it and stabbed it through the bones of his face before he had time to flinch. Again, they fled from me before I could bring them all down.

"You are rather good, Richard," William said, pointing at his own cheek. "Though, you took a wound there."

I felt my face and my fingers slipped into a gash beneath my left eye. As is often the way with wounds, I could not recall any specific blow that might have caused it.

"It is nothing," I said, as the hot blood welled down to my neck.

"Perhaps you might try drinking the blood of these next fellows?" William said. "You may find it helps, you know?"

And more came at me. I pushed out into them and kept moving along the portcullis, keeping my back to it so that they could not fully surround me.

I was tired. My arms seemed to move slowly and I missed a spear strike and it punched me high on the chest, causing me to miss a cut aimed at a Mongol neck. The interruption of my timing caused my defence to fall apart and I was struck on the head and arms and then a rain of blows knocked me hard against the portcullis. Mongol soldiers fought mostly in silence but they were now shouting and the roar of voices filled the tunnel, filled my head as the pain of their attacks thundered in my head. With horror, I realised I had fallen to one knee, and the fear drove me up to my feet again and I threw them off from me, lying about me with a sword in one hand and a broken spear in the other.

When they retreated, I fell against the portcullis, sucking air into my lungs and shaking all over.

Blood ran into my eyes and I felt the sharp-cold pain of a cut on my forehead somewhere.

I dropped the spear and raised my left hand to my face but there was something wrong with my trembling arm. A gash on my wrist pumped blood over my hand and down to the floor in a thick stream. The mail at my left shoulder was torn open and a wound beneath gaped, shining black in the darkness.

A fallen Mongol at my feet groaned and crawled away. I took a step to him and stamped down on his neck to immobilise him, then stabbed my blade through the side of his neck. I had to be quick while the others argued about who would attack me next. No doubt they were enjoying the fight, otherwise they would have finished me with a storm of arrows. The injured man groaned as I dropped my sword and pulled the man up by his filthy coat with one hand and held him while I sunk my teeth into the wound on his neck where his blood spurted.

The warm blood filled my mouth and my belly

It made me strong, and my wounds felt hot as they began to heal.

A hail of arrows crashed into me.

The Mongols had perhaps been horrified by blood drinking, or they were simply done with testing themselves against me and repeatedly failing. All I knew was the storm of a score of arrows, and then a dozen more, hitting my helm, my leg, the portcullis behind me, and many hit the body of the dying man in my hands. I retreated to the portcullis and used the body as a shield, ducked behind it. Arrows stuck in his clothing, others hit his flesh with a wet smack. The force of the arrows pushed me back into the portcullis while I held on to the body, though it shook with the impacts. An arrow stuck in my lower leg, and another hit me in the shoulder, slipping deep into the wound beneath the ripped mail. The pain was exquisite and I wailed and hugged the body to me as my legs failed and I went down. The archers had spread out to either side and peppered me from angles that my meat shield could not defend. My helm was hit again and my skull rang with the pain, my vision clouded with silver-white snow.

Perhaps I blacked out. Lost my senses, at least. A voice roared at me to get up. The smell of fresh blood filled my nose.

A mass of Mongols picked their way toward me in a wide arc, swords, and daggers drawn.

Something was by my head, demanding attention.

William had pushed his bared forearm through a square gap in the portcullis. He had cut his wrist and blood welled and gushed out of it, covering his hand with glistening, dark blood.

"Drink!" he roared at me.

I did not hesitate. I grabbed his arm, sank my teeth into his wrist and sucked the hot blood down.

It had been sixty years since I had last drunk my brother's blood. I remembered how it had given me greater strength than any mortal blood. And once again, it was like drinking lightning, like consuming the whirlwind. Shards of ice and fire ran like lightning through my veins, to the tips of my fingers and filled my head with clarity of vision, clarity of thought. Every sense burned and the world became hard-edged and bright like the midday desert sun. Every muscle felt as if it would burst, as if I had grown to twice my size. I felt like a giant, though I knew I was not. A great passion for murder filled every part of me, and I had to kill, had to tear down every man and every building in the city.

I stood and threw the arrow-filled Mongol body at a man in front of me as if it was no heavier than a stone, knocking the man down and the one behind him. Most of the others froze in shock and I ran into the men, a red mist descending and my sense of self fading. I was all passion and no thought. It seemed as though God or the Devil was in my bones, and I grabbed the men and smashed them with my hands. I drove their heads into the portcullis, into the walls. I threw them up into the ceiling and snapped their necks and crushed their skulls. My fists broke their faces into bloody pulp and I stamped their throats and chests, crushing them underfoot. Though they fled from me, I was faster than the fleetest of them and killed a dozen, and then two dozen, even before they could flee into the light beyond. It was so bright out there that the glare hurt my eyeballs and I shielded my eyes, looking for more men to murder.

Beyond the escaping Mongols, the sounds of battle filled the air. They were being killed from the rear also, and the great mass of them scattered away from where I stood, cringing against the walls of the tunnel. They were brave men, but they were right to be afraid of me and I chased them down also, dashing their brains out against the blood-smeared walls while they wailed and screamed and prayed to their barbarian gods.

The stench of blood was glorious. I drank from the tattered neck of a head that I had ripped from its body, the last of the blood within streaming into my mouth and over my face. But soon there were no more men to kill and, though it yet raged, I felt the bloodlust of William's blood diminishing.

Someone was calling my name, a distant sound that echoed through the groans of the men who were dead but did not yet know it.

A man strode toward me and I turned and seized him, lifting

him so that I might bite his throat out and fill myself once more.

"Richard, stop!"

A woman.

Eva cried out and then she was at my side, holding my arm.

"It is Thomas, Richard," she cried. "You hold Thomas. He is a friend, Richard. You must let him go."

His grimacing face came into focus and I dropped him, pushing him away so that he fell. Eva backed away from me and the fear in her eyes shook me further out of my rage.

Looking about me, I saw a slaughterhouse. Bodies everywhere, walls and ceiling sprayed with blood and the floor underfoot splashed with it from the disembowelled and dismembered men and horses that filled the tunnel. Someone finished off a dying horse, cutting off the horrendous sound of its suffering.

My surviving companions, bloodied and battered, stood about the entrance in the light of an orange sunset. Beyond them, Mongols rode hard away from us down the roadway toward the distant middle gatehouse, fleeing the bloody horror. Orus supported a wounded Khutulun. Stephen had somehow survived but was covered in blood and had the mad, blank post-battle stare. Hassan leaned on a spear, without helm and with tattered armour hanging from him. There was no Jalal, Radi or Raka. I remembered that I had seen Abdullah fall and indeed, he was also absent. No doubt lying dead back there on the road with the three Assassins.

I had abandoned my companions for William.

Recalling my brother, I turned and ran to the portcullis. William was still on the other side, grinning at me, at the carnage that I waded through. Behind him, small groups of other men drifted toward the portcullis, Mongols or Turkomens, staring at the blood and gore and smashed bodies. Their voices were raised in protest but they stood and did nothing, for now.

"Why?" I shouted at William. "Why give me your blood?" I grabbed the portcullis and glared through it at him.

"You are my brother," he said as if that explained it.

"I will still kill you," I said. "I will still hunt you to the ends of the Earth."

He took a deep breath. "I wish you would not. For it is to the ends of the Earth that I am going, and I do not believe you will fare well there. Look at what a mess you have made in this city. Go home, Richard."

"The ends of the Earth?" I asked. "Where is that? You are fleeing Hulegu, no?"

"Hulegu and Mongke have other brothers. One of them is Kublai, and he controls the East. He means to conquer all Cathay and he can do it, with my help. There are a hundred cities there the size of Baghdad, and a thousand grander than Paris. If Mongke should fall, Kublai will become the Great Khan, again, with my help."

"You will not be able to control him," I said. "No more than you could Hulegu, nor any of these others who you have given the Gift."

He smiled. "I do not wish to control him. I will make myself a prince and do my work in peace. All I need is wealth, I see that now. Wealth, and land. You should return to Christendom, brother, you are not capable of surviving in foreign lands, amongst foreign people. You have too much hatred in your heart."

"I will never stop coming for you," I said. "God desires you dead, and I am His instrument."

William sighed. He looked around at the Turkomen who gathered closer to him. No doubt they were wondering who he was and why we were conversing.

"Is there any chance you would return the favour and let me drink your blood, brother? I would greatly love to feel that power. I would make short work of these men, would I not?"

"My only regret in seeing you cut down before my eyes," I said, "will be that it was not my own sword that ended you."

He sighed again and spoke rapidly. "A deal, perhaps?" He held up a hand as I began to protest. "I gave my blood and turned at least thirty, serfs and lords, between Nottingham and Acre. Do you want to know who they are, where they are, so that you can hunt them?"

I hesitated. How could I deal with a devil such as he? I was a fool to even consider it, I knew that much. But how much destruction could thirty immortals do to my homeland? To Christendom as a whole? What deviousness were they working on my people even as we spoke?

"You can never turn me away from my pursuit of you," I said.

"Perhaps I could postpone it?" William said. "All I need is two hundred years, brother." I laughed with scorn but he continued. "What is such a span to the likes of us?"

"You could turn a thousand men into immortals in such time," I said.

"But no Christians," he said.

"You would turn your Cathay armies against Christendom," I said.

"Never," he said. "I swear it."

I laughed at his lies.

"I will tell you where our grandfather lives," he said.

That gave me pause. "You are filled with lies."

"Never to you, brother." He tilted his head. "Have you ever known me to tell a lie?"

A clanking noise echoed around the tunnel and William glared at me.

"Quickly, Richard. Swear you will not follow me to Cathay and I will tell you where to find our ancient grandfather. And I will tell you where my Gifted are."

I punched my fist into the portcullis so hard that the entire thing shook and my skin split, leaving blood on the wood. "Agreed. I swear it. But I shall kill you the moment you return to Christendom."

He grinned. "Our grandfather is in Swabia. In a forest, living in a cave. The locals live in terror of him."

The portcullis shook and shifted up as the chains took the strain. William began backing away.

"Who did you make immortal?" I shouted.

"A French lord named Simon de Montfort," William said, raising his voice and still retreating. "An English knight named Hugh le Despenser. Both of them men after my own heart, you will find."

"Who else?" I roared.

But he turned and ran. He ran through the massing crowd of Turkomen and they made only half-hearted attempts to stop him. He struck down a man or two and sent them flying as he ran. The portcullis shook and began to rise, slowly. So slowly.

"Richard," Eva said, at my shoulder. "We must go." She stared at the massed soldiers on the other side.

"We can kill them all," I said, unwilling to let William go without more names.

"Perhaps," she said. "But your men are hurt. Exhausted. They need you."

I looked at her. She was injured. She had no sword. The others behind me were in a similar poor condition. And there was the stark absence of the men who had already fallen.

The portcullis shook and rose further, winched up from some mechanism beyond the ceiling. I slammed my hands against it, sensing that I had somehow been bested by my brother once more.

"We need horses," I said to my men. "Supplies."

"And quickly," Thomas said. "Before he gets too far."

"Quickly, yes," I said, as we moved away from the tunnel. "But we are not pursuing him."

They stared at me.

"We must retreat from this place," I said. "Eventually, we shall return to the Kingdom of Jerusalem. We must gather our strength and take our time doing so, waiting until our moment is right. And then we must kill Hulegu at a place of our choosing."

"What about your vile, murdering brother?" Thomas said, raising a shaking finger to point down the tunnel of the gatehouse.

"He has gone to the East," I said. "And I will kill him when he returns."

"When will that be?" Stephen asked.

"One day," I said. They were outraged. Furious, even, and they had every right to be. "We will slaughter the Khan and his men, first."

Orus smiled and looked at Khutulun. She nodded. "Hulegu now."

None of my people were happy with our failure. My failure. And yet I am certain they were relieved to be leaving that horror of a city.

Moving as a group, we slipped further through Baghdad toward the gate, avoiding contact with enemies where we could. As night fell, we rounded up a horse for each of us, and a few spares, killing the men guarding them. We wrapped ourselves in Mongol coats and followed Orus and Khutulun through the final gate into the mass of the surrounding army and rode in the moonlight as if we were an arban about an official task. We were challenged only a few times, and Orus shouted responses that satisfied our enemies. It was in our favour that the armies were so disparate, from so many nations and cities, and all expected to see strangers amongst them. Still, I was shocked by the size of the forces that stretched here and there for miles. All come to share in picking clean the monstrous great carcass of the greatest city in the world.

Then we were free, riding on or parallel to the Damascus road until we turned off to hide out in a village a hundred miles away.

There we drank blood from the Saracen villagers and took over their meagre homes while keeping them prisoner. Hassan pointed out that it would be better to kill them outright in case they alerted roving Mongol patrols to our presence but I had seen quite enough murder for the time being. Instead, we ate their goats, mended our gear.

And we waited.

Following my abandonment of my companions on the road in Baghdad, I found that the relationship between me and each of them—other than perhaps Orus and Khutulun, who had a barbarian's immorality—, had changed. There was no denying I had committed a great sin by fleeing from them when they needed me to fight to save them and they would all trust me even less than they had before. The only one I truly cared about was Eva and she did not wish to discuss it, assuring me that it was not important. I knew she was lying but I was happy to accept the falsehood.

Stephen was shaken by the whole terrible event and had faced certain death by the screaming Mongols all around him. It was indeed remarkable that he had survived but he did not forgive me for putting him in that situation nor, of course, for leaving him to die. I think that he also mourned Abdullah.

The Saracen had taken a Mongol axe in the top of his head, splitting his skull in two. I had never much liked the man, despite finding a grudging respect for him in time, yet I felt particularly guilty for his death. Despite being banished for a social impropriety, he had cared enough about his homeland, his city, his people, to stay and fight when he could have done anything else and many thousands of his countrymen had given up. After all his snivelling and complaining, the man had discovered an admirable moral core to his soul but thanks to my actions, he would never be able to develop further. At least he did not have to witness the complete annihilation of his city.

There was no doubt that the esteem in which Thomas held me had declined. The man was always reserved but his demeanour became rather cooler for quite some time. On the other hand, he was a man who well understood the importance of duty and the conflicts that could arise between one duty that clashed with another.

Hassan was deeply angered because he had lost Jalal, Radi, and Raka and all three had died in order to protect him, their master. Even so, Hassan had almost himself been cut down. I could well imagine that he cursed me and chastised himself for ever trusting a Frank like me but he silently seethed instead. It seemed likely that any night he would cut my throat in my sleep but Eva thought otherwise.

"He will very likely do it," she said. "But not until we have killed Hulegu."

Later, I found out what had happened in Baghdad after we escaped it.

The Christians who assembled in the Nestorian church and some of the foreign visitors were spared, but the Mohammedan population was subjected to almost complete extermination. The Christian soldiers from Georgia and Armenia took great joy in it, for killing Saracens was what God wanted. And no civilised man could contend otherwise.

When all in the city were dead, and all the wealth plundered, then the palaces and the mosques, the university and libraries, the homes and the markets, were set on fire. The contents of the Caliph's treasure house were loaded into two vast wagon trains, with one sent to Mongke Khan in far-off Karakorum, and the other sent to a city called Maragha in the north of Persia where Hulegu would make his capital.

During the week of slaughter, Hulegu held a banquet with the Caliph in the palace itself. Hulegu pretended that the Caliph was the host and that Hulegu was the guest. He mocked the caliph for not using his treasure to pay soldiers to protect his city. For what was treasure worth if you could not keep it?

When the city was finally in ruins, the Caliph and his sons were sewn up in beautiful carpets and trampled to death beneath the hooves of the horses of Hulegu's immortal retinue.

The Vizier, Abdullah's uncle, was retained in his office and served the Mongols. He faced the impossible task of rebuilding the city. He began immediately and worked to the best of his ability for three months.

He attempted this task for three months only because then the Vizier died.

The Shiites said he died of a broken heart because his city had been destroyed. The Sunnites said it was due to the guilt and shame he felt at betraying his caliph, and that he could not live with that decision.

The truth is that I killed him myself.

Although my companions and I argued over the risks involved, ultimately, I believed it would be worth it. We crept back to the city after most of the armies had moved off to new pastures and slipped through the few Mongols that remained. After three months of plundering, there was nothing left to protect, so no one was guarding anything with any great dedication. The Mongol garrison troops within the city were spread out and living in half-demolished and burned palaces, carousing and drunk as lords all night and lying insensible in their own piss through the day. It was remarkably simple to avoid any trouble.

While the others guarded the approaches and held our horses ready for the escape, Hassan and I walked almost right up to the Vizier's bedchambers before cutting down the armed servants who attempted to thwart us. Hassan had been angry for three months, since the deaths of his men. Angry at me for the failure of my Baghdad strategy, for my tactical errors and abandonment of them during the sacking, and he was angry at the world and at himself. He rejoiced in the killing of the Vizier's men and I was glad that he was taking it out on them rather than me.

Letting ourselves into the enormous, marble room, the most powerful man in Baghdad fell to his knees before us, weeping and begging for his life.

"We are here for your treasury," I told him and he told us all we needed to know about how to take it.

"God is greatest," he said, praying through his tears.

"Was it worth it?" I asked him.

The Vizier seemed almost relieved when my dagger pierced his neck.

I drank a little from him and passed him to Hassan, who

savagely sucked down the blood before tossing his body across an ornate couch. We were already long gone by the time anyone raised an alarm. Perhaps no one ever did.

The wealth that had been left to the vizier by the Mongols was in the form of gold, silver, and gem stones locked in the much-reduced treasure room to be used for rebuilding the city. All that treasure, we stole, packing it into bags shared between two dozen horses that we rode and led out from the ruins of Baghdad without being challenged once, nor even pursued.

A mercenary act on the face of it, perhaps, but I needed a large amount to buy horses and equipment, to find places for us to live, and to pay for slaves to serve us and to provide blood for my people. And I had to pay vast sums for information on the whereabouts and activities of Hulegu while we planned our assault on his palace and the final assassination of him and his men.

It took us seven years.

But then, in early AD 1265, we were ready for the final assault on Hulegu Khan and his immortals.

PART SIX
MARAGHA FEB
1265

I WAS THE FIRST ONE TO CLIMB the border wall of Hulegu's palace compound, my fingers clinging to the cracks between the dark stone in the black moonless night. The compound was within a city, and there were thousands of people in homes and in the streets all around us, and guards and servants within the palace walls. My weapons were wrapped tight so they could not make a sound, and I wore no armour. Dressed in a close-fitting tunic in the Persian style, with a rider's trousers beneath and a Mongol hood and coat over it all, I was able to move swiftly in relative silence. Beneath me, hanging suspended from my belt, was a heavy sack and the sound that it made brushing against the stone as I climbed seemed loud enough to wake the dead. I prayed that it would alert no one, as the rest of my company scaled the wall behind me or waited their turn to mount the wall in the shadows below.

Years of planning and preparation had preceded my scaling of that wall, and I was just about as nervous as I had ever been in my life. It seemed to me that anyone within fifty feet would be able to hear the thumping of my heart and I had to remember to breathe in and out or else I would have suffocated myself from apprehension. I felt like a weak-kneed squire riding toward my first battle.

A chunk of mortar broke off beneath my fingers and I crashed against the wall, cursing under my breath. The sack I was carrying bounced off the wall and the contents jostled inside. From somewhere below, I heard the nervous hissing of my comrades.

Stealthiness had never been my forte. Always, I had been made for the direct approach and the intricacies and timings of our infiltration had me rattled. If the slightest thing went wrong, we would be assaulted on all sides by numbers that we could never hope to overcome. Gathering myself, I climbed on.

On the other hand, if everything went according to plan, then it would end in an orgy of tremendous violence all the same.

And that was something I was familiar with.

As my hands reached the top of the wall, I pulled myself up and peeked over into the cluster of service buildings with yellow lamplight glowing from windows and doors, and the marble mass of the grand palace itself.

It was quiet below and so I whistled faintly and listened as my companions began their climbs. Sliding over the top, dragging the sack carefully behind me, I slithered down into the shadows and waited for the others to join me.

How we came to be scaling that wall on a cold night in early 1265 involves an assassination, the Mongol Empire's first great defeat, and a massive civil war.

* * *

So much had happened since Baghdad fell. So much had changed.

After sacking Baghdad and massacring its people, Hulegu Khan intended to go on and conquer the rest of the Mohammedan lands and then to subdue Anatolia and destroy Constantinople. Once that great bastion of civilisation on the edge of Europe was gone, there would be nothing stopping them pouring across Christendom all the way to the Atlantic coast. The knowledge of those plans, won through interrogation of captured soldiers and bribed merchants and diplomats, instilled in me both a terrible fear and a determination to stop the khan at all costs, even if it meant my own life. But I knew that I must be patient, for I would get only one chance to put an end to him and his men.

Hulegu left three thousand Mongols in Baghdad to rebuild it but without the Vizier in charge, they accomplished nothing. I had seen their greatest city, and Karakorum was a pathetic, barbarian place. For all the wealth they had plundered, for all the multitudes of engineers and artisans from civilised peoples that they had pressed into slavery for them, the Mongols remained incapable of building anything of note, let alone rebuilding the greatness and beauty of Baghdad. In fact, even a hundred years later it remained mostly a ruin. And the people living around the city could no longer even be supported, as the Mongols had destroyed the intricate irrigation systems around the city and they were never rebuilt. Armies bring diseases and eat up the land like locusts, and vile plagues and famine remained after the Mongols left.

Other Mohammedan princes witnessed this destruction of Baghdad from afar, and it certainly appeared as though they felt any resistance to the Mongols to be hopeless. After Baghdad, Hulegu led his armies north to Tabriz to regroup and the remaining princes of Syria and Anatolia came one by one to offer their submission. For a time, we intended to assault him there but he remained on a war footing, with hundreds of thousands of men surrounding him and so instead we watched and waited.

After a period of consolidation lasting almost a year, Hulegu resumed his advance, this time towards the coast and Aleppo. His immortal second in command, a Mongol lord named Kitbuqa, commanded the vanguard and Hulegu himself commanded the centre of three grand armies. On his way to the coast, Hulegu finally subdued upper Iraq, where there were still holdouts. The Mongols reached Aleppo in January 1260 and took the city in mere days, although the town's citadel held out for another month. In that campaign, Hulegu was assisted by the King of Lesser Armenia and Crusader Bohemond VI of Antioch and Tripoli. The Mongols extended their power south into Palestine and it appeared to everyone that the entire Mediterranean coast would fall to them.

Watching it all happen from afar made me feel sick to my stomach. Most appalling of all was the relative weakness of those who attempted to stand against him and the ease with which Hulegu's forces overran them. I wondered with dread whether even the Kingdom of France and her allies could resist such a relentless onslaught. How long would Paris stand? Would Rome even take up arms?

But in truth, the Mongols were a long way yet from Europe and not all the Saracens had fallen. The great Sultan of Syria and the Mamluks of Egypt represented the only remaining chance for the Mohammedans. Hassan, even though they would have considered him as a dangerous heretic, wanted us to help the Mamluks just as we had hoped to help the Abbasids.

I said no.

We were done with that. Done with attempting to ally with the enemies of Christ and done with relying on anyone other than each other. Thanks to the Vizier's treasury, we had wealth enough to survive and to bide our time, and I told Hassan in no uncertain terms that is what we would do. Hassan grumbled but came to agree. Though his thirst for vengeance was as powerful as any of ours, the Assassins were well-versed in patience.

And then, across the world in the East, the Great Khan Mongke died.

It was many months before all Mongols heard and none of them knew that this death would signal the beginning of the end of a unified Mongol Empire.

The Great Khan had taken up the assault on the great nation

of Cathay. News took a long time to travel, of course, but I heard eventually that he had died assaulting some Cathay fortress. There were a dozen whispered stories about how he had come to his end. We paid merchants for news and some told me that Mongke died of cholera during the siege. Another said he had shit himself to death in an endless bloody flux. Another told us that Mongke had drowned in a warship in the high seas while his armies besieged an island fortress. Another story said he was crossing a river, another swore he was being transported across a lake in a barge, and the vessel was destroyed by enemy fire, or it was a simple accident. A Hungarian silversmith fleeing his Mongol masters swore that Mongke had been killed by an arrow shot by an archer during an attack on an eastern castle, and then later the Hungarian's wife said the Great Khan had been incinerated by an explosive bomb launched from a trebuchet.

But I knew the truth.

William had killed him.

The timing was too perfect for it to be otherwise. By my calculations, it would have taken about a year and a half for William to travel from Baghdad all the way to the Mongol assault on China. There, he had somehow managed to poison Mongke. Poison was a method of murder familiar to him and no doubt the Great Khan's lifelong abuse of wine had thoroughly weakened his constitution. And surely the number and sheer variety of stories indicated that the Mongols spread misinformation to cover up what they must have known to be a shameful assassination that demonstrated a terrible failure in state security. Or perhaps they believed Mongke had simply drunk himself to death. Thousands

404

of other Mongols had gone the same way before.

But I was sure. It was a remarkable assassination, and one perhaps greater than any Ismaili Assassin had ever achieved, though Hassan insisted that it had to have been one of his own four hundred fedayin who had finally succeeded in their mission.

Why, Hassan had challenged me, would William have done this thing?

"Chaos," I said.

Following the death of the Great Khan, once again the worldwide campaigns of the Mongols came to quite a sudden halt. Chaos ensued.

And chaos was what William thrived on. Mongke's death in 1259 led to a four-year civil war between two of his brothers, Kublai and Ariq Boke. William had told me in Baghdad that he meant to throw in with Kublai, and with William's support, Kublai eventually won the succession war.

Although he never sought the position of Great Khan for himself, the struggle for the succession took Hulegu away from Syria and Persia, and he left his subordinates in charge. I was sure that Hulegu now knew that he and his core group of bodyguards and lords were immortal and he could afford to take his time. It was clear that he meant to become lord of all lands from Persia to France, and so he left the Middle East and headed home with most of his armies.

One of his immortals was named Kitbuqa. This man was left in command of a single tumen of about ten thousand men and, with this small force, he made the fatal mistake of attacking the Mamluks.

The Mamluks were newly in power in Egypt and were the vanquishers of the King of France in his dismal failure of Louis' crusade eight years earlier. Those Mamluks were not like the other Mohammedans the Mongols had faced. In fact, they were a slave army taken mostly from the steppe people of the north, especially the Kipchaks. These former steppe people understood Mongol tactics, and even employed them against the Mongols. Not only that, the Mamluks had the advantage of being equipped with the highest quality Egyptian armour and weapons and had much finer and more powerful horses than the Mongols did.

The Mamluks were led by a man named Baibars, under the Sultan Qutuz. Baibars would be remembered as a great leader of the Egyptians, though he was, in fact, a tall, fair-skinned and light-haired former slave stolen from his Kipchak people near the Black Sea when only a boy. Baibars knew that the great Hulegu and his officer corps had gone to the East and so they baited the Mongols into attacking by doing the one thing that was guaranteed to draw them in. They beheaded the Mongol envoys, which as any horse nomad could tell you, is how you categorically declare war on the steppe.

In September 1260, the two forces clashed in what came to be known as the Battle of Ain Jalut. The site was known as the Spring of Goliath, and it was the very place that King David flung his stone at the Philistine champion.

It was an appropriate coincidence.

Strangely enough, although my companions took no part in it, we were not very far away when it happened, as the battle took place in Galilee and we were only thirty miles from there, on an estate near Acre. When the armies met, the first to advance were the Mongols, supported by men from the Kingdoms of Georgia and the Armenian Kingdom of Cilicia, both of which had submitted to Mongol authority. The two armies fought for many hours, with Baibars provoking the Mongols with repeated attack and retreat, without committing and losing too many of his men. It was said that Baibars had laid out the overall strategy of the battle since he had spent much time in that region as a fugitive earlier in his life. When the Mongols carried out another heavy assault, Baibars and his men feigned a final retreat, drawing the Mongols into the highlands to be ambushed by the rest of the Mamluk forces concealed among the trees.

The Mongol leader Kitbuqa, already provoked by the constant fleeing of Baibars and his troops, committed a grave mistake. Instead of suspecting a trick, the foolish Kitbuqa decided to march forwards with all his troops on the trail of the fleeing Mamluks. I believe that Kitbuqa's immortality had gone to his head and it led him to make rash decisions. Whatever the reason for his foolishness, when the Mongols reached the highlands, the hidden Mamluks charged into the fray and the Mongols then found themselves surrounded on all sides.

The Mongol army fought very fiercely to break out but it was too little and too late. Kitbuqa and almost the entire Mongol army perished.

"One of our immortal enemies, Hulegu's right hand, Kitbuqa, has fallen," I said to my companions when we heard the news.

"I do not understand," Khutulun kept saying, for it was the first time that the Mongols had lost a battle. "I do not understand." Orus likewise scratched his head. All they had ever known their whole lives was Mongol victory, from one end of the Earth to the other.

"They can be beaten, then," Thomas said to me later. "It is possible." For all his hatred of them, he seemed almost disappointed. I think that, in his mind, he had made them into something like demons and now he found that they were men after all.

But Hulegu would soon return and we all expected him to crush the Mamluks. In the Mongol civil war, Hulegu supported his brother Kublai and then returned through Persia to take up his war against the Mohammedans.

Knowing this, my companions and I prepared to kill Hulegu as he approached through the lands of Palestine. I spent considerable wealth in exploring a number of potential ambush sites in the hills, and even hired a few desperate mercenaries to help us scout likely areas. It was a dangerous place to be roaming around, with bands of Mamluks, Mongols, and brigands clashing on the borders.

But Berke, brother of the deceased Batu and the leader of the Golden Horde of Mongols on the steppes of Russia, had recently converted and now called himself a Mohammedan. After Baghdad fell, Berke was angry at the insult to his new faith and he moved to attack Hulegu, who had to make his way up to Azerbaijan to defend against this new enemy.

Which took Hulegu far away from us once more.

The presence of a serious threat from fellow-Mongols on his northern flank boxed Hulegu in, and he settled down once more and decided to wait out his cousin Berke, who was already old and who Hulegu, being immortal, would easily outlive. In the cities he had won along the Tigris and Euphrates, Hulegu put his viceroys into power, and rewarded some of the helpful Shiites. Thus establishing his vast dominion, Hulegu declared himself to be the Ilkhan, and his empire as the Ilkhanate. This word il-khan meant subordinate khan. The term had been agreed to by Hulegu, in exchange for in practice having complete autonomy from Kublai. It was said by those we bribed that, behind closed doors, Hulegu laughed that Kublai was concerned with appearances where Hulegu cared only for real power. And Hulegu ruled his vast Ilkhanate not from Iraq but from western Persia and the city of Maragha.

Maragha was up north, near the Caspian Sea. Northeast of Mosul, northwest of the ruined Alamut and south of Armenia and close to the enormous saltwater Lake Urmia. The lake had a number of large islands, the largest of which was about six miles long. An island that I would later visit.

The city of Maragha was situated in a narrow, north-south valley at the eastern extremity of a fertile plain between the valley and Lake Urmia just twenty miles to the west. The land all around in fact was rich with vineyards and orchards, all well-watered by canals led from the river, and producing great quantities of fruit.

It was no wonder that Hulegu was content to wait out the Mongol civil wars and the Mamluk power grab in such surroundings. It was not only the great abundance of the land but the strategic location of the city that allowed him to cover any attacks from the Golden Horde to the north, as well as govern his

Persian subjects to the southeast and control his newly-conquered peoples to the southwest in Iraq and Syria.

We knew that the time for us to kill the Ilkhan was approaching. He was ruling from one city and most of his armies were disbursed hundreds or thousands of miles away.

And yet the Hulegu was very careful with his security. Such a conqueror had made thousands of enemies, even millions. And it was not only the Ismailis who were capable of poisoning their enemies or murdering them in their beds. And so we watched from afar as he ruled and, under Hassan's guidance, we slowly and carefully built a network of spies. Slave traders, merchants, musicians. The jugglers and acrobats. Physicians and masons. Anyone who would travel through the region, first of all. Then we found people who could approach or even enter the city and provide information on the layout of the streets, the important people, and so on. Eventually, we bought off a man named Enrico of Candia who provided a steady stream of slaves to the rulers of Maragha and so could provide a wealth of insider information.

Enrico was a Venetian by birth, though he claimed to have left as a boy, never to return. He had grown rich transporting slaves across the Black Sea in all directions and had grown fat and enormously wealthy ever since coming under the protection of Batu Khan. Since Batu's death, he had come over to Hulegu's side following a falling out with Batu's brother Berke. Hassan and Stephen, both devious men by nature and in practice, believed that Enrico had feigned this conflict with Berke and was, in fact, spying for him. We were therefore concerned about trusting him in any way.

"What if he serves Hulegu and yet only pretends to Berke that he serves him?" Stephen said to Hassan, one evening as we ate together in our home in the Kingdom of Georgia.

It was easy enough in those times and in that part of the world for me to pose as a wealthy French mercenary, especially with such a mixture of foreign peoples in my entourage. Especially, also, as the opposing armies of the Golden Horde to the north and Hulegu's Ilkhanate to the south were at risk of coming to blows in the lands that lay between them, like Georgia. With a fabricated reputation for martial brilliance and reliability that we had sent ahead of us, the local lord had provided me with a perfectly acceptable residence so that I and other soldiers of fortune like me would be on hand should hostilities break out.

"Perhaps our man Enrico serves both masters?" Hassan said. "Giving information to both Hulegu and Berke, and so serves only himself?"

"Might it be that he trades information to anyone who can pay?" Eva suggested. "The Latin magnates of Constantinople, his fellow Venetian traders, and the Saracen lords. It would seem that Enrico of Candia knows everyone. Surely, we may expect to find him accommodating. We should pay him well, not ask too much of him in return, and grudgingly provide him with a plausible story about why we wish to know about the palace. Something that he would not feel honour bound to sell us out for."

"What might such a thing possibly be?" Thomas asked.

"Horse thieves," Eva said. "We will steal the Ilkhan's most valuable horses right out of his stable, for breeding in Acre, where good horses are a fortune."

Hassan sighed, and pinched his nose, for he had little regard for the wisdom of women, especially when it was sound. "And if we make contact and he sells us to Hulegu, what then of our entire undertaking? We must be cautious."

"For God's sake," I said to the group, and banged my hand on the table, causing them to turn to me all at once as the plates and cups rattled. "Stephen, go to his people and buy us some blood slaves for ourselves, will you? The usual type. Mutes or morons, if possible. Foreign savages if not. We shall continue to move cautiously but we must act, and not sit around talking about the matter."

Two years later, I still did not know whether the Venetian Enrico of Candia was loyal to Hulegu or not. Whether he had sold us out, and whether we were walking into a trap. And that thought, along with a thousand other worries about our assassination plan, played on my mind as I scaled the wall of Hulegu's palace on a cold night in February 1265.

* * *

Maragha was not a large capital but it had a high city wall and four sturdy gates. The outer wall to the north had a small postern gate big enough only for men and not horses, and we had promised a fortune to a certain Kipchak guard if he would but open it to us on that night. Praise God, the young fellow held up his end of the bargain. Orus seized him, and whispered threats should we find he had sold us out to his masters. When the terrified Kipchak swore to Christ—for he was a Nestorian—, that he had done precisely as we had required, Orus expertly cut the young man's throat.

I have killed uncounted thousands in my life and been witness to many times more deaths, but it is the dishonourable ones such as that squalid murder which have plagued my dreams down the centuries. An inauspicious start to our infiltration, and it unsettled me all the more as it felt as though our venture was tainted with the underhanded act. But it was an act of necessity for, once he had let us in, we could not let him go lest he be captured and give us up, nor could we tie him up lest he be discovered and do the same. And so, a treacherous blade to the gullet it was, and his body we shoved into a dark doorway.

I told myself that the incidental deaths of the innocent were necessary in order to save Christendom from Hulegu's horde. We would kill hundreds to save millions.

Slipping into the city through the postern was straightforward. Making our way through the streets was likewise a relatively simple matter and we did so swiftly and without challenge. Alas, there was but a single gate into the walled palace compound and so over the wall we went, climbing like lizards up the stones with our gear hanging from sacks behind some of us. We had a lot of men to kill, and we needed the means to do it. For they were not ordinary men, but Hulegu and his immortals, and they would die hard.

The others followed me, dropping as quietly as shadows down the inside of the wall into the dark soil and ornamental bushes near to the base of the wall.

I counted down Eva, Thomas, Stephen, Hassan, Orus, and

Khutulun. We were all there, and all ready.

One of the Mongols that William had turned had been killed by the Mamluks and our information suggested Hulegu had twelve immortals left alive to serve him.

Every one of them was in the palace with him that night. Eight of them were Hulegu's personal bodyguards, collectively known as the keshig, and they were with him or near to him almost all the time and had been for years. By all accounts, they were battle-scarred brutes who terrified the courtiers. But the other four immortal lords had been recalled from their regions of Hulegu's Ilkhanate. It was the Mongol new year celebration, and they would feast together and discuss the Ilkhan's strategic priorities for the following year.

It was the first time Hulegu's immortals had all been together for many months and we knew we may never have a better opportunity.

There were seven of us and thirteen of them, so already we were at a numerical disadvantage as far as immortals of the blood went. Another disadvantage was that one of my men was Stephen, who I had trained to fight with basic competence in the intervening years but who would never be anything like a true warrior, even with his immortal's strength. And I had two women on my side. Deadly and skilful though they were, neither Eva nor Khutulun had the strength to match an immortal man of similar skill. And Hulegu's keshig bodyguards and lords were all seasoned soldiers.

Not only that, there would be mortal men in Hulegu's hall. Retainers, servants, supplicants, family members, soldiers, bodyguards, and slaves. Every Mongol court was a jumbled web of alliances and relationships and anyone we found in that hall would have to be killed, too. At worst they would fight us, and at least they would get in our way. For all I knew, I was leading my six companions against two hundred men or more.

Waving at them to follow, I led my company along the inside of the wall, between it and the lines of heavily-pruned fruit bushes that bordered the Persian style palace gardens. It was an absurd indulgence for a Mongol prince but Hulegu had settled into a luxury that would no doubt have been beyond the imagining of his barbarian fathers out on the savage steppe. An indulgence that displayed the confidence he had in his position, far enough from his enemies than no army could surprise him, and security in his own immortality. He would not be the only Mongol seduced by the degenerate wealth of the people he had conquered with such contempt.

I crept along beside the rows of ornate bushes, bent double and listening carefully for any signs that we had been seen by the patrolling night guards. If the alarm was raised before our attack was begun, then our chance of success would be gone, and the chance that any of us would escape would be close to nought, for we would be cornered and assaulted by hundreds of soldiers.

But we had our advantages. Assuming that none in our network of spies had been compromised or had been an enemy all along, then we would have surprise on our side.

Also, many Mongols would become fall-down drunk on an ordinary night in the ordus and we had timed our assassination to coincide with the celebration of the new year. Orus and

Khutulun swore that everyone at court would have feasted all day on milk, cheese, mutton, roast horse, rice and curds and especially endless mountains of buuz, which were steamed dumplings stuffed with meat and were the only halfway edible food in the vile Mongol diet. They would certainly be stuffed to the guts and guzzling down gallons of fermented horse milk and rice wine. Our informants had told us that Hulegu's men mixed blood into their drinks to make an intoxicating potion they revelled in, to the confusion and repulsion of all who were not immortals. The gluttonous brutes had been hunting and banqueting for several days already and so they would surely be suffering from their excesses.

Whereas we had been practising. At Hassan's urging, we had rehearsed our roles in the assault on the palace many times. We had discussed it at table, we had even staked the ground in estimated dimensions of Hulegu's hall and acted out our parts as if we were revels or guisers performing for each other so that we could coordinate the timing of our attacks. We practised fighting in confined spaces. We all practised throwing. Eva and Khutulun became expert at tossing fist-sized stones into distant baskets.

Alert to every sound, I heard the cooks in the kitchens behind the palace shouting at their servants while they roasted meats, the smell of which filled the air and made my guts churn. Figures hurried here and there. A muttering boy dragged a basket of firewood along the ground toward the servants' entrances at the rear of the palace. Two men carried a freshly-slaughtered goat from one building to another, laughing about something as they went.

416

When we reached the centre of the north wall, we paused and unwrapped our weapons from the strips of wool or sheepskin that had kept them from clanging or rattling during our incursion. After all of us were ready, I nodded to Stephen.

For just a moment, Stephen's features in the gloom reminded me of when he had been a bookish English monk too afraid to even approach me on the ship in the Black Sea. He nodded back at me and hurried past us, all alone in the shadows, toward the palace stables with his heavy sack clutched to his chest. Whether he buckled under the pressure of his mission remained to be seen.

Looming above us in the darkness, Hulegu's palace seemed rather bigger than it had when we had staked out the dimensions on the ground.

After Stephen vanished into the gloom, the rest of us headed straight toward a specific servants' entrance at the rear of the palace, listening hard for any sign of the guards or anyone else who might discover our intrusion and raise the alarm. The kitchens were close by now, just across a courtyard, and the fires within were casting light from under the door and smoke from above the roof. A door in the kitchens opened, throwing a shard of yellow light slanting across the ground, and a young man came out. I waved my people down and we ducked low on the path. The lad carried a heavy jar in his arms, no doubt filled with wine for the celebrating lords within the palace. Tensing, I prepared to run him down and destroy him before he could raise the alarm. But he continued on across the courtyard, kicked open a door into the palace, and headed inside.

I let out the breath I was holding and waved my people to

follow me. My nervousness only increased as I went. Killing enemy soldiers had rarely bothered me, even when I was young but I knew innocent people would die in our attack and I could not shake the feeling of guilt. I kept telling myself that they would be victims of war and their incidental deaths would help to avoid a great many more deaths in the future and so the sin would be mitigated. Besides, they would only be Saracens, Persians, Mongols, mostly, and Armenians and I would be saving all Christendom west of Jerusalem from the irresistible invasion of the Mongol lords of war.

Assuming, of course, that our attack worked.

We moved swiftly and slipped up to the palace itself. All but Thomas and Hassan, who continued on around the building, heading for a side entrance to the other side of Hulegu's hall. My steadiest man, the old Templar was a great comfort to me and watching him disappear alone into the darkness stirred my heart greatly. He and Hassan were heading further into the palace than the rest of us and their task was immensely dangerous. I felt certain that I would never see them again, and I wished I had spoken to Thomas of my high regard for him. Then again, what was the point of such things? We all die, and either we will see each other again or we will not. And either way, God knows the truth and surely that is all that matters.

What a foolish old man I had become, feeling so emotional and apprehensive. An indulgence I could not afford.

Inside the servants' entrance was a large chamber where food and wine was prepared for the hall upstairs. The room was lined with shelves, and dried meats and herbs were hanging from the beams. Lamps hung from chains gave off a good light. Already, I could hear the cacophony of raised voices talking further within the building and above our heads, muffled by the stones and timbers of the building.

The boy who had carried the jug of wine across the courtyard was at a bench along the wall, ladling the contents into smaller serving jugs. I saw and smelled at once that it was not, in fact, wine but fresh blood he was transferring. Two old women in servants clothing turned from preparing a huge platter of roasted meat on a workbench and stared at me with confusion written on their faces. The fact that they appeared to be innocent Armenian servants doing their duty caused me to hesitate to do what was necessary.

My companions pushed into the room after me while I stood staring at the three servants, wondering if I might not have them bound and gagged instead of dispatched. One of the old women dropped to her knees with her hands raised in supplication as our intentions dawned on her. The other screwed up her face in anger and took a deep breath.

She did not have time to utter a cry, for Khutulun pushed past me and cracked the woman's head open with the hammer side of her axe, and then buried the blade into the skull of the other one. Through it all, the boy stood stock still, arms by his sides and his eyes screwed shut. Khutulun whipped her axe blade from the old woman's skull and hacked into the lad's face, dropping him like the women. Wiping her blade on her coat, she turned and sneered at me, her expression mocking my weakness. I had a foolish urge to protest that I would have killed them had she not intervened but Eva grabbed the sack from my hand and shoved me into motion.

Without further idiotic delay, I headed into the servants' stairwell and ran up the timber stairs, the others right behind me. It was dark and narrow and the boards creaked underfoot and though we attempted to be quiet, we sounded like an invading army as we ascended.

A man's voice growled something above and I ran up the last few steps, drawing my dagger.

It was a Mongol soldier, dressed for war. A kezik, a guard protecting his lords within the nearby hall. And though he was there to stop unauthorised entry and to fight intruders, he was not truly expecting to have to do so. Since the dawn of time, almost every guard who ever stood on duty has served an unremarkable watch where the greatest danger to him is being found dozing by his commanding officer. There are a few moments where his expectations conflict with reality and he must adjust to the fact that he will have to shake himself for sudden violence.

Those few moments were all I needed.

I leapt up the steps and slammed my dagger up under his chin and forced him clear from the landing area into the antechamber, bearing him down beneath me with my hand over his mouth. His dark eyes were wide in shock that he was being killed.

Orus jumped over me and brought down the second kezik with a terrific blow from his mace. The crash the man made as he hit the wall and bounced onto the floor was sure to bring more men from within the hall to investigate. The kezik's dented helm rolled across the floor until Orus stamped on it.

The kezik beneath me stopped struggling and I savoured the smell of his blood and watched as his eyes faded and he breathed his last breath into my face. It reeked of sour wine and onions.

Khutulun and Eva continued on up the stairs to the gallery above, their feet making a terrible din.

The revelry within the hall continued unabated but I could not feel relief. At any moment, they could discover us. Thomas and Hassan, or Stephen, could already have been killed or—even worse—captured.

Our dead keziks had been guarding the rear door into the hall where Hulegu and the other lords celebrated the new year. A small, sturdy door of dark wood was all that separated me from my enemies. Orus stood before it, a mace in one hand and a bulging sack in the other.

"Bar the door," I hissed at him.

He turned with a confused expression. "How?"

Certain that he was being foolish, I stepped beside him, cursing his stupidity.

Yet he was correct.

Our paid informants had sworn that the doors at either end of the hall could be barred and yet there was nothing to suggest that had ever been possible. Merely an ornate iron latch.

I took a deep breath and clapped Orus on the shoulder. "Do not let even a single man through," I said and relieved him of his sack, for I would need the contents in short order.

Before I ascended the next stair to the gallery, I glanced back at the young Mongol warrior. He stood with a mace in his left hand, and his sword now drawn in his right. A single man to hold that small antechamber against a horde who would be desperate to escape.

He turned and looked at me over his shoulder. For once, he did not grin. Instead, he nodded once, slowly and in response, I bowed my head.

I took the final stairway in a few leaps to find Eva and Khutulun crouched at the top of the steps. Another servant lay dead, face down against the wall with blood pooling beneath him.

I had reached the gallery, which ran along one side of the building just beneath the edge of the vaulted ceiling, with a beautifully carved balustrade at waist height, that looked down onto the hall below. At the far end of the gallery I knew was a stairway leading to some other part of the palace beyond the hall but I had to trust that Hassan and Thomas would do what they could to block or distract any reinforcements from that end once the assault began. In its normal function, such a gallery could house musicians, at other times it was where lords could look down on those inside the hall without having to mix with them.

It would also, I hoped, provide the perfect platform for committing a massacre.

The voices down in the hall were loud and the stink of the men and their vile food filled my nose. Laughter and arguments suggested that they were all steaming drunk and I prayed that we had timed it correctly so that their inebriation would inhibit their strength and coordination. Judging from the sound alone, there could have been fifty or a hundred men below me. Perhaps more.

With any luck, we could launch our attack without them ever

knowing what hit them.

"Quickly, now," I whispered to Eva and Khutulun.

We yanked open the sacks and began to unpack the contents. Inside, we had ceramic pots twice the size of a man's fist, each one wrapped in its own pouch of soft sheepskin of the highest quality. The soft coats protected the thinly-walled pots from breaking prematurely, and also prevented them from clanking together and giving us away. We shoved the pouches back into the leather bags and tossed them aside while lining up the pots on their flat bases. Each pot had a tube of waxed paper jutting from the top. The tube of waxed paper was filled with black powder that fizzed and burned like the devil when it was lit.

From inside my coat, I took the length of slowmatch I had lit before we made our final approach on the city. It was a short length of twisted hemp impregnated with some alchemical substance that allowed it to retain an ember within for many hours which could then swiftly be utilised to light a fuse. I had been repeatedly assured of their impeccable reliability.

Mine was cold.

I blew on it but it was completely out.

"Bloody useless Saracen bastard," I said, meaning Hassan, who had procured the devices from the surviving Syrian Assassins. "How do yours fare?" I asked Eva and Khutulun.

But then there was a shout from the far end of the gallery.

A Mongol guard stood staring at us, open-mouthed and outraged at our presence. No doubt the dead servant next to me also helped to give the game away. Another kezik came up beside him and there were more armed men behind filling the space.

Ripping my sword from the scabbard, I ran at them. I knew I would be in full view of anyone in the hall who looked up but there was nothing else I could do.

I felt the plan crumbling into pieces. So close to success, it had instead fallen to failure.

All I could do was fight on, fight through. It was all I knew. It was my profession. My passion.

The first Mongol drew his sword but I slashed my own blade across his face and he went wheeling back into the men crowding behind him. By God, I thought, there are so many of them. Too many to kill before the alarm was raised, if it was not too late already.

I kicked the next man's legs out from under him and stomped on him as I lunged at the men behind. The floored man rolled away and I half fell, raising my blade to defend against the dagger swung at my head. I kicked out with such fear and anger that the man was sent tumbling over the balustrade and down into the hall below with a crash.

The revelry stopped all at once, like the last candle being snuffed out.

I slashed at the remaining men, catching one and the rest jumped back from the gallery onto the landing beyond.

Behind me, Eva and Khutulun squatted, hunched over the rows of pots.

A cry went up from the hall, jeering and angry at the fallen man and I peered over the balustrade, leaning on the pillar of an arch.

The great hall was packed with Mongols. At a glance, it was

well over two hundred men, plus almost as many servants or slaves, most young girls. The revellers lined the hall on either side of the centre, most sitting on benches or on rugs and furs on the floor. It was laid out like a ger, only there was no women's side. What women there were mixed in amongst the men, and I saw none being treated with anything close to respect. There were no honoured wives, no domestic side to proceedings. Just slave girls.

I searched quickly for the lords amongst them. The ones who William had turned into immortals. There were many men dressed in silk finery, surrounded by clusters of followers and which of them were my targets, I could not easily tell.

Then again, it hardly mattered.

Most of them were staring at the body of the man who had fallen onto a group carousing below the gallery. Almost as one, however, every face in the hall was turned upward in search of the point from which the unfortunate fellow had tumbled. Of course, they all saw me.

At the top end—the end we had entered, and the one with the door guarded by Orus—sat Hulegu, surrounded on all sides by his keshig bodyguards who were dressed for war.

The Ilkhan, the most powerful man on Earth, other than, perhaps, his brother Kublai.

His eyes met mine and grew wide.

Holding my arms out by my side, I leaned over the balustrade and raised my voice to a powerful roar that echoed in the now-quiet hall. "Hulegu Khan! I am Richard of Ashbury. Your crimes are legion. And now your death is at hand!"

I doubt anyone understood my words precisely but Hulegu

certainly caught the crux of my declaration. He jumped to his feet and jabbed a finger up at me, scowling in pure hatred and barked out orders.

All about the hall, men bestirred themselves to attack.

Our key inside man, the slaver Enrico, had assured me that the only men with weapons would be Hulegu's immortal keshig but it was not just those eight soldiers who leapt to their feet and rushed across the hall toward the gallery. It seemed as though fully half of the drunken savages in the hall staggered across the benches, trampling slaves and servants as they charged my position. The first of them jumped up to grasp enormous painted fabrics hung on the wall and clambered up hand over hand.

A sword stabbed toward me from the side and I jerked away from it, bringing my blade up to defend the vicious attacks from the Mongols beside me up on the gallery. I could not defend the balcony from the men swarming up the wall hangings, as well as the men already up on the same level as me. Forgetting the hall for a moment, I rushed into the Mongols clustered near me in order to cause disorder amongst them and so destroy them rapidly. Cutting as fast as I could, slashing across their hands, their faces and shouting some wordless cries of fury. I stabbed one through the throat and he ran, blood gushing through his fingers, into the men behind him. While they threw him down, I killed them, too. Blood gushed out on the timbers underfoot amongst the writhing bodies.

"Richard!" Eva shouted from behind me.

The first men from the hall were climbing over the balustrade and I ran back along the gallery to cut them down. It was loud with shouts and jeering from the drunken merrymakers down below who were confident that they were themselves under no threat, that they would witness a short hunt followed by the violent execution of a Frankish interloper. They had no idea that it was their own horrifying deaths that were coming.

All along the balustrade, Mongols were dragging themselves up and over the railing. I cut the first man on the back of his exposed neck and his head came clean off, the body falling away. I cut off the hand of another man and crashed my blade into the skull of the next. On I ran to the next and smote him, and the next. They were drunk and slow and I was an immortal knight, faster than anything they could have imagined. I kicked a very fat man in the face and then the whole teeming bunch of them fell as one, as if by God's own hand.

The rope suspending the wall hangings had snapped and the row of fabrics all collapsed under the weight of dozens of climbing men, and they fell tumbling into a pile at the base of the wall. Many of the spectators cheered and laughed at their comrades.

Not all were unaware of their danger. A group of men hammered on the main hall door but it seemed they could not force it open from the inside.

Well done, Thomas. God save you.

But the rear door that Orus guarded, behind Hulegu's dais, was being advanced on by a group of men determined to rush out, climb the stairs and attack me from that side. Worse still, the Mongol bodyguards, armed and armoured though most without helms, now stood in a line below me, looking up.

Seeing me once more looking down, Hulegu roared and his

eight keshig jumped into action, throwing themselves against the bare wall and scrambling up against the stonework. One climbed the remnant of the wall hangings rope at the far corner.

I knew then that it was over. I could not fight eight immortal warriors, not all at once in a confined space. They would surround me and overwhelm me and I prayed that they would kill me outright so that I would be spared the sight of Hulegu's face, smug in his victory. Nevertheless, I prepared to kill as many as I could before I fell and hoped to give Eva and Khutulun the time that they clearly needed.

A pot sailed through the air from the end of the gallery in a great arc trailing smoke and a fizzing, smoking fire.

It smashed on the wall just above the rear door and the evil liquid inside gushed out and down for a moment before it was ignited by the waxed paper fuse. The sound was like a demon being thrust out from Hell, and the explosive ball of flame engulfed the men beneath in a shroud of boiling flame. Their screams filled the hall from floor to the timber roof high above. Safe from assault, the door was guarded by a raging fire. Flames leapt and bounced close to Hulegu's dais and he skipped away from it.

While the Mongols were frozen in horror or shrieking in fear at the sight of their fellows writhing in agony, another incendiary pot flew, angling right across the hall from end to end. This time it smashed beside the main door and tossed out fire like a beast searching for men to consume. The fire drove the men there back from their efforts to break out and as the people within saw that both exits were aflame, every man and woman, lord and slave, panicked. Screams of terror echoed from the rafters.

Two more fire pots flew and both doorways were further engulfed in explosive flame. Eva and Khutulun were throwing them as rapidly as they could get the fuses lit and so more and more followed quickly, smashing into the floor or into people or benches everywhere in the hall. Each fire pot belched out so much fire that every one of them immolated a half dozen people or more. The screaming crowd gathered in groups, clutching each other. What tempting targets they made. When these groups were hit, they all died.

The roaring of the fire grew, as did the screams and cries of agony and pure terror. Smoke billowed up in plumes and built steadily, quickly filling the hall with thicker and thicker smoke and the flames danced higher and licked the walls and the roof beams above.

All the while, the strongest and bravest Mongols clambered up the wall to the gallery, and I fought to keep them from overwhelming us. I cut and shoved and kicked like a demon. Some made it up over the balustrade momentarily and I killed them or threw them back into the ocean of fire below.

An armoured, immortal keshig leapt up and threw himself over onto the gallery close to Eva and Khutulun. He paused, looking between them and me, as I ran at him from the other end. He wisely chose me but had foolishly turned his back on Eva, who stood up behind him and swung her dagger into his neck and punched out his throat in a shower of blood and gristle. Without missing a beat, she snatched up a fire pot and tossed it down the wall into the other immortals climbing up.

But not all of them. Another keshig lunged from where he clutched to the rail and I thrust my sword into his open mouth and pushed it hard into him, my blade getting caught in his teeth and skull.

I was getting tired, and sucking in lungfuls of filthy, hot smoke and the sweat and tears running into my eyes stung and partially blinded me. My strikes were growing sloppy as my arms grew tired and the fear of the flames grew rapidly toward panic. Simply put, I was getting carried away and I paid for my carelessness when the keshig I had run through the mouth flung himself away and ripped my sword from my hand.

Two others clambered over the balustrade onto the gallery either side of me and I ran to one in order to throw him down. Before I could grab him, he slashed my arm open near the shoulder. Grasping his sword arm, I drew my dagger but he clamped onto my wrist and held on so hard I could not shake him off. I let go of his arm and punched him square in the face hard enough to crush his nose and spread the split flesh halfway across his face but still he clasped me. The other immortal stomped toward us. His braids and long moustache were singed and his skin burned but still the mad bastard grinned as he reached us. All I could do was retreat and use the body of the man entwined with me as a shield.

Dread filled me when, behind the grinning savage, half a dozen men at once climbed over onto the gallery.

The Mongol I grappled with butted me hard in the face with his helm, breaking my nose as I had done his. As only a man who has experienced such a thing will know, the pain of a broken nose is quite exquisite and uniquely disorienting. My eyes filled with tears and I was blinded. In panic at my sudden vulnerably, I seized him by the head with both hands and sank my teeth into his face and ripped off his cheek, upper lip and a good portion of his crushed nose. His screams filled my mouth, as did his blood and I drank it down for a moment, then heaved the writhing, faceless bastard at the keshig behind, just to slow him down as I backed away and wiped blood from my eyes.

When my vision cleared, I saw that he was no longer grinning. In fact, his face was contorted in fury and, sword held ready, he strode forward to cut me down.

A fire pot smashed into him. The blistering heat of the flame rolled over me and the keshig became a screaming torch, while the blaze covered the gallery from side to side in a wall of fire. I backed up to Eva and Khutulun, who were almost out of fire pots. Four sacks of the evil things and they had gone through them with admirable rapidity. Both were drenched in sweat and coughing from the smoke, eyes running, and their hands were burned.

"We did it," I shouted at them.

The entire hall was engulfed. The heat was incredible and most of the people within were already long dead.

Eva clapped me on the back and pointed into the hall, shaking her head.

I looked down through the shimmering, boiling air to see Hulegu drinking blood from a dying woman's neck before pausing to shout orders. The Ilkhan was blackened with oily soot and his clothes were tatters where they had burned on him, showing bright pink skin beneath. He directed a group of loyal men who attacked the rear door with their fists and feet. With horror, I realised they were all but through the timbers. The fire had burned the door, weakening it and though it was all aflame and the fire licked and burned the men who tried to break through, they did it for their lord, for their Khan. They killed themselves, died in agony, so that he might live.

"He will get away," I shouted at Eva.

Lighting the fuse, she hurled her very last fire pot at him. Her aim was perfect and it was certain that he would be drenched in flame and killed.

Hulegu raised up the dying woman and ducked behind her. The pot exploded on the woman and a ball of fire engulfed him. Yet he stood and tossed the screaming, flaming woman aside before jumping into a group of servants cowering at the food of his dais. He seized another girl to use as a shield, holding her aloft as easily as a wineskin. His boots and one trouser leg had caught alight but one of his surviving men threw his own body around his lord's limbs to smother the flames.

"Come on," I said to Eva, as Khutulun threw her last pot down into the screaming masses. The heat and smoke were almost unbearable and we needed to retreat down the stairs, join Orus and go into the hall to kill Hulegu by the sword. I raised my voice to shout over the roar of the flames and the screams. "We have to go down and—"

A group of shrieking Mongols rushed through the wall of flames on the gallery and brought me down beneath the weight of them.

They brought the fire with them. The men were all burning as

432

they fought me and their burning clothes and hair licked my skin and the pain seared through me. A blade cut into my head, glancing off my skull.

A dagger was punched into my lower back and I arched and bucked, throwing the men off of me. Eva killed them and dragged me out from under them while Khutulun put out the fires on me with her hands and then yanked the dagger from my kidney.

I screamed and shivered with the agony of it as they pulled me to my feet. The burns were excruciating.

"Blood," I said, or tried to. Eva was already dragging a burned, bloody, dying man up to me and I drank a few mouthfuls from the puncture wound in his eye, enough to give me the strength to move.

As we fled from the gallery, I peered into the hall one last time. The masses of flames and smoke obscured the details but surely everyone was now dead. Nothing could have survived such an inferno. The flames had caught the beams and joists of the ceiling alight and flames jutted up at the roof. It would soon all collapse in and bury any survivors in masses of burning timbers.

We stumbled down the stairs and Khutulun cried out. A wail from the depths of her soul.

Orus was dead.

Lying against the wall of the antechamber amongst a pile of dead Mongols, his head almost severed under his chin and his eyes staring wide, mouth hanging open. His clothes smouldered. Thick, black blood from wounds on his chest welled out.

The door into the hall was a burning ruin, the charred remnants hanging on the hinges, with fire pouring out of it at the top and rolling upward along with billowing black smoke. The hall beyond was a mad wall of bright orange flame.

I paused by Orus but a moment, for I was filled with a rage that made the fire in the hall pale in comparison.

Hulegu had escaped me.

Throwing myself down the stairway into the storage area, I kicked through the door and ran out into the black night. After the cacophony and incandescence within, I was hit with the bitter darkness and it was like plunging into a winter lake. My eyes were filled with the glare and I could see almost nothing and the stench of smoke was everywhere around me.

A bell was ringing, clanging frantically, and people shouted all around the palace and in the city beyond. Unseen hooves and feet drummed in panic on the paving as people fled the massive conflagration.

But I staggered on toward other sounds. Fainter sounds. Footsteps, laboured breathing. The sounds of men hurrying away. As I followed, my vision cleared and I discerned the outlines of three men I was pursuing, cutting across the servants' courtyard toward the royal stables. All three limped or shuffled as they hurried away, wounded and burned.

Two immortal keshig turned when they heard me coming after them. Hulegu glanced back and snarled an order before continuing on.

It was only as they attacked that I recalled I had no sword. No proper weapon at all, and no armour either.

One hulking bodyguard was silent and armed with an axe, and the other big sod roared some Mongol insult and swung his sword wildly as he rushed in.

It would have been prudent to retreat and procure a weapon but I was very far from rationality by then and in my madness, I believed that I could fight through them with my bare hands.

I dodged the blow from the axe and shifted away from the wielder but was forced to block the sword of the other man with my forearm. It was that or lose my head. The blade hit the bones of my wrist and, as we both moved, it ripped downward along my forearm and tore off a great flap of muscle and skin before biting deep into the bone. While his sword was bound in my arm, I grabbed his wide-open mouth with my other hand and yanked with all my might, ripping down in fury. His jawbone came off in my hand along with the stretched, tattered skin from his temples, cheeks and neck. I tossed it away and he fell, making a horrendous, gargling scream and clawing at the ruin of his throat.

The axeman winged his weapon at my face and I jumped back, yanking the first man's sword from my arm. I tried not to think about the sight of the flesh from half of my forearm flopping back and wet, like I had been peeled.

With a sword finally in my hand, I rushed the keshig, grappled with him and slid the point of my blade up into his groin and wriggled it in, cutting the great vein there, as well as gelding and, eventually, disembowelling him also.

Astonishingly, the man with no lower face climbed back to his feet and came at me making a gurgling, keening sound from his chest. His eyes were screwed up in desperate rage as he threw a pathetic punch at my face. I stabbed him in the chest. As repulsive as it was, I needed blood and so I drank from his ruin of a neck while he struggled with the last strength of his life, drowning in his own blood. After spitting out an enormous, slimy clot or a length of vein, I tossed him to the ground and looked for Hulegu.

"He went in there, Richard!" Eva shouted, running up behind me. She pointed across the courtyard to one of the nearby kitchen buildings.

Without wasting time on thanks, I chased after Hulegu and kicked my way inside. I saw right away what it was. The low-ceilinged, one-room building was for housing a group of blood slaves. It was dark, lit by only a couple of smoky lamps. There must have been forty or so men and women chained to the two long walls, with piles of straw for beds.

At the far end, Hulegu Khan limped alone through the filthy room and barged his way out of the door.

He was still heading for the royal stables. Hulegu meant to take his swiftest horses and to ride off into the night, to find his armies out in the country where he would be safe from me.

Following at a full sprint, I kicked open the door and rushed back outside. I found myself at the edge of a large, paved courtyard.

Where I stopped.

Ahead, the palace stables were ablaze. Great red-orange flames jetted up and lit up the night, throwing manic shadows and lights all around. Horses bolted away from the roaring fire toward the front of the palace complex, directed by brave stable hands but many other servants fled in panic.

God love you, Stephen. You did it.

Silhouetted against the flames, stood Hulegu.

He had his back to me and I stalked toward him.

Rapid footsteps sounded behind me. I could tell at once that it was not Eva's familiar gait, so I jumped to the side and whipped around with my blade up and ready.

Khutulun ran past me and struck Hulegu in the base of the spine with her sword, thrusting him forward off his feet. He landed on his face and she was on him, flipping him over onto his back and pulling her sword back while spitting a furious stream of insults in the Mongol tongue, while he snarled up at her like an animal and writhed in pain from his wound.

I seized Khutulun by the shoulder and dragged her away before she killed him. She turned on me, mad vengeance in her eyes, and shook her sword in my face while she raged.

But I was too gripped by my passion for the death of that man, and I would not be denied. My own anger was very great, and though she had lost far more to him that I had, I was the lord and would make her submit to my will. I struck her in the face, kicked her legs out and stole her sword. She screamed and tried to attack me but Eva jumped in and restrained her while I turned on Hulegu.

His wild, barbarian features, twisted in rage, were cast in mad shadows by the slanting, dancing red light of the flames. His arms flailed and grasped at the ground but his legs were motionless due to the wound to his spine. A pool of blood spread through his silk coat low on his body, and a shining shadow of blood leaking from his body grew and spread beneath him.

"My brother made you," I said. "And now I will unmake you."

He growled in his own language and spat a mouthful of blood

437

onto his chest. Hulegu's contempt turned to bitter laughter. I sensed that he was mocking my judgemental tone. And he was right. I had just murdered hundreds myself, including innocent slaves.

But I already knew I was not a righteous man. Just as I knew that he was an evil one. All of a sudden, I was filled with a powerful loathing, for him, for his entire people. For William.

I slashed my dagger across his throat and dragged him upright while his fists hammered ineffectually against my head. My rage consumed me and I sank my mouth into the gushing wound and sucked down the hot blood, which spilled over my face and soaked my chest. His blows grew weaker and I stopped to look him in the eye. Hulegu's mouth opened and closed and his eyes glared at me even as the light began to go out from them. I tossed him to the ground, snatched up my dagger again and planted one foot on his chest while I sawed through his neck with my blade. I was shouting at him, but I do not know what I said. When I ripped his head from his body, I held it aloft and sucked the last remnants of blood from the tattered neck. Finally, I tossed it to the ground and spat on his corpse.

I let out a huge sigh and looked up at the smoke billowing into the night sky.

It was done.

When I turned, Eva and Khutulun were holding on to each other and their eyes glinted red with the light from the inferno of the palace stables. Behind them, the palace itself was being swiftly consumed by the vast conflagration and the roofs were already collapsing, throwing sparks and flame into the black night.

438

"Richard?" Eva said. "We must flee."

I nodded. "You go." I pushed past her, snatching up my stolen sword and heading back to the outbuilding near us. "I will see you at the meeting place."

She stared at me, aghast, as I strode back into the hall of the blood slaves. Those inside cowered away from me on their filthy piles of straw. Of course, I was drenched in blood and no doubt looked like a horror. While they wailed, terrified of me and the fires all around their prison, I moved to pull their chains from the iron rings affixed to the timber walls. A young man shivered in terror as I used my blade to prise the ring out. The Mongol sword bent and I tossed it aside and gripped the ring and pulled.

"What in the name of God are you doing?" Eva said from the doorway.

"Go," I said, through gritted teeth. "Please, go."

She came closer, incredulous. "Leave them, for the love of God, Richard. We must flee in the great rush of the people or we shall be isolated and captured. You know this. Leave these slaves."

"I will not," I said, growling as the ring wriggled loose and came free. The idiot blood slave stayed where he was, eyes wide and shivering. I tossed the ring into his lap so that he could carry the chain with him. "Go, you damned fool." I said it in Arabic and when he still did not move, I grabbed him and threw him to the door and moved to the next slave. She was a hideously ugly young woman but her eyes said she understood her freedom was at hand. I grabbed the ring by her with both hands, planted my feet and heaved backwards.

"You are a bloody fool, Richard!" Eva shouted as she pulled

out her dagger and stomped to the next slave.

Instead of killing him, she used her dagger to hack at the iron fixture next to his head.

Khutulun had no compassion in her, no Christian conscience or moral consideration for the weak. And yet she also came back to help. Working together, we freed the blood slaves from their chains very swiftly and followed the last of them out.

The palace complex was in chaos, and we joined the flow of fleeing people without being challenged. Our agents in the city had started small fires in various quarters when they saw the flames in the palace. They had the effect that Hassan had sworn they would. The danger of fire panicked the residents and soldiers in the city. When we made it beyond the palace gate we fell into the crush of people pushing and shoving their way out. We were covered in blood and burns and blackened by smoke and I assumed we would have to fight our way clear at some point. Yet, the people were Armenian Christians and Persians and Mongols and people from all over the region and the lands that Hulegu had dominated and thus everyone was a stranger to everyone else. So, although some people around us gave us suspicious looks, we escaped unchallenged into the suburbs and then into the rural farmland just as the sun began to lighten the sky.

Hulegu and his men were dead and Eva and Khutulun had made it out with me.

Whether Thomas, Stephen and Hassan had survived, we had no idea.

* * *

Our meeting point was an isolated fisherman's house many miles to the west on the shores of Lake Urmia that we had taken over days before. We chased down an escaped horse and, later, another one, and the three of us made it to the house before midday.

Stephen was already there. The shrewd young man had used his fire pots to thoroughly burn the stables and had ridden one of Hulegu's magnificent Saracen mares all the way to the shore before dawn. He was wide-eyed and shaken by it all and filled with the disbelieving giddiness that men experience after surviving battle.

Inside the house was a large table stained with fish blood, a few stools and benches and the supplies we had stashed there. Chief amongst them was the wine, which I drank with great enthusiasm.

Khutulun spent the day alone, on the shores of the lake, deeply affected by the death of her brother. I wondered whether she regretted trading Hulegu's life for his. Those in mourning contemplate past moments shared with the fallen but they also lament facing the future without them. If she was considering the future, perhaps she already regretted her immortality and the bareness that came with it.

"She should come inside," Eva muttered. "She will draw attention to us."

"Leave her be," I said.

None of us truly expected to see Thomas or Hassan but late in the day the old Templar appeared on the horizon. I rode out and brought him in. He trudged all the way across the plain wounded and thirsty and cold and he collapsed once inside the door. After I gave him my own blood, he recovered rather quickly.

"Hassan sacrificed himself so that I might escape the palace," Thomas explained while he drank some wine. "We defended the hall door against more men than I could count. They all wanted to free their khan. We abandoned the position when the door turned to flame and yet we were pursued by a great number as we fled. Hassan pushed me through and closed a door, defending it from the other side so that I might make my escape without him." Thomas shook his head. "A Saracen. Sacrificed himself for me. A Templar."

Stephen nodded as if he understood. "The Assassins are obsessed with death. All they want is to enter Heaven."

"No," I said. "His home was destroyed. His family. Everyone he knew was dead. All he had left to do with his life was to end it."

"And what is left for us?" Thomas asked. "Half of our task is done. It has taken so long. And now we must find William."

"No," I said.

They looked at me.

"William has gone to the East. He swore that he will be gone for decades, at least. Centuries, perhaps. If he returns at all."

"So that is it?" Thomas said, growing angry. "He saved your life with his blood in that Baghdad gatehouse and you just forgive his crimes?"

"I forgive nothing," I said, keeping calm. "William will certainly die. And yet, he will wreak his evil on a distant people.

His mischief will be directed amongst the Mongols and their enemies in the East. When he returns, I will kill him."

None of them wanted to face that journey eastwards again.

"So," Stephen began. "What do we do until then?"

I looked at them. Stephen, Thomas, Eva and pursed my lips, considering whether I should speak what had long been on my mind.

"Do you mean to slay us, now?" Thomas asked. He spoke softly, with no challenge in his voice. It sounded as though he would have almost welcomed it. "To be rid of all those given the Gift of the blood?"

The truth was, I had considered it. I had ruminated upon it, on and off, for years. By my hand as well as William's, there had been a great proliferation of immortals walking the Earth, and I felt that it was my duty to put an end to all of them, including the ones from my own blood. Other than Eva, of course.

Spreading my open hands, I spoke softly. "It never crossed my mind," I said. "However, we know from Bertrand and from William himself that my brother left dozens of immortals in Christendom. Knights and lords and God only knows who else. They must be stopped. No one will stop them if I do not."

"If you do not?" Eva asked. "You alone?"

I held her gaze for a moment. "Stephen, my good fellow, would you be so kind as to ask Khutulun to come inside now. There is something I would like to propose to you all."

All but Khutulun sat on the benches on the other side of the table from me. They were all exhausted and should have been resting. But I needed to speak and I think they needed to hear it.

"You were each thrust into this existence, in one way or another, through the actions of my brother." That was true for Eva and also for Thomas. I looked at Stephen and Khutulun, who had joined me voluntarily and then begged me to grant them the Gift, each for their own reasons. "Some more than others, perhaps. And yet we have remained bound together for years. You have followed me for thousands of miles, through horrors and hardships. You men renounced sworn oaths because you knew you had a higher calling. A greater moral duty, to destroy a particular form of evil that no one else could. You swore to defeat that evil. And now you have." I cleared my throat, hesitant to continue in case they refused what I was about to offer. "But perhaps it is time to exchange new oaths. Perhaps, I would swear to you that I would protect you from all who would do you harm and provide for you wealth and the blood you need to survive. And perhaps you would swear to serve me and do as I command, where it serves the cause of our Order."

"Our Order?" Thomas said, frowning.

"An Order, yes. An Order dedicated to a single purpose. We would make oaths to dedicate our lives to destroying all immortals that William de Ferrers has made. First in Christendom, and then wherever else we may find them. And we swear to kill William himself when he returns from the East."

Stephen was nodding enthusiastically. The others did not immediately protest, at least.

"And if he does not return?" Thomas said. "What then?"

"Then we will swear to pursue him to the ends of the Earth and cut off his head wherever we find him."

I wanted to say more. I knew I had said it all rather badly, and I wished to explain how it would give us a common purpose, and it would mean that we continued to rely on each other but I fell silent.

"I will swear it," Stephen said, eagerly. "I will swear the oath. We can do great things together, I know we can. Yes, I will swear it."

Thomas pursed his lips. "It would be an honourable duty." He inclined his head.

"You want me to live in your land?" Khutulun asked. Even filthy and unkempt, and in a dark hovel, her beauty shone like the moon and the stars. "I will not do this. I will return to my people."

Eva's head snapped sharply to me and I knew what she was thinking. That I could not let her go. She was a blood drinker. She would never age, so far as we knew, and she was a killer besides. Clever, dangerous. To let her go would immediately undermine everything I wanted to establish. It was easy to read Eva's thoughts in that fleeting glance.

Khutulun should be the first immortal executed by our new Order.

"Very well," I said, instead. "Go home. Be with your people." I leaned forward and pointed a finger at her. "But if you make any trouble. If you become another Hulegu, I will kill you, too."

Khutulun laughed in my face, her expression utterly contemptuous. "I will wait until the Ilkhan's funeral. Only then will I go." She held my gaze, daring me to challenge her even though she surely knew I would best her.

How she had gotten wind of my plans, I could not comprehend, for I had been careful not to tell her. Then I looked at Stephen, who was studiously inspecting a point on the ceiling.

"Stephen, you great blabbering fool," I muttered. "Are your virtues so easily overturned by the handsomeness of a woman's face?"

Eva barked out a bitter laugh. "Why do you look at the speck of sawdust in your brother's eye and pay no attention to the plank in your own?"

I smiled. "A fair question."

"Khutulun," I said to her, "it is important that you understand. If you make any other immortals with your own blood, or if you use your strength against Christian kingdoms, or if you speak of me or our Order to anyone, I shall not hesitate to slaughter you. Do you believe you could stand against me?"

She tossed her braids and scoffed but she lowered her head in submission. "I understand. I have no further interest in you or your Order."

After living together with her, fighting beside her, teaching her our languages and training her to fight more effectively, she could throw us off so easily. Perhaps it was because her heart was broken from her loss. Perhaps it was the unassailable gulf that existed between our two peoples. Or perhaps it was that she was only ever a black-hearted Tartar with a beautiful countenance.

"By what name should our Order be known?" Stephen said, suddenly.

"It will not be known," I said to him and to all of them. "It will be a secret known only by the members of the order. But its name amongst us will be the Order of the White Dagger."

Eva's head snapped up at that, her eyes shining. Thomas looked to the heavens, perhaps recalling that it was as he was being sliced open by my brother in the Khan's palace that little Nikolas had used my dagger to attack William.

"You have named it this," Stephen said, "because your fine dagger has upon it the image of Saint George and we will be dedicated to protecting Christendom from the dragon that is William's men. Perhaps we should call the Order after the saint?"

I shook my head before he had even finished speaking. "No, Stephen. We will protect Christendom from the dragon, that is true, and we will seek to uphold knightly ideals. But we, too, are the dragons."

We waited near to Maragha for the dust to settle. Without Hassan to help organise the network of informants, it was difficult but we watched and waited and saw how the Ilkhan's great funeral was planned. It took place on the huge island in Lake Urmia. Only the inner circle of the Ilkhanate's Mongols was in attendance, including Hulegu's sons, all sired prior to William's Gift, of course. The eldest, Abaqa, became the ruler of the Ilkhanate. Following his death after seventeen years, another of Hulegu's sons became the ruler, Tekuder, who was also at the funeral.

The ceremony also featured the sacrifice of twenty-seven beautiful virgin girls. Their blood was poured across the burial site and then entombed with Hulegu.

Entombed along with vast amounts of treasure.

We did not want all of it. Indeed, we could not have

transported so much as half of it without buying masses of slaves and horses and wagons to carry it and then we would have required an army to protect it.

But we crossed the lake at night, hopping from island to island in our two small boats. I was tired by the time we got there but I had energy enough left to kill all of the honour guards and slay the barbarian priests chanting and praying for the soul of their departed lord.

Of all the gold and silver and fine furniture and cloth that was buried, we took only the precious coins and the gemstones, and the finest jewellery.

It was a fortune, and we would need it.

I allowed Khutulun to take more than I should have because Eva was right and I was always a fool for women.

But there was enough left over to pay for passage across the Black Sea, and even to pay for comfortable cabins on a ship to Venice. We could afford to pay for plenty of healthy slaves for the journey who we bled every other day or so. That was how, after many days at sea, we came back to Christendom. Back to the lands where we all belonged, amongst people like us, where we could begin once again to track down and slaughter the spawn of William de Ferrers.

And that was when my dear Eva left me.

PART SEVEN
VENICE
1266

THOUGH WE HAD CALLED at numerous ports on the journey home, disembarking from the ship at Venice felt like I had finally returned to civilisation. Though the Venetians were a haughty, arrogant people and were interested only in trade, and power over the Genoese, with whom they had been at war, their remarkable city was a fine sight to see after so many years in foreign lands. The urchins surrounded us the moment I set foot on the dockside, asking where we had come from and touting their wares. A few of the more desperate tugged on my sleeves until I clouted them about the ears.

"Best wine in the city, sir," they would say. "Come, follow me and you will see."

"Our rooms are clean. How many beds do you need, lord?"

"Such food we have, sir, you will never leave Venice."

"Are you looking for a woman's company, my lord? My master's house has all that you could desire."

The cleverer ones spoke French, and one or two even had a stab at English. And yet for all the familiarity I felt for the place and for the people, it was not England. It was not even France.

My companions and I had a task to complete and oaths, made to one another, to fulfil. There were two lords that we knew of, in France or in England, who we had to hunt down.

Stephen had been talking to me for months about his grand ideas for how to maintain the efforts of the Order of the White Dagger over many decades or even centuries, should we need to do so. A day after arriving in Venice, we sat all together while we ate at a busy tavern overlooking the lagoon. It was time to make a final decision about where we went after Venice.

"We should most certainly establish ourselves as merchants," Stephen said, gesticulating with a chunk of bread. "And we should absolutely do so in London. Use some of our wealth to purchase an appropriate sturdy dwelling, perhaps buy a ship, buy and sell goods. And then we have an explanation for the wealth that we have and for our presence in society."

"You are always so keen for us to be merchants, Stephen," I said. "What do you even know of it?"

He waved his bread around. "It cannot be a difficult thing. Look at the fools we have met who are as rich as princes. But surely you see that we can have public wealth and means in this way without the responsibilities that come with obtaining land in fief from some baron who we would have to answer to?"

"Do you think that the merchants of London, or anywhere, will simply allow us to join them?" I pointed out. "Do you know how closely these merchants guard their trade? They do not know us."

Again, he was unconcerned. "We can convince them."

"How?" Eva asked, peering at him over her cup.

He grinned and shrugged. "Every man wants something. We will have to find out what each man wants and then give it to him. And so we will become established in London."

"Why not Paris?" Thomas asked.

I nodded. "London is the worst place on all the Earth," I said, and then remembered Karakorum. "Almost."

"We are English," Stephen said, then coughed. "Other than you, Thomas. We would do better with London as our home."

"We have not needed a home these last years," I said. "We can continue to move from place to place, as we need."

Eva sighed. "Always, we have needed somewhere, have we not? Why continue to live like steppe nomads when we do not have to."

I tried to get them to understand. "I had a home," I said, thinking wistfully of distant Ashbury. "It is all very fine for a while but your servants, your friends, your lord, will all begin to notice that you do not age. And that is not something you can easily explain away. Why make a home at all? Why become established in a place when we would be run out of it within a few years? Perhaps even earlier than then. After all, it is likely that our blood slaves would speak to the servants of other masters in the city of our regular bloodletting. Gossip can be deadly in a town of meddlers like London."

He nodded, excited to tell me what he had evidently been thinking for some time. "The blood slaves have never been a problem so far, Richard. A little bloodletting is good for everyone, is it not? The gossip might say we are overly concerned for our servants' health but no more. Anyway, my thinking is that we operate two homes, in different parts of the kingdom. And I could live alone in London while you all continue to search for William's immortals wherever the scent leads. After some years living in London, when my eternal youth begins to be remarked upon, I would move to the second house across the country and call myself by a different name, leaving the London house in the hands of a capable steward. And then, after a few years when most of the existing merchants have died, I can return to the first home in London and continue to support your ongoing searches with the necessary funds. When I so return, I could claim to be the son of myself, do you see? As you yourself have done, Richard. And so we may inherit by legal means that which we would already own." He dipped his bread in his wine and sat back to chew on it.

"Sounds complicated," I said. "Complicated plans fail."

"Not always," he said, trying and failing to charm me with a grin. "Not in Maragha."

I shook my head, still feeling uneasy with his ideas but unsure precisely why. His blind confidence, perhaps, which was certain to come crashing down when it met with the complexity of reality.

"So," Thomas said. "You wish to be an idler in London while the rest of us trawl the Kingdom of France and the rest of

Christendom for William's spawn, is that it?"

I laughed but Stephen made a show of being greatly wounded by the suggestion. "Indeed, no, sir," Stephen said. "I would apply what I have learnt from our dear departed lord of Assassins. We all saw the value of the knowledge we gained through speaking to merchants, troubadours, doctors, and any itinerant traveller, did we not? Imagine the very same thing, only for Christendom."

"Men's tongues wag only for coin," I said. "And thus, you would burn through our fortune in a matter of years. Already, Stephen, you have purchased two homes for yourself in your mind's eye. And you imagine that our order's wealth would survive such expenditure?"

He sat back, satisfied with himself. "And that is why I must also become a successful merchant."

Eva stared at Stephen thoughtfully. At the time, I believed that she was as grudgingly impressed as I was by the cunning young fellow's creativity. And yet, my wife was having quite different thoughts.

Before leaving Venice, we spent time depositing and withdrawing wealth from the Templars and banking houses. We had those names to pursue, and we agreed first to head overland into France to track down Simon de Montfort, the French lord who William claimed to have turned. We decided that Stephen was to travel on alone by ship to England and there set himself up in the manner which he had been envisioning for many years.

That is to say, the decision was made for Stephen to travel alone but that is not what happened in fact.

And there was another thought on my mind I had not been

able to truly ignore for years, no matter how often I attempted to dismiss it. When I came close to catching my brother in that gatehouse in Baghdad, he had made a claim so preposterous that it could not possibly have been the truth.

William had spoken to me of what he called the Ancient One. A man he claimed was our grandfather. A man who could be found in Swabia, perhaps three hundred miles north of Venice. Across difficult terrain but not a long journey, certainly not compared to the distances I had travelled before.

I was sorely tempted to head north.

* * *

"I recall quite clearly what William said," I muttered to Eva, speaking softly. "He said that our true grandfather lives, and he is thousands of years old. Thousands of years. The things he has seen. The power that he has. You would learn a lot from him, brother, if you would but go to him. That is what William said to me in the gatehouse in Baghdad."

"And what do you think he meant by that?" Eva asked me, stretching her long, naked body beside me.

We lay in bed with the morning sun streaming in through the open window. In the street below, Venetian voices shouted and the tangy scent of the waters mixed with the smell of fish being cooked on the dockside.

It would be one of the last times we shared such a moment together.

454

"I have been thinking of it often," I said. "All these years, I believed that God had made me as I am. I believed that either God or the Devil made William immortal after the Battle of Hattin, and He made me the same so that I had the strength to put a stop to William's evil. A long time ago, the Archbishop of Jerusalem told me that very thing. I swore an oath to my brother's wife, Isabella to avenge her and her children, and I swore revenge for William's murder of my first wife. But the notion that my blood was changed, was given this power by God... well, that is a notion I have accepted ever since and so my purpose is not simply a moral good but a God-given duty. The Lord changed my blood so as to create balance with William's evil. And so the evil that I have done, the slaughter that I have done, that was ultimately just. But what if none of that is true? What if I was never gifted this power but was born with it, through this man who is the father of our father? What does that mean for my soul?"

I fell silent, irritated at my intellectual deficiencies. I had half a mind to ask Thomas what he thought or even, God forbid, Stephen. But these were questions, or vulnerabilities, that I could express only to my wife.

Eva waited until she was sure I had stopped speaking. "You are losing your wits by using them so much. Twisting yourself into knots for no more than a few mad words by a twisted man."

"William has a way of making me dance to his tune, does he not?"

She sighed, thinking. "Perhaps you imagine his abilities to be greater than they are."

"How so?"

"What is the likelihood that you have some secret ancestor still living in Swabia? It is an absurd notion. So why would he say such a thing? Perhaps he was speaking whatever words formed in his mouth, without thought, and he never even dreamed up the notion before he spoke it. Perhaps he does believe it because he is mad. Which clearly he is. And it could be that he was deceived himself by some decrepit old trickster. You imagine that he has some grand plan that he is unleashing on you and so you give his mad words credence when you should simply forget them."

I listened to an argument break out on the dockside beneath the window. It was rather heated, especially for so early in the morning. But that was the normal manner of social interaction for Venetians.

"It is indeed a bizarre claim," I said. "Our true grandfather is thousands of years old, and he lives still. The outlandishness of it alone makes me believe there is something to it. If he was going to lie, would he not have made it credible?"

"You may be right about him manipulating you," she said. "His words always get their claws under your skin. Could it not be that some of his spawn are in Swabia? He is sending you to them so that they can kill you."

I sat upright. "That is it. By God, that is it. It is so obvious, why did I not see it? I am a fool. Of course he has laid a trap. We should go there, immediately, find these immortals and slay them."

Eva rolled over and faced away from me. "Why do what William wants? If it is a trap, by going to Swabia you may very well be charging headlong to your death."

I could not understand her reticence. "This is why I founded the Order. We must go to Swabia and kill these immortals."

"Immortals who may not even be there. You are giving his words credence when the truth is unknown. His other admissions are far more credible. He turned knights in France and England and we have their names, do we not? This is far more credible, as it mirrors his previous actions. You should focus on those men first, and then see what they have to say about the immortals of Swabia."

I nodded, though she was not looking at me. "That is a reasonable course to follow. One immortal thoroughly questioned will lead to more. We should do precisely that." I clapped her slender flank and grinned, banishing thoughts of William's cunning. "What would I do without you, my love?"

She climbed out of the bed and pulled on her undershirt.

"We should go out and find some food," she said over her shoulder. "And some strong wine."

My smile fell from my face. "A little early for strong wine, is it not?"

She did not look at me. "We shall both want wine."

Her words and demeanour filled me with dread.

All through the journey, Eva had been wistful, and distant. She had never been an overly-affectionate woman but it seemed as though she spoke her thoughts less and less. We would not make love for weeks or months, even when we had the chance, and then she would suddenly seize me in a great lust and cling to me with a desperate passion. Other times, she would weep and then deny it. Although she also often seemed her old self—sturdy, confident, wise—I believed her changed from how she was before we set off into the steppe years before. I clearly recalled the Eva I had grown to love as we travelled from England to Spain, Italy, and Outremer, fighting in local wars and making our way in the world. She had been different when we ranged deep into Mongol lands, and those of the Assassins and the Saracens. And then there was the Eva who I had now. Aloof and gloomy.

Being a mere ninety-seven years old at that time, I had not yet begun to understand the mind of a woman and so I did not know what to make of it all.

I suspected that the toll of spending so much time amongst Godless peoples had worn her down. It certainly had me. And I was apprehensive about the world we were going back to yet I could not wait to see the French countryside and travel amongst my own people, or people almost the same as mine. Why Eva did not feel the same, I could not say.

Whenever I attempted to ask her about it, I would find myself angering her.

"You should be happy," I recall informing her in our cabin on the way home. "French taverns serve proper food. Think on that. Think on riding all day in the rain before drying our boots on the hearth while we eat roast mutton and drink good wine from Bordeaux."

"Think on what you like," she said, not looking at me. "Do not direct my thoughts, so."

"You are only bitter that we have not lain together for such a long time," I said, grinning and reaching for her. "Come here to me."

She slapped my hands away. "Come to yourself instead. And keep your tongue behind your lips so I can get some bloody sleep."

There was a strong chance that it was the murder we had done in Maragha. Such a sin weighed heavy on me and on Thomas and it was not either of us but Eva and Khutulun who had lobbed the fire pots and so delivered the inferno to the Mongols and their innocent slaves. Women are not created for war, and despite all her skills with the blade and her unfailing, uncomplaining toughness, Eva was certainly a woman.

Yet, when I broached the notion of penance, she cursed me and said that our quest for William's monsters, our very continued existence was our penance. And although I did not quite understand what she felt, I agreed to let the matter lie.

There was another great sin that I had committed. One which I pretended to myself and to God that I had not done. And yet I had carried with me, for years, the guilt and the shame of my abandonment of her in Baghdad. I had looked at her, my wife, surrounded and assaulted on all sides, and I had left her to die. No matter that I justified my actions post hoc by telling myself her strength and skill would always have saved her from the horde. I left her to die.

It was my greatest sin, though it already had such mighty competition. What is more, the abandonment had accomplished nothing. William had eluded me anyway.

That decision that I made must surely have demonstrated to Eva, beyond all words that I could ever utter, that my quest for vengeance against William would also come before her, my wife.

Ours had never been a proper marriage. Looking back with

the power of hindsight, I saw how I had treated her in many ways just like the squire that she often pretended to be and indeed served as. I had neglected to provide her with what she needed. A wife is subordinate to a husband, of course, but while the male domain is the world, the married woman's realm is the home. A marriage is for producing and raising children, but even for those who are barren, a woman, a wife, rules her home, she commands the servants and directs the meals and company, creates income from the assets, manages the economy of the household. She has that power. She serves that role, as the man serves his in turn as provider and protector.

But Eva had never had her own place, her own realm. Her own life. Never had anyone to command, anywhere to grow, and had been at my side like a servant more than a wife.

I was such a fool. A fool for women, people liked to say of me, ever since I was a boy. It was meant to imply that beauty made me stupid, and that has been true from my first decade to my last century. But in truth, it was more than that. I was foolish in all ways, where women were concerned.

And I had not seen any of that at the time.

Which is why it hit me with such terrible force and brought me so low when it happened. We sat opposite each other across a small table in the morning sun outside the tavern near to our rooms. It overlooked a quiet, narrow inlet and though there were people all about, they were going about their daily business and paid us no mind. The wine was good, and Eva drank off three full cups before she had the courage to say what she had to say.

"I will not travel with you into France," Eva said, looking me in the eye. "I am going to England, and there I will establish one of the two houses that we will run for our order."

A thousand thoughts ran through my head. Mostly, I was simply confused. "Why have you not spoken of this to me before now?"

"Cowardice. I feared saying all that I must say. And I feared your reaction."

My heart began racing as I struggled to comprehend what she was getting at. "You have not yet said all you must say?"

Her courage faltered and she looked away for a moment. "When William killed me, and your blood brought me back, you saved me. We were together. We have been together ever since." She sighed. Eva had never been gifted with speech. "I am tired, Richard. Tired of always travelling. Tired of dressing this way. Pretending to be a man, to be your squire. You will not stop your quest. The thought of trailing from town to town in the search. I cannot do it. I will go to London, and make a house there, or I shall go to some other town. My oath to the Order stands. I am committed to our purpose. My life will be dedicated to finding and ending all of William's spawn. But I will live my own life."

"Your own life?" I said, stuttering like a boy. "And not a wife to me?"

She looked at me again. "Not a wife, no. I shall pose as a widow, in order to have the appropriate station. I will take no husband."

Suspicion crept into my thoughts. "Is this some scheme to marry Stephen?"

Eva stared in astonishment, then laughed in my face. "He is a boy. I want nothing of love from him. But, in truth, yes, I also wish to learn more from him."

"Learn?" I said. "What could you learn from him? He is a boy, as you say. You could never learn from him what you have from me."

"He is a boy in his heart. But his mind is devious and he burns with ambition. He is clever."

"And you wish to be around him, rather than me?" I could not believe my ears.

"It is not him that I want," she said, growing irritated. "I will live my own life but will correspond with him, visit with him, coordinate our efforts. You see, it is his cunning I wish to cultivate. Cunning that can be turned into power."

I struggled still to understand. "You want power?"

She waved her hand and shook her head, growing impatient. "You have listened to Stephen, but you do not take him seriously, so you do not take his ideas seriously. Imagine it. Look at us. We still have not aged. How long will we live? Decades more, certainly. Centuries, perhaps many centuries. Imagine what we can build in that time. We would have to be careful, pretending to be small people while hiding our wealth and our connections, but with the knowledge to find all of William's spawn. And then, when they are all dead and our oaths are complete, God willing we will still be here. What else might we achieve with what we have been given? With this Gift?"

Stephen's ambition had infected her. I should have seen it earlier but perhaps I could have done nothing even if I had known where it would lead. Although, I could always have cut off

Stephen's head and thrown him into the sea before we ever reached Venice. Perhaps that would have kept Eva by my side over the centuries.

But it may also have condemned England to a tawdry existence on the edge of the world, rather than becoming the greatest empire that ever would bestride it. Stephen and Eva made that empire. With my help, of course.

In Venice, sitting before my wife under a pale blue sky, the stench of the lagoon and with a cloud of flies determined to die in my cup of wine, I had more selfish concerns. "We took oaths," I pointed out. "To be undone only by our deaths."

"We have lived together for fifty years, Richard." Her eyes grew damp. "A lifetime of marriage for mortal men and women. We have been faithful to each other, in all ways. I think God will forgive us."

Eva had decided. She was not asking permission, as a woman should, which was typical of her forthrightness. Quite rightly, she had not considered our marriage to be an ordinary one. It struck me suddenly as quite astonishing that she had lasted as long as she had. Even before I had met her she had received some simulacrum of a knight's training and had served as a bodyguard for her perverse father. But no other woman in all the world would have entertained for a moment's thought what she had embraced with me as we fought and killed across the world.

"You will need blood," I said. "Every few days. You must be prepared. I will not be there to give you mine and you must not be without for too long."

I do not know why but at that she burst into womanly tears.

The first time I had ever seen her weep.

* * *

In the face of the rampant Mamluks under Baibars and his successors, the Crusader kingdoms in the Holy Land would not survive for very much longer.

The remaining Syrian Assassins were initially overjoyed by the Mamluk defeat of the Mongol armies. Of course they were. Hulegu had destroyed hundreds of their castles in Persia and had slaughtered everyone who had lived in them. For a time, the Mamluks were an avenging force, delivering a righteous blow against the Mongols.

But when the Mamluks had subdued the Mohammedan peoples of Syria, Baibars turned his attention to wiping out the heretic Assassins between 1265 and 1273. Even with their fine castles, the Ismailis of Syria could not resist the might of Egypt and their new allies, and they ceased to be an independent military or political force. Baibars did not exterminate them as Hulegu had done to the Persian Assassins, and so the Ismaili Assassins struggled on in Syria, keeping their faith but lacking any power in the world. Indeed, they survived only by being subjected to the authority of Baibars and the Mamluks and agreeing to carry out the political murders that the sultan ordered.

Saracens turning on each other should have been a good thing for Christendom. But the Assassins were so easily subdued that it barely slowed down the Mamluk assault on the Crusader

464

Kingdoms.

The Mamluks raided Antioch in 1261. Nazareth fell in 1263 and Acre was encircled, only surviving due to ongoing supply from the sea. Caesarea and Haifa fell in 1265 and then all our remaining inland Crusader castles could not survive. In 1271, it was the White Castle of the Templars and the magnificent Krak des Chevaliers, Beaufort and Gibelcar that fell. Without reinforcing Christian armies to save them, the greatest fortifications could not survive the Mamluk siege engines.

The Mamluks even employed a Syrian Assassin to murder the chief baron of Acre, Philip of Montfort in 1270. Unholy savages that they were, the fedayin struck down poor Philip while he prayed in his chapel.

From being the terror of the Holy Land, feared by the Abbasids, Persians, Mongols and Crusaders alike, the Assassins ended up becoming nothing more than hitmen for the sultan. A truth demonstrated by their attempt on the life of my future king, Edward I of England.

Prince Edward, as he was then, joined the Crusade that was to undo the conquests of Baibars.

And who was the great saviour of Christendom come to save the Crusader Kingdoms? The great King Louis IX launched a new Crusade to smash the Mamluks and was even seeking to coordinate with the Mongols of Persia who had inherited Hulegu's empire.

And yet, the great fool messed it up once again. Louis diverted the Crusade to Tunis with the intention of converting the sultan there to Christianity. No doubt they convinced themselves it was for good and noble reasons, and not due to their fear of facing the ferocity and ability of the Mamluks. Either way, they paid for their cowardice when the army was struck with the bloody flux. The pestilence tore through the men on the North African shore and even took Louis himself. Good riddance. An ignominious end to an incompetent crusader.

Prince Edward of England, son of Henry III, and a man destined to become a truly great king arrived in the Holy Land in June 1271. He led a force on Louis' Crusade to Tunis but was not willing to accept that failure and so sailed on to Acre. His army was small but the Mamluks rightly feared the might of Christian knights and so Baibars decided to have this English prince killed.

Edward struck into the Plain of Sharon, near Mount Carmel and coordinated with the Mongols, who sent a tumen of ten thousand to Syria to support him. But without the leadership of Hulegu, the Mongols quickly withdrew in the face of the Mamluk counterattack, leaving Edward to negotiate a peace with Baibars.

The Mamluk peace was negotiated to last ten years, ten months, ten days and ten hours. This is the timeframe allowed for hudna, the truce that is allowed to interrupt jihad if there is a justified tactical advantage for the Mohammedans to temporarily halt their duty to annihilate the infidel. Such practices show very well their fundamental deceptiveness and cunning. As does their continued love of political murder.

Not satisfied with the peace, Baibars sent a Syrian Ismaili fedayin to assassinate Prince Edward of England. The Mamluk governor of Ramla pretended to be willing to betray Baibars and sent a messenger with gifts for Edward. With a cunning and patience that Hassan would have been proud of, the messenger was admitted many times into the prince's presence while the false negotiations were undertaken. Even though he was searched for weapons, the fedayin's patience had caused Edward and his men to let their guard down. A knight who claimed to be there later told me how it happened.

Edward was unused to the climate and reclined on a couch in no more than a cotton tunic. The fedayin, posing as a messenger, approached in order to pass the prince a document, a false letter supposedly from this traitor Mamluk lord. Edward took the letter and asked the messenger a question regarding its content. The messenger bent over the reclining prince, directing Edward's attention to a line in the letter with one hand, and with the other, he drew a concealed blade, cunningly hidden on the inside of his belt.

He thrust this blade at Edward's chest.

But the future King of England was no ordinary man. He had a lifetime of martial training honing his instinct and he was a big, powerful fellow.

With remarkable speed, Edward twisted so that the blade caught him on his arm instead of his chest. Quickly, the prince struck the treacherous Saracen to the ground while tearing the man's dagger from his hand. Edward, showing a decisiveness that was fundamental to his character, immediately used the enemy's weapon to stab the fedayin. Before Edward could restrain them, his servants smashed the Assassin's brains in with the prince's footstool.

Though he was furious, Edward considered himself to be

unscathed. But he was thinking like an upstanding Christian, and not a treacherous Mohammedan.

For the Assassin's dagger had been poisoned.

Edward became seriously ill.

His flesh around the wound on his arm began to fester and oozed a steady stream of thick, stinking pus. No supposed antidote worked and his condition deteriorated. Finally, his surgeon simply cut away all the rotten flesh from around the original wound and his robust constitution enabled him to overcome the poison in his system.

The very moment he was well enough to travel, he left the Holy Land forever and returned to the civilised people of England.

What if the fedayin's poison had taken Edward's life? What then for England? His younger brother, Edmund, was also on the Crusade. Presumably, he would have become King of England. Edmund was a good man. Solid, dependable. A dutiful second son all his life. But he was no Edward, and I doubt he would have conquered the unruly Welsh and hammered the mad Scots into submission.

Thanks to God, and to the Plantagenet robustness, Edward survived and returned home. In time, I served in many of his campaigns and did more than my fair share of the work.

The monks William of Rubruck and his elderly companion Bartholomew left Karakorum in the summer we had, back in 1254. Both of them somehow managed to make it to Tripoli little over a year later and eventually to Rome and finally home to Paris, although the shrivelled-up Bartholomew died immediately after.

At some point, Rubruck wrote an absurdly long and detailed letter to King Louis about everything that had occurred. Years later, Stephen claimed to have read a copy of the letter that had belonged to another Franciscan named Roger Bacon and said it mentioned nothing at all about an English knight and the trouble he caused. Poor Thomas as leader of the expedition was also excised entirely, as was Bertrand. Even Stephen was barely mentioned in the rambling narrative. Considering how we had abandoned him, in one way or another, such hurt feelings were to be expected. Amusingly, King Louis seems to have taken no actions based on the content of Rubruck's letter, and no other lord, priest or monk read it either. Rubruck returned to obscurity as a monk for the rest of his days. One might say his great efforts were entirely wasted other than the fact that his mission provided cover for mine and so ultimately helped to rid the world of Hulegu.

Tragically, our great city of Acre fell to the Mamluks in 1291. After so long stemming the tide of Saracen expansion, the Crusader kingdoms were finally no more.

Failure.

Our people could no longer resist the ferocity of the Mohammedans and the kingdoms of Christendom turned against each other rather than uniting to drive out the invaders from the Holy Land. Even though I had seen their fanaticism first hand, and for so long, I did not imagine that they would eventually take Constantinople and threaten to overrun Europe itself.

One of the most severe consequences of the loss of the fall of the Crusader states would be the fall of the Templars. Their collapse in the face of the Mamluks and the Mongols brought them into disgrace and the order was much criticised by those who wanted someone to blame. Pressure on the Templars grew from many sources until Philip IV of France arrested every Templar in France in 1307. The vile French king seized the order's assets, tortured and tried the men and eventually burned the final master to death in 1314. Thomas took it hard, of course, for he remained a Templar at heart even after decades serving the Order of the White Dagger. For a time, he was convinced that Philip IV was one of William's immortals and I was willing to believe that the cruel bastard was a vampire. But it turned out not to be the case, as far as I know. In time, the hurt of it faded but Thomas never got over the betrayal. Without the Templar's presence linking different kingdoms together in resistance to the Saracen expansion, successive states would be isolated, overwhelmed and conquered in turn. We needed the Templars. May Philip IV burn in the hottest fires of Hell for eternity.

It would be two hundred years before I returned to the East but I would again fight to protect Christendom from the rampaging Turk.

* * *

It was many years before I heard what happened to Khutulun. She returned to her people as she had intended, and found a great Mongol named Kaidu who was an enemy of Kublai, who William was supporting. Kaidu was the leader of the House of Ogedei and

470

Khan of the Chagatai Khanate. Khutulun must have chosen him because of his opposition to Kublai, and William, and also because he was a war-loving steppe warrior at heart, just like she was. No doubt when she presented herself to Kaidu, he would have wanted her for his wife but she certainly refused because she became famous as the daughter of Kaidu. When I heard that, I laughed, for I can well imagine this Khan's confusion and ultimate compliance to her demand. The lie could have been made quite easily. I imagine her riding alone across the step and claiming that her mother was some woman that Kaidu had taken years before. Whether that was the way of it, or whether he believed her or not, he certainly claimed her as his own.

In return for this dishonourable act of deceit, she offered him her brilliance as a warrior, a tactician, and political strategist.

With her help, by 1280 Kaidu was the most powerful ruler of Central Asia, reigning from western Mongolia to Oxus, and from the Central Siberian Plateau to India.

In time, stories of her ability made their way to Christendom.

There was a lowly Venetian merchant and conman named Marco Polo who claimed to have visited the court of Kublai Khan. I know for a fact that he never travelled further than the shores of the Black Sea, and his accounts of the East were stolen from hundreds of braver men, who themselves had only heard the tales second or third hand, while he plied them with cheap wine in the Venetian trading colonies. This Marco Polo was a man who wished to be a great traveller but he also lacked the courage to venture from safety. As a collector of stories, he made a great impression, however, it was not he but another man who wrote

471

down those collected stories which were presented as the experiences of the fraudster Polo himself.

Whatever his personal lies and deceit, he at least got some things correct. He described Khutulun as a superb warrior, one who could ride into enemy ranks and snatch a captive as easily as a hawk snatches a chicken. She fought with Kaidu in many battles, particularly those against Kublai and William. The story goes that Khutulun insisted that any man who wished to marry her must defeat her in wrestling but if he failed she would win his horses. That certainly sounds like her as she knew that no man on Earth could ever defeat her. Well, I supposed I could have done but whether she would have married me is another matter. But through this cunning challenge, she spent years winning horses from those competitions and the wagers of hopeful suitors and it is said that she gathered a herd numbering ten thousand.

There are a half-dozen stories of who was her eventual husband. Some chronicles say her husband was a handsome man who failed to assassinate her father and was taken prisoner. Others refer to him as Kaidu's companion from another clan. A Persian chronicler wrote that Khutulun fell in love with Ghazan, a Mongol ruler in Persia.

So many contradictory tales surely mean one thing. She had no husband. No doubt many eminent men professed their certainty that they would be the one to claim her, and thus these stories spread. But she had no interest in such things and wanted only to fight and kill and be a great warrior.

Kaidu had fourteen sons but Khutulun was the one from whom he most sought advice and political support. Indeed, he named her as his successor to the khanate before he died in 1301. When Kaidu died, Khutulun guarded his tomb. But his sons hated her brilliance, hated her ageless beauty and strength and they feared whatever dark magic prolonged her youth. Above all, perhaps, they knew she was not of their blood, so the sons of Kaidu banded together all their men and they killed her, though she is said to have killed a hundred of them before she fell.

If she had stayed with me, fought with us in our order, she would likely have lived longer. But she would not have lived the life of a Mongol warrior and that was all she wanted. Her death at the ungrateful hands of men she had made great caused me to feel a terrible surge of hatred and a thirst for revenge on them. But by the time I heard, it had already long come to pass. Besides, I am sure her death was also glorious and I smiled to imagine the ferocity and virtuosity with which she would have fought to her last.

What of her enemies, Kublai Khan and William de Ferrers? The Great Khan slowly and relentlessly conquered all China and established the Yuan dynasty and became Emperor of China as well as the Great Khan of the Mongols. That conquest was perhaps the most remarkable of all the achievements of the Mongols, for the Chinese were the most advanced, the most numerous and the most well-defended people the world had ever known. Indeed, their cities were so well defended, by walls so high, wide and strongly-built that William advised Kublai to send word to the Ilkhanate for the great trebuchets used by Hulegu to smash the walls of Baghdad. With those weapons, the Great Khan was finally able to break through city and after city and complete the conquest.

Kublai was astonishingly successful, and yet he also experienced great failure. His attempted conquests of lands that would become Vietnam and Japan ended in disaster. His favourite wife died and that broke his heart and his spirit. A few years later, his son and heir also died and this calamity broke what remained. The most powerful man on Earth indulged his gluttony and grew disgustingly fat and riddled with gout and God only knows what else. He died in 1294, aged 78.

William, it seems, had learned his lesson. He had not made Kublai into an immortal and had instead served in a quieter role, advising and steering. Manipulating and assassinating.

After Kublai came his grandson. And after him, a series of young successors who each ruled for only a short time. Some were more capable than others but all were severely lacking in the glory and ability of their forefathers, becoming no more than administrators of their enormous empire. Like all Chinese dynasties, the Mongol Yuan dynasty turned inward and became obsessed with the machinations of the court. While they called themselves Khan as well as Emperor, they soon became nothing like steppe nomads and lost that which made them unique. Still, the Chinese always knew they were ruled by northern barbarians, no matter how sinicised they became, and after only a hundred years they were overthrown.

So many Yuan Emperors died young and died early into their reigns. What was William hoping to accomplish by his machinations? Always, he tried to remake the world, and remake the people of the world, into what he wanted them to be. William wanted naked power. He wanted to be worshipped. But he dressed it up in grand notions of religiosity or civic glories for ordinary men. I do believe that somewhere in his black heart he wanted to build great things, to change the world for the sake of some confused, empty notions of change and progress. That is why he always told men precisely what they wanted to hear. And yet because of his evil nature, all he ever truly did was destroy. Just as his efforts to shape the Yuan dynasty ended in their overthrow and destruction.

William would return to the West and begin to wreak his evil on the people of Christendom once more but it would not be for some time.

But in his prolonged absence, we still had many immortals scattered throughout the kingdoms of Europe to find and to kill.

* * *

William's immortals had to die. We had two names only from William but I knew well what I would do. The plan was a good one. I had been repeating it for months, even years.

Take either man alive, or even both of them, and torture them for the names of all the others that they knew. Then I would behead them and chase down the next one. Thusly, I would clean the corrupt filth from all of Christendom.

I knew of Simon de Montfort. He was a French lord and also Earl of Leicester in England. He was one of the men who joined Innocent's Crusade and took part in the shameful sacking and conquering Constantinople decades before.

The other was an English knight named Sir Hugh le Despenser. I half-remembered some fellow named Despenser but it had been a long time since I had been in England.

When Thomas and I rode into France and asked after de Montfort, we eventually discovered that the man I knew of had died fighting the Cathar heretics, almost fifty years earlier.

"Then our work is done for us," Thomas said. "Fifty years ago, or nearly."

"Perhaps," I said, partially relieved and also enormously disappointed. "Yet, these immortals can be tricky. William would have chosen the most cunning of men."

The old de Montfort's son, also the Earl of Leicester, had lately been stirring up trouble against King Henry III. No matter how often I had heard it, I was still astonished that the little boy I had known before my self-imposed exile was still the King of England, now an old man. This new Simon de Montfort had risen in rebellion.

"He is the true ruler of England," said a giggling, fat, Burgundian townsman in Dijon. "Henry is nothing."

The story was confirmed a number of times before it dawned on me.

"The son is the father," I said to a bewildered Thomas. "Do you not see? They have done the very same thing that we have proposed to do in order to pass our wealth down from generation to generation. The very same thing, or something similar. This new Simon de Montfort is the same man as the father. William must have granted him the gift, he lived for some time and then decided to pretend to die." With sudden inspiration, I could imagine how it could be done. "You or I could do the same thing, Thomas. On the battlefield, you are run through and fall dead. A trusted man takes your body away, perhaps gives you blood to drink. And much later you return, claiming to be your own son, now grown. I am sure it could be done."

"This is all a fancy," Thomas said, for he always lacked imagination. "You believe this only because Stephen suggested it for us."

"William said that they were men after his own heart," I replied. "And this Earl of Leicester has seized England for himself. Does that not sound like something William would do? Our duty is to slay this de Montfort, and to thus save the King and his kingdom."

Thomas remained sceptical until we discovered that de Montfort's right-hand man in the rebellion was none other than Hugh le Despenser.

Our joy at discovering both our quarries were already flushed into the open was short lived. When we neared Paris, we found out that the rebellion had been crushed in battle, and both de Montfort and le Despenser were slain.

"Perhaps they are feigning death once more," I suggested. "We should observe the men who claim to be their sons. Perhaps they have simply pulled the same trick once more."

As I would eventually discover, I was wrong about that and the vampires de Montfort and Despenser were truly dead. Our best chance for smashing William's immortals was snuffed out.

But we continued on to England in order to investigate.

Whenever I had imagined coming home, I had pictured myself walking through damp woodlands and colourful meadows, with the hills of Derbyshire as my horizons.

In fact, our ship crossed the channel and hugged around the coast of Kent and then up the Thames into London. It was a truly vile place, and only ever became worse as the centuries rolled by. It was a city for the grasping, the ambitious, and the perverse. Seekers of power and pleasure. Desperate men and women living in filth, breathing in the smoke and stench of rotting shit while dreaming of one day winning great wealth and marrying their son to an impoverished lady. A city of pimps, jesters, smooth-skinned lads, flatterers, pretty boys, effeminates, paederasts, singing girls, quacks, sorceresses, extortioners, night wanderers, magicians, mimes, beggars, and buffoons.

Stephen was right at home.

Stepping off the boat was just like it was in every other port between Calais and Acre. A swarm of skinny boys shouting questions and saying welcome back, sir, or welcome home, as if they recognised you.

And yet...

It was different. The stench was more powerful than anywhere but Paris, nevertheless there was a familiarity to everything that confused me at first. The sounds of so many English voices raised in cries as men laboured on the dockside or shouted their wares from the public cookshops just up the way along the waterfront. I found myself drawn to the smell of hot pastry and the savoury aroma of boiled beef.

"What can I get you, squire?" the cheery man in front of his

478

shop said as I drew to a stop in front of him. He was plump and ruddy cheeked, as was appropriate for an English vendor. "Fresh game and fowl, the best in London, as I'm sure you know, squire."

I could smell suet, onions, eggs, and butter, and I wiped the drool from the corners of my mouth. The roasted birds looked wonderful but I pointed to a dark, glazed pie big enough to feed a dozen. "What is in that?"

"Beef and kidney, squire. The finest cuts, by God's hooks, they are. Onion stewed for half a day until it—"

"I shall take it."

I fished coins from my purse while the fellow scratched his head. "You'll be sending your servant to pick it up, will you, squire?"

"Hand it over."

He was uncomfortable and unsure but he took my coin readily enough and handed the thing over like he was passing me a child and I tucked it into my arm. The smell was glorious and I could not resist a moment longer. Punching through the thick, inedible crust, I pulled out the rich, savoury filling within and shoved a fistful into my mouth.

"Steady on, squire," the shopkeeper said.

The taste of it was remarkable. Salty, tender meat, slippery with the rich juices.

Fifty years. I have not been home in fifty years. Half my life.

In my mind's eye, I saw the hall of Ashbury Manor filled with smiling faces. I recalled sneaking into the kitchens of Duffield Castle to snatch some of the stewed beef before it was spooned onto the platters and being caught by the cook. He cracked me on the skull with an enormous wooden spoon. Standing there on the busy waterfront I laughed out loud, like a madman. I was filled with emotion. So much so that I almost wept.

Fifty years.

"Here, Thomas," I said. "You must share this with me. This is the taste of England."

He wrinkled his nose. "Then perhaps we should have stayed in France."

England had been in turmoil for decades but the rebellious barons had finally been crushed and the remaining rebels cornered and destroyed by King Henry's son, Prince Edward. The prince was already in his late twenties and a man in the prime of his life. A man who had been campaigning against the rebels for years, and who had fought in half a dozen pitched battles. Once the rebellion was over, and the country was finally at peace, Edward left on his crusade which would end in his attempted assassination at the hands of the subjugated Ismaili fedayin.

King Henry grew ill and died when his son was on the way back to England. When I had left, fifty years before, Henry had been a young boy under the regency of William Marshal. While I had remained ageless in my absence, he had ruled for decades and died a decrepit old man. I was pleased that he had lived and ruled for so long but I felt very guilty for abandoning him when he had clearly needed me. If I had stayed in England, or returned sooner, I would have been on hand to kill the vampires de Montfort and Despenser and end their rebellions.

That guilt was one reason why I perhaps lost a little fervour for the aims of the Order of the White Dagger. When Edward became king, I found myself fighting for him against the Welsh and later against the Scots. It was simple to find the employment of a lord to keep me funded and occupied, and at other times I was paid as a mercenary directly by the Crown. Always, I said to my peers and lords that I had grown up in the Holy Land, the grandson of an English knight named Richard of Ashbury.

No man had heard of him.

Once Acre fell, in 1291, I knew I would have to come up with a new story to tell. But as long as you fought well and did not seek to climb above a low station, few men cared where you came from. Everyone always assumed the worst. Why else would a wandering Englishman be cagey about his origins if he was not some form of criminal? But a man-at-arms' trade is the murder of the king's enemies, and so sinners were always welcome.

In all the fighting, I pushed my knowledge and experience onto the men I fought with. I had learned from the Mongols that mobility was vitally important in war. Likewise, I championed the use of the small horses called hobelars as the best means for moving men rapidly in a campaign. At first, they told me I was mad but over the years I saw the changes happening until men treated it as so obvious a thing it was not worth so much as commenting on. Likewise, thanks to my experience with the Wealden archers against the French and witnessing and hearing accounts of the Mongol arrow storms, I pushed always for bringing more and more archers with us. Again, at the start of Edward's reign, I was mocked for wasting resources on such men but, in just a few decades' time, we could not recruit enough of them.

In between campaigns, we searched for the immortals of Christendom that William had created.

Stephen wormed his way into London and began to quietly establish himself as a man of standing, though he had to be warned repeatedly to stop bringing so much attention to himself. My dear Eva set herself up first in Exeter, possibly because it was so far away from London, and then in Bristol. When we crossed paths, we both pretended that we were happy. Both of them inconspicuously cultivated contacts with the itinerant folks who returned regularly to the cities. Through the words passed between them, Thomas and I tracked down reports of bloody crimes and suspicious outlaws. For some years, Stephen and Eva would swap houses and trade lives, each pretending to be the relative or descendent of the other. For a few years between wars, I myself ruled the townhouse in London that we had taken for our order. It only confirmed what I had already known; that I was not well suited to city life.

Finding the spawn of William was hard work. Most leads led nowhere and it would be some years before we found a true vampire once again. It would be in the reign of Edward's grandson, Edward III, and during his wars against the Kingdom of France. After the elder Edward died, the crown passed to Edward II who was rather a disappointment, to say the least. He very nearly undid all of his father's gains.

But, just as the soft Henry had produced the iron-hard Edward, so his weakling son produced a lion in his turn.

Ever since he was a young man, and before any of his famous deeds were done, I had great affection for Edward III. Despite the protestations from Thomas, Stephen, and Eva that I was abandoning my oaths to the Order of the White Dagger, I had thrown my lot in with him early on and I was at his side when we seized the would-be usurper, Roger Mortimer.

And I would fight for him when we campaigned against the French, defeating them time and again thanks to our mobility, our unity of action, and the power of our archers.

It would be at our great victory at Crecy that I discovered a foul vampire on the battlefield and the Order of the White Dagger would bend our will to capturing and killing the monstrous bastard. Our quest would be interrupted by the disaster of the Black Death and for the sake of the Order I would have to journey through unprecedented death and horror in the hopes of finding salvation.

But that is a story for another time.

I had not known how much I had missed England until I had returned there. From the savages of the east to the madness of the Greeks, and the volatility of the Italians, I had been amongst strangers for half my life. Returning to my own country, campaigning alongside men who were just like me, it made me never want to leave ever again. In fact, I would be ready to venture forth again after a mere couple of centuries but for the time being, all I knew was that it was my land. I was an Englishman. And the English were my people.

Finally, I was home.

AUTHOR'S NOTE

Richard's story continues in *Vampire Knight the Immortal Knight Chronicles Book 4*.

If you enjoyed *Vampire Khan* please leave a review online! Even a couple of lines saying what you liked about the story would be an enormous help and would make the series more visible to new readers.

You can find out more and get in touch with me at dandavisauthor.com

BOOKS BY DAN DAVIS

The GALACTIC ARENA Series
Science fiction

Inhuman Contact
Onca's Duty
Orb Station Zero
Earth Colony Sentinel

The IMMORTAL KNIGHT Chronicles
Historical Fiction - with Vampires

Vampire Crusader
Vampire Outlaw
Vampire Khan

GUNPOWDER & ALCHEMY
Flintlock Fantasy

White Wind Rising
Dark Water Breaking
Green Earth Shaking

For a complete and up-to-date list of Dan's available books,
visit: **http://dandavisauthor.com/books/**

Printed by Amazon Italia Logistica S.r.l.
Torrazza Piemonte (TO), Italy

13680946R00280